I dedicate this book to Trevor, with love, and to the friendly and kind people of Aldeburgh

No man knows what he will do till the right temptation comes.

Henry Ward Beecher

David, Age 10 years

I hate speaking to people. Why do they want me to? She's the worst. She goes on and on. Pushing her face close to mine. Speak to me, David. I'm your mother. I love you. I love you. We went for a drive and walked by a river, there's a bridge. I like it; the way it's made, the stones fitting together. When we come back home she touches me. Her hand pats my cheek. I hate it. It makes my flesh creep and I feel sick. Leave me alone. I push her. I run up the stairs to my room. I close the door. I'm all panty I can't breathe. I sit on the bed. If she comes up, I'll run away. I sit and listen. Nothing. I feel better. I'm alone. I like to be alone. No one to try and make me speak or touch me.

I go to my desk. I put paper on the easel and I take out a pencil from the drawer. I sharpen it to a fine point. Then I sit down. I hold the pencil in my hand. I feel good. I am happy. I see the bridge over the river, I see all the stones, I see the water running, the plants growing on the banks. I can see it all.

I put the tip of the pencil on the paper and I draw. First the bridge. This stone is shaped like a wedge, next to it is one like a coffin. I draw and draw. I can't stop. I mustn't stop. I can see the water dancing, the smooth boulders and pebbles lying on the river bottom, the water-weed moving from side to side. I draw and draw. Then I stop. It is finished. I like it. It's good.

It's all I want to do. I don't want to have lessons with the tutor. I don't like him. Why do they want me to talk? If I talk, they talk back. It goes on and on. I like talking to myself. I laugh when I say things to myself and they can't hear me. I know lots of words. I like saying them to myself. I practise the words in my room, whisper them into my pillow. It's my secret. I like secrets.

Chapter 1

Monday, March 8, 1971

Frank Diamond stopped the Avenger GT at the entrance to the Pemberton's house. He shouldn't consider taking this case on. Were they ready for this? Laurel hadn't said no, but anything to do with children, well, it was too soon after the terrible revelations at Blackfriars School.

He looked round; it seemed a prosperous area of Aldeburgh, as he'd been expecting; a quiet road above the High Street; houses set back from the road with tall hedges giving privacy, pavements clean of debris and the only person he could see, a woman pushing a well-sprung pram.

He drove onto a gravelled drive which curved towards a three-storied, brick house, built in the 1900s, he guessed, definitely pre-First World War. Several twisted mock-Tudor chimneys pointed to the cloudy sky like the arthritic fingers of a doom-laden prophet. It was strange, sometimes when you first saw a house you sensed the house was saying something to you. His first glimpse of his cottage, a few miles from Dunwich, braving the North Sea on top of Minsmere cliffs, said welcome. The Pemberton's house presented a cold unfriendly face; it said go away.

1

He slid out of the car, picked up his briefcase, and locked the door. He glanced at the Avenger and sighed, as an ex-lover might sigh when he looked at his present girlfriend and thought of the one who'd gone before. He'd sacrificed the blue Mustang: it was too conspicuous for a private detective.

The oak front door was opened almost as soon as he'd released the bell-pull.

'Mr Diamond?' asked a woman, neatly dressed in a white blouse and navy skirt. She was tall, about five feet seven, with dark, permed hair and thick brows.

'I am. Mrs Pemberton?' Frank asked.

The woman smiled and shook her head. 'No. I'm Ann Fenner, Miss Ann Fenner, housekeeper.'

This huge pile and servants as well? He didn't know solicitors earned that kind of money. No need to worry about non-payment of fees.

Miss Fenner led him into a spacious hall; there was a wide staircase leading to a double minstrels' gallery. 'Please take a seat, Mr Diamond. I'll let Mr and Mrs Pemberton know you're here.' She seemed very composed and efficient.

The upright hall chair was uncomfortable. He sighed, not looking forward to this interview. The case was nearly two years' old, two years' cold. Was there anything more he, Laurel and Stuart could do? Go through the motions, take the money – a very generous sum – and then, after a suitable period, give their sincere regrets they'd made no headway? He didn't want to do that. He should have refused the case after he'd looked into the background, but the mother's tearful pleading over the phone made refusal impossible

Miss Fenner reappeared. 'Mr and Mrs Pemberton are in the library. Can I take your, er … coat?' she asked, eyeing his leather jacket.

He wondered if Stuart was right, perhaps he should buy some clothes more suitable for meeting clients. If he did, he'd have to get a short back and sides as well, and he wasn't having that.

'No, thank you.'

Miss Fenner, showing the first signs of any emotion, looked relieved. She opened a door on the left of the hall. 'Mr Diamond,' she announced, remaining in the room.

A tall, lean, moustachioed man rose from a leather chair and offered his hand. 'Thank you for coming, Mr Diamond. I'm Adam Pemberton.' He was dressed in a well-cut tweed suit, with a green tie that looked like a badly knitted piece of string.

He led him towards a woman who'd remained seated. 'Carol, this is Mr Diamond.'

He judged Carol Pemberton to be in her early or mid-thirties, at least ten years younger than her husband. She was one of the most beautiful women he'd met. Like a refined Elizabeth Taylor. She was tall, not as tall as Laurel, and certainly not Laurel's build, she was as slender as a poplar tree. Her oval face, with perfectly symmetrical features and deep blue eyes, was framed by black hair swept back in a chignon. He knew he was staring. 'Mrs Pemberton.' As he shook hands he tried not to look at her too intently.

Her husband sighed. Probably fed up with the effect his wife had on men. 'Can I offer you some coffee?' he asked.

He nodded. 'Thank you. Coffee's always welcome.'

3

Adam Pemberton turned to Miss Fenner. 'Ann, please see to that.'

'Thank you for agreeing to look for David. I'm sorry if I over-reacted on the phone. I'll never give up hope he'll be found. We've heard such good things about you. I just know you'll succeed,' Mrs Pemberton said.

Her voice was soft and low, but now he was closer he saw lines were etched at the corners of her eyes.

'You don't look like a detective,' she said, smiling as though she didn't mind his long hair and leather jacket.

'Forgive my wife,' Adam said. 'She always speaks her mind.' He indicated a seat.

'Sometimes it's useful not to look like a detective.'

Carol nodded, smoothing down the black skirt over her thighs.

Miss Fenner returned with a tray of cups, saucers, coffee, milk and sugar. Mrs Pemberton poured and Frank drank his quickly. He wasn't in the mood for small talk. Adam Pemberton certainly wasn't, he was fidgety and impatient. Frank opened his briefcase. 'I've studied the police case notes of your son's disappearance and also those of the detective agency you employed. As you know I was unwilling to take on the case: they both did a thorough job. If my partners agree we take the case, I must have your agreement that if, after a suitable period of time, say a month, no progress has been made, we'll unfortunately be unable to continue. However, I want to assure you I'll do everything I can to open up new lines of enquiry, and even if a lead is slight, I'll follow it up.'

Carol placed her cup on a table and leant forward, eyes shining, clutching her hands together. 'I do hope they'll agree. I know you'll find him; I'm sure if it.'

4

Adam frowned. 'Carol, my dear, you mustn't place such a burden on Mr Diamond.' His lugubrious face, mouth turned down at the corners, didn't reflect his wife's certainty. 'I must tell you, Mr Diamond, I have given up hope of seeing David alive. I just want to know what happened to him, to find him, and to bury him, so he lies at peace.'

Why is he so sure David's dead? Most parents never give up hope until they see the lifeless body of their child.

Carol put her hands over ears, closed her eyes and shook her head repeatedly. 'No, Adam, you mustn't say that. It's too cruel.'

Adam shrugged.

Frank waited until she'd regained her composure, then took a notebook and Biro from his briefcase. 'I know you've been asked the same questions many times, but I do need to know about David. I'd like to find out what kind of child he is, and I'd like to see his room and spend some time in it alone. Is that agreeable?' He looked at them.

Carol nodded her head vigorously, but Adam pulled down the corners of his mouth. He stood up. 'I haven't got anything new to say. We've been over this so many times, all my answers and thoughts are in the case notes. You say you've seen those? I'm sure Carol can answer your questions. I must do some paperwork, I've a client to see this afternoon.'

Didn't he want to find his son? Frank decided it would be more productive to talk to Carol alone; Adam's taciturn mood might inhibit her words and thoughts. The fact she was extremely attractive had nothing to do with his decision. Who was he kidding?

'If that's what you prefer, Mr Pemberton, and Mrs Pemberton is agreeable …?' He raised an eyebrow.

She nodded eagerly. 'Shall we go to David's room? We can talk there.'

'No. As I said, I'd prefer to spend some time alone in David's room.'

She looked puzzled, hurt. 'Very well. We'll go to the sitting room.' She looked at Adam, who nodded and she kissed him on the cheek. 'I'll see you at lunch, dear. Will you stay for lunch, Mr Diamond?'

'Thanks, very kind of you, but I need to get back to the office. If we take the case. I'll make arrangements to come back and talk to you, Mr Pemberton, at a later date.' Not a likeable man. Why had a beautiful, kind woman married such a grump? Money? Some hidden attraction?

Adam nodded and turned towards a large desk under a window.

Carol led him to an over-furnished room; there were several settees, many small tables and Turkish rugs scattered over the polished wooden floor. She pointed to a Knole settee upholstered in green satin.

He balanced on the edge and hoped he didn't humiliate himself by sliding to the floor.

Carol sat on an armchair opposite to him. She looked beautiful and eager to please. 'What can I tell you?'

He wasn't sure how to approach the subject, it could be tricky and he didn't want to upset her. 'I need to know everything about David. I'm sure the answer to his disappearance will lie in his own personality. I noticed in the police case notes he has difficulties with reading and writing. Could you tell me more about that?'

She frowned. 'Why is that important? It can't have any

bearing on why he disappeared. Yes, he isn't very good with his words, and he's a great disappointment to Adam, but he's a very special boy.'

He nodded sympathetically. 'He looks like you. A beautiful child.' She blushed, looking downwards. The photographs in the files showed a tall, slender boy with his mother's colouring, oval–shaped face and dark blue eyes. But the face, although worthy of a portrait by Caravaggio, was not feminine: the chin was strong and the mouth determined. 'I know this is difficult but I need to build a picture of David. I need to understand him. Tell me about him. When did you discover he had problems?'

She sighed and rubbed her hands over the pencil skirt. 'He was a beautiful baby, as you can imagine. Adam was so proud. A son and so handsome. He was a quiet baby, everyone said I was lucky; he hardly cried and seemed to sleep most of the time. But as he grew I noticed he didn't seem to see me, when I smiled at him and made those stupid noises mother's make, he didn't react. It was as though he lived in his own world and wouldn't come out.' Her fingers were scrunching the fabric of her skirt. 'We thought he might be deaf, but tests showed his hearing was normal.'

'When did he start talking?

'He was almost three before he said his first word. He doesn't talk very much now. He doesn't like talking; but when he does talk he makes sense.' She leant towards him. 'But he has another way of communicating. David makes up for all his faults by his special gift. He draws and paints. The art teacher at his new school says he's never seen such a gifted child. I think he's a genius.' Her eyes were shining. 'Look, I had one of his drawings

7

framed for this room.' She pointed to the wall to his right.

He rose and walked towards it. She followed. It was a pencil drawing of a stone bridge. The execution was excellent, the proportions, the shading, the light glinting off the river flowing between shrubbed banks, spoke of maturity and expertise. 'David did this?'

Her face glowed at his obvious disbelief. 'He did. I took him for a drive one day, then we walked along a river bank. We stopped to look at the bridge, but only for a few minutes; when we came home he went straight to his room. When I came up with milk and biscuits he was doing this drawing. He didn't stop until it was finished. As you see it now.'

'From memory?

'Entirely.'

This gift was not mentioned in any case notes. Could it be important? 'Have you any more of his drawings?'

'Hundreds. I'll show you. Most are in his room.'

'This drawing is architectural. Did he always draw buildings?'

She frowned. 'Usually, but sometimes he'd sketch people.' The corners of her mouth turned down, as though she'd a bad taste in her mouth.

He wanted to ask her why she didn't like these drawings, then decided to see for himself. 'What about schooling? It must have been difficult to find a suitable school for David.'

She leant back, her shoulders slumped, her eyes briefly closed, as though reliving past difficulties. 'We couldn't send him to school at five. Later, Adam wanted him to go to his old boarding school. He has contacts there, he said he'd talked to the headmaster and he thought with one-to-one tuition they'd be able to help him, but ...' She opened her hands, palms upwards, shrugging her shoulders.

'You didn't want him to go?'

'Adam has very strong views. Usually that's a comfort and a help as I'm afraid I sometimes find it difficult to reach a decision. This situation caused a major rift between us. I knew going to a school at that age, he was only eleven, wasn't right for him. I don't completely understand my son, but I love him. I believe he's a very special boy, with a special gift. In the end, Adam agreed David would be taught at home by tutors who understood his difficulties and his special talent. In return I agreed when he was thirteen David would go to a boarding school, but only if we could find one which suited his special requirements.'

'And you did?'

'Yes, we were lucky, there's a school about twenty miles from here: Chillingworth. It specialises in taking boys from eleven to eighteen who have difficulty in fitting into the normal educational system.' Frown lines appeared between her eyebrows.

'You were happy for David to go there?'

Her mouth twisted. 'I would have kept him at home, but I could see Adam's reasoning: David had to learn to mix with boys of his own age. I must admit I fretted after he'd gone. At first it seemed to be working. I wouldn't say he was happy at the school, but he didn't complain, and he loved the art lessons; the teacher praised his work and we'd arranged for him to have extra tuition. He uses mostly pen and pencil, and he does like water colours, but he's not keen on oils. He started pottery and the teacher said he could try sculpture the next year.'

9

'He started in the September?'

'Yes. The first term seemed to go well and he made a few friends. One boy he was especially fond of was Peter.' She shook her head and frowned, as though she couldn't understand the friendship.

'And the next term?'

'He went back after Christmas without any fuss. But at half-term when he came back something had changed. He clung to me like a limpet and wouldn't let me out of his sight. Adam was angry at his behaviour.' She bit her lip and her cheeks flushed. 'He even wet his bed a few times, which he hadn't done since he was nine.'

Poor little bugger, he thought. Both the police and the detective agency had made enquiries at the school, but it hadn't led anywhere. 'But he went back?'

'Yes. But when he came home for the Easter holidays he said he was never going back there. There were terrible scenes. When I tried to find out why he didn't want to go back he would run to his room and wouldn't speak to me. The day before he was due to go back to school he ran away.'

As she talked a tear slid from each eye. Liquid pearls over alabaster cheeks. She was getting under his skin.

'Did he take anything with him?'

'He has a knapsack, he took that, art paper, pencils, some money, a pullover, spare socks, food he'd taken from the kitchen, and a pocket knife that belonged to Adam. Quiet a fierce thing. He was wearing his favourite jacket, a cagoule I bought him for a Christmas. Adam didn't like it as it had a hood.'

This kid was no fool. 'That's a list of a boy who knows what he's doing.'

She unselfconsciously wiped away her tears with a handkerchief. 'I though it showed he'd carefully planned his escape; it showed maturity.'

'There was no thought he'd been abducted?'

'No, certainly not. The police were sure he'd come home when his food and money ran out and he was cold and hungry. They only began to take his disappearance seriously when this didn't happen and there were no sightings of him.'

Anything could have happened to him: taken by a complete stranger; he was a beautiful lad and there were more than enough perverts who, if they saw him looking lonely or lost, wouldn't turn up the chance to abuse him. And afterwards? Bodies lie undiscovered for years and sometimes are never found. Could he have made his way to Ipswich and then to London? Twenty odd miles from Aldeburgh to Ipswich and then another seventy-five to London. He wouldn't be able to walk that far. Could he have hitched a lift? Made a life for himself on the streets of London and still be alive? Frank didn't think this was likely. Or could he have become despondent, felt life was too difficult, and taken his own life? Then his body would have been discovered, unless he'd jumped into a deep river or lake, somehow weighing his body with stones. Two years. Something should have turned up by now. Could he have been abducted and then sold on? Possibly abroad?

He turned to Carol. 'Would you show me David's room? I'd like some time alone, if you don't mind.'

She stared at him, frowning, then nodded.

He followed her up the wide staircase to the minstrels' gallery. Her legs were slim, the high heels emphasising her slender ankles. There was more than one reason he shouldn't take the case.

Chapter 2

Laurel ran down the staircase of Dorothy's house, now her home; the smell of coffee met her. Time for a break, thank goodness. Something to distract her from depressing thoughts. She hoped they wouldn't agree to taking on the case of the missing boy. Why hadn't she spoken out? Why hadn't she expressed her fears? Was she afraid of looking weak? After the discovery of the murders of young girls by Philip Nicholson at Blackfriars School last September, she didn't want the agony of finding another dead child. On the other hand, if they found him alive, and returned him to his parents, that would be wonderful. She squared her shoulders. Get real, theirs was a new business, they couldn't afford to be picky.

She pushed open the kitchen door. Dorothy, frowning, was plonking cups and saucers on the table. She wasn't the only one in a bad mood.

'Smells good.'

Dorothy snorted, took a percolator from the stove and poured coffee, some into cups and some on the pine table. 'Bloody hell.'

'Something wrong, Dorothy?'

Dorothy sat down on a chair, her back ram-rod straight. She pushed back her grey hair from her forehead 'Sorry,

Laurel, this postal strike has driven me mad.'

'It's over now. You won't need to drive to Ipswich with the post.'

'What we'd have done without the private mail service I don't know. Well! Seven weeks, and still they'll only take first-class mail – I'd shoot the lot of them.'

Laurel sipped her coffee. 'Then we'd never get our postal service back.'

Dorothy's shoulders slumped. 'I've been a grump, sorry. It was the last thing we needed just as we were starting up the agency.'

'Despite the strike, we've done well. We're breaking even.'

Dorothy smiled. 'I've enjoyed working with everyone, being part of the team and listening to you, Frank and Stuart talk about the cases we've had. Much more exciting than being a school secretary. I know Frank is satisfied, but are you? You've seemed a bit down lately. Is it the missing boy case?'

'It is, but I've given myself a stiff talking to. Just a bit close to everything that happened at Blackfriars School.'

Dorothy stood up and smoothed her blue jumper down over a navy tweed skirt. 'I thought as much. It's still raw, but we can't afford to give in to morbid thoughts, although every time I go to Emily's grave I shed tears. Philip Nicholson got what he deserved. Thank goodness he went to trial; I couldn't have stomached it if he'd had a cushy time in some mental hospital.'

Dorothy's twin sister, Emily, had been strangled by Nicholson, one in a series of horrific murders by the former headmaster of Blackfriars School.

'Laurel, I'm going to ask you a favour.'

14

'Go ahead; I'll help if I can.'

Dorothy leant across the table. 'Do you know Nancy Wintle? She lives in Aldeburgh, lived there all her life.'

'No, I don't think so, but I've heard you mention her. She's a widow, isn't she?'

'She is; married James Wintle, nice man and a good doctor. I'm very fond of Nancy, she's older than me, must be seventy, but there's no side to her, not like some of the Aldeburgh folk.'

'What's the problem? Can't *you* help her? Hasn't she any children?'

'Yes, a son, he's a doctor in Carlisle; she doesn't see him very often. She's confided in me to some extent, but she wants to talk to you or Frank. She didn't want Stuart, being as he's local. She'd prefer a woman.'

'And I'm the nearest thing.'

Dorothy laughed, her usual good humour restored. 'You may be built like a blonde Amazon, but there's no doubt you're a woman.'

'What did she tell you?'

'Not very much. It's to do with her brother, she's worried about him.'

She frowned. 'This doesn't sound our kind of case; we can't interfere in family relationships.'

Dorothy sighed. 'I know, but Nancy seems … it's out of character … she's frightened. I'm not sure what she's frightened of, but it's not like her. I'd take it as a special favour to me if you'd talk to her.'

Laurel reached across the table and took Dorothy's hand. 'Of course I will. I could see her this afternoon, I've nothing on.'

'Thank you, Laurel. I'll phone her now.' She bustled

15

out of the room.

It's better to have something to do and it was a sunny day. She could do some shopping in Aldeburgh; perhaps the fisherman might have an early lobster.

'That's fine, she'll expect you at two-thirty.'

'What can you tell me about her brother? Is he younger or older than Nancy? Hold on, I'll get a notebook.' This could be a waste of time professionally, but every new case must be taken seriously, and she'd do anything for Dorothy.

She settled at the kitchen table, biro poised as Dorothy lit a cigarette and took a deep breath of Players Navy Cut.

'He's her younger brother, by about four or five years; Samuel Harrop, a retired Harley Street surgeon. He left Aldeburgh when he went to university in London and never returned, except to visit Nancy and her husband; they all got on well together. When he retired he and his wife, Clara, came back to Aldeburgh to live. As well as being close to Nancy, it was the music which attracted him: Sam loves classical music and he's especially fond of Benjamin Britten; can't stand his music myself, not a bit tuneful. Nancy was overjoyed, she's always been so proud of Sam, and being an older sister she's always treated him like a little boy, much to his wife's displeasure. Can't say I care for Clara. She's made quite a name for herself since they moved here. Big noise in the church, the WI, and any other society she thinks is good enough for her.'

Laurel looked up from her notebook and stared at Dorothy. 'Dorothy Piff, you aren't normally bitchy.'

Dorothy sniggered and took another puff of her cigarette. 'Don't care. I've seen the way she treats Nancy.'

16

'I won't be going into this case with an unbiased mind if you keep on like this.'

Dorothy shrugged. 'Don't you trust my judgement?'

'More than mine. Although both of us were fooled by Nicholson.'

'As was everyone else, apart from Frank.'

'Don't keep reminding him.'

She put her coffee cup on the draining board. 'Do you want anything from Aldeburgh?'

Dorothy raised the forefinger of her right hand. 'Could you take the post in? Would you believe it? The post office will be closed for several days for decimalisation training! Good Lord, it's been nearly a month since the changeover – they should have grasped it by now. I need to do two more invoices, won't take me long.' She retreated to the dining room which served as a communal office and boardroom.

Laurel looked out of the kitchen window. Two blue tits were examining a nest box, some dwarf daffodils, heads folded, were showing streaks of yellow, and scudding clouds cast racing shadows over the lawn. A good day for a little light detective work.

Laurel parked near Aldeburgh's Moot Hall, opposite the fishermen's huts. She was glad she'd put on a warm coat, it was dry and sunny, but there was a nippy breeze. High waves were rushing in, falling on the beach, sending pebbles dancing, and seagulls, either perched on the nearest hut, or wheeling overhead, were raucously crying for food. She looked at her watch: just gone two, plenty of time to check on the day's catch, though by this time most of the good stuff would have been sold.

She climbed the concrete steps to the wooden hut; the display on trays outside looked meagre: two rockfish, some undersized Dover Soles and a few mackerel. The gelatinous smell of dead fish was stronger inside. 'Afternoon, Mr Fryer. Is that all you've got?'

'What had you in mind?' Mr Fryer was a lean, middle-aged man, skipper of his own boat and the first choice for fish by the residents of Aldeburgh.

'What have you got hidden in your fridge?'

He grinned. 'Can't fool a detective, can I?'

After some friendly banter, she bought several medium-sized Dover soles,

He handed her the change. 'Better check it, Miss Bowman. I'm still struggling with them 5ps and 10ps. Give me the old sixpences and shillings any day.'

Laurel asked him about Nancy.

'Nancy's all right, despite her funny hair-do. Well liked is Nancy.'

'What about her brother, Sam Harrop and his wife. Do they ever come in here?'

Mr Fryer nodded as he ripped off the skin from a Dover sole and stepped outside to chuck it to the screeching seagulls. 'He's a quiet chap, doesn't say much when they come to buy fish, but she's a snob, treats me like dirt, and barters over lobsters as though she's dealing with a bloody Egyptian carpet seller. Acts as though she's doing me a favour buying the bloody lobsters, she pokes at 'em and says they don't look fresh to her.'

She put the fish in the boot of her car. So Dorothy wasn't the only one who didn't like Clara Harrop. As she walked past The Jubilee Hall the music of a string quartet poured into the street. Soon be time for the music festival, then the town would be throbbing.

Nancy's cottage was one of the terraced houses on the right side of the High Street as you went towards the main car park. It was part of a group of five houses placed between a restaurant and a greengrocer's shop. All the cottages doors were brightly painted, pots of bulbs and herbs on the pavement, and window boxes containing pansies, crocuses and daffodils. Laurel's nose twitched; the aroma of fresh bread and savoury Cornish pasties drifted towards her from the nearby Smith's Bakery. She hadn't felt hungry at lunch time and only had a couple of biscuits and a coffee, now she was ravenous. A pasty would go down well after the interview.

Nancy's cottage had a blue, lapboard door with a brass knocker in the shape of a dolphin and a matching brass name plate: *Sea Salt*. Blue hyacinths, fully in bloom, filled the window box and the pots round the door. All neat, tidy and ship-shape. No wonder she and Dorothy got on. She knocked.

Nancy had difficulty in prising the door open. 'Give it a shove, would you? Let me move back a bit.'

Laurel put her shoulder against the door and leaned on it. She nearly fell into the front room.

'Well done, Miss Bowman. Dorothy said you were strong. Wish I was.'

Nancy Wintle was like a flamboyant sparrow, dressed in brightly coloured tartan trews and a white polo-necked sweater, her hair a mass of short pink curls showing glimpses of a matching pink scalp. 'Thank you for seeing me. Do come in.'

The front room was small, crammed with antique furniture: two Georgian armchairs close to a two-bar electric fire, a sideboard with silver-framed photos, and a table with four chairs, all mahogany and of good quality. In contrast a large, white television sat glowering in a corner.

She saw her interest. 'It's a colour television,' Nancy boasted, 'Got it for the World Cup in Mexico last year.'

She suppressed a smile as an image of Nancy sitting in front of it, gyrating a rattle, sprang to mind. She picked her way through the crowded room.

Nancy pointed to one of the armchairs. 'Please take a seat.'

The electric fire was belting out heat from both bars. 'Would you mind if I took my coat off?'

'Ah, an outdoor girl. Of course, remiss of me. I do feel the cold, I'm afraid. Not too much flesh on me nowadays.' She took Laurel's coat and danced nimbly between the furniture and hung it on a hook on the back of the door. 'Would you like some tea?'

Laurel sat down and angled her legs away from the fire's dry heat. 'No, thanks. Shall we get down to business? Dorothy says you're worried about your brother. I'm not sure we'll be able to help, but everything you say will be in confidence although, if we do take this further, then all members of Anglian Detective Agency will share the information. Are you sure you want to tell me about your worries?'

Nancy hopped to the chair opposite Laurel, hitched up her trews and sat down; she leant forward, her brown eyes gleaming like well-polished pebbles. 'Yes, now I've met you I'm quite sure I want to tell you and ask you to investigate. Dorothy said you were a trustworthy woman and I like your business-like attitude. I know you won't

20

think I'm a batty old woman.'

She wasn't so sure.

'Dorothy's told you about my sister-in-law, Clara?'

She nodded, but didn't say anything, wanting to hear what Nancy would say.

Nancy took a deep breath as though preparing for a dive into deep water. 'This is difficult to say ... I think Clara is going to murder my brother.'

Chapter 3

Frank lifted his gaze from Carol Pemberton's ankles to flashes of nyloned thighs; the slit in her pencil skirt opening and closing as she climbed the stairs. He didn't like the effect she was having on him. Did she realise how attractive she was? In his experience, most desirable women were well aware of their charms.

At the top of the stairs she turned left and hesitated before a door. 'I always hope when I open this, David will be sitting by the window, paper on an easel, utterly engrossed in drawing some scene from memory. Then he'll turn round and smile at me.' She opened it. 'Every time I hope, and every time the room is empty, waiting for him to come back.' She opened the door.

The woman was torturing herself, but how beautifully and eloquently she expressed her grief. Too beautifully? Too elegantly?

She stood in the doorway, moving her head from left to right, as though searching for him. But the large room was empty. She waved him in. 'Do you want me to show you where he keeps his things?' she asked hopefully.

He smiled at her and shook his head. 'I'll treat everything with respect and leave it neat and tidy. I may be some time. Is that all right?'

Frown lines appeared between her eyebrows. 'What do

you hope to find?'

'I don't know. I may find nothing new, but it'll give me a chance to absorb something of David's personality. It's surprising how, when you see and touch someone's clothes and possessions, you seem to absorb something from them, and that person becomes clearer to you.'

Her eyes widened. 'Are you psychic? I wanted to consult a medium but Adam wouldn't let me.'

Thank God for that. 'No, not at all. Sorry if I gave that impression.' Did she look disappointed?

'I'll leave you. Shall I send up some tea or coffee?'

Would she never leave? Did he want her to? If it was another bedroom, in another place, he'd want her to stay. 'No, thank you.' He shut the door behind her, sighed with a mixture of guilt and relief, and leant against the door. He needed to find out about her relationship with her son, and that went for the boy's father as well. He must ask other people about the family dynamics. What about talking to Ann Fenner, the housekeeper? What relationship, if any, did she have with David? Did coping with the boy's difficulties lead to friction between David and his mother? The boy and his father? Between the parents? Could David's behaviour, his tantrums, have driven one, or both, over the edge? Perhaps David hadn't run away from home – perhaps he never left the house. That was one area that hadn't been explored by either the police or the detective agency. Did David really hate the school? There were several areas opening up for exploration.

He turned and looked at the room. Any teenager would be in heaven to have this room for their own, although some might find it too large, lacking cosiness; it might make some children feel insecure.

The decoration was sophisticated for a child. The white woodwork and subtly shaded wallpaper reflected an adult taste – his mother's? He'd expect a thirteen-year-old boy's room to be a reflection of his personality, full of his interests: football posters, pop groups' photographs, models of cars or sailing boats.

He remembered his own teenage bedroom. The contents and state used to drive his mother mad. His interest in biology meant any interesting artefacts he found on walks were displayed on shelves: rabbit skulls, bird's feathers, even owl's pellets, along with bits of moss, leaves and wild flowers in jam jars. His prize possession, a Dansette record player, stood on top of a chest of drawers, with records of Johnny Ray and Fats Domino beside it. On the back of the door he'd stuck photos of women he'd fancied, cut out of his mother's film magazines: Audrey Hepburn, Catherine Deneuve, Gina Lollobrigida. He'd preferred the wilder sexual allure of foreign film stars to blander Hollywood beauties, although he'd fancied Maureen O'Hara, but he'd gone off red-headed women after Nicholson's obsession with them.

This room was too tidy, it told him nothing. Was it exactly as David left it? He strolled to a large window which overlooked the back of the house: expanses of lawn, a tennis court and a rectangular pond with a stone statue of Neptune, complete with trident, overlooking the sterile water. Certainly superior to Dorothy's dolphin burping green slime in front of Greyfriars House, but not as much fun or character.

He took a camera from his briefcase and started to photograph the room and the view from the window. He hadn't asked permission to do this as he didn't want to be refused. He'd found photographs useful when the team were discussing cases. Often one of them saw something the photographer hadn't noticed, and it also gave all the team a better understanding of the case. He wasn't the world's best photographer, Laurel was much better, but at least he was one step ahead of Stuart Elderkin. He'd produced some extraordinary snaps: views of people's feet, clouds in the sky and once a reflection of himself in a shop window.

He frowned; Stuart and Mabel's relationship seemed to have hit a sticky patch. Marriage plans were on hold and although Mabel had moved into Greyfriars House to take over the catering, Stuart hadn't yet let his bungalow.

Frank was fond of them and although the detective agency could work without one, or both of them, it would be a pity if the team broke up. It had seemed ideal when Dorothy, Stuart and Mabel had proposed they should be part of the agency, with Dorothy as secretary as well as providing Greyfriars as their base, Stuart as another detective, and Mabel looking after all of them. The bonds they'd formed during the Nicholson case had shaped them into the perfect team.

He refocused on the room. All the furniture was made of a pale wood: maple? ash? He started his search by opening drawers in a chest to the right of the door. The top drawer was full of socks, all neatly paired; light cotton summer socks, mostly white, arranged to the right, and to the left winter woollen socks, black, brown and grey. No pair of socks looked old and worn, no sign of baggy edges round the ankles or darned heels. Could these socks belong to a thirteen-year-old boy? No, a devoted and obsessive mother presented this drawer to the world.

The second drawer held underwear, pants and vests, cotton and wool, and to the right a pile of handkerchiefs, all in apple-pie order. He couldn't believe the content of these drawers reflected the boy's personality. If they did there was nothing to get hold off.

The third drawer contained jumpers, neatly folded, a layer of tissue paper between each garment. Soft grey lamb's wool, a deep maroon crew neck, a beige V-neck; these weren't the clothes of a young boy; they were the week-end wear of a bank manager. Where was the colour a child would revel in? He still had his yellow Snoopy sweater, with *'To dance is to live and to live is to dance'* printed on the back. He'd still wear it, but it had shrunk, or he'd muscled up. Where was the fun in this room?

He opened the wardrobe and brushed his hand through clothes on hangers. More of the same: boring trousers, jackets, suits, shirts and ties. Where were the jeans? The t-shirts? The track suits? A row of sensible shoes and boots, neatly arranged on a rack, some with shoe-trees, were at the bottom of the wardrobe. These were the clothes of a middle-aged man, a dull middle-aged man, not a teenager. Poor kid, did he get a chance to express himself? He remembered creating havoc at home when he was David's age by using his birthday money to buy a mock-leather jacket and skin-tight jeans. His father had sworn at him and threatened castration if he ever appeared in public dressed in 'those hooligan clothes'. He thought he looked cool and tried unsuccessfully to comb his curly hair into a DA

'What kind of hair-cut is that?' his dad had asked
'It's a DA.'

'What's a DA?'

'A duck's arse,' he replied.

'You're the arse, if you ask me.'

Parents!

This search was getting him nowhere, except he realised the boy was controlled by *his* parents, at least regarding his clothes.

Under the window was a desk: large, modern, matching the other pale wood furniture. A narrow top drawer took up the entire length of the desk with three smaller drawers on each side of a knee-hole. A short easel sat on the top.

Frank opened the top drawer. There were drawings, piles of them, mostly in pencil, some in pen and ink. He carefully pulled them out and laid them on top of the desk. All were well drawn, beautiful in their execution; scenes of town and city buildings, modern skyscrapers, eighteenth-century coaching inns, street scenes with buses and cars, shop fronts, department stores and country scenes of thatched cottages, tiled houses with plaster work on the walls and the spires and towers of churches. The workmanship was sophisticated, the detail obsessive and minute. He thought he could discern, by the increasing control of the pencil, the later works from those David had drawn at a younger age. He took a few snaps of those drawings he liked best. Laurel would be interested in this aspect of David. Had she ever taught or known a child with such talents? This might make her more willing to try and forget her natural antipathy to any case connected to children or schools. He hoped so. Also, there was something else: the drawings were obviously from the same hand; he was sure he'd recognise David's work if he met it again, just as he'd recognise the work of Turner. He bit his lip. Was that too strong? He didn't think so. The beige sweaters and the brogues didn't match this outpouring of talent.

He sat on a chair in front of the desk, sifting through the drawings, looking for …? He wasn't sure what he was looking for. Something that would leap from the thick, cream paper and say: this isn't right, this is suspicious, or this poses a question. Why did he run away? Why was he afraid to go back to the school? Did he run away? All he saw was an incredible talent, but nothing in the lines of buildings, churches and houses raised alarm, only admiration for the skill of the young boy.

He opened the top right-hand drawer: pencils, row after row of pencils; all carefully gradated according to the hardness of the graphite. Long thin pencils, sharpened to points as fine as the end of a darning needle, to short fat pencils, the graphite ends soft for shading. A wave of sadness and melancholy washed over him. When he was a boy at school, the art master had given each pupil three pencils of varying hardness, they were to choose a partner and try to sketch their likeness using only the three pencils. Nothing else was needed. He showed them drawings he'd done of some of them, using only the same three pencils, and asked them if they recognised their classmates. This aroused instant excitement and as the master held up each portrait in turn there was loud shouts, laughter and the red-faced boy, the subject of the portrait, squirmed in his seat. The last portrait was Frank's. There were gasps, no laughter, just muttering. Frank could see the boy in the portrait was him. He was scowling, the knot of his tie loose, the mouth full-lipped, sulky, eyelids half-closed, with thick lashes framing his eyes. The master had coloured in his irises, the only colour used in all the portraits of the boys. The emerald eyes seemed obscene, staring directly at you. He'd been shocked by the portrait. He didn't recognise himself. It was like him, but not him.

The art master put away the sketches. 'Well, there you have it, boys. You can see how with a limited range of pencils, you can produce sketches that are recognisable.' They split into pairs and spent the rest of the lesson either acting as the subject or as the artist. Frank couldn't remember who he partnered, or if they had any success, but his memory of his portrait remained with him. It was hard being a teenager: wanting to break away from parents, school, conventions, but not having the independence to do anything about it. How much more difficult for a teenager with problems like David? Little blighter had the balls to run away when he didn't want to go back to his school. Or perhaps he didn't want to stay at home and be controlled by his parents? Be a teenager again? No way. A mass of insecurity, not knowing who you are, full of sexual urges and the lust for adventure but having neither the means nor the know-how to fulfil them.

He opened the second drawer down: pens and nibs, bottles of ink, mostly black but a few coloured inks: red, green, and brown. Also erasers. This search was getting him nowhere, except to reawaken memories of his own teenage years. The bottom right hand drawer contained neatly folded cloths, some ink-stained. He rummaged below them, but there was zilch. His shoulders were tight with frustration. There was nothing to get hold of, no clue to David's personality or to the reason for his disappearance.

He shrugged his shoulders and wriggled in the seat, trying to release stiffness and tension. His spirits sinking, he turned to the left side of the desk. The drawers were full of more sketches, but smaller than those in the central top drawer. He carefully lifted them out and examined each one in turn, looking again for any clues, anything which he thought unusual. They were mostly drawings of parts of buildings: a few stone steps and iron railings, a chimney pot, a brick pathway leading to a wooden gate, a Georgian front door, with a lion mask knocker. He sifted through them, replacing them one by one in the drawer. Nothing. He glanced at his wrist watch. He'd been in the room nearly an hour. Carol was bound to appear soon, demanding to know what he'd found. The answer would be absolutely nothing, except her son was obsessively neat and tidy and lived in a room more suited to a middle-aged bachelor or a monk.

He wandered back to the window, looking out but not seeing the garden and pond. He tried to imagine he was David: dominated by his parents, over-protected by his mother, a disappointment to his father. A secretive boy, keeping his thoughts and desires to himself. His passion: art. He soaked up the outside world, retaining images within his brain and releasing them in an explosion of pencil on to paper. What must he feel if everything in his life was pored over by his mother, nothing was private, no part of his life was entirely his own? Every child has secrets from their parents, things they don't want them to know. Something they might be ashamed off but desperately want to do: smoke a sneaky cigarette with their friends, enjoy a solitary wank over a picture of a topless model, a thousand-calorie chocolate bar on the way to school, or a hot date with the school tart. What girls did in their teenage years he wasn't too sure of, he'd have to ask Laurel; he was sure she'd give him a comprehensive list from both her own experience and from all the girls she'd taught.

What were David's secrets? He might have had some at his boarding school, but here? He'd have to hide them. Where? In this room? He turned back from the window and viewed the room from a fresh perspective. What would David want to hide? Where could he hide it?

He took off his leather jacket and hung it on the chair in front of the desk. He'd have to be quick and thorough. He didn't want Carol catching him taking the bedroom apart. He took his jacket off the chair, threw it on the bed and put the back of the chair under the door handle. He'd wriggle out of that one if he had to.

He took a torch from his briefcase and started with the wardrobe. Pushing clothes aside he tapped on the panels, listening for hollow sounds and shone the torch beam over them. Nothing. He moved to the chest of drawers, pulling all the drawers out and exploring the carcass of the chest, the back and the undersides. Nothing.

He put the drawers back and used the same technique for the desk. Nothing. He caught a glimpse of his face in the wardrobe mirror: red and sweaty. He turned to the bed, a single divan covered in a pale blue silk eiderdown. Just the thing for a teenage boy! He folded it back over his jacket and felt under the mattress. Nothing. The lower part of the bed was a storage area accessed by pulling out a drawer by silver handles. The cavernous drawer was empty. He pulled it out as far as it would go and lying on the floor shone the light of the torch onto the underside of the bed. Neatly stuck to it was a bulging envelope about fourteen by twenty inches. His heart beat quickened as he leant across the drawer and peeled off the tape. The envelope dropped into his hand. He quickly got up, pushed back the drawer and remade the bed. He looked at his wrist watch. He'd been in the room well over an hour. There was no way he could examine the contents and not be disturbed. He didn't want Carol to find him doing that. It might contain evidence if the case turned serious. He shoved the envelope into his briefcase. If necessary, he'd have to put it back. He took the chair from the door, put on his jacket and wiped his face with a handkerchief, trying to bottle up the excitement racing through his body. What was in the envelope?

Chapter 4

'You think Clara is trying to murder your brother?' Laurel repeated. 'Are you sure?' She wished she hadn't taken up Dorothy's request to talk to Nancy Wintle. 'That's a very serious charge.'

Nancy's face wrinkled, distress making her look like a walnut. 'You don't believe me, do you? I knew no one would believe me.'

Nancy's genuine misery and the hopelessness in her voice made Laurel reach out and take Nancy's hand in hers. 'Please don't think that, Nancy. I'm shocked, I must admit, but please tell me everything you can. Why do you think Clara is trying to kill your brother, her husband?'

Nancy's face relaxed, but her eyes gleamed with unshed tears. 'Thank you. I've been trying to pluck up courage to tell someone, I've nearly told Dorothy many times. Now I've come to a point when I'd rather everyone thinks I'm as mad as a hatter rather than do nothing. If Sam died and I'd not tried to help him, I'd never be able to live with myself.' She withdrew her hand from Laurel's. 'I need a drink, and I don't mean tea.' She went to the sideboard, opened a cupboard door and took out a bottle of Scotch and two cut-glass tumblers. 'Can I tempt you?'

Laurel usually drank her whisky as a nightcap, but she

33

could see the label on the bottle was Glenlivet. 'You can. With some water if possible.'

Nancy went to the kitchen and returned with a jug of water, and soon they were opposite each other again.

'Your health,' Nancy said, raising her glass containing two fingers of liquid, none of it water.

'And yours.' Laurel sipped the Scotch, rolling it round her mouth before letting it trickle down her throat. The drink had been a good idea: Nancy looked more relaxed. 'When you're ready, Nancy. Can you tell me when you first suspected something was wrong?'

Nancy placed her glass on the floor and went over to the sideboard.

Not a refill already?

She picked up two silver-framed photos, sat down and passed one to Laurel. 'This is a photograph of my wedding day. Sam is next to me.'

It was a black-and-white photograph: Nancy slim and pretty, with blonde hair and a happy smile, gazing up at her new husband, James Wintle, a tall, serious-looking man who looked tenderly at his bride. On the other side of Nancy was a lanky teenager, a good-looking boy with thick blond hair and a wide smile. Samuel Harrop, looking happy for his sister.

'You were a lovely bride and your brother was a good-looking boy. Is he still handsome?'

Nancy frowned. 'Unfortunately, yes.'

What does that mean? She didn't ask her to elaborate – not yet, and passed the photo back to Nancy who gave her the other one.

'This is one taken, oh, a few years ago. It's Sam and Clara.'

34

Against a background of a pebble beach and a calm sea, Sam, still recognisable as the boy in the previous photograph, stood by a tall woman. There was a space between them as they faced the camera, arms by their sides. Sam's hair was still thick, but the coloured photo showed there was more silver than blond; the charming smile was present. He looked the kind of surgeon who'd put his patients at ease. His wife's brown hair was fashionably styled, her grey suit well-cut and her expression enigmatic. The face of a future murderer?

Nancy picked up her glass and took another swallow. One finger down and one to go.

'Tell me about Sam as a boy, before you got married. Were you always close?'

Nancy smiled. 'Our mother died soon after Sam was born. I was five. Helping to look after him helped me cope with her loss. We had a nursemaid, but I enjoyed helping to bathe, feed, and play with him. I'd rush back home after school to be with him. I can see him now, lying in his cot; he'd wave his arms when I came in. I've always loved him.' Her voice wavered.

'Dorothy said he went to London, to university and didn't come back to Aldeburgh much.'

Nancy's lips disappeared as she sucked them in, as though she was biting back the words she wanted to say.

'What is it, Nancy? Is there something else about Sam and Clara you find difficult to deal with? I do need to know everything that may be relevant if I'm to help you.'

Nancy took a deep breath and her body quivered. 'There's something about Sam I've never told anyone before, but I think it may be the reason she's ... trying to get rid of him.'

The anguish in her eyes was alarming. Laurel nodded. 'I'm not here to judge Sam. If you want me to take this further, I'll only pass on this information to the others if I think it's relevant to the case.'

Nancy wiped her eyes. 'I couldn't bear it if everyone knew … and Sam would hate me. Everyone looks up to Sam. If this became general knowledge his reputation would be destroyed. Would Dorothy have to know?'

This was getting difficult. 'Dorothy's part of the firm. You know she's discreet.'

'I know; I'd trust her not to say anything; but I'd find it difficult to face her.'

What has Sam done? Something to do with his days as a surgeon?

Nancy clasped her hands together, like a small child saying bedtime prayers. 'Sam … is a … homosexual. There I've said it.' A shiver ran down her body from her shoulders to her small feet.

She didn't know what to say. Was this true? Was Nancy sure? Sam was married … not that that meant he couldn't have relationship with men, but what about Clara? Had she only recently discovered this? Was that why she wanted to get rid of him? That is, if Nancy was right.

'When did you find out Sam was homosexual?'

Nancy wouldn't meet her eyes. 'It was just after I married. James, he told me. Sam, before he went to university, used to visit us regularly, at our new home. He worshipped James, I'm sure that's why he read medicine. I could see James became uncomfortable with Sam coming round so often, and he started to go out of the room and leave me with him.' She took a sip of whisky. 'I

36

was cross, I thought James was rude, and I could see Sam was upset. One day after Sam went home I told James what I thought of him.'

Nancy was calm as she told her story. It had the ring of truth. This was far more complicated, and interesting, than Laurel had expected. 'James told you of his suspicions?'

'It was more than suspicions; he had proof.'

She calculated the date of the revelation. 'This was before the law changed, wasn't it? When homosexual relationships were illegal?'

Nancy nodded. 'When James told me I was furious; I couldn't conceive such a thing. I knew nothing of homosexuals, apart from them being the butt of dirty jokes and ghastly court cases in *The News of* the *World*.'

'But James persuaded you it was true?'

Nancy sighed. 'Partly, but I wasn't convinced. James was worried for Sam; he knew Sam wanted to make a career in medicine, and if his sexuality was exposed, that would be the end of that. He made me aware many prominent men were homosexuals, most, if they were discreet, were able to lead successful lives, but sometimes loneliness and a need for sex, love or both, drove them to reckless actions, and blackmail and exposure sometimes followed. He wanted to make sure Sam knew about this, but he didn't feel it was right for him to talk to him.'

'You said James had proof. Can you tell me what it was?'

'Sam wrote him a love letter. He asked James not to tell me. He didn't show it to me, said he'd destroyed it and he'd told Sam never to write anything like that again. He didn't think Sam had … done anything, with anyone, but he wanted me to talk to him.'

37

She leant back in her chair. What a difficult situation for a young, naïve bride.

'Do you know any homosexuals, Laurel?' Nancy asked hopefully. 'They're not all depraved, are they?'

She laughed. 'No more than any other person. I'm sure some are horrible, but so are some people who society would call normal. Yes. I've met a few, lesbian couples in both cases: two teachers, and a couple who ran a pub. Couldn't ask for nicer people, and the teachers weren't interested in young girls, they were in love with each other. Also, when I was a student, one friend, Tony, was gay.'

'Gay? What does that mean?'

Laurel bit her lip; of course, Nancy mustn't know what it meant nowadays. 'It's another word for homosexuals, usually men. They prefer to be called gays than homos or other derogatory words.'

Nancy sighed. 'What a shame, such a nice word.' She shook her head. 'Go on, dear.'

'We often went out drinking together; it was relaxing knowing he wasn't interested in me as a woman, and I think he felt the same. Mind you I could always tell if a manly dish came into a pub as his pupils dilated.'

Nancy laughed. 'So this doesn't disgust you? You aren't put off by what I've told you?'

'No, I'm interested. Did you talk to Sam?'

Nancy took a long, deep breath. 'Yes, I finally summoned up the courage. I told Sam how much I loved him and hoped he wouldn't be offended. My greatest fear was he'd hate me and we'd lose each other.' She clasped her hands again. 'He cried. He'd been afraid James would tell me and I'd hate him. I told him we both loved him and

38

wanted to help and support him. I explained everything James told me.' She sat in silence, a few tears tracking down her cheeks. She pulled a handkerchief from her trews pocket and wiped them away.

'Did you and Sam remain close?'

'Yes, but it was never quite the same. The next year he went to university in London. He promised me he'd be careful; said he'd never run the risk of anyone finding out.'

'When did he marry?'

'He was thirty-eight and well established in Harley Street. He came home specially to tell me. When he said he was getting married I thought something had happened to him, a miracle, he was normal, I wouldn't have to worry about him. But before I could tell him how happy I was he was cured, he told me Clara knew he was a homosexual, but was happy to marry him for the status and wealth he'd provide. It wasn't a real marriage.'

Laurel raised her eyebrows. She didn't know what she been expecting to hear from Nancy but this tale got more complicated and unbelievable by the minute. 'So Clara provided a cover? Do you think Sam had relationships with men?'

Nancy looked at her, her brown eyes dull with pain. 'Yes, I'm sure he did. I think he liked Clara and they shared several interests. Both loved music, it was one of the reasons for returning to Aldeburgh: the music festival and he adores Benjamin Britten. She enjoyed running their house and mixing with his colleagues. I don't think she's interested in sex, so the marriage suited her.'

'Then why do you think she's trying to kill him? As his widow, she wouldn't have as much clout. What's convinced you she's going to murder him?'

Nancy hung her head. 'Sam's ill. He hasn't told me what's the matter, but I think it's serious. The last time I saw him he said he needed to talk to me alone. He needed to tell me something.

'I think Clara overheard him and since that day I haven't been able to see him. She makes excuses: he's too ill, he's out, he doesn't want to speak to me. Lately when I phone I can't get through. I'm afraid I'll never see him alive again.'

Laurel turned and waved goodbye to Nancy, who was standing on her doorstep, trying to look cheerful. What was she to make of what she'd heard? Thoughts were sliding round her brain like returning elvers to their home river; too many thoughts and not in much order. Her mouth was dry from the whisky, as if she'd sucked on a lemon halfway through a hockey match.

On her way to her car, near the Moot Hall, she walked up the High Street to see what was on at the cinema. The Misses Smith's tearooms were open and as, in the excitement of Nancy's revelations, she'd forgotten to buy a pasty, she decided this was the next best thing... The chimes of a bell vibrating on a copper coil summoned one of the Miss Smiths from the kitchen. Laurel was placed at a table near the window; she was the only customer. While she waited for her pot of tea and plate of cakes to appear, she made notes on the meeting with Nancy. Some of what she'd heard rang true: Sam's homosexuality, Clara's willingness to marry him in exchange for status and money, but Clara trying to kill Sam? Why would she want to do that? This was the part of Nancy's story she found hard to swallow.

A waitress, complete with lace-edged apron, placed cup, saucer, teapot, hot water and a milk jug on the table; Laurel chose a chocolate éclair and a piece of ginger cake. She needed a sugar boost. What would the others think of this case? Would they want to take it on? Dorothy would want to help Nancy, and Laurel wanted to find out more about Sam and Clara. Tomorrow morning the team were meeting to discuss new cases and those in progress; she wanted to take Nancy's case further and hoped the rest of the team would agree.

Laurel sipped her tea, the astringent brew washing away the metallic taste in her mouth. How much her life had changed in six months. Then she was a new member of the teaching staff of Blackfriars School: the Senior Mistress. Now she was a partner in a detective agency, the other partners people who'd either been police officers or who worked at the school. Frank, a detective inspector leading a murder case, Stuart his sergeant, Dorothy the school secretary and Mabel the school cook. Now they were a team, using Dorothy's house in Dunwich not only as their base, but as living quarters for Dorothy, Mabel and herself, Stuart to follow, when and if he and Mabel married. Frank, wanting some independence, stayed at his cottage on the cliffs overlooking Minsmere beach.

What would have happened if Dorothy, Stuart and Mabel hadn't made their offer to be part of the partnership she and Frank had formed?

Laurel poured hot water into the teapot. So far it had worked well: Stuart was the third detective, so they could take on more cases; Dorothy looked after all the paperwork, freeing more time for investigations and

Mable cooked, shopped and took care of them. The only fly in the ointment was Mabel didn't seem too keen to name a date for the marriage, and this was making Stuart miserable. They were such a good team, friends as well as colleagues; she didn't like to think what would happen if the team split up.

Chapter 5

Tuesday, March 9, 1971

Frank drove between the open, wrought-iron gates, decorated with silhouettes of hooded monks, and parked in front of the round pond with its central dolphin burping spouts of water. Greyfriars House, the beating centre of Anglian Detective Agency. He shook his head and smiled. He must talk to Dorothy and ask her if the agency could pay to have the fountain restored to its original efficiency. She'd already updated several parts of the house: an outer scullery had morphed into a darkroom and the spacious dining room was turned into an office, with four desks, each with its own telephone. The largest desk was hers with a new electric typewriter, and nearby a Xerox duplicating machine, and all the other up-to-date accoutrements needed by an efficient secretary. The dining table doubled as a conference point for their weekly meetings, as well as formal meals.

Today Dorothy would have laid each place not with cutlery, but blotting paper, pencils, sheets of foolscap and duplicated notes for the meeting. She'd put every scrap of her formidable energy into easing the jobs of the three detectives and making Greyfriars into a hub of efficiency. The work helped her to cope with the recent loss of her sister, Emily.

Was it only last September when everything had come to a head? He didn't regret resigning from the police, not one bit, especially when Stuart had joined him after his retirement. Two policemen, an ex-Senior Mistress, a school secretary and the school cook. What a combination. He shook his head again. A good team. There'd been a few mistakes, not many and non-serious, also a few successes. Finding Amy Frame's teenage daughter when she'd run away, and the recovery of stolen antique jewellery; both those cases had been satisfying. What would the morning's meeting throw up? He hoped the team would support his proposal to carry on with the Pemberton case, they'd have to – he'd promised Carol he'd look for David.

Carol. He'd never been keen on the name Carol, until now. Suddenly it seemed a charming name. He remembered following her up the staircase, the tightening of his jaws, the difficulty of breathing normally, and the realisation of the effect she was having on him. He desired her. Usually his desires were followed by boredom and the need to escape from the relationship. You're not a good person, Frank Xavier Diamond, he thought, echoing his mother's frequent chides. He'd have to be careful not to allow his carnal feelings to show: was Carol the kind of woman who'd enjoy being ogled? Perhaps, but Adam Pemberton might kick him off the case if he thought he'd taken a shine to his wife.

Something delicious was being cooked in the kitchen; there were aromatic smells of baking fruit and pastry: Mabel was getting ready for their coffee break. In the boardroom/dining room Stuart Elderkin was already seated at the table, his loaded pipe ready beside the blotting paper in front of him, his well-built frame comfortable in the elm captain's chair with its broad seat and encircling arms. Dorothy was placing a financial report on each of the blotters.

'Morning, Frank,' Stuart said, 'any luck with the missing boy case?'

Dorothy looked up, her spectacles on the end of her nose. 'I've got a suggestion to make on that one, if we take it on.'

'Good morning. I think you'll both be interested. Where's Laurel?'

'She went out for a run, and needed a shower. Here she is. I can hear her coming down the stairs,' Dorothy said.

The dining room door swung open and Laurel, red-faced, her damp hair pulled back in a pony-tail, burst into the room. 'Hello, Frank. That blew the cobwebs away, it's still chilly but good for running.' She pulled a chair up to the table.

Frank smiled inwardly as he contrasted Laurel, her tall frame clad in a navy sweater and cords, to the elegance of Carol. Every time he saw Laurel he was bowled over by her: attractive, with long blonde hair, just under six feet tall, with broad shoulders and narrow hips. Her build, courage and intelligence had been more than a match for Nicholson, but it had been a close call. She could have been the last of a long line of his victims.

'I'll get Mabel,' Stuart said.

He raised his eyebrows at Laurel. She screwed her nose up, as if to say, 'Don't ask me.'

The first two items on the agenda were quickly dealt

with: a financial statement and plans for a second bathroom and the conversion of a smaller room to be used for interviewing clients. All were passed.

'These are very reasonable quotes, Dorothy,' Frank said.

'Dirt cheap, if you ask me,' Mabel said.

Stuart laughed heartily, too heartily.

Dorothy tapped her nose, looking pleased with herself. 'Local contacts, member of the church. Well, Frank, you're item three. The floor is yours.'

He consulted his notebook and told them everything he'd discovered at the Pemberton's house, except he didn't mention how beautiful Carol was. 'I found this envelope taped under the bed. I removed it without asking permission.' He also didn't tell them there was one drawing he hadn't brought with him. It remained in his cottage. Why didn't he want to show it to them? He wasn't sure himself.

'Not lost your old habits, I see,' Stuart said.

'Old bad habits,' Laurel said, shaking her head in mock horror.

He shrugged. 'Finding David is more important than playing with a straight bat. The boy hid them for a reason. He didn't want his parents to see the contents. I may have to return them.'

'Shouldn't we put on gloves, or something?' Mabel asked.

'Paper doesn't take prints, love,' Stuart replied.

They leant forward, faces eager, intrigued, wanting to see what was in the envelope. God, I love this job, thought Frank.

'The envelope contains drawings by David of different

46

people. I'll pass the drawings round without making comments and then when we've seen all of them, I'll tell you who's who. Some of the drawings are of people I don't know, but I think we can make guesses at this point. The format varies: some are only faces, others, head and shoulders and there are a few full-length sketches.'

He opened the envelope and carefully pulled out the drawings. He passed the first drawing to Laurel, watching her face as she studied the picture. Bubbles of oxygen seemed to rush through his brain. His heartbeat quickened as he looked at the drawings again.

Nothing was hidden, David had drawn these people as though their thoughts were laid bare on their faces for all to see; their characters revealed: goodness and evil, generosity and greed, lust and innocence. Frank leant back in his seat, waiting for the team to absorb the details. He was sure he'd hit the mother lode. David's disappearance must have something to do with these drawings.

The last drawing completed the circuit. Laurel was frowning, blinking her eyes; Stuart Elderkin tamped down tobacco in his pipe and lit a match; Dorothy was shaking her head as she reached for her packet of cigarettes and Mabel's eyes were filled with tears.

'I've got a bad feeling about this,' she said.

Stuart reached for her hand. She pushed his away.

Frank pretended he hadn't noticed. 'I'll take you through the drawings of the people I know.' He placed the drawing of Carol in the centre of the table. 'This is Carol Pemberton, David's mother.' He'd captured her beauty but the face that stared at them from the paper was not the face he'd seen yesterday. The eyes were wide, staring, making her look as though she suffered from an over-

47

active thyroid. Her black hair was loose, floating round her head in an electrified cloud and her lips were drawn back showing small teeth. She looked terrified, or possibly ...? He thought of the drawing he'd kept back. He hoped it wasn't true.

'Perhaps we shouldn't read too much into this, it could be the product of the vivid imagination of an adolescent boy. Mrs Pemberton, though upset at times, was calm and reasonable when I interviewed her,' he said.

'Is she as beautiful as this?' Laurel asked.

'It does her justice,' he replied. He moved on to details of his interview with her.

He placed the second drawing by the side of the first. 'This is Adam Pemberton, the father, another fantastic likeness.' The lugubrious face with its down-turned mouth was perfectly caught, but at the corner of each eye a tear was forming. The stiff Englishman was made human by the slightest touch of a pencil. The boy had shown his father's deep sadness. He told them what he'd learnt about Adam. Why is Adam so sad? Was it because of David's inability to read and write, or the state of his wife's mind?

He took another drawing and laid it on the table. 'This is Miss Ann Fenner, the housekeeper.' He explained he'd only seen her briefly and she hadn't made a deep impression on him. She'd been polite, efficient in making and bringing in the coffee, but had shown no emotion, or curiosity about his visit. He tapped the drawing. 'She looks quite different here.' She was smiling, laughter lines creasing the skin round her eyes and mouth, her head tilted back showing a strong, long neck.

'It looks like David related to her, someone he trusted,

someone who liked him and who he liked back,' Laurel said.

'She looks normal, not like his mother and father,' Dorothy said, following up her comment by inhaling on her cigarette.

'Stuart, I think you'd be the best person to talk to Ann Fenner if we take on this case. I don't think she thought much of me,' he said.

'She looks a respectable woman. Did you have that leather jacket on?' Stuart asked.

He nodded, pulling a face.

'No wonder she didn't take to you. We want to find out about her relationship with David. Anything else?'

'Any gossip about the parents, also if you can find out about the tutors David had, especially in the last two years before he went to school. Addresses or telephone numbers would be useful. One of them might shine some light on the family,' he said, as he picked up more drawings. 'The rest of the people I don't know, but I guess some of them are staff and pupils at Chillingworth.' He spread out the remaining drawings below the others.

'I know one of them.' Stuart said, pointing to a full-length portrait of a man dressed in a suit, collar and tie and black gown. 'That's the headmaster, Ralph Baron.'

'How do you know him, Stuart?' Dorothy asked.

'It was a few years ago. One of the pupils died. Nothing suspicious. Found in his bed by one of the other pupils. Some kind of heart failure. Everyone was very upset.' He looked at the expressions on the other members of the team. 'I know what you're thinking. There was a post-mortem, nothing nasty was found.' The silence round the table said it all. They looked again at the drawing of

Ralph Baron.

'Is he as tall as he looks?' Laurel asked.

'Bit taller than you, Laurel, about six two,' Stuart replied.

They looked again at his portrait.

He was certainly slim with the build of a whippet, or a long-distance runner, and looked ready to leap from the page and jump a few hurdles. David had captured the intensity of his character, he fairly fizzed off the paper. His hair looked fair, straight. Definitely short back and sides with a low parting on the left and hair combed across his scalp. The face was long and thin, bushy eyebrows, a Roman nose and a generous mouth with full lips, which seemed incongruous in such an ascetic face. And the expression? Difficult to judge. Was this a person David liked? Frank frowned. The eyes said yes, he'd given the man kind, friendly eyes; the lips said no: they were lascivious and slightly twisted.

'Frank, can I interrupt before we look at the next drawing?' Dorothy asked.

Frank nodded.

'I read all the previous case notes, as we all have, and as I was going through the *East Anglian Daily Times* yesterday I came across a job advert—'

'Not leaving us already?' Stuart quipped. Mabel glared at him and he took some deep puffs on his pipe and looked the other way.

'Chillingworth School are advertising for a secretary, part time. What do you think? It might be useful to have someone able to snoop round.'

'Well spotted,' Frank said. 'If we decide today to take the case, and after Stuart and I've been to the school, we can decide whether it would be a good idea.' He hesitated. 'Mind you, you might not get it.' He ducked as an eraser flew through the air. The mood lightened.

'Time for a coffee break?' Mabel asked

Stuart picked up some plates and followed Mabel. 'That was a really lovely Chelsea bun, Mabel.'

There was a muffled reply from Mabel and the closing of the kitchen door.

'What's the matter with them?' Frank asked Laurel and Dorothy.

'I don't know,' Laurel replied; she looked at Dorothy.

'Mabel hasn't confided it me, but I'm sure she's still fond of Stuart.'

'Women!' Frank said, puffing out his cheeks, then blowing air like a surfacing whale. 'You could have fooled me.'

Laurel dug him in the ribs as Stuart came back into the room; he avoided everyone's eyes and slumped into his chair.

Frank collected the drawings they hadn't looked at; everyone took their seats waiting for Mabel.

She bustled in. 'Sorry to keep you waiting. I was putting a casserole into the oven: lamb hotpot. One of your favourites, Stuart.' She looked at him. He didn't reply, but shot her a baleful look.

They're worse than a pair of spotty teenagers, Frank thought.

'Mabel, you're spoiling us. I'll have to up my running if you keep on giving us so much delicious food.'

'Thanks, Laurel, glad someone appreciates my efforts.'

'Mabel!' Dorothy said.

Mabel flushed. 'Sorry.'

'Let's look at the rest of the drawings,' Frank said.

The one he'd selected was a woman dressed in a uniform which suggested she might be a nurse or possibly a school matron: starched uniform, with a fob watch displayed on her ample bosom and a neat cap pinned to a thin head of hair which was scraped back from her face, possibly into a bun. The mouth was tight, no sign of teeth, the nostrils flared, as though she'd detected a random fart. Large eyes, probably brown from the amount of graphite used, were surrounded by lash-less lids. The eyes were expressionless, staring into space, showing no emotion, neither caring nor disdain. Frank thought he wouldn't like to see her approaching with a bedpan, or worse a thermometer.

'Could be the school matron,' Laurel said.

Dorothy shivered.

'That's the end of the adults. The last two are children.' He placed them side by side on the table. The portrait on the left made him feel sick. It had when he'd first seen it, and its effect on him hadn't changed.

The child looked young, possibly nine or ten, although Carol had told him the youngest children in the school were eleven. This boy was terrified. There was a frozen expression of fear on his face, shown by the wide eyes, enlarged pupils, the half-open mouth, lips drawn back in horror at what he was looking at, or what was about to happen. The way David had used shading to create shadows made his skin ghostly white, his cheek bones sharp as knives; you could almost hear his terrified whimpers. Frank gripped the edge of the drawing and placed it back in the pile of drawings. 'I hope David has a vivid imagination; no child should feel this terrified.'

'I wonder who he is,' Dorothy said, lighting another cigarette and taking a deep pull.

'If he's a Chillingworth pupil we'll find out. He's not the boy who died, is he?' Frank asked Stuart, knowing the answer but wanting to break Stuart Elderkin's silence.

'I would have said, if he was,' Stuart snapped.

Frank glanced at Laurel who bit her lip.

He ploughed on. 'Last one. The only one with a name.'

Written in a childish but firm hand, in a jumble of capital and lower case letters, was the name Peter. It was a full-length portrait of a slim boy, about fourteen, who was smiling, his light-coloured eyes, probably blue, looked at you directly, and his small mouth curved with happiness. He was the kind of child mothers smiled at and old ladies patted on the head.

Laurel put out her hand. 'Can I have a closer look, please?'

She'd seen what he'd seen.

'Unless I'm mistaken this boy, Peter, has Down's syndrome.'

Dorothy leant forward and Stuart looked up.

'You mean he's a mongol?' Mabel asked.

Laurel nodded. 'Yes, I think so. Although the signs are not obvious: he's got a round face, and his hair, which is probably blond, looks thin. It's the eyelids, that droop at the corners that give it away. I've seen several children with Down's syndrome; I worked at a special school when I did my teacher training. Peter's physical signs of the condition are slight compared to the children there, at least that's how David has shown him. Also, if you look carefully at the corner of his mouth you can see a bubble of saliva.'

'Carol – Mrs Pemberton – said David had a friend called Peter he was especially fond of; I don't think she approved. Now I know why,' Frank said.

Laurel bridled. 'It's not Peter's fault he's got Down's syndrome; it's inherited through the chromosomes. The children I worked with were lovely; well not all of them. They were a mixed bunch, just like any other class.'

'Don't get snotty with me, Laurel; I was giving you a reason for Mrs Pemberton's dislike, not mine.' He immediately wished he hadn't said that.

'Then Mrs Pemberton doesn't sound like a very nice person … even if she is beautiful.'

What was happening? Their meetings didn't usually degenerate into swapping insults. He took a deep breath. 'I wondered why he's the only person David has given a name to? David obviously has difficulty writing, but he'd wanted this boy to have a name. I think he was someone important to David. Someone special.'

Laurel nodded. 'I think they were friends. Perhaps they were attracted to each other because of their disabilities: David, the boy who has difficulty reading and writing, but is a genius with a pencil, and Peter, the boy with Down's syndrome, who'd not only have difficulties with reading and writing, but also in coping with many other aspects of normal life. What a strange friendship, if that's what it is. But understandable. Two misfits supporting each other. Able to be themselves when they were together.'

'That's a brilliant analysis, Laurel,' he said.

'Poor little buggers.' Stuart reached for his pipe.

'If Peter is still at the school he may know why David

ran away,' Dorothy said.

'Or David may have told Peter about his family, perhaps the reason for his disappearance lies there,' Frank mused.

They all gazed in silence at the drawing of Peter.

Frank studied their faces. The moment seemed right. 'I'd like us to take this case on. Do I have your agreement?'

Four pairs of eyed looked into his. Four heads solemnly nodded. Relief flooded through him and deep in his guts desire and lust made his muscles tighten. He'd see Carol again. And again. And again.

Chapter 6

Wednesday, 10 March, 1971

Although it was after lunch Samuel Harrop was lying on the settee dressed in pyjamas and a dressing gown. He tried not to move, as every muscle contraction, however slight, sent waves of sickening pain crashing through his body. He looked at the rosewood clock on the matching sideboard. Five minutes past two; in twenty-five minutes he could have another dose of morphine. He mustn't weaken and take it before then, he must keep his mind clear until he'd seen Nancy. He couldn't, wouldn't, tell anyone else. She'd be appalled, but he knew she'd still love him and would do what was right. He must get Clara to let him see her.

He carefully turned his head to look round the sitting room, his favourite room in the house. The French windows leading to a grassy slope, rich with primroses, the Art Deco furniture he'd collected over a number of years, the streamlined Paul Frankel sofa, in ebony and black lacquer and the matching armchairs. Near the wall was his music centre and his collection of records and tape cassettes. He'd loved to lie on the settee, the French windows open, the sea breeze coiling round the house, wafting the curtains. He'd close his eyes and listen;

perhaps a favourite Benjamin Britten opera, the rich voice of Peter Pears filling the room. Now the windows were locked and he couldn't open them and he dreaded hearing any music as it prompted thoughts that soon all would be silence.

Immediately he'd seen Nancy and was sure she'd do what he wanted, he would commit suicide. He'd hidden a bottle of morphine many months ago and he would make an end to it. He was a coward and he'd be leaving Nancy to deal with the fallout of his confession. He grasped the arm of the settee as a wave of pain twisted his gut. Would telling her put her in danger? Only if only *he* knew he'd told her.

Why wouldn't Clara let him see Nancy? Nancy knew about their false marriage. This last month Clara had made him a prisoner in his own home, she'd dismissed the cleaning lady and the gardener, and he was too physically weak to escape. She'd even removed the phones so he couldn't ring for help. He must reason with her, bribe her, promise her anything as long as he saw Nancy. He couldn't, mustn't, die without making reparation. Nancy would be horrified, disgusted and frightened but she would see justice done.

He glanced at the clock again: it was time. Through the open door of the sitting room he heard Clara's footsteps on the tiled floor of the hall. She came into the room and paused in the doorway. 'It's time for your medicine.'

As always, she was immaculately dressed and groomed. Her brown hair was swept back into a hairstyle reminiscent of Maria Callas, her favourite soprano; on her it seemed like a helmet. She wore a jade-green wool suit and black high heels.

'Shall I fetch it?' she asked.

He nodded. She turned and left the room, returning shortly with a tray on which was a medicine bottle, two glasses, one empty, one containing water, and a spoon. She placed them on a small table near him.

He forced himself to sit up. As he moved the smell of his unwashed and decaying body made him gag. This morning Clara had refused to help him bathe, and he was so weak he was afraid if he got in the bath by himself, he might sink beneath the soapy water and drown. Clara didn't love him, but he'd thought she was fond of him. Now he knew she despised him because he was weak, dying and she hated the ugliness of his approaching death.

He measured the morphine with the spoon into the empty glass, just enough to take the edge off the pain, but not enough to bring even a brief oblivion. He wouldn't let Clara give him his medicine: he no longer trusted her.

He washed the bitter taste away with the water in the other glass. 'Clara, I need to talk to you.'

She sat on one of the armchairs, planted her feet firmly on the carpet and stared at him, her face expressionless. 'I'm not letting you see Nancy until you tell me what you want to see her about.'

'Clara, I haven't much time left. Before I die there is something I must tell Nancy. Lives depend on it. I should have told someone before, but I was a coward.'

She leaned towards him, her face flushing. 'Why can't you tell me? What is it? She knows you're a homo. What else is there to tell? What do you mean, lives depend on it?'

Sam flinched at her description of him. His throat tightened and the room seemed to press in on him, the armchairs turning into squat black toads. He was hallucinating. 'Please, Clara.'

She leant against the back of the chair, hands resting on the arms; in emerald green with her crown of hair she was like a queen, ruling over his life.

'I promise to fetch Nancy if you tell me what you are going to tell her. I don't want to look a fool when she finds out you haven't told me. I think that's the least I deserve. I am your wife and I've acted my part all these years. I know you've had lovers, but I've never done so, no scandal has come through me.' She paused. 'I promise to fetch Nancy if you'll tell me what you're worried about.'

He'd have to risk it. At least one person would know the truth and even if she didn't bring Nancy, perhaps her conscious would make her reveal his secret.

He lowered his head, so he couldn't see her face and told her.

She drew her feet towards each other, until it looked as though her legs were glued together.

'Who's behind all this?' Her voice was calm.

He told her.

She sat still for several minutes. 'I'll go and see Nancy now.'

He looked up. Her face was rigid like chiselled ice.

'Phone her. She'll come straight away. Let me phone her. Where are the phones?'

'No. I want to see her before you speak to her. I won't tell her anything. You must do that.'

Fear fluttered through his chest. 'Please don't leave me locked in. Something might happen while you're out and I won't be able to escape.'

Clara shook her head. 'I'll bring her back soon, I'll leave now.' She walked stiffly from the room. A few minutes later he heard the turn of the key in the front door and then the sound of her car pulling away.

Would Nancy come to see him? Clara seemed determined. Was she going to Nancy's? Where else could she be going? He leant back, the cold leather pressing against his dying body as though it wanted to wrap him in a skin coffin. He longed to be covered by a feather-filled eiderdown, to press the morphine bottle to his lips, let the liquid trickle down his throat, rest his head on a soft pillow and to slip into a final sleep, and oblivion.

If she wasn't going to Nancy's, where was she going? To *him*? He shouldn't have told her. Why would she do that? To challenge him? Or warn him? Could she be going to ask for help? Help to shut him up? God in heaven was she capable of doing that? He mustn't think like that – it was the morphine twisting his brain. Supposing he died before he told Nancy, and Clara didn't tell anyone? The horror would go on. What could he do?

Chapter 7

At midday, Laurel parked Dorothy's Morris Traveller outside the Harrops' Edwardian house. She'd asked Dorothy if she could borrow her car as the Morris was less conspicuous than her Ford Cortina. At the meeting everyone had agreed she should take on Nancy's case, and after consulting Nancy, she'd decided to try and make contact with Sam Harrop when his wife, Clara was out of the house.

She was parked on the opposite side of the street to the house, a discreet distance from the drive. She looked at her watch. Ten past one. She ate the Cornish pasty she'd bought from Smith's Bakery, savouring the crisp pastry and the peppery contents. She made sure none of it dribbled onto her best blue suit; she'd not worn it since her first days at Blackfriars School, but she'd reasoned if she did bump into Clara she wanted to present a respectable picture. She put the greasy paper bag into the waste bin on the floor and opened a side window to let out the smell.

It was now quarter to three and she was bored. She opened up *The Times* newspaper which she'd brought to hide her face with, and flipped through a few pages. Nothing but bad news: a Belfast milkman gunned down in front of children; a life sentence for a squaddie who'd raped and killed a ten-year-old child and Lionel Bart fined £50 for possessing cannabis. She looked at the TV programmes: *Softly, Softly* at eight followed by a party-political broadcast. She groaned.

If she bumped into Clara she'd got her lie ready: she was looking for a Mr Froggatt, and must have got the wrong address. She sighed and wriggled, trying to find a comfortable position. She'd have to get used to doing stake-outs; she hoped they weren't a regular feature of her work.

There was short, sharp shower of rain. When it was over she opened the door, and walked past the house. There was a female silhouette at one of the upstairs windows, and a Golf VW in the driveway. Clara's car. She walked back and got in her car again. Perhaps this was a waste of time and Clara wasn't going out today. She looked at her watch: ten to three. Time was moving as slowly as a limpet.

The distinctive noise of a VW engine cut through the air and the car's bonnet edged out into the road. Laurel peeped from behind the hastily raised newspaper. It was Clara, alone, wearing bright green with her hair done up in an enormous bouffant. She drove away. Where to? Hopefully it wasn't a short journey.

Laurel waited a few minutes in case she'd forgotten something and returned. She checked her handbag: notebook, pen, camera. She wished she hadn't worn high heels along with the suit; they weren't ideal for sleuthing.

The house was elegant, three stories high, with a flat castellated roof; long, wide windows lightening the grey stone walls. Three shallow steps led up to a dark blue front door, and lead pots on either side contained topiary box. Should she press the brass bell? Or circle the house first, looking in through the windows?

Nancy told her Clara had dismissed the cleaner and gardener several weeks ago, so there should only be Samuel Harrop in the house. She hoped she could make contact with him for Nancy's sake. Supposing he wasn't here? Would Nancy be justified in calling in the police? They'd talked about the possibility, but it was something Nancy didn't want to do. She wanted to protect Sam's reputation.

There was no one in the front downstairs rooms. Nancy had said Sam was ill; he might be in bed. She'd *have* to ring the bell if she couldn't see him at the back of the house and hope he could get downstairs.

Laurel walked down the left side of the house; there was a narrow grass path and her high heels sank into the turf. She hoped Clara would think they were aeration holes made by the gardener on his last visit. The lawn at the back of the house sloped gently up to a flat plateau; primroses studded the bank. The first room she came to was the kitchen; there was no one there, and the door leading into it was locked. She looked through the keyhole, no key on the other side. She moved on. French windows, their curtains drawn back, showed a large room, its furniture stylishly black, very 1920s. She moved closer, pressing her nose against the glass so she could see into the corners of the room.

She nearly missed him. He was a stooped figure near a music centre, his cream-coloured dressing gown matching the flocked wallpaper. His right hand was raised towards a shelf stacked with music cassettes. She gently tapped on the window.

He slowly turned round. His eyes, the whites yellow, were full of fear. Laurel hardly recognised him from the photos Nancy had shown her. He was a frail, ill, old man; his hair no longer thick, was hanging in greasy locks round his face; his skin yellow, and so fine and tight over the bones of his skull she thought if she could reach through the glass and touch it, it would disintegrate like antique silk. He staggered towards the window, hope in the dull eyes. He must have a liver disease: cirrhosis? cancer? Poor man, he looked wretched.

She smiled at him and waved her hand as you would to a small child you didn't want to panic. He reached the window and pressed a hand to it, as though to support himself, or perhaps wanting to make human contact. He mouthed something. She couldn't hear his words. She nodded and smiled again, then took out the notebook and biro from her handbag.

She quickly wrote in capitals and held the pad so he could see the words.

NANCY SENT ME

He nodded his head and said something, it might have been 'Good,' or 'Thank God.' She mimed to him, pointing at him and pretended to write on the pad, hoping he'd latch on. He looked puzzled, his eyes vague, his mouth open; he shook his head.

She wrote CAN YOU WRITE? on a fresh sheet and held it up to the window. Understanding dawned in his eyes, he nodded and slowly turned away and shuffled towards a dark wooden sideboard on which a clock read twenty-five past three. Time had changed pace: now it was rushing forward like an incoming rip tide. Clara might be back at any moment.

Sam rummaged in a drawer, his movements slow and juddery. He seemed to have found what he wanted, turned back, then doubled up, his face creased with pain. He leant against the sideboard, panting and looked at her. She thought he said. 'Don't go.' She smiled and nodded. What she felt like doing was finding a shovel, breaking the window, putting him in her car and taking him to Nancy. Hold on, girl, she told herself. Look what happened the last time you let impetuosity get the better of you, stupidly continuing to read the log book when you should have left the cottage and contacted Frank. That nearly got you killed. This is an investigation, not a rescue mission. We need to find out more about the situation and I mustn't move without consulting Nancy.

He started to straighten up, as though the pain had lessened. He shuffled to the window.

Laurel printed on her pad:

CAN YOU GET OUT?

He shook his head, the piece of paper dangled from his fingers as though he'd forgotten about it.

I WILL GET NANCY AND BRING HER HERE, she wrote.

He stared at the words, then slowly wrote on his piece of paper, and held it up for her to see. The writing was shaky, uneven and the line veered lop-sided down the page.

No need She is coming. Clara fetching her.

She stared at him. He nodded and a ghost of a smile

touched his lips. So Clara had changed her mind. Was that where she was driving to? To fetch Nancy? They might be back at any time. If they saw her it would embarrass Nancy and probably infuriate Clara. She wrote another message:

I'LL GO NOW. NANCY WILL BE SO PLEASED TO SEE YOU.

His eyes swam with unshed tears. He wrote on his paper.

Who are you?

She scribbled quickly, wanting to be gone:

LAUREL BOWMAN – NANCY'S FRIEND

She didn't think letting him know she was a detective would calm him down. Suddenly his face changed, and his head started to shake. Was his pain increasing? The paper in his hand shook as though it had a life of its own. He turned his head and looked towards the music console and pointed, his arm vibrating like the marionette conductor of an invisible orchestra.

The sound of a car turning into the drive made Laurel gasp; she tapped on the window and waved goodbye. He stared at her, his mouth open and closing, as he tried to tell her something.

She moved to the side of the house and waited. There was the sound of two car doors closing, one after the other. Then a turning key, the front door opening and closing. She waited a few seconds, then bending low she scuttled to the front of the house, and peeped round the wall. All clear. Clara's car was once more on the drive. She and Nancy must be inside and hopefully with Sam. She ran down the drive and breathed a sigh of relief once safely inside Dorothy's Morris. She took a deep breath. That was close.

She imagined Nancy's face as she saw Sam, how the pleasure of seeing him would be tempered by how ill he looked. He was dying. No doubt about that, but now Nancy would be able to help care for him, if Clara let her. What should she do now? No point in waiting for Nancy to come out, Clara would drive her home. She would ring Nancy later and ask her how the meeting had gone. Would she still think Clara wanted to kill Sam? Surely, she would see this was a genuine illness and perhaps Sam hadn't wanted her to see how ill he was. Clara was merely obeying his wishes. Perhaps her dislike of Clara had coloured her judgement. She frowned – Nancy was a balanced person. This case looked as though it'd come to a swift conclusion; a pity as she didn't want to be involved looking for the missing boy; anything to do with a school brought back too many memories of dead children.

Chapter 8

Stuart Elderkin parked his Humber Hawk near The Moot House on Aldeburgh's sea front. This was where he'd arranged to meet Ann Fenner, the Pemberton's housekeeper, after phoning her that morning. Luckily Wednesday afternoon was her half-day off, and as she was free for the rest of the day, she'd agreed to meet him. She was adamant she didn't want to talk to him in Aldeburgh, so Elderkin suggested a drive to some other place.

'Looks like she doesn't want the Pembertons to know we're meeting,' he told Frank after supper the night before.

'Interesting!' Frank said.

'Thought I'd take her to Southwold.'

'Really? It's a bit far, but if you can find anything that will help us, it'll be worth it.'

'Leave it to me, I know how to charm the ladies,' he said.

Frank raised an eyebrow.

I did once, he thought.

Stuart glanced at the car clock, two twenty, he was ten minutes early. Sudden rain lashed in from the North Sea, cold and flinty; the noise on the windscreen made him think it would turn to hail. He'd offered to pick her up outside the Pemberton's house, but received a firm refusal. Had she told the Pembertons she was meeting him? Why didn't she want anyone in Aldeburgh to see them together? All this secrecy suggested she must have something important to tell him. He hoped his deductions were right; the case needed something concrete; David's drawings were suggestive of undercurrents of tensions and fear, but they weren't evidence, and could be the imaginings of a gifted but over-active imagination.

There was a tap on his window. Ann Fenner, eyes squinting against the driving rain, umbrella flapping in the wind, stood beside the car. Stuart smiled and signalled towards the other side of the car. He leant over and opened the passenger door. No point in him getting drenched as well.

She stayed outside the car. 'I'm sorry, Mr Elderkin, I'm going to make everything wet.'

He took the umbrella from her, shook it, and put it on the floor in the back. 'No problem, Miss Fenner, drop of water won't harm my old war horse.' He hoped the leather seats wouldn't stain; he'd have to give them a good polish.

He pointed to her plastic raincoat which was dripping water. 'Would you like to take that off?'

She nodded. Elderkin placed it on the back floor with the umbrella, and as she slid into the passenger seat he noted she was wearing a black-and-tan checked coat, low-heeled black shoes and gloves. Smart but sensible. He'd chosen his clothes carefully: clean white shirt, maroon tie, grey suit and he'd brought his Dannimac and a trilby. Clothes to reassure and nothing that would frighten the birds. Not like Frank's.

'How about driving to Southwold? Or is that too far? There are some nice tea shops there. What do you think, or have you got another appointment?'

She turned to him with a broad smile. 'Really? I'd love that. I like Southwold but I haven't been there for ages.'

His chest expanded. It was good sitting next to a woman who wasn't glaring at him, or disagreeing with his opinions. 'Then off we go!'

Soon they were on the A12, heading north.

'Do you drive, Miss Fenner?'

'I've a licence, but no car, I'm afraid.'

'Do you ever drive the Pemberton's car?'

'No. I've offered to do shopping, or to take David out before he disappeared, but Mr Pemberton prefers me not to drive their car.'

He left it there; he didn't want to talk about David until he could see Ann Fenner's face as she answered his questions. It was enjoyable driving with a placid woman by his side. Doreen, his late wife, had been a peaceful, sensible woman; always made him feel as though he was in charge, the head of the household, even if it wasn't true. Doreen was a quiet manipulator, but her diplomacy meant she never challenged his ego, such as it was. Dear Doreen. Now Mabel was a different kettle of fish. More like an angry lobster at times. He felt a twinge of guilt. Should he be enjoying another woman's company when he was engaged to Mabel?

He'd known Mabel for years, before she married and he'd always admired her. My, she'd been a good looker. A bit flighty, quick-tongued and with such definite opinions. He hadn't been confident enough to ask her out, and before he knew it she was married to a local

70

fisherman with his own boat. When her husband drowned at sea, a few years after Doreen died, he'd sent a card of condolence and attended the funeral. Some months later she'd stopped him in Aldeburgh's High Street to thank him, and he's taken her for a coffee.

When Susan Nicholson was murdered and Blackfriars School became the hub of the investigation he became closer to Mabel. She was still a handsome woman and an excellent school cook. He was tired of catering for himself and thought Mabel would fit the bill for Mrs Elderkin Mark 2. It wasn't until she was attacked by Nicholson and nearly died he realised he loved her. He didn't think, at his age, he would feel love again, but he had. When she'd accepted his proposal, and they'd joined Frank, Laurel and Dorothy in forming the detective agency, he felt his life had started again.

Why had Mabel changed? She'd started avoiding him, and sometimes said hurtful things. He knew Frank, Laurel and Dorothy were embarrassed by her behaviour. She was contrary, sometimes saying something nice, building up his hopes, then dashing them down again with a brusque reply. What could he do? If he had it out with her she might break off the engagement. Could he ask Frank to help him? But *he* wasn't too hot on personal matters, afraid some woman would tie him down, make him buy a three-piece suit and cut off his long hair. What about Laurel? She was good at dealing with people. Perhaps if she could find out what was wrong with Mabel he'd try and put it right. It would be embarrassing: a fifty-five-year-old man asking a much younger woman to help him sort out his love life. He'd been sure Mabel loved him, but now? As Frank would say: *Women.*

The rain eased as they turned on to the A1095 for Southwold, the sky streaked with blue.

'I think we're going to be lucky, Mr Elderkin.' Ann Fenner smiled at him and pointed out of the window.

Stuart decided he needed to abandon ruminations of his domestic troubles and concentrate on the case. Perhaps a bit of buttering up might help Ann Fenner open up about what went on in the Pemberton household.

'Indeed, we are,' he replied. 'I'll park near the lighthouse. Would you fancy a walk along the prom before we find somewhere to have tea?'

'Could we? That's really kind of you, Mr Elderkin. I do like Southwold: the pier, the beach huts and the lovely little shops. This is a real treat for me.'

Her words were heartfelt; he felt sorry for her, she mustn't have much of a social life, he hoped she was well paid. He wondered if she'd ever been married and perhaps gone back to her maiden name after the marriage ended, by death, divorce or desertion. It wasn't relevant to the case, was it? Mustn't think like that, everything was relevant. Could a past husband or lover have kidnapped David, and Ann Fenner was involved? But there hadn't been any ransom note. Supposing the boy had died accidentally after the kidnapping? Bit far-fetched but he mustn't let a woman's flattering words seduce him into sloppiness. It was Mabel's fault: if she hadn't been so shirty lately he wouldn't be so easily swayed by the soft words of another woman.

They walked through the small Edwardian seaside town. Although the holiday season wouldn't start until Easter, which was four or five weeks away, the streets were busy, with small queues at the bread shop and fishmongers.

He sniffed the air. 'Ah, Adnams brewery is in business.'

Ann Fenner laughed. 'You like your ale, do you, Mr Elderkin?'

She seemed to have shed ten years, her face relaxed and smiling.

'I do like a pint or two, but not on duty, you understand. Lovely smell, malting hops, although some folk don't like it.'

'Mixes well with the sea air, adds a touch of gaiety to the place.'

As they walked down the narrow streets, stopping to look in several of the many antique shops, he realised people must take them for a couple, perhaps a married couple. He didn't find the idea unattractive: she was a well-set up woman, easy to talk to, and she seemed to have an even temper. A reliable source of information? He hoped so. After a stroll up and down the front he found a quiet tea shop and ordered tea and buttered scones. He wondered if Ann Fenner was a good cook.

He let her drink the first cup of tea and eat a scone, then he took out his notepad and biro. 'Would you mind if I made notes, Ann? Can I call you Ann? My name's Stuart. Can't trust my memory anymore.' It wasn't true, but he didn't mind playing the old codger if he got the right result.

'No, of course not, and I'd like you to call me Ann, but will you tell Mr and Mrs Pemberton what I say?'

Stuart poured hot water into the tea pot and gave it a stir. 'No reason for that unless this case gets referred back to the police, and someone is accused of a crime.'

She sat back, her fingers holding tight to the edge of the table cloth. 'What do you mean, a crime? David ran away. How can anything I say be relevant to a crime?'

Whoops. Not a good beginning. 'Sorry, Ann. We're not expecting to find a crime's been committed, I was just theorising in answer to your question, putting the worse slant on the case. No need to worry about what you say being passed back to your employers.' Had that smoothed the way?

She took a sip of tea, frowning and didn't reply.

Oh heck. He was silent, then buttered a second scone. They weren't as good as Mabel's, bit dry.

Ann took a deep breath. 'I want to talk to someone about David. I did talk to the police and the private detectives who took on the case, but ...' She looked at him, biting her lip.

'You could have told them more?'

She nodded. 'I'm not sure if what I've got to say is relevant. Also, Mrs Pemberton always insisted on being there when I was asked questions, and the police and the private detectives didn't seem to think I'd have anything important to tell them.'

Stuart took out his pipe and matches. 'Would you mind if I light up, Ann? Helps me to think.'

She relaxed. 'No ... Stuart. I love the smell of tobacco. My late husband smoked a pipe, although ...'

Although what? A widow. 'I tell you what, why don't you tell me everything you want to tell me, and I'll ask questions if I'm not sure what you mean. That'd be better than me giving you the third degree, wouldn't it?' He chuckled, tamping some rough-cut into his pipe and lighting up, leaning back in his chair as though ready to

74

hear a good story.

She smiled at him. 'You're very good at relaxing people, aren't you? A woman feels safe in your company, Stuart.'

He wasn't sure if that was what he wanted to hear. A touch of danger always spiced up any relationship. He nodded sagely and puffed on his pipe.

She took another sip of tea, then placed the cup firmly on the saucer. 'I'll start at the beginning, shall I?'

'Always a good place to start.'

'I came to the Pemberton's six years ago. When my husband died I needed to get a job: for the money and to stop me going mad ...' She reddened.

Again the hesitation, as though she wanted to say more but was embarrassed or afraid. It was always useful to talk about matters not related to the case before you started in earnest. It helped you to learn the pattern of voice. 'What did your husband die of? Was it an accident?'

She looked down, avoiding his eyes. 'No, he died of lung cancer. It's a death I wouldn't wish on anyone.'

So that was why she was embarrassed, her husband had smoked a pipe. He clenched his teeth against the stem of his. If Mabel set the date for their marriage he'd seriously think of giving it up, but if she didn't ... a man had to have a few pleasures, even if they weren't good for him. He smiled at her. 'Tell me, what it was like when you first started your job at the Pembertons?'

She swallowed and nervously licked her lips. 'I was lucky to get the position: I'd not worked for several years, but my last job was in a big hotel, I was in charge of the housekeeping: the laundry, bedlinen, dining-room linen, flowers, and supervising the chambermaids. My old manager was still around and gave me a good reference. I wanted to be with a family, we didn't have children and I liked the idea of helping to look after a young boy. I didn't realise how different David was to other children.'

'Didn't the Pembertons tell you about him when you went for an interview?'

Ann Fenner shook her head. 'I saw him very briefly; I thought he was a lovely boy, but shy. I didn't realise Mrs Pemberton didn't want me to have much to do with David. My job was to run the house, cook meals and supervise the other people who work for them.'

'They are?'

'A cleaner comes in three times a week, a gardener, and a woman occasionally cooks when I have my time off. I have one-and-a-half days off a week. The whole day varies according to what entertaining the Pembertons are doing. Since David disappeared they haven't had people round very often, so usually I get Sundays off.'

'What are they like to work for?'

'They pay well and they're generous with the housekeeping, there's no scrimping on the quality of the food, although Mr Pemberton checks the accounts thoroughly, as you'd expect he would.' She pulled at her right cheek. 'Even when David was here, it wasn't a happy household. Perhaps it's me, I've not been much fun since Bill died; I shouldn't expect other people to cheer me up.'

'Tell me about David. What was he like when you first went there?'

She smiled. 'You've seen his photo?'

Stuart nodded.

'Then you'll know what a handsome chap he was ...

76

is. Whenever I met him in the house I'd say, 'Hello, Master David.' That's how Mrs Pemberton wanted me to address him. I felt like the servant woman in *David Copperfield*. I realised he was different; he didn't talk very much. Sometimes Mrs Pemberton would lose her temper with him and poor Mr Pemberton would look so upset. I never heard him shout at David.'

From the different tones of her voice: cold for Mrs Pemberton and warm for her husband, Stuart detected a difference in feeling to each of them. 'Did David ever speak to you?'

'Not at first. It started because of my cooking. Sorry to blow my own trumpet, but I'm a good cook and I introduced meals I thought would appeal to a young boy, especially extra nice puddings.'

Stuart wanted to ask what these were, and how good was her apple pie. He restrained himself. 'What happened?'

'I was in the kitchen looking through my cookery books to find a recipe for plums; the Victoria tree in the kitchen garden had produced a glut and I wanted something different to plums and custard.'

Stuart Elderkin thought of Doreen's plum pie. 'Plum pie's nice,' he ventured.

Anne laughed. 'I'd found a recipe for plum and almond tart; I think the flavours of plum and almond are harmonious, and I was so absorbed reading the recipe I didn't hear him come into the kitchen, until his hand, finger, pointing at the recipe, came into view.

'"Are you going to make that?" he asked.

'I jumped and my hand went to my throat. "Master David, you've given me a fright." He giggled. I realised

77

he must be able to read at least some of the recipe and he'd spoken a short, clear sentence. I decided not to comment and acted as though this was normal.'

'Clever woman,' Stuart commented.

Ann Fenner blushed and smiled. '"I don't like you calling me, Master David, it's silly," he said.

'"What do want me to call you?"

'"Just David."

'I nodded and pointed to the book. "Do you think you'll like this recipe? I noticed you left some of your plums and custard."

'He moved closer and studied the recipe closely, tracing each line with his finger. "What's shortcrust pastry?"

'I explained.

'"I'd like you to make this. It sounds good."

'He could read, slowly, but he seemed to understand most of the words and he'd said more words in one minute than I'd heard in the five months I'd been there. I was so excited I wanted to rush out and tell his parents, but something stopped me. Why was he talking to me when he wouldn't talk to his parents? How would they feel if I told them he'd freely talked, almost chattered, to me? Did David want me to tell them? Would he feel betrayed if I did? I didn't know what to do.

'"I shall make it tomorrow," I said.

'He smiled at me and I smiled back. It was so natural, a child looking forward to a nice pudding. I had difficulty holding the tears back.

'"Can I come and see you again?"

'My heart swelled with joy. "Any time, David and we can look at more recipes."

'"Thank you. I'll come when *they* are out, or *they're* busy and they think I'm in my room."

'The joy died. This wasn't right and if they found out David was secretly visiting me I might lose my job, but I couldn't tell him that.

'"Is this a secret between us, David? You don't want me to tell your parents you've been talking to me?" I was hoping he'd shake his head and say it didn't matter.

'Instead he beamed at me. "Yes, our secret. I like secrets. If you tell *her* she won't let me come and see you. She doesn't like anyone doing anything for me, she likes to do it all herself." The tone of his voice showed he didn't like that.

'"Very well, come and see me when you can, you'll always be welcome." I knew it was wrong and dangerous, but I couldn't betray him and I suppose I was flattered he'd trusted me. He smiled once more, turned away and went out of the kitchen without saying another word. I almost believed I dreamt the episode it was so weird hearing him talk in such a mature manner, and hearing the cold tone of his voice as he spoke about his mother. I must admit from that moment my feeling towards Mrs Pemberton changed and what I learned later made me dislike her more.'

Stuart blew out his cheeks. This was really interesting: a boy who could talk but chose not to and who seemed to dislike his mother. 'What you've told me, Ann, is very helpful, it shows us another side to David's character. I think we need another pot of tea, or …' He looked at his watch. 'The Crown will be open. Shall we go there, have a beer and perhaps some fish and chips?'

'I thought you didn't drink on duty?'

79

'This isn't a duty, it's a pleasure, and I'd like to hear about David's behaviour before he ran away and also you can tell me what Mrs Pemberton did to make you dislike her. What do you say?' This was a profitable afternoon: new slants on David and hopefully some dirt on Mrs P, not to mention agreeable company, a pint and some good grub.

Ann Fenner looked torn. Did she think she'd said too much already?

'Are you sure? Haven't you got to get back to the office?'

'Why go back when I've got good company, and the prospect of a pint of Adnams?'

She laughed and smiled up at him. 'If I didn't know better I'd think you were flirting with me, Stuart Elderkin.'

'Perhaps I am. There's no law against it, is there?'

'Not yet, but they may make one soon.'

Stuart got up, paid at the till, and took their coats and his trilby from a hat stand. He passed her coat to her. He opened the café door and she preceded him, a girlish bounce to her step. Remember you're a detective, he thought, and an engaged man.

Chapter 9

Frank's appointment with Ralph Gabriel Baron, headmaster of Chillingworth School, was for two-thirty, the same time Stuart was meeting Ann Fenner. He'd tried to see Baron in the morning, but the woman who spoke to him on the phone was adamant: this was the time offered, take it or leave it, and although she didn't use that phrase, the meaning was clear.

After the sickening crimes committed by Philip Nicholson, headmaster of Blackfriars, Frank and the rest of the team, especially Laurel and Dorothy, were jumpy about investigating a case involving a school. However, David hadn't disappeared from the school so Frank hoped the answer didn't lie there. He knew from Carol, Peter was a pupil at the school, but was the frightened boy also a pupil? or was he a figment of David's imagination?

As he turned onto the B1128 from Westleton, the rain stopped and strong spring sunshine lit up the bare branches of the trees. At Yoxford he turned onto the A12. Near Farnham, before the River Alde passed under a bridge on its circuitous way to Aldeburgh, he turned left, and a few miles from the main road turned left again. An inconspicuous school sign, placed low on a brick wall, indicated the way. The driveway was narrow and twisted between clumps of trees, mainly oak, which grew close to the road, obscuring the view ahead. He thought he could see the green growths of emerging bluebells; they'd be a wonderful sight in May.

The trees thinned, revealing a small manor house set back from a gravelled rectangle; several cars and a school minibus were parked on it. Frank slowed down and stopped on a grass verge so he could get a clear view of the house; he opened a window to let in fresh air. A blackbird leant back as it pulled a worm from the ground. With raucous cries, a second blackbird dive-bombed the first, and a frantic fight started. He smiled and hoped the worm escaped.

It was a handsome Jacobean house, built in red brick, three stories high with Dutch pediments, their stepped brickwork rising above the roof. Three tall chimneys flanked each side of the central pediment, with more chimneys at the ends of the house. The windows, with stone surrounds, were tall, their panes of glass glittering in the sun. The house looked in good repair. How do they manage to maintain a house this size to such a high standard, he wondered? The pupil numbers were small; he must find out what the fees were. He parked near the main entrance, an imposing door with two roundel windows above, and looked at his watch: ten past two, he'd given himself twenty minutes of snooping time.

The main door was kept open by a cast-iron doorstop. He stepped into an empty hall, marble-floored, wooden panelled, with doors on either side, one signed Headmaster's Office. He wasn't seeing him here; the interview was to take place in Baron's private rooms. Ahead was a corridor leading to a flight of stairs. There was a mixture of smells: lavender furniture polish and traces of whatever they'd eaten for lunch; he sniffed as he tried to guess; not the usual smell of school dinners, but something savoury and vaguely peppery. Goulash? It seemed unusually quiet for a school; he knew there weren't many children, but where was the bustling secretary? the child on its way to the headmaster's office? the officious caretaker?

Frank was about to chance his arm and open one of the doors when the clatter of footsteps on the stairs held him back. A slim young man, about twenty-five, with floppy blond hair, wearing a paint-spattered smock, strode into the hall.

'Hello. Can I help you?' he said.

Frank introduced himself and his business. 'I'm meeting Mr Baron in his private rooms. I'm a little bit early, but I don't want to put anyone out.'

'I'm Gordon Stant, I teach art and music.'

This is a bonus, he thought. 'Did you teach David Pemberton?'

'Who?'

He explained.

'No. I started here last September. How awful. His parents must be distraught.'

Pity. 'Did you meet the previous art master?'

'No, when I came for an interview he'd already left.'

'When was that?'

He frowned and pulled a face. 'Er, last June. I say, I don't think I should be answering all these questions. Shall I take you to Mr Baron?'

Frank smiled at him. 'Don't worry, just passing the time of day.' There were many paintings and original prints as well as copies of famous paintings by artists such as Van Gogh and Renoir on the walls of the hall. He'd pointed to them. 'Someone likes works of art. They certainly brighten things up. Is this your influence?'

'No. It's Mr Baron's; he believes in the civilising effects of art on the boys … of course I approve,' the schoolmaster replied.

Frank glanced at his wristwatch 'I'm still early. Perhaps you'd give me a quick tour. It's a lovely example of a small Stuart manor house, one of my favourite periods. When was it built?'

Gordon Stant's face relaxed. 'About 1700; it is fine, one of the reasons I took the job, the chance to work in such a lovely building. How much time have you got?'

'Plenty,' he said. 'I presume the rooms have been modified for school use?'

'Actually, because the number of pupils is small, a lot of the original features have been kept.' He opened a door to the right. 'These rooms were originally the servants working quarters: the kitchen, pantry, buttery, servant's hall and service room. The kitchen's been kept and the servants' hall is the boys' dining room.'

'I thought servants were confined to the basement?'

'There is a basement, there's a staircase to it from the servants' hall.'

The room they'd entered was a classroom, with ten desks, a blackboard and easel, complete with chalk and eraser in the easel's groove. Light flooded in from the mullioned windows showing a linoleum floor, several cupboards and two bookcases filled with brightly backed books. There was a door opposite.

'Where does that go?'

'This was the buttery, there was a beer cellar below.'

84

Frank tried the handle; locked.

'I say, you can't go where you like! No one goes down there, I'm told the steps are unsafe. We can't risk a child falling down and breaking its neck.'

'Sorry, just my natural curiosity.'

'Perhaps I'd better take you—'

He did an ignore. 'So where are the rest of the classrooms?'

Stant turned and led him back into the man hall. 'On the left. This is the Great Hall,' he opened a door, 'it's used as a gym and also for assembly. The former parlour and drawing room are the other classrooms.'

'Where are all the children?' Had they been spirited away by someone playing a flute?

'It's Wednesday afternoon,' Stant said.

Frank raised his eyebrows. Yes, he knew that.

'Games afternoon. Gary Salmon, the sports master, has them on the field. They do exercises and go for a run.'

'Brave man. Are the pupils mostly biddable? Or will some of them hide in the bushes?'

Stant laughed. 'I wouldn't blame them, I hated games. They don't play team games, it's a case of them letting off steam and keeping fit. Also, they're too frightened of Mr Salmon to misbehave. Goodness, he frightens me.'

Does he now? Perhaps David was also frightened of Mr Salmon. Too frightened to go back to school?

Stant grimaced. 'I say, I shouldn't have said that! I think I'd better take you up to Mr Baron's room.' He reddened. 'You won't mention that, you know … about Mr Salmon, will you?' he muttered.

'I never heard you, Mr Stant. I suppose you have other duties, keeping watch over the flock at night?'

Stant pointed him towards the corridor and staircase. 'I supervise prep sometimes, but the kids mostly play games, if they're not messing round. You probably know they have difficulties in one way or another?'

He nodded. 'But you don't have to do dormitory duty?'

Stant shook his head. 'That was another reason I took the job, most of the teaching staff sleep out, and our lodgings are paid for. There isn't enough room to house all of us in the main house.' He started to climb the stairs. 'Please follow me.'

The wide stairs, the banisters polished by schoolboys' hands to a smooth patina, led to the first floor and a long corridor above the east terrace.

He stopped and looked out of a window; a well-kept lawn gently sloped down to fields, and in the distance a track-suited, tall, muscular man was performing keep fit movements and in front of him, boys wearing shorts and singlets were mimicking him. 'Mr Salmon?'

Stunt grimaced and nodded. 'This way.' He turned right along the corridor. 'The dormitories are on the north side of this floor; the south side is used for offices and Mr Baron's room, the sanatorium and matron's office and the rooms of the resident staff.'

'And they are?'

'I'm sure Mr Baron can answer all your other questions.' Stant was looking uncomfortable.

The wall of the corridor opposite the windows was panelled in oak, stained black by time, or inadequate cleaning, or both. No paintings or portraits were present, unlike the rooms and corridors of the main part of the school.

'Why did Mr Baron want to see me in his private quarters not in his office?'

The man shrugged his shoulders. 'Not sure. Wednesday afternoon is his free time. Probably wanted to stay in his private room; if he appears in the main school he'll get waylaid with some problem or other.'

The narrow corridor opened into an octagonal space with windows set in to four of the walls looking out over the school grounds to woods beyond. A circular metal staircase twisted up from a recess in the fifth wall. The master knocked gently on a door set between two panelled walls. The door swung open.

'Good afternoon, Mr Diamond. Please come in. Thank you, Mr Stant.' He nodded to the master, who turned abruptly on his heels but not before Frank had seen the look of devotion in his eyes.

The first impression of the man was of energy and power. Mr Baron was tall and slim. He moved silently, leading Frank to the centre of a large room. From previous case notes Frank knew he was forty-five; he looked younger.

'Please take a seat, Mr Diamond.' He pointed to a leather armchair, one of a pair, matched by a three-seater sofa; the furniture was grouped round a hearth in which logs burned in a cast-iron grate; a beautiful rug lay before the fire. The rest of the room was elegantly furnished and included a baby grand piano under an oriole window. Was the furniture supplied by the school? If it was his own, teaching salaries must be looking up. He'd better get Laurel to rethink her choice of career.

He sank into the armchair. The soft leather was comfortable and a faint smell of a floral polish scented the air.

'Can I offer you some refreshment? Tea? Or would you prefer something stronger?' Ralph Baron indicated an oak dresser with silver trays on which stood decanters wearing matching silver labels: whisky, rum, brandy and gin.

Frank could have murdered a pint of Adnams but he didn't think that would be on offer. 'Tea would be fine.'

As Ralph Baron moved to the table and picked up a telephone, Frank studied him. David's drawing of him was accurate, apart from not showing the expensive watch he was wearing – a Rolex Oyster?

He turned to Frank. 'How do you like your tea? Lemon or milk?'

God's teeth. He wasn't too keen on tea and certainly not the pale lemon stuff with a floral perfume. 'Assam, if you have it, please, milk and no sugar.'

Baron turned back to the phone. 'A pot of Assam and my usual, Mrs Weston. Perhaps a few scones?' He listened and smiled. 'Thank you.'

Frank scanned the room again during this brief phone conversation. The walls were covered in paintings: some of the oils looked like old masters, the majority were watercolours. They made the room look more like an art gallery than a personal space.

'I see you're admiring my collection, Mr Diamond.'

More clocking it than admiring. 'You've certainly been busy, Mr Baron.'

'Do you like art? Are you a collector?' The tone of the voice suggested he didn't think Frank would say yes.

Frank didn't feel in the mood for an in-depth discussion on matters artistic, but he wanted to make a connection to Ralph Gabriel Baron. He needed to be able to talk to the staff and pupils and upsetting the headmaster wouldn't help. He liked the art produced between 1830 and 1920, anything before or after he found too religious or to abstruse. Time to flannel. 'It's something I've always been interested in, but so far I haven't had the time or the spare money to indulge in buying works of art. You have some beautiful paintings.'

Baron's eyes lit up, and his full lips parted in a smile.

So far so good.

'Do have a look round while we wait for the tea.' He rose from his chair, moving with an athlete's grace, and walked to a row of watercolours on the far wall.

Frank followed him. He hoped he wasn't in for a grilling or even worse a long, boring lecture on different water colour techniques. He noticed not only did Baron sport an expensive watch, but his shoes looked handmade.

'If you had the chance what kind of work would you collect, Mr Diamond?'

'Probably modern art, abstract,' he lied. There wasn't any in the room, so he hoped he was on safe ground. 'I'm looking forward to going to Andy Warhol's exhibition at the Tate.' He wasn't but Laurel had mentioned it recently.

Baron's lips twisted and turned down at the corners. 'Oh, dear. Not for me. Anything after 1900 I'm afraid I'm not interested in. Although …'

Frank looked at him quizzically. 'Yes?'

Baron's face darkened. 'Nothing. Nothing. Do look at some of these watercolours.' He pointed to several, saying the name of the artist, and telling Frank why the paintings were so special.

Samuel Prout, Edward Lear, David Cox. Frank knew

some of these names and he sealed them in his memory for checking later for desirability and value. Baron's face was lit up with desire and ownership, his hands caressing the frames of each picture.

There was a knock on the door and a middle-aged woman wearing a green overall entered carrying a laden tray which she placed on a table. Her face was stern, unsmiling.

'Thank you, Mrs Weston,' Baron said.

The woman nodded, giving Frank an appraising glance, her dark eyes cold and hostile.

Frank wondered if his tea might be poisoned.

'Anything else, Mr Baron?' she asked. Frank wasn't sure of the accent.

'No, thank you, Mrs Weston.' She left and Baron poured the tea which they drank at the table.

'I can't quite place Mrs Weston's accent. Is she foreign?' Frank asked.

Baron looked up from buttering his scone, his eyebrows raised. 'Very astute, Mr Diamond. You have a good ear, especially as she only spoke four words. I'm not sure which middle-European country she originated from; she's a widow, married an Englishman after the war and she stayed here.'

'Does she live nearby?'

Baron frowned. 'She lives in, she's the school cook.' He bit into the scone, chewed furiously, then swallowed. 'Mr Diamond, I think we ought to get on with whatever you came about. I have several things I need to do this afternoon.'

The change in his attitude was sudden. Why? A question about an employee? He hadn't liked Frank's interest in Mrs Weston. Did Mrs Weston know David? Was that it?

'Certainly, I'm grateful you could spare me the time today. As you know the Pembertons have—'

'Yes, yes, I know all about that. The police, and later the detectives the Pembertons hired, came to the school. Haven't you read their notes?'

Getting shirty. Why? 'Yes, but I must try to find David. You told Mr Pemberton you'd give your permission for me and my partners to talk to the staff and pupils who knew David. You did agree to that?' He risked a mouthful of tea. It was well flavoured and strong. Baron wiped a non-existent crumb from his full lips with a linen napkin.

'I did.' He sounded as though he wished he hadn't.

'Excellent. We'll be as discreet and as quick as we can.' Perhaps a little white lie might help. 'I'm sure we won't uncover anything new, but I have to try for the Pembertons' sake.' He shrugged his shoulders apologetically, trying a winning smile.

Baron's shoulders relaxed and his face lightened. 'Good.' He pushed the plate towards Frank. 'Scone?'

He declined. 'Excellent tea, congratulations to Mrs Weston.'

The frown came back. What was it about that woman that made Baron nervous? How was he going to find out about Peter and the frightened boy? He couldn't show the drawings to anyone. He wasn't supposed to have them. He could ask about Peter, but the name of the other boy was unknown. This was not a time for questions, Baron would be the last person he interviewed.

'Would it be convenient to come in tomorrow and talk

to a few of the staff?'

Baron shot up from his chair as though the starter's gun had gone off. 'No. We've two lots of prospective parents visiting tomorrow, and we're too busy on Friday. You can come on Monday.' He walked to the door and opened it, signalling the interview was over.

Damn. Baron would have time to possibly influence anyone who might have information. But why would he do that? 'Very well, thank you. Would you be able to arrange rooms for us to talk to the staff and pupils?'

Baron nodded. 'I must insist a member of staff is present when you talk to any pupil.'

Double damn. 'Of course. I'd be grateful if I could have a list of all the staff and pupils who were at the school when David was.'

Baron smiled. 'You'll find several of them have left, both staff and pupils.'

'I expect that's normal in a school?'

Baron smiled again. 'Yes, that's normal.' He waved his hand, ushering Frank from the room.

As they walked down the corridor which overlooked the playing field a door opened and the woman in the nurse's uniform came towards them; it was the woman David had drawn. She didn't look any more pleasant in the flesh.

'Good afternoon, Headmaster.' She had a slight accent also.

Baron nodded and was about to walk past her, but Frank stopped. 'Ah,' he turned to Baron, 'your school matron, I presume,' He shot her a smile and stuck out his hand. 'Frank Diamond.'

Baron juddered to a halt. 'Nurse Gammell, this is Mr

Diamond. He's a private detective who will be coming back to the school next week to ask the staff and pupils about David Pemberton.'

Nurse Gammell's face remained expressionless. 'I look forward to talking to you then, Mr Diamond.'

Frank didn't believe her.

Chapter 10

In the dining room of Greyfriars Laurel put down the phone. It was the third time she'd tried to contact Nancy, hoping to hear what had happened when she saw her brother, but each time there was no reply. She must still be at Sam's; she hoped she and Clara were going to work together and make the time Sam had left as comfortable and as pleasant as possible. She was happy for Nancy as it looked as though her fears about Clara was unfounded, although she must have been shocked when she saw Sam, as the poor man was obviously not far from death. She sighed; it meant her work with Nancy was over and now she'd be involved with the David Pemberton case. She'd have to get on with it and not be such a wimp. The thought of going into a school and questioning teachers and pupils made her stomach clench, but she was skilled at working with children and her experiences of schools generally would be useful. She shook her body, like a colt rising after a roll in a meadow, getting rid of bits of grass. No more negative thoughts.

There were sounds from the kitchen, and a delicious savoury aroma. How lucky they were to have Mabel. Frank said he'd never eaten so well; his mother hadn't been a great cook, in the university canteen meals were chips and more chips, and when he was with the police meals were often erratic, eaten on the hoof, and heavily weighted towards fat and carbohydrate. At least once a week Frank cooked for himself at his cottage. Said he didn't want to lose his touch; Stuart vouched he was red hot on omelettes. So far, she hadn't been invited for dinner à deux.

She opened the kitchen door. 'Hello, Mabel. Smells delicious. One of your fish pies?'

Mabel was attacking a pan of boiled potatoes with a masher. 'Hello, dear. Yes, just got to put the top on.'

She sat down at the table and watched Mabel cover the contents of a large dish with the mashed potatoes, rough up the surface and liberally sprinkle it with grated cheese. She stepped back, and admired the finished dish. 'There, that's done. I'll put it in the oven later.'

'That's one of Stuart's favourites, isn't it?'

Mabel turned and looked at her. She flopped down in the chair opposite Laurel. 'He likes most of my dishes,' she said. She wouldn't meet Laurel's eyes and looked down at the table frowning, picking up dropped flakes of cheese with a damp finger and eating them.

Laurel wasn't sure if she should say something, but someone had to. Mabel was older than her, she'd been married and widowed, but something was badly awry between her and Stuart. She remembered how happy they'd both been when Stuart announced their engagement in this very house, soon after Mabel had come back from hospital, after Philip Nicholson had been arrested for several murders, and the near fatal attack on Mabel. She, Frank and Dorothy had been so happy for them.

'Mabel. I realise it isn't any of my business, but can I

help? You know how much you and Stuart mean to me. If you tell me to shut up I will, and I won't be offended.' She looked at Mabel who'd raised her head and was staring at her with teary eyes. She reached out a hand and Mabel took hold of it, gulping with suppressed emotions.

'I don't know who to talk to, Laurel … you've never been married, you can't understand …'

She took a chance. 'I was engaged once.'

'It's not the same, dear. When you're living with someone …'

'I know I haven't had your experiences, but I do understand about wanting someone and how strong those emotions can be.' God, she sounded like a marriage guidance counsellor.

Mabel's grip tightened. 'Oh, Laurel, if I could only find the courage to—'

The kitchen door swung open.

'Hello, you two. What are you plotting? Wow, that smells good,' Frank said, as he breezed in.

Mabel pulled back her hand and quickly rose from the table.

Laurel felt like attacking him with the masher.

Laurel poured Dorothy a gin and tonic and a Jameson's for herself. Mabel was sitting in an armchair sipping a sweet sherry and Frank was looking out of the sitting-room window holding his glass of beer to the fading light. They'd agreed to share the day's discoveries after supper. Stuart Elderkin hadn't yet come back from his appointment with Ann Fenner.

Mabel got up. 'We can't wait any longer. That pie will be dry soon. We'll have to start without him,' she said

96

crossly.

'I'm sure he'll be back before we've finished our drinks,' Dorothy said. 'He's never late for meals, too afraid he won't get his fair share.'

Mabel sniffed and went to the kitchen.

'Stuart said Ann Fenner didn't want to meet in Aldeburgh, he thought of taking her to Southwold.' Frank said.

'That explains it, lucky her, they've got some nice tea shops there,' Dorothy replied. She turned to Laurel. 'Any luck with Nancy's problem?'

She shrugged. 'I think Nancy's worries are over. Hopefully it's all sorted out by now. She was going to see her brother this afternoon. I'll give you all the details later.'

'That's a relief.'

They turned their heads at the sound of the front door slamming; Stuart Elderkin came into the room. 'Not late, am I?'

'Good day?' Frank asked.

Stuart pursed his lips and nodded. 'Tell you after supper,' he said smugly.

'I'll let Mabel know you're back and I'll lay the table. Shall I get you a beer, Stuart?'

Stuart rubbed his ample stomach. 'Might squeeze one in, Laurel. Thank you.'

Laurel passed round the fish pie for second helpings. 'One of your best, Mabel. Where did you get the queenies from?' She was conscious Mabel looked miffed, mainly because Stuart had asked for a small helping of pie. He was living dangerously.

'The fishmonger in Aldeburgh had some; he had big scallops, but these little ones are sweeter, I think.' She glanced toward Stuart, but he was doodling on the tablecloth with his knife.

'Ever tried grilling them with butter and garlic?' Frank asked. 'Only trouble is you need a lot of them and they're the devil to clean.'

Mabel didn't reply to him.

Laurel decided it was time to get on with the evening's business. 'Shall we make a start, Frank?'

'Wait 'til I get my notebook,' Dorothy said, rushing from the room.

Mabel snatched up the plates, not asking if they'd finished. 'I'll clear up, we can have cheese and biscuits later, if *anyone* wants them.' She glared at Stuart.

When everyone was back Laurel went first and told them about her visit to Sam's. There were murmurs of sympathy for Samuel Harrop when she described his condition.

'Poor man,' Dorothy said, 'such a brilliant surgeon.'

Then Frank told them of his afternoon at Chillingworth.

'What do you make of the set up?' Stuart asked.

'I'm not sure, something doesn't seem right. We start interviewing Monday. Want to join in, Laurel, being as you think you won't be needed by Nancy anymore?'

'Yes, of course,' she said brightly.

Dorothy turned to Stuart. 'Was your afternoon with Ann Fenner successful?'

Laurel wished she'd used a different word.

Stuart lit up his pipe, settled back in his chair and told them what Ann Fenner had said about David. 'It seems when he wants to talk he can. In Ann Fenner he found a sympathetic ear.'

Dorothy nodded approvingly. 'I've never met the woman; seen her once or twice in Aldeburgh, but I'm impressed. She sounds a sensible, kind woman.'

Stuart puffed on his pipe. 'She is.'

'Did she tell you why her feelings about Carol Pemberton were hardened?' Frank asked.

'Yes, it took a bit of persuading, but under the influence of a few sherries at The White Lion, she finally spilt the beans.'

As they waited for Stuart to have a final puff and then knock out his pipe in the fireplace, Laurel glanced at Mabel. The anger had died to be replaced by a look of worry and sadness. Did she think she'd lost Stuart by her behaviour? She had treated him badly over the last few weeks. If only Frank hadn't come into the kitchen when Mabel was about to tell her something important.

Stuart sat down, looking grave. 'I don't know if what Ann told me has any bearing on David's disappearance, but it explains his attitude towards his mother. If you remember the Pembertons hired a number of tutors to teach David until he was thirteen. Ann Fenner is convinced Carol Pemberton had relationships with at least two of these men.'

Laurel glanced at Frank. His eyes narrowed and his nostrils were pinched. She'd seen the softening look on his face when he'd put the drawing of Carol Pemberton on the table earlier in the week; she'd wondered then if he was attracted to her, but knowing Frank's attitude to women and his professional scruples, it hadn't worried her. But now? He hadn't said anything personal about Mrs

Pemberton – usually if a woman was attractive or sexy he might make some comment, but not this time. She *was* beautiful; the drawing showed a fragility which most men would respond to; the white knight rescuing the fair damsel syndrome. Not a response *she'd* encountered very often. Frank riding to her rescue over the sands of Minsmere beach to help her dig out Nicholson was the nearest she got to that. Was she jealous? She had to admit there was a faint pain under her ribs, but she hoped it would soon go away.

'Can you give us more details, Stuart?' Frank asked.

Stuart nodded and leant forwards, placing his small hands on the table. 'She didn't know the first tutor very well as he left about two months after she arrived. At first she thought it was good for Mrs Pemberton to have someone nearer her own age to talk to when Mr Pemberton was at work, but then she noticed the two of them often left David in his room working on his drawings and they, Mrs Pemberton and the tutor, would be in the sitting room; she'd hear them laughing and talking, but then there would be long periods when she didn't hear anything, although she knew they were there. She felt uncomfortable about that.'

Frank shrugged. 'That's a bit thin. I don't think we can read much into that.'

'There's more,' Stuart said. 'That tutor was dismissed, not for messing round with the boss's wife, but David took against him; shut himself in his room and wouldn't come out for lessons, although everything seemed to go well to begin with.'

'Did the boy know about his mother and the tutor?' Mabel asked. 'Poor child. How do you cope with that at his age? And with his difficulties?'

Stuart turned towards her, his face softening. He smiled at her. 'He probably did what he always did, he got a sheet of paper and a pencil and drew it out of his system.'

Laurel saw Frank flinch. Something had struck home.

Mabel smiled at Stuart. 'Sometimes you're a very clever man, Stuart Elderkin.'

'I was when I got you to agree to marry me.'

Laurel held her breath, expecting Mabel to come back with a barbed reply, but all she did was widen her smile. Whew! Things are looking up.

'What else did Ann Fenner tell you?' Dorothy asked.

'The next tutor, name escapes me, but it's in my notebook, was the first one who lived in. Ann said he was young, about twenty-three. He'd graduated from Oxford, and was hoping to make a living writing, but until, if and when he was published, he decided to try private tutoring. He'd had a bash at teaching in a school, but couldn't manage the kids.'

Frank was running a hand over his cheek as though deciding whether or not he needed a shave. 'Did Ann like him?' he asked

'She did, said he was gentle with David, seemed to relate to him, and David responded. On one of his secret visits to Ann he said he liked the new tutor. Then after about five months it changed, and Ann Fenner thinks she knows why.'

Dorothy shook her head. 'Same story?'

Stuart nodded. 'You're right, but this time Ann saw them at it, so to speak.'

'Do you trust her?' Frank snapped. 'Could she have

fallen for the tutor herself and not got anywhere?'

Stuart looked shocked. 'Ann Fenner! I don't think so. A woman who wears a sensible winter coat and carries an umbrella isn't a femme fatale. She's a widow and she obviously loved her husband, talked about him with real affection. I think she's a lonely woman, but she's no sex pot.'

'She sounds nice, Stuart,' Mabel said. 'I must see if we can help her. What do you think, Dorothy?'

Dorothy pulled back her shoulders. 'Stuart's a good judge of character, we'll think of something.'

'That's my girls,' Stuart said, grinning broadly.

'Will you please finish your report, Stuart,' Frank barked.

Stuart stared at him. 'Hold your hat on. What's got into you? No need to snap my head off.'

Frank briefly closed his eyes, his hands gripping his knees. 'I'm sorry, Stuart, I must be tired.'

You're never tired, Frank Xavier Diamond, Laurel thought. Something or someone has got to you, and you're not used to that. Just when it looked as though Mabel and Stuart had made it up, Frank was upset about something and that something is the news that Carol Pemberton is a nymphomaniac. Normally he'd be delighted by a bit of information like that; it didn't solve the case but it shed light on one of its principal players.

Stuart continued. 'One night, Ann Fenner said she couldn't sleep; she'd eaten a cheese sandwich late and she got terrible heartburn. It was after one in the morning, she went down to the kitchen to get some Andrew's Liver Salts—'

'Should have tried Milk of Magnesia,' quipped

Dorothy. Mabel giggled.

Frank glared at them but Stuart smiled indulgently. 'My, you ladies! No need to be embarrassed, we're all grown up here.'

Laurel wasn't so sure.

'As I was saying, she crept down the stairs, afraid of waking anyone, when she saw a faint light under the library door; she thought the standard lamp had been left on. She opened the door and there they were on the rug in front of a dead fire.'

'Did they see her?' Dorothy asked.

'She wasn't sure. Certainly, Mrs Pemberton didn't because according to Ann she was stark naked, on her back, her black hair loose, spread over the rug, and he was on top. They were too … er, engrossed to notice, or even hear the door opening, but she did wonder if he looked up briefly, and saw her.'

Frank was silent.

'What did Ann do?' Dorothy asked.

'She made a rapid retreat up the stairs and put up with the heartburn all night, plus a shocked nervous system. She says she didn't know what to do. She thought about having a word with the tutor, but she was worried he'd tell Mrs Pemberton; she couldn't bring herself to say anything to the husband, it would be her word against his wife's. She even thought of trying to find another job, but she didn't want to leave David.'

'Is there any connection we can see between Mrs Pemberton's unfaithfulness and David's disappearance? Could David also have made a similar discovery and said he would tell his father?' Laurel asked.

'It's another thought,' Stuart said.

'You mean she might have done him harm? Got rid of him? Surely no mother would do that,' Mabel said. 'What do you think, Frank?'

Frank coughed, and reached for his glass of water, but before he could reply the phone on Laurel's desk rang. Dorothy was nearest. She listened. 'It's Nancy for you, Laurel.'

'Good, I've been trying to get her. Hope she wasn't too shocked by Sam's appearance. Hello, Nancy, how did it go?'

'Go? What do you mean? Did you see Sam?' Nancy's voice was worried.

'But you've seen him, haven't you? Clara came for you.'

'What are you talking about? I've been out all day. Ivy Merryweather rang me up at lunch time, she's had a flood, her boiler burst, I've been helping her mop up. She doesn't have a phone so I couldn't ring before. I've just got back. I rang straight away to see if you'd seen Sam.'

Laurel's heart thudded against her ribs. 'I'll come over at once, Nancy. I need to explain something. Then I think we ought to go to Sam's.'

'At this time of night? I don't think Clara will be pleased to see us.'

'Trust me, Nancy. Get ready to go out. I'll be with you in half an hour.' She put the phone down.

Frank had moved to her side.

She gulped. 'Nancy hasn't seen Clara, so either Clara went to Nancy's and she was out, or she went somewhere else. She certainly came back with someone. I heard two car doors close. I thought it was Nancy with her. I don't think Sam should be left without medical help another night. I'm taking Nancy to him. I'll force Clara to let us in.'

Frank took her arm. 'You've got a bad feeling about this, haven't you?'

She nodded.

'I'll drive, it'll be faster.'

Stuart Elderkin rolled his eyes. 'You're not in your Mustang, remember.'

'Anything we can do? Do you want me to come? Nancy might be glad to see me,' Dorothy asked.

'Be prepared to come over to Aldeburgh if necessary,' Frank said, as he made his way to the door.

In the hall Laurel grabbed her handbag and a waterproof, as it was raining again. She was relieved Frank was coming with her, but unfortunately it reminded her of the time they had come back from Aldeburgh and found Mabel almost dead on the beach below the steps of Blackfriars School.

David, Age 12 years

I hate her. She is bad. It is wrong to do that. You can only do it with your husband. I want to tell Daddy. I don't know how to tell him. Why did she do it? I've read about it in the newspaper the gardener leaves in the shed. I can read a lot of words now. My tutor, the bad man, he taught me lots of words. He's a teacher. Teachers should be good. He was bad to do it with my Mummy. Why did he want to do it?

The newspaper says lots of people do it when they shouldn't. Doctors, vicars, people my Daddy votes for. Sometimes they do bad things to boys. I'm not sure what they do. I know what the tutor did. I saw them. He gave me lessons, then Mummy told me to go up to my room. He and Mummy talked and I did my drawings.

I was hungry. It was tea time. I went to the kitchen to find something to eat. I passed the door of the library. I wanted to get a book. The door wasn't closed. I peeped through the crack. They were kissing. A long kiss. He was touching her all over. I felt sick. I went back to my room. What was happening? Would Daddy have to leave? Would the tutor be my new Daddy? No. It was wrong.

That night I couldn't sleep. His room is near mine. I heard his bedroom door open, and he went down the stairs. I waited. I counted to twenty. I can count to a hundred but I didn't. I crept down the stairs. I was scared. The library door has a keyhole. I looked through it. My mummy was on the floor. She didn't have any clothes on. He was on top of her. He was moving up and down. She put her legs round him. She doesn't love Daddy any more. What will happen?

I went back upstairs. I took a piece of paper and pinned it to the easel. I got out three pencils, one fine, one medium and one thick. I drew it out of my head on to the paper. I will have to hide it. If she found it what would she do to me? I want to tell. If I tell Daddy will he hate me? Does he know?

The next day I still feel bad. I go into the kitchen. Miss Fenner is sitting at the table. I like her. I can tell she likes me. She doesn't say much to me. I remember when I first spoke to her. She called me Master David. *She* made her do that. I didn't like it. Miss Fenner makes nice things to eat. She is always the same. She doesn't shout and she doesn't cry. I talk to her. She was shocked when I first spoke to her. I laughed and she smiled. She makes nice puddings. I like her.

I will be thirteen on the twenty-third of July. I will go away to school in September. Daddy is taking me to visit the school soon. I am afraid. I've never been to a school. You have to listen to teachers and you have to answer questions. I do that with the tutors. I am glad I am going as there will be no more tutors. Mummy will have to stop being bad.

Daddy comes in from work. He is sad. I wish I could tell him. He knows I don't like anyone touching me. Sometimes he puts out his hand. Then he pulls it away. I think I love my Daddy. I go upstairs and draw a picture of

107

him and one of Miss Fenner. I put them with the others. It
is my secret. I like secrets.

Chapter 11

Frank pulled away from in front of Nancy's house, Laurel sitting in the back of the car with Nancy, trying to reassure her it was going to be all right. She'd told Nancy what had happened at Sam's that afternoon, but when she'd told her how ill Sam looked, Nancy went white and needed a glass of whisky before they set off.

Frank was glad to be active; he didn't want to think about what Stuart Elderkin had told them about Carol. How was he going to tell them about the drawing he'd kept back? How could he explain why he'd kept it back? It was hidden in a drawer in the bedroom of his cottage. Was it because in his heart he knew it was a drawing of Carol and some man, who wasn't her husband, having sex? He'd tried to put it down to the adolescent sexual fantasies of David. Possibly an Oedipus Complex with the boy imagining himself as the man making love to his mother. How could he show it to them now, when Ann Fenner's description of Carol Pemberton and the tutor making love on the library rug perfectly matched the drawing? But how had David known about them? He must have found them together, just as Ann Fenner had. In the drawing you couldn't identify the woman, all you could see was the hair spread out, and her arms raised, her hands gripping the shoulders of the man. He was above her, falling dark hair obscuring his face; his body was youthful, the chest almost hairless, nipples erect and skin pale and smooth. David had captured a moment of intense passion. What effect had that had on him? To see his mother being fucked by his teacher? Part of him was outraged for the boy, but another part of him was seething with jealousy and lust. He didn't like the effect the drawing had on him: one of uncontrollable desire. He liked to have control of any situation and before wanting Carol, he'd never lost control of himself. He inwardly groaned.

He automatically followed Laurel's instructions to the Harrops' house, silent, half-listening to Nancy whispering to Laurel. She seemed a nice lady, grateful he'd come, saying it was good to have a man to take charge. He wasn't sure what Laurel made of that. If there was any physical danger she was as good as him at dealing with it, probably better.

'Don't park in the drive,' Nancy whispered.

He pulled up in the road out of view from the windows of the house, although as far as he could see there were no lights showing. The rain had turned from drizzle to a slanting, cold downpour, lashed by an easterly wind, bringing with it the sharp smell of the sea.

The gravel crunched under their feet as they walked towards the house.

'That's Clara's car,' Laurel whispered.

The house was in darkness. He switched on the torch he'd brought with him. 'We'll ring the bell; they must be in the back of the house. OK, Nancy?'

In the light of the torch Nancy's pink hair was flattened against her scalp; she looked frail and

110

frightened. 'Oh, Laurel. I'm so worried. What if Clara won't let us in? Supposing she won't let me see Sam?'

Laurel wrapped an arm round her. 'I'm sure we can sort it out. Frank's very good with people, he'll be able to explain to Clara. She must see sense.'

Blind faith, he thought. His belief in himself was decreasing by the minute. 'It will be all right, Nancy.' He pressed the bell. Several times. Then after a few minutes and no response he attacked the large cast-iron knocker. The blows echoed back to them.

'Let's go round the back. Sam was in the room with French windows this afternoon,' Laurel said.

'His favourite place,' Nancy muttered. 'Where he listens to his beloved music. That's why they retired here: the music, the concerts, going to Snape Maltings, always ending up at The Oysterage at Orford for supper. I expect he's playing something now, and that's why they haven't heard us. I do hope we won't give them a fright when they see us.'

He glanced at Laurel. He was sure they were thinking along the same lines.

They made their way down the side of the house, Laurel holding on to Nancy, making sure she didn't trip. There was no light in the kitchen and the blind was drawn. The room with the French windows was also in darkness and drawn curtains obscured any chance of seeing inside.

Nancy trembled, her teeth chattering with the cold and probably nerves. 'Oh dear, what shall we do? Wherever are they? Do you think Clara's taken Sam to hospital? But her car's at the front of the house. Do you think she got an ambulance? Surely she'd have rung me?'

'Frank, I think we need to get in,' Laurel said.

111

Nancy clutched her arm. 'We can't, dear, we haven't got a key.'

'Laurel, I think Nancy ought to wait in the car. Take the torch. I'll stay here.'

Nancy turned to him, her eyes wide with fear, her hair plastered to her scalp. She looked ten years older than when they'd set off only twenty minutes ago. 'What are you going to do? What do you think has happened? Oh, Sam! Please be all right, Sam.'

Laurel took the torch from Frank and tried to move Nancy away from the French windows. Nancy fluttered her arms against Laurel's hold. 'I shouldn't have told you. This is my fault. Clara's found out and she's taken him away.'

Laurel blinked away the cold rain beating into her face.

This was a nightmare, he thought.

Laurel looked as though she wanted to pick Nancy up and carry her to the car. They had to get into the house. Now. As quickly as possible.

'You must do as Frank says, Nancy. At once. Come along, this is no time to make a scene.'

She hadn't lost the bossy, I'm a teacher and know best touch. He smiled.

Nancy straightened up. 'No need for that tone, young woman. Dorothy said you were a nice person, now I'm not so sure!' She allowed herself to be pushed towards the car.

'Bring back what I may need,' he said.

Laurel nodded, looking ready to put Nancy in an arm lock if there was further trouble.

He felt round the edge of the French windows while he waited.

A light came round the corner. 'I locked her in. I don't think she'll be sending me a Christmas card. These any use?' She showed him a large screwdriver and a tyre wrench.

'I think the direct method is called for. Ready?' he said.

'Go ahead. If it's a mistake we can get the glazier in tomorrow. The firm can afford it. Or do you think we should call the police?' She pointed the light at the window.

He shook his head. 'Let's hope we don't need to call them when we get in. Stand back.' He covered his eyes with one arm and smashed at the pane above the handle with the tyre wrench. Several times. Exploding, cracking, shattering. He expected neighbours to rush out. Tinkling sounds as shards of glass fell to the ground, prevented from falling inwards by the curtains. He knocked out jagged edges at the sides of the pane as Laurel held the torch steady.

Satisfied, he pulled back the curtain and felt for a key. He grunted, moved closer to the door, pushed his arm in further. 'No key.'

'Sam said he couldn't get out,' Laurel said, her voice squeaky

He smashed the lock, then he pushed against the door. It moved, but there was still resistance.

'Bolts, probably top and bottom,' he said.

Laurel groaned. 'Any minute now PC Plod will come round the corner and arrest us for burglary.'

'Not forgetting locking up an old lady in a car.' He picked up the wrench. 'Want a bet? Top, bottom or both? Loser buys double whiskies for winner.'

113

'Both,' Laurel said.

'OK, I'll go for top, old people don't like bending down. Watch out, the glass might come down on your head.' He bashed at the top pane. The noises seemed louder than last time. He had to stand on tiptoe to reach in. He found the bolt and was surprised it slid down easily. The door still didn't open, although it bent a little as he pulled it. 'You win. Drinks on me.' He bent down and smashed the bottom pane.

He pulled the door open, large pieces of glass exploded on the stones outside the window.

'Thank God for that,' Laurel said.

He opened the door and more shards pinged off the stone flags; he pulled back the heavy curtains, they felt like velvet. Laurel shone the torch round the room. It was as she'd described it to him: the black Art Deco furniture, the music system and Sam's collection of records and tapes.

There was an acrid smell.

'Someone's been burning paper,' Laurel said, as she shone the beam of light over the room. The moving shaft of light stopped. 'Frank!'

An arm hung over the side of the black settee, its fingers loose, pointing to the floor.

'Don't move until I've put the light on, and watch where you're treading, Laurel. Don't touch anything. Please shine the light on the wall so I can find the switch.' He was reverting to Detective Inspector Diamond, just as Laurel had changed back into a teacher to control Nancy. Old ways die hard.

He fumbled in his pocket for a handkerchief, it wasn't pristine but it would have to do. Avoiding the settee, he

114

made his way to the wall switch Laurel had focused the beam on, and pressed it down. Light flooded the room from a central modern chandelier.

Lolling on the settee was the gaunt figure of a man, his face hidden by a crumpled black-and-white cushion, its partners on the other end of the settee and the armchairs.

Frank carefully lifted the cushion. 'Is this Sam?'

'Yes.'

The other side of the cushion was stained with blood and saliva. Sam's face was blue, his eyes bursting from their sockets, bits of black-and-white threads round his snarling mouth and between the incisors. Blood oozed from his nose and mouth, and his bitten tongue stuck out from between the retracted lips.

'He fought, didn't he? He didn't want to die,' Laurel said, tears trickling down her cheeks.

He looked at Sam's emaciated arms and stick-like legs, revealed where the pyjama trousers had pushed up, his swollen belly obscene in contrast to the rest of him. The yellow skin and eyes gave clues to the disease which would have soon killed him.

'Could Clara have done this?' he asked.

'Nancy said she thought she wanted to kill him.'

'Why would she do that when it was obvious he hadn't long to live? Where is she?'

Laurel stood looking down at Sam, the torch, still on, dangling from her hand.

'Laurel, would you phone the police? I can't see a phone in here, there's probably one in the hall. Keep the torch on until you find the light switch.'

He watched as she opened the sitting-room door. He heard the click of a switch.

'Frank! My God, Frank.'

He rushed to her. She was looking up, her eyes wide, her face blanched. Hanging from a rope fastened to the banisters at the top of the staircase was the body of a woman dressed in green, her neck stretched, the head inclined to one side, her pale face partly obscured by dark, loose hair. Her blackened tongue poked from her mouth, leering at them.

Laurel turned away and Frank held her close. 'Is it Clara?'

He felt her head nod.

'Cut her down, Frank, for God's sake cut her down.'

He needed to get Laurel away from the swaying body. But where? Not to the other corpse in the sitting room. He couldn't see a phone here. Bloody hell, didn't they have one at all? 'Laurel, you'll have to find a neighbour and ask to use their phone. I can't see one here. Don't let Nancy come in. Dial 999 tell them the address and there are two dead people. Could be a murder and suicide.'

She pulled away from him. 'I know what to do, thank you. I'm not an idiot.'

That was better.

'Why don't you sit with Nancy in the car, until the police arrive.'

'What shall I tell her? She's cold and wet, and she was in a state before this. Shall I ask the neighbours, if I can find any, if she can go into their house for a while until we can take her home?' She paused. 'I could ring Dorothy, she'd come over. Perhaps Nancy could go back to Greyfriars. I don't think she should be by herself.'

'Excellent. Although the police may want to interview her as soon as possible.'

'Bugger the police.'

'My own sentiments entirely.' He squeezed her shoulders. He opened the front door which had a Yale lock and an old-fashioned key in the key hole. The Yale was on, but the key hadn't been turned.

'Good luck.'

He would have time to take a closer look at the bodies and a snoop round before the flat-feet came.

Chapter 12

As soon as Laurel was through the front door Frank went back to the sitting room with its awful presence. Sometimes a dead body seemed to have more substance than the living person. In death Samuel Harrop couldn't be ignored. Frank looked round the sitting room and then examined the body more closely. There was no doubt the man had fought and struggled with whoever had suffocated him. If this was Clara's idea of a mercy killing, she hadn't given him a peaceful death. The poor man, with his frail body and wasted muscles, would have been easy meat. His clothes were disarranged, probably happened as he struggled; the dressing gown open, and his pyjamas gaping, his distended abdomen bulging between the open flies. Why did Clara kill him when he was only a few weeks, if that, from death? Why give him such a terrifying end if she wanted to spare him pain? Sam had been a specialist, a doctor; he'd have the means to end his life if he wished, or Clara could have used that method to end his life. It didn't add up.

He could tell from Laurel's expression she was blaming herself, thinking if she'd acted sooner, or made sure Clara *had* contacted Nancy, this wouldn't have happened. She would take it badly; she might want to leave the partnership, thinking she wasn't good enough for this kind of work. He must talk to her. Perhaps he was getting ahead of himself and he was reading her wrong, but he didn't think so. He knew she didn't want to be involved with the David Pemberton case, and thought herself inadequate because of her sensitivities.

He looked carefully at Sam's body and bent down to look at the hand still trailing over the edge of the settee. Some bright green strands were caught in the thumb nail. As green as the wool suit on the figure suspended by its throat in the hall. He couldn't see any material under any of the other nails. The closeness to the body made bile rise in his throat as the first threads of death filled his nostrils: the smell of ammonia from the urine Sam had released in his death throes, his unwashed body already decaying, and the burnt paper smell from the fireplace all mingled to form a potent and retch-inducing stink. He wished he'd had his silver vinaigrette with its inner pad soaked in lavender oil. He had used it at post-mortems when he was a detective inspector; he could do with it now.

He moved to the fireplace, knelt down and looked at the ashes; the acrid, powdery smell was stronger here. He couldn't make out what had been burnt. Why burn documents when it didn't matter what was in them as you wouldn't be here to care? Unless they contained information which would ruin your reputation. Presuming it was Clara who burnt the papers after killing Sam, why care about your reputation when you've just committed the worse crime possible?

He bent closer. Some of the edges of the papers were untouched by the flames; he couldn't be sure but they looked like bank statements; he could make out a few capital letters: an I, next to it a D, then a burnt space, then

119

another D, an unburnt space, more burning, then finally a K. There was something familiar about the letters. He rubbed his hand over his mouth, concentrating. MIDLAND BANK. His own bank. Why would you, after murdering your husband, start burning bank statements? For light relief? He'd better not try that one out on the police when they arrived.

He wasn't looking forward to this role reversal. Was he up to being a witness? Or even a suspect? They'd have to explain why they broke in. Would they be believed? He left the fireplace and quickly moved to the hall. He didn't have much time. Clara's hands, level with his eyes, dangled by the sides of her body, fists clenched. Using his handkerchief, he turned over one of her hands and looked at her nails. They were beautifully manicured and coated with unchipped dark pink nail polish. Often suicides by hanging, once in the throes of death, try to pull the rope, or cloth, from their necks. Clara's nails had survived not only the struggle when she smothered Sam, but her own death. He wasn't happy. He hoped the police would be unhappy, too.

The smell of death was increasing; even though it could only have been hours since they were both alive. Clara's nyloned legs were stained with excrement and urine, her sphincter muscles relaxing in death, releasing the contents of her bladder and rectum. Some of it had pooled on the marble hall floor. A terrible way to die. You had to be desperate to have the courage to tie the knot, and in this case, climb over the upper banisters and hurl yourself into space. Wouldn't a woman such as Clara have realised what a pathetic and undignified figure she would make, swinging from a rope, legs dangling, showing her stained underwear? From what Laurel had told them in the meeting Clara valued her status as Sam's wife and prized her position in the town. It was not a neat death. Another fact that didn't add up.

He climbed the stairs to try and get a look at Clara's face, the rope and the knot. The rope looked new, or unused. It should be easy to find out when and where she bought it, or perhaps it had been around some time; the dismissed gardener, or cleaner, might be able to help. The rope was firmly tied to the oak banisters; they'd taken her weight without any sign of damage. He couldn't see the knot under her chin. Pity. For the first time since he'd left the police, he regretted his decision. He wanted to investigate these deaths. He was afraid the easy answer would be accepted: mercy killing followed by suicide. It might be true, but there were other alternatives. Although who or why someone would want to murder Sam and Clara he hadn't a clue.

He looked at his watch. The police would soon be here. He ran down the stairs and looked at the other ground-floor rooms. A dining room, no sign of any violence; the kitchen, nothing interesting except for two glasses and a medicine bottle, half-empty. Again he used the handkerchief; the bottle contained morphine; he sniffed the glasses. One of them had held the drug. Why not give him an overdose instead of killing him with a cushion?

A smaller room looked like a study; Sam's? There were shelves of books, mainly medical, also scientific periodicals and books on opera and classical music. More interesting was a filing cabinet, its drawers pulled open; the named files were empty. Even if each one had contained only ten sheets of paper, they'd have produced more ash than the amount in the fireplace. Someone had emptied the files in a hurry. Was it Clara? Or had someone else taken away the contents of the files and burnt some uninteresting papers in the hearth in the hope the police would think that's where all the contents of the filing cabinet had landed up?

There was the sound of a car pulling up; he hurried back to the hall and waited for the bell to ring. He ostentatiously used his handkerchief to open the door.

A short, squat man, dressed in a Gannex raincoat and trilby, glared at him. Behind him were two other men, both in plain clothes, one of them was Johnny Cottam, a young constable who had been promoted to a detective constable after the Nicholson case. Good, someone he knew and trusted. Behind them were two uniformed constables.

'You're Frank Diamond?'

Ah, a James Cagney look-a-like. 'Yes.'

The man barrelled past him, his wide shoulders catching Frank as he strode into the hall. He came to an abrupt halt before the body of Clara. He whirled round. 'I'm Detective Inspector Revie.'

'I've heard about you.'

'And I've heard about *you*.'

'Nothing good I hope?'

'Correct.'

He tried not to smile. Revie took off his raincoat and trilby and threw them to one of the PCs, who raised his eyebrows. Revie's hips were as wide as his shoulders, but his body looked hard under the navy suit. His small, bright blue eyes stared beneath straight, dark eyebrows and the Marcelled waves of his dark hair shone with Brilliantine.

Revie turned to Cottam. 'Contact a pathologist. Try and get Ansell if you can. He's the best.'

Cottam hesitated on the front door step, looking as if he wanted to ask a question, before leaving.

Revie went up in Frank's opinion. Ansell had been crucial in the forensic evidence he'd produced to get a guilty verdict in the Nicholson case. Perhaps there was some hope of a sensible conversation with Revie.

'Right, Sonny Jim, where's the other body and what the hell were you and that woman doing breaking into the house?'

On second thoughts, perhaps not. He pointed to the sitting room. 'My name, by the way, is Mr Diamond and my associate is Miss Bowman.' No point in pandering to a bully.

Revie's small eyes became even smaller. He turned and shouted into the night. 'Cottam, come back and drive *M*r Diamond to Leiston police station. Where's Miss Bowman?' Cottam came back in, looking bemused.

'She's with Nancy Wintle, Sam Harrop's sister, presumably at a neighbour's. Did she give you the address? Nancy didn't see the bodies, we kept her in the car.'

'So you and Miss Bowman were in the house together? Did you touch anything?'

Frank explained about the light switches, he didn't mention the glasses or bottle in the kitchen.

'Right, Cottam, find Bowman and take her with you. Don't let them talk to each other.'

Frank could see it was going to be a long night.

Chapter 13

Friday, March 12th, 1971

Laurel sat at her desk in the dining room of Greyfriars, pretending to read through the notes on the David Pemberton case. She tried to concentrate, but other images swam before her eyes: Nancy's grief-stricken face, Clara Harrop's body hanging at the end of a rope and the hideous expression on the face of the dead Sam Harrop; also, she couldn't get the sickening smells of their bodies out of her nose. Worse of all was the guilt of her failure to get hold of Nancy and to return to the Harrop's house on Wednesday afternoon. Everyone was reassuring her she couldn't have acted in any other way, but if she'd followed her instinct and got Sam out of that house, he'd still be alive, and so would Clara.

Dorothy came into the room. 'Mabel's making some tea. Would you like a cup? It's nearly four, you've been sitting there long enough. Come on, Laurel, buck up. This is no time for introspection, we've got work to do.'

Laurel didn't know what to say or do. She felt numb. Normally Dorothy's bossiness would have roused her to make a pithy remark, but not today. She looked up. Dorothy was frowning at her, her glasses on the tip of her nose. Thank goodness for Dorothy. She was upset for

Nancy, but she wasn't wallowing in it; she didn't blame herself for starting the investigation off by asking her to help. She tried a smile.

Dorothy smiled back. 'That's better. Leave the paperwork.' She moved closer and whispered, 'Come and help me with Mabel, she's a bit upset.'

'What about?' she whispered back.

'Something to do with Stuart, I think.'

She shook her head. 'Those two, you'd think they were teenagers the way they're carrying on.'

Dorothy giggled. 'Romeo and Juliet: I can see Mabel on a balcony, and when young Stuart appears she pours hot tea all over him.'

Laurel sniggered. 'Dorothy Piff, to think you were once a respectable school secretary.'

'It's mixing with the like of you and Frank that's brought me down to this level.'

They were still laughing as they came into the kitchen.

'I'm glad someone's happy,' Mabel said, pouring tea into three cups. 'Though how you can laugh when Frank's at the station being grilled by that Revie man, I don't know. Next thing we'll hear is he's arrested for murder.'

Dorothy sat down, pulled out a packet of cigarettes and matches from her pocket and lit up. 'You honestly think Revie will get the better of Frank? If they arrest him, they'll have to take Laurel in as an accessory. Come on, Mabel, pull yourself together. This is a terrible situation, but no need to make it worse.'

Mabel plonked a plate of biscuits on the table, her face pinched and unhappy. 'I didn't have any time to make a cake, you'll have to make do with shop bought biscuits.'

'I don't mind,' Laurel said, 'I like shortbread.' Mabel

glowered and she realised she'd said the wrong thing.

'I'll have to have more money for the housekeeping if prices keep going up,' Mabel moaned.

'Are you doing anything tonight, Laurel?' Dorothy asked.

Laurel raised her eyebrows. Now what? 'Nothing, except to wait for Frank to come back from Leiston police station.'

Dorothy sipped her tea, then took a long pull on her cigarette. 'I'm going into Aldeburgh. There's a meeting at the Jubilee Hall about the possibility of building another nuclear power station. Easterspring's only been going for five years, so it will be ages before they start to build a new one, but they want to ease the way for the next phase. Would you like to come with me? I want to see the director, Dr Luxton, and hear what he's got to say.'

It wasn't something Laurel felt strongly about, but perhaps she should. It would get her out of the house and away from moaning Mabel, and possibly another embarrassing scene when Stuart got back. 'Yes, I'll come with you. What time's the meeting?'

'Seven o clock.' Dorothy glanced at the kitchen clock. 'We could leave soon and have a bite at The Cross Keys before it starts.'

'Along with all the other people who've decided to do the same,' Mabel muttered.

'Mabel, what's the matter with you?' Dorothy asked. 'Is it Stuart?'

Mabel slumped in her seat. 'I think he's fed up with me.'

Laurel stopped herself from saying, I'm not surprised.

'Why do you think that?' Dorothy asked, patting

126

Mabel's hand.

Mabel breathed in deeply. 'Someone told me they'd seen him in The White Lion, in Southwold, having a drink with a woman. They said they seemed thick with each other. I can't blame him, I haven't been very nice lately, have I?'

Laurel grasped her other hand. 'Oh, Mabel, that was Ann Fenner he was with, the Pembertons' housekeeper. He was only questioning her about David. I'm sure Stuart loves you, but you've been giving him a hard time.'

Mabel's chin dropped, a tear sliding down her cheek. 'I didn't realise it was her, but they said he was enjoying himself; they were eating fish and chips.'

Dorothy glanced at Laurel; they both bit their lips.

'Why don't you come with us to Aldeburgh? The meeting might be boring, but we'll have a meal first, and you'll see lots of your old customers. They'll all tell you your daughter-in-law's batter's good, but not as good as yours,' Dorothy said.

Mabel blinked. 'What's on the telly tonight?'

Dorothy consulted the *Radio Times*. '*The Virginian* followed by Eric Sykes.'

'Do come, Mabel. You can tell me who everyone is,' Laurel said.

Mabel smiled at them. 'Thanks. I think I will. But what about Frank and … Stuart when they come back? What will they have for their supper?'

Laurel sniffed. 'They're big boys, they can fend for themselves; also, Stuart might appreciate you more if you're not here, absence makes etc. etc.'

'Right, it's settled. I'll leave a note for them.'

'We could call in at Leiston police station and see if

we can rescue Frank,' Laurel said. Why had Revie wanted to see him again? They'd both made detailed statements yesterday.

Dorothy shook her head. 'Frank will do it his way. I bet he's got that Inspector Revie on board by now.'

'We'll hear all about it later, or tomorrow morning. Right, ten minutes to get ready, then off we go. I'll drive,' Laurel said.

Laurel, Dorothy and Mabel walked the short distance from the Cross Keys to the Jubilee Hall, both in Crabbe Street. The narrow street, close to the sea front, was crammed with people waiting to get into the meeting. They joined the queue, which because of the meagre pavement, spilled onto the road.

'Lovely old building,' Mabel said. 'I like it better than that Snape Malting, that's too far away from the town.'

'They've made a good job of rebuilding the concert hall after it burnt down last year. Such a shame,' Dorothy said.

'They still have concerts here during the music festival, don't they?' Laurel asked.

'They certainly do, but I hear Mr Britten isn't too well,' Dorothy said.

'He's never looked strong, poor man,' Mabel replied.

Laurel was surprised by the spaciousness of the hall with its deep stage and orchestra pit built underneath it. The rows of metal and leatherette chairs began to fill up.

'Let's get on the front row,' Dorothy whispered. 'Sometimes these science boffins aren't very good public speakers. We want to hear what's going on.'

Laurel led the way and they bagged seats in the centre

of the first row.

Dorothy wriggled. 'The seats are as uncomfortable as I remember.'

On the deep stage was a long table, with a microphone, glasses and a jug of water and three chairs.

Mabel got up. 'Just going to have a few words with some people I know. Don't let anyone pinch my seat.'

'I thought that was Stuart's prerogative,' Laurel said. She received a playful tap round the ear from Mabel.

'It's good to see her looking like her old self,' Dorothy said. 'Something is bothering her, I don't think it's anything to do with Stuart, not directly, I think she's worried about something, but she can't, or doesn't want to, talk about it. Stuart is as puzzled as anyone. I do hope they can sort it out, for their sakes and the agency's. I'd be so upset if one or both left.'

Laurel's stomach tightened. 'You don't think it would come to that? I really need everyone at the moment; I know I'm being lily-livered and logically I know I'm not responsible for the Harrops' dying, but …'

Dorothy squeezed her hand. 'You coped magnificently with Nicholson. Have faith in yourself. We've all got faith in you.'

Those few words lightened her spirits. She must push thoughts of inadequacy behind her and concentrate on the search for David Pemberton and possibly, if the Harrops' deaths were suspicious, finding out what happened to them and who did it.

Mabel came back to her seat as three men mounted the stage and took up their positions in front of the now silent audience. The man in the middle stood up and took hold of the microphone. 'Welcome to the meeting.' He introduced himself as a Suffolk County Councillor, acting as chair; he introduced the man on his right, the director of Easterbrook Power Station, Dr Luxton, and the man on his left as the Deputy Director.

Dr Luxton was a tall thin man, balding with a Plantagenet face; he gazed at the audience through owl-like glasses and wore a green tweed suit, white shirt and plain brown tie.

A boffin, looks and all, thought Laurel. He didn't look well; there were shadows under his eyes, and the corner of his right eye regularly twitched.

'How long has he been at Easterspring?' she asked Dorothy.

'Came when it was commissioned in 1966.'

The County Councillor waffled on about the prosperity the building of Easterspring had brought to Leiston and the surrounding area, how it had saved the town and how by the end of its life it would have generated enough electricity to power England and Wales for six months.

'Which six months was that?' Mabel asked in a whisper, 'April to September?'

Laurel suppressed a laugh.

'Dr Luxton will now speak on the work of the power station and the future of atomic energy in England and in this part of the country in particular,' the County Councillor said, passing the microphone to Luxton.

Luxton unfolded his body and leant towards the audience.

Terrible posture, Laurel thought. He looked nervous for a man with such power and responsibility; his eyes were shifting from side to side as if he was looking for someone in particular. Then he seemed to get a grip of himself and spoke in a pleasant cultured voice about the work of the station.

He briefly mentioned the history of nuclear power, the role of the British Nuclear Design and Construction, backed by English Electric, Babcock and Wilcox and Taylor Woodrow, in the building of the plant, and then baffled everyone with details about total generating capacity, the rate of oxidation of internal reactor-core components, and steam produced by boilers and turbo-generators.

Laurel's concentration drifted; she wished they'd sat a bit farther back so she could look round and see if she knew anyone in the audience.

'Although it will be many years before we need to replace this power station …' Luxton stopped speaking. He was staring towards the back of the hall, his mouth open in mid-sentence.

Laurel turned, directing her gaze in the direction of Luxton's stare. A few people were standing at the back of the hall, obviously latecomers. One person stood out, she'd seen his face before: seen it on paper, the drawing of the headmaster of Chillingworth School. Ralph Gabriel Baron.

'Dorothy, look who's at the back of the hall,' she whispered.

Luxton had regained his composure and was talking about a new power station to be built next to the present one, to be called Easterspring 2, an advanced gas-cooled reactor.

Dorothy craned her neck. 'You mean Mr Tucker, the art gallery owner?'

'No. No. Which one is he?'

'Look he's waving to me now. Nice man, always in a good humour. Oh, yes, I see who you mean. My word, that boy got him off to a T.'

'Oh, dear, he's fainting!'

Mabel's words made Laurel and Dorothy turn back to the stage. Luxton had collapsed across the table, the microphone fell to the floor, and loud metallic sounds reverberated round the hall. The chairman tried to pull Luxton into his seat whilst the Deputy Director retrieved the microphone.

Laurel didn't think; years of dealing with physical crises on the playing field, in the gym or the school playground, sent her towards where she was needed. She got up and went onto the stage. 'Can I help?' She didn't wait for the chairman's reply. She managed to lower the ungainly body of Luxton onto the stage floor and placed him in the recovery position. He was surprisingly light for his height: skin and bone. She loosened his tie and checked he was breathing. His breaths were shallow and his face pale, filmed with sweat. Could be a panic attack. He'd seemed nervous at the beginning of the meeting, then he'd settled down, but when he'd seen Baron he'd lost control. What was needed was a paper bag.

'Ask if anyone in the audience has a paper bag,' she ordered the chairman.

'What?'

'Just do it.'

The chairman turned to the Deputy Director. 'You heard what the lady said, ask the audience.' The noise from the floor was increasing, some people were making for the door, some were coming up to the stage, their expressions either concerned or curious.

132

'Oh, for goodness sake.' Laurel grabbed the microphone. 'Has anyone got a paper bag? Sounds mad, I know, but I need one.'

Mabel rummaged in her handbag, and produced a brown paper bag full of something. She came to the stage and handed it to Laurel. 'I brought some bread for the seagulls, forgot to give it to them.'

Laurel gave her the thumbs up, tipped the stale bread onto the stage floor and placed the bag over Luxton's mouth and nose. 'Take some deep breaths,' she whispered in his ear, hoping blood was returning to his brain and he would come to shortly.

A tall, dark-haired, good looking man, carrying a doctor's bag came onto the stage.

'Thank heavens,' the chairman said.

The doctor looked at Luxton and Laurel. 'Panic attack?'

'I think so.'

'You a medic?'

'No. Former head of PE.'

The doctor nodded. 'Girls?'

Laurel nodded, still holding the bag to Luxton's face.

'Plenty of experience then,' the doctor said.

Laurel eyeballed him. 'He's coming to.'

Luxton groaned, then retched. Laurel and the doctor helped him to sit up.

'Let's get the poor man out of the limelight. This is embarrassing for him,' Laurel said.

'You,' the doctor addressed the chairman. 'Take his right arm, and you,' pointing to the Deputy Director, 'get a chair for him in the wings.'

Laurel decided she'd try to get into *this* doctor's

practice. She hadn't signed up with one and was constantly nagged by Dorothy to get herself fixed up.

Luxton had recovered sufficiently to stagger, with help, out of the range of the audience.

'Sit down, man,' the doctor ordered. He pushed Luxton's head down between his knees. 'You'll feel better soon.'

The chairman scuttled back to the stage. 'Ladies and gentlemen.' He was speaking into the microphone. 'Please be seated. Dr Luxton has recovered but is unable to continue his talk. However, the Deputy Director ...'

The man's an idiot, Laurel thought.

'Will continue the talk.'

Laurel looked at the doctor who was taking Luxton's pulse. He raised his eyebrows as if he agreed with her estimation of the chairman's capabilities.

'Not too bad. Can you talk?' he asked Luxton.

Luxton nodded. 'Yes. Thank you. Both of you. I don't know what happened. I've never fainted before.'

'How will you get home?' Laurel asked.

'I live in Thorpeness. My deputy can drive me home.'

'Is there anyone there?' the doctor asked.

Luxton gulped. 'No, I live alone.'

It figures, thought Laurel, only a bachelor would wear such a horrible suit.

The doctor frowned. 'In that case, I think we need to get you to hospital. I don't want you by yourself in case you have another attack. Or have you a friend who could stay with you tonight? Tomorrow you need to get a full check-up. I don't think it's serious, but better safe than sorry.'

'Perhaps your deputy could stay with you?' Laurel

asked.

Luxton's face crumpled. 'No. He's got a family. I don't think he'd want to do that.'

The doctor looked at Laurel. 'You OK to stay with him? I'll see the deputy, sounds as if the meeting's packing up, and I'll get him some water.'

'There's some on the table.'

The doctor shook his head. 'You'd have thought the chairman would have brought the poor chap a glass by now!' He stalked off.

Laurel put her arm round Luxton's shoulders. He flinched. 'Are you all right now, Dr Luxton?' She slowly withdrew her arm.

He leant back against the back of the chair. 'Yes, thank you. Did you come to my rescue when I fainted? I saw you sitting on the front row. What's your name?'

'Laurel Bowman. I used to be a PE teacher, so I've got some knowledge of first aid. Luckily someone got hold of a doctor.'

'Don't you teach now?'

'No.' She didn't feel like elaborating. His breathing was becoming shallow again. 'Dr Luxton, take some slow deep breaths. Try not to get worked up if you can.' He looked round and his right eye started twitching. He looked frightened, as though whatever had brought on the attack was returning to his mind.

'Can I help you? Something is bothering you and making you feel unwell. Perhaps if you told someone, they might be able to help you sort out the problem. Sometimes when you talk to someone about what's worrying you, it immediately shrinks in size and you find you can deal with it.' It was like talking to a fourth year who was convinced life was over because they had a spot on the end of their nose, or her best friend had gone off with the boy she fancied.

He looked at her as though he was longing to tell her, his mouth trembling and tears filming his eyes. 'I can't tell anyone. If I told you, you'd wish you hadn't helped me, you'd hate me so much you'd wish I'd died. I wish I *was* dead.'

Good heavens. She must tell the doctor and make sure the Deputy Director understood how serious this was; he seemed unstable, delusional. What had he done to make him feel like this?

'Please don't feel like that. Whatever it is I'm sure you can put it right. Try to get some rest. Are your parents still alive? There's nothing like going home and being spoilt for a few days.' She knew she was offering platitudes and from the look on his face, nothing she'd said was getting through.

The doctor came back with the Deputy Director. 'Come along, Dr Luxton, you're going home with your colleague. I'll come with you to his car.'

As the two scientists left the stage, Dr Luxton leaning on his deputy, Laurel called the doctor back and told him what Luxton had said.

'I'll have a word with his friend, tell him not to leave him by himself. I'll make an appointment to see him tomorrow if his own doctor can't fit him in.'

Laurel shook his hand. 'Thanks. By the way, have you got room for another customer? I haven't signed up with a practice yet.' No use being a shy violet.

'Delighted ... Miss?' he said, glancing at her left hand.

'Laurel Bowman.'

136

'Oliver Neave. So, you're *the* Laurel Bowman, who sorted out Nicholson?'

'I'm afraid so.'

'Welcome to our practice. Although perhaps it'd be better if you had my partner, Dr Scott, as your doctor.'

Laurel's shoulders sagged. She'd obviously made a poor impression. Then she saw the twinkle in his eyes and the friendly smile. 'Of course, if you think that'd be best.'

'I do. Now I'd better catch up with Dr Luxton, before he's whisked off. Goodnight and thank you for your prompt and kindly actions.'

Laurel went back to the hall. Dorothy and Mabel were waiting for her and talking to them was the man Dorothy had said was Mr Tucker, the owner of the art gallery. She'd often looked in the windows of his gallery, it was on the same side of the High Street as Nancy's house, towards the post office. It was up-market, with painting and sculptures tastefully arranged; the prices well beyond her.

They turned as she approached.

'How is he?' Dorothy asked.

'Much better, but still not fit to be by himself.'

'Laurel, this is Ben Tucker, Ben, Laurel Bowman.'

Tucker shook her hand. 'Well done, you were up on that stage in a trice. I suppose we must expect such prompt action from the lady who put an end to the terrible deeds of Mr Nicholson.'

His fluting voice was clear, his accent well-bred, suggesting an education in one of the best private schools, followed by a degree at an Oxbridge university. Physically he was short, about five eight, rotund, with crinkly grey hair, neatly barbered, with a widow's peak

137

above a pleasant fleshy face; his light brown eyes, small mouth and elvish ears, made Laurel think of a jolly pixie. A rather old pixie.

She smiled at him. 'Thank you.'

'Ben's invited us to have coffee with him before we go home. Do you feel up to it, Laurel?'

The thought of a strong cup of coffee was tempting. 'Sounds good. I could do with something. That poor man was in a terrible state. Do you live far, Ben?'

'I'm staying for a few days at the Wentworth Hotel. We can have coffee and something a little stronger, if you wish, in the hotel lounge. Shall we go, ladies?'

The hotel was a short walk, past the Moot Hall, on the road to Thorpeness at the edge of the town. Ben Tucker received the full attention of the hotel's receptionist, and on seeing the lounge was busy, he ushered them into the bar. Coffee was ordered, with a brandy for Dorothy, a cherry brandy for Mabel and whisky for Laurel and Ben.

'Goodness me, what a night. High drama indeed. I thought this would be a boring meeting. Far from it. This poor man was in a state, you say, Laurel?'

They were seated in low, comfortable leather chairs round a small table. The waiter had brought dishes of crisps and peanuts; a fire was glowing in the nearby hearth. All relaxing after the unsettling encounter with Dr Luxton.

'Yes. I feel worried for him, but I was impressed by Doctor Neave, he seems extremely capable.'

'From what I could see he was equally impressed with you, Laurel,' Dorothy said.

Mabel winked at her.

'Aha!' Ben said. 'That's two conquests tonight,

138

Laurel.'

'Two?'

'Why, I'm the second. Like dear John Betjeman, I've always admired strong, determined women.'

Laurel couldn't be annoyed; he said it with such good humour and a sense of fun, she and the other two laughed.

'Did poor Dr Luxton tell you what had made him ill? I know him slightly; he's bought a couple of pictures from me. Such a clever man, and good at his job, I hear. Does Dr Neave think he's got a bug?' He leaned towards her, his voice full of concern.

Laurel frowned. 'No, I don't think he'd got an infection. He seems to be very worried about something.' She stopped. It didn't seem right to discuss him.

'You don't think he's worried about the power station, do you? Goodness, we don't want any mistakes made there. Do you think he's well enough to be in control of such an establishment? I've always had my doubts about nuclear power. I know the good points, but if anything happened ...' Ben Tucker shook his head.

'I really couldn't say, Ben,' Laurel replied. 'I'm sure Dr Neave will sort him out when he sees him tomorrow.'

Dorothy finished crunching some crisps. 'He seemed to get worse when he saw someone at the back of the hall, didn't he Laurel?'

Ben's eyes rounded. 'Oh, I hope it wasn't me – I was at the back. I came in a bit late and I thought I'd stay there so I could sneak out if it got really boring.'

'No,' Dorothy said, 'It was – Ow!'

Laurel had given her a swift kick. Too much was being said. Facts that might have a bearing on the case. Although how anything to do with Dr Luxton could tie up with David Pemberton she couldn't see.

Ben laughed. 'Quite right, my dear,' he said to Laurel. 'Ever the detective – I believe that's your new profession?'

Laurel flushed. 'Yes.'

'I'm glad Dr Luxton's seeing Dr Neave tomorrow. I hope he's not being left alone tonight?' Ben said.

'No, he's going home with his deputy,' Laurel said.

'Any more coffee?' Ben asked.

They all refused.

'I think we ought to be going,' Laurel said.

'Yes, Frank should be back from the police station by now. As for Stuart, I expect he's tucked up in his bed in Leiston,' Dorothy said.

Ben Tucker leant back against the leather chair. 'Of course, I'd forgotten, Laurel. Not only have you had to deal with a fainting director of a nuclear power station, but you discovered the bodies of the Harrops. Who would have thought such a tragedy could happen here, in a quiet little town like Aldeburgh? Your nerves must be strong indeed. What did the police say? Mercy killing and suicide I suppose. You must love someone very much to be driven to such extremes.' He cocked his head towards her.

'I really don't know what the police think. I made my statement. It looked like the situation you describe.' She shuddered. 'It was awful.'

'Time we were off. Thank you for the coffee and drinks, Ben. Right, girls?' Dorothy rose from her chair.

Ben bounced up. 'I'm sorry, I shouldn't have brought up that subject. Let me get your coats.'

As he helped Laurel on with hers, a difficult feat due

to their differences in height, he whispered, 'Do come and see me in my gallery. I may have some work for your agency, although I know you've got your hands full at the moment.'

Was there anything Ben Tucker didn't know about Aldeburgh and its inhabitants?

Chapter 14

Detective Constable Cottam guided Frank towards Revie's office in Leiston police station.

'What does he want to see me about?' Frank asked. 'He went over my statement *three* times yesterday.'

Cottam's lips twitched. 'He's been in purdah since Ansell's pathology reports came back. Something stinks.'

Not the most appropriate comment, Frank thought. 'How are you getting on with him?'

Cottam frowned. 'I thought he was a bullshitter to begin with, but he's pretty shrewd in some ways. Not made my mind up yet. Wish *you* were back on the job.'

Frank smiled at him. 'Johnny Cottam, you're a bit of a bullshitter yourself.'

Cottam knocked on a door and opened it. 'Mr Diamond, sir.'

Revie was sitting behind a wooden desk with a telephone and an open file on it. The room was sparsely furnished: two chairs in front of the desk, a grey metal filing cabinet against a wall, one wooden shelf with books and periodicals leaning drunkenly against each other, and a window overlooking flowerbeds in front of a busy road.

Revie got up. 'Sorry to drag you back again. Like a cuppa?'

His Birmingham accent seemed more pronounced

today and the lines on his face deeper. Was the offer of a drink a sign of a friendlier Detective Inspector Revie? It was just past four, so why not?

'Thanks, I'd prefer a coffee, if that's possible and a choccy biccy would go down well.'

Revie turned to the lingering Cottam. 'You heard the man, and no pinching a biscuit, they're for visitors.'

'Yes, sir.' He closed the door.

Revie frowned. He must have clocked the look Cottam gave him. 'Sit down, Mr Diamond.' Revie moved back behind his desk, sighed and drew up his chair close to it and leant towards Frank. 'I expect you're wondering why I asked you to come back?'

He tried to look puzzled, but couldn't help replying, 'Is it about the post-mortem reports?'

Revie's face coloured and he closed the file on his desk with a snap. 'Who told you that?'

'No one,' he lied. 'I couldn't think of any other reason you'd want to see me again, unless you were going to arrest me.'

Revie glowered at him. 'That *would* be a pleasure.'

He decided he'd better shut up or Revie might just do that.

'I'm expecting Ansell shortly. You worked with him on the Nicholson case, didn't you? What do you think of him?'

'Professionally?'

'Bloody hell, I don't want to know about his sex life or what football team he supports.' He pointed at Frank. 'I suppose you're pleased about Liverpool beating Bayern Munich, the other night?'

Frank nodded. 'It's a good score, 3-0, but it's only the

first leg.'

Revie sniffed. 'Back to Ansell, did he do a good job for you?'

Revie was looking for help, for reassurance; perhaps there was hope of some kind of a working relationship. It was what he needed, what the agency needed. Better go carefully from now on, cut the crapping around and treat the man seriously, show him he was dealing with a good ex-copper.

'He was excellent; in fact, I was pleased when you asked for him at the Harrops' house. His evidence led to the conviction of Nicholson. He's a hard worker and doesn't mind how much extra time he puts in to get the results you need.' He wanted to ask what Ansell had found, but decided to play the diplomat.

Revie grunted. 'Good. Yesterday you said you wouldn't be happy if the inquests on the Harrops' deaths came in as mercy killing and suicide. I gave you short shrift and told you to give your statement and bugger off.'

'Yes, I seem to remember it went like that.'

'I want to know why you thought it would be a wrong verdict.'

'You've changed your mind?'

'I might have.'

Frank settled back in his seat; Revie was still leaning towards him; in Frank's book that meant he was genuinely interested in his answers. 'First of all, why did Clara kill Sam when he only had a short time to live? I could be wrong, perhaps the end wasn't as near as his appearance suggested. What did Ansell say about his general condition?'

Revie opened the file on his desk. 'Cancer of the liver,

very advanced, secondary growths in the pancreas, lungs, and bones. Said the poor bugger would have died in a week or two; he must have been in terrible pain.'

'I hope he was taking morphine?'

'Yes. There was some in a bottle in the kitchen and we found a good supply hidden upstairs. Looks like he was well prepared for the end.'

Frank's shoulders relaxed. Revie didn't need to give him so much detail. Excellent. 'But why kill him by smothering? She could have dosed him up with morphine. And he wasn't ready to die yet. There was something he had to do. He wanted to see Nancy, his sister, for some reason: to say goodbye? Or to tell her something he didn't want to take to the grave?'

Revie nodded. 'But Clara didn't want him to see Nancy. She didn't want him to talk to Nancy, or anyone else.'

'Why was there no telephone in any of the rooms?' Frank asked.

'We found two in locked cupboards, she'd made sure he couldn't contact anyone. Also she'd dismissed the cleaner and gardener.'

Frank nodded. 'Yeah, I knew about that. Poor old Sam, on his last legs, was a prisoner in his own home.'

'Any idea what she was worried about?' Revie's small, blue eyes became smaller as he squinted at Frank.

Frank turned the question over in his mind. Sam's homosexuality would have to come out, but if he told Revie, Laurel would be furious and Nancy would feel betrayed. 'I presume you've talked to Nancy Wintle?'

Revie rolled his eyes, suggesting they hadn't learnt much from her. 'Yesterday. She's in a right stew, can't blame her. She was fond of her brother. Mind you she'll be a rich woman when all Sam Harrop's affairs are settled. He left everything to her, with a reasonable allowance for his wife, but as she's dead as well, Mrs Wintle cops the lot. In my book that makes her the prime suspect.' He leant back in his chair and laughed. 'Can you see her stringing Clara up? She'd have a job pegging out the washing.'

Frank smiled. 'She's got a cast iron alibi, in case you change your mind. I think you need to talk to Nancy Wintle again – diplomatically.'

Revie scowled, then smirked. 'Too hard, am I?'

'You need to ask her if there was anything her brother was hiding from people.'

Revie stared at him. 'He was married.'

Frank shrugged his shoulders. 'I can say no more.'

There was a knock on the door and Cottam appeared carrying a tray with three cups and a plate of biscuits. Behind him was a tall, thin man with light brown hair curling down to his collar. 'Hello, Frank! Gosh, didn't expect to see you. Been called in for consultation, or are you going to be arrested?'

Frank was pleased to see Martin Ansell was more confident and cheerful than when he'd first met him the previous September. The success of his work on the Nicholson case and his impressive court appearance had done his self-esteem and reputation a power of good. However, Revie didn't look to be happy with his remarks.

'Please sit down, Dr Ansell. I've summoned Mr Diamond so he can answer more questions.'

The relaxed atmosphere had disappeared with Ansell's flippant comments. Frank needed to go carefully with

Revie if he was to get what he wanted from him. 'I'm here to help, if I can, Martin. I'm grateful Inspector Revie has given me this chance to be more involved.'

A look of understanding passed over Ansell's face. 'Of course. Sorry for the *faux pas*, Inspector Revie.'

Revie's lower lip pushed out and he shrugged.

Frank wondered if he knew what a *faux pas* was, but he seemed mollified.

'I've read your post-mortem reports, Dr Ansell, but before we go into details, help yourself to a cuppa and a biscuit. The coffee's Frank's.'

How pally, he'd been promoted. He sipped the coffee which tasted like mud dredged from the bottom of a stagnant river. 'Delicious, thank you.' If his mother could hear him he'd be sent to the priest for a confession and ten Hail Marys.

Revie placed his mug on the desk, adding to several other stains on its surface. 'Let's take Sam Harrop first, shall we, Martin?'

My, this was getting cosy. It would be nicknames next. Marty, Franky and Nicky. The three musketeers, or the three stooges. His mind was wandering: the grillings yesterday and lack of sleep were taking their toll. He shook his head vigorously. 'Sorry, lack of sleep.'

Revie sneered. 'You're getting soft; not used to proper cases now, are you?'

Frank metaphorically bit his tongue, but couldn't keep his teeth clamped long enough. 'It's all the sex, Nicholas. But I expect you're too old to remember.'

Ansell spluttered into his tea.

'I've had more shags than you've had hot dinners,' Revie retorted.

Ansell carried on spluttering, making the other men laugh.

'Right, let's cut out the macho stuff and get on with the job,' Revie said.

Frank thought he might be able to like Revie … eventually.

'As you know, Sam Harrop was smothered,' Ansell said, wiping away biscuit crumbs from his chin. 'If this is skilfully done and whatever was used to smother the victim removed, the murderer might get away with it, but the victims need to be young, very old, or incapacitated, it's not an easy job on a fit person. Although Mr Harrop was very ill, he fought the murderer. The skin round his mouth and nose were pale, this is due to the pressure used, but the rest of the face showed cyanosis, colouring by the blood cells. There was saliva, blood and tissue cells on the cushion. There were no marks on the victim's face, so the cushion was the only weapon used.'

Revie frowned.

'I mean the murderer didn't use their bare hands. If they did, you'd expect to see scratches, nail marks or lacerations on the victim's face.'

'Got you,' Revie said.

'The act was violent. There was a lot of bruising on the lips, gums and tongue. I also saw bruising in the mouth and nose. There were haemorrhages in the face and eyes and he'd bitten his tongue in the struggle.'

'How long would it have taken?' Frank asked.

Ansell grimaced. 'Three to five minutes.'

Revie looked as though he was about to spit on the floor. 'Bastard! What was Clara doing if someone else was killing Sam?'

'Either she was already dead, or incapacitated, or she was looking on,' Frank replied.

Ansell shuddered and Revie pulled a face.

'My guess is, she was already dead,' Frank said.

Revie's sharp eyes became sharper. 'Explain.'

'She didn't want Sam talking to Nancy. Perhaps she went to someone she knew who also didn't want Sam to talk, and she asked for help. The way she treated Sam before he died shows she was a cold-hearted bitch. Perhaps she sought help to shut Sam up, but—'

'Surely, she'd want his death to appear as natural or a suicide,' Revie interrupted. 'We know Clara Harrop left Sam in the house, Miss Bowman saw her drive away. She thought she'd gone to Nancy Wintle's. Clara comes back with someone. Miss Bowman heard two car doors close. She assumed it was Nancy with Clara, but it must have been the murderer.'

'If we knew where Clara went we would be closer to finding out what happened,' Frank said.

'I can't give you any proof that it wasn't Clara who murdered Sam. The green threads from Clara's suit were found under one of Sam's nails.'

'Nail? A nail, not nails?' Frank asked.

Ansell's face twisted. 'Yes. Only under the right thumbnail. It's possible only that nail caught her sleeve as he struggled with her as she was smothering him, and I think to most people that would be conclusive. Clara murdered him.'

Revie drummed his fingers on the desk. 'Let's go over Clara's suicide. Are you completely happy it was a suicide?' he asked Ansell. 'Your report suggests otherwise.'

'Murder by hanging is extremely rare. A fit and healthy adult victim would need to be made unconscious by injury or a drug; a child or a very weak adult could be hanged without resorting to either of these. Clara was a strong, fit woman, as her autopsy proves. Even unconscious, it would need strength to carry her upstairs and to heave her over the banisters.'

'What weren't you happy about, Martin?' Frank asked.

'There was fracture dislocation between the third and fourth cervical vertebrae. You'd expect to find this type of injury in a judicial hanging, usually suicide by hanging is due to asphyxia, or the jugular veins are blocked, or if a thin cord is used and it presses deep into the tissues, the arteries serving the brain are constricted. The commonest cause of death in hanging is a combination of asphyxia and constriction of the veins.'

Frank looked at Revie. 'Interesting but no proof she didn't take her own life.'

Revie grimaced. 'Martin, you mentioned a bruising on the neck.'

Ansell sighed. 'The bruising was under the knot, a slip knot by the way, under the right ear, so it could have been caused by the knot tightening as she fell from the banisters.' He paused, scratching his neck, exactly in the spot he'd described. 'I wasn't happy; the shape of the bruise didn't look right. If I was pushed in court, I'd say it looked more like a bruise you'd get if a knife-hand strike had been performed.'

'A knife-hand strike?' Revie asked, eyes widening.

'The old karate chop, beloved of Bruce Lee and other martial arts gurus,' Frank said. 'Delivered with the side of the knuckle of the small finger.'

'Lethal?' Revie asked.

'It can be,' Ansell replied, 'or a skilled fighter can induce unconsciousness.'

'Long enough to string someone up and toss them over the banisters?' Frank asked.

'It's possible, but I can't provide you with enough evidence to bring a verdict of murder by person or persons unknown at the inquest.'

Chapter 15

Saturday, March 13th 1971

Frank looked at their faces as they sat round the dining room table at Greyfriars: Laurel, despite an early morning run, looked peaky, Dorothy seemed fine, Stuart self-satisfied and Mabel subdued.

'What will you do, Frank, if Nancy doesn't tell Revie about Sam? If they were murdered, I can see how important it is Revie knows Sam was a homosexual, but he can't prove it was murder, can he, from what Ansell's said?' Laurel asked.

Frank shook his head. 'Not at the moment.'

'If it was murder and suicide, then what's the point in revealing Sam's past? It would hurt Nancy to have his reputation blackened for no good reason,' Laurel said.

Dorothy patted Laurel's hand. 'Nancy's in a state at the moment, but her son from Carlisle is staying with her for at least a week. Once she's calmed down, if she thinks there's anyway she can help to find out who did this to Sam and Clara, I'm sure she'll tell Revie as much as she can.'

'What's next?' Stuart asked.

Frank got up. 'I'm phoning the Pembertons this morning; before we go to the school on Monday I need to report back to them, and also ask a few questions.' He hesitated, then sat down again. 'I'll go over what I'm going to ask, and I can add any questions you think of.'

Laurel looked at him, her lips tight. 'Yes, that's what we usually do before one of us goes off to question someone.'

Not the usual cheery Laurel. He wasn't in the mood for other people's ups and downs. He wanted to go back to the Pembertons, had done all week, but at the same time he was dreading it. He wanted to see Carol, half-hoping a second meeting would not have the same effect as the first. He was still unwilling to believe what Ann Fenner had said about her, even though David's drawing of the woman and the man making love, could be Carol with one of David's tutors. He felt like a teenager with a crush: wanting to be near her, wanting to stroke her face, her hair, wanting to hear her voice, to hold her hand, and to look into her eyes and see his passion reflected back at him.

'Of course. I want to know how much the fees are, better than asking the school—'

'It's nearly two years since David was there; they'll have gone up by now,' Laurel interrupted.

Frank grimaced. 'Yes, I realise that, but it'll give me some idea of the yearly income of the school. As I said the other day, the upkeep of the school, staff salaries, heating and lighting and all the other expenses, don't add up. They'd need to be charging a hefty annual fee to cover the costs. It may be functioning as a charity, but even so.'

'OK,' Laurel said, still stony-faced.

What's the matter with the woman? All that stuff with the fainting Director of Easterspring seems to have upset her. Not like Laurel. 'I also want to find out more about Peter. Mrs Pemberton did mention his name, so hopefully I can find out more about him before Monday.'

'If we could talk to Peter we might be able to find out why David ran away,' Stuart said.

'It'll depend on how well he can communicate, or even understand your questions,' Dorothy said.

'Just because he's got Down's syndrome, if indeed he has, doesn't mean he's an idiot!' Laurel fumed, shaking her head and glaring at Dorothy., who looked shocked.

Frank ignore Laurel's outburst. 'I'll try and get the names and addresses of David's last two tutors; they may be able to throw some light on his personality, although the last one left when David first went to Chillingworth.'

Stuart sniggered. 'Are you going to ask Mrs Pemberton about *her* relationship with them?'

This time *he* got the benefit of Laurel's glare.

Frank decided it was a good time to make a phone call.

The call was answered by Ann Fenner, but Carol was obviously nearby, for as soon Miss Fenner said, 'I'll see if—' Carol Pemberton's voice was in his ear.

'Mr Diamond, good to hear from you. Any news? Any developments?' Her voice was low, almost a whisper, as though she didn't want Ann Fenner to hear their conversation.

'Mrs Pemberton. No, nothing new yet.' Nothing he could tell her. 'Would it be possible to see you and your husband either today, or tomorrow? We're going to Chillingworth on Monday and there's information you may be able to give me that would be useful before we interview some of the staff and pupils.'

There was no immediate answer; they hadn't been cut off as he could hear her breathing. 'Is it just you?'

'Yes, unless you'd like to meet some other agency members?'

'No. Come over this afternoon, about three. Is that suitable?'

Frank walked back to his car which was parked in front of the fishermen's huts near Aldeburgh's beach front. He'd walked to Thorpeness and back, killing time before his appointment with the Pembertons. He'd escaped from Greyfriars before lunch, returned to his cottage, had a shower, changed his clothes and headed for Aldeburgh. He'd treated himself to a pint and a fisherman's pie in the Cross Keys, but he was regretting this as his stomach was contracting with nervousness, and he felt light-headed and slightly breathless. This was ridiculous.

He switched on the ignition, took a deep breath, and tried to put not only the car into gear, but his mind as well. Turn off the emotions, turn on a professional attitude. Treat all words said with analytical acuity, get rid of the mushy brain.

Ann Fenner opened the door. 'Good afternoon, Mr Diamond.' Her smile was wide and friendly; Stuart had worked his magic. 'Mrs Pemberton is in the sitting room. Can I take your coat?'

'No thank you. Mr Pemberton?'

'I'm afraid Mr Pemberton had a long-standing engagement. He'll be back tomorrow evening.' Her voice seemed to hold a warning. She must know he'd been told about Carol and the tutors. She led him to the sitting room.

'Mr Diamond, madam.'

'Thank you, Ann.' She turned to him. 'Good afternoon, Mr Diamond. It's a little early but I fancy a drink. Ann, would you bring me a gin and tonic?' She looked stunningly different. Her hair was loose, floating like a black cloud round her beautiful face. Her short, patterned dress, with long flaring sleeves and low V neck line made her look young, girlish. Frank swallowed.

'Ice as usual, madam?'

'Yes. Mr Diamond, will you join me?'

This wasn't what he'd expected. No Mr Pemberton and the offer of an alcoholic drink. Gin wasn't his favourite tipple. 'I wouldn't mind a whisky, thank you.'

'Ann, please see to that, and when you've finished in the kitchen you may take the rest of the day off. I won't need dinner tonight.'

'Are you sure, madam? Tomorrow's my day off, but I don't mind working tomorrow if you need me. Mr Pemberton might want a hot meal when he gets back, rather than the cold buffet I usually leave.'

Carol waved her hand impatiently. 'No. I'd like some time by myself. Please don't disturb me for the rest of the weekend.'

Ann Fenner nodded and left the room.

Carol approached Frank, holding out her hand. 'Sorry about that, Ann is such a fusspot at times. As you gathered my husband isn't here, however I'll try and answer all your questions. Please sit down.' She pointed to an armchair.

Frank was glad it wasn't the settee. Ann Fenner's remarks, Adam Pemberton's absence, the suggestion they might be in for an alcoholic session, all sent alarm bells

156

ringing; the trouble was the music was enticing and former good resolutions were slipping away.

Carol seemed composed and made small talk until Ann Fenner appeared complete with silver tray, glasses, an ice bucket, a bottle of Gordon' gin, one of tonic, and a bottle of Laphroaig, which she placed on a coffee table near Carol. He looked at the bottle of Scotch; two doubles and all his inhibitions would disappear. Carol passed him a good three fingers of Scotch and gave herself an equal measure of gin, two cubes of ice, and not too much tonic.

He opened his briefcase. If he'd known about this situation, what would he have done? Run a mile? Or not bothered with the briefcase at all?

He opened a notebook and tried to speak in a normal tone. 'Mrs Pemberton, would you mind telling me the annual fee you paid Chillingworth School?'

She frowned. 'I can't see that's important. Let me see ... Adam dealt with that side. I think it was about fifteen hundred a year. I'll check, if you like.'

Frank scribbled in his notebook. 'No, that's fine, just trying to get as much background as possible. You mentioned David had one particular friend at the school, Peter. I got the impression, although I may be quite wrong, it wasn't a friendship you approved of. Could you tell me more about Peter? Did he ever come here? Did David ever go to his home?'

Carol was sitting on the settee; she edged closer to him. 'I knew you were astute as soon as I met you, I said so to Adam. You're able to read people, aren't you? Just from a tiny inflexion in my voice you knew I didn't approve of Peter.' She leant towards him and a rich, flowery perfume drifted up from her body. The skin of her face, neck and the swell of her breasts above the v neckline of her dress was smooth and creamy.

Frank looked down at his notebook, not seeing what he'd written. 'Can you give me more details, please.'

She leant back, smiling. 'Certainly. I didn't think Peter was a suitable friend. I didn't invite him here, and as Peter was an orphan, there was no way I was going to let David visit him in the holidays, even if it was possible. I didn't ask.'

Frank's professional antennae came back into action. 'An orphan? I don't know anything about that.'

'Oh, yes. The governors of the school are philanthropic. They reserve a few places each year for children from orphanages, those who have no relatives, and are boys with disabilities, like Peter.'

'What was wrong with Peter?'

'He's a mongol. Very low IQ, you know. I didn't think it was good for David, with his problems, to mix with boys like that. The whole point of sending him to school was so he'd make friends with boys like himself. I know all the boys have problems, but Peter's are …' The pitch of her voice had risen, it was sharp and edgy. He was glad Laurel wasn't here; she wouldn't have been able to control herself, especially in her present mood.

'Do you know why David liked him?'

She shook her head, black hair falling like a velvet curtain. 'No, I don't.'

Frank frowned. He didn't remember any reference to Peter in either the police report or the one from the detective agency. 'That's fine, I'll see if I can speak to Peter at the school.' He took another sip of his drink. Carol was one-third down hers.

'What on earth do you hope *he'll* be able to tell you?'

Frank smiled then shrugged. 'Probably very little, but we need to explore every lead.'

She relaxed, crossing her legs; her skirt riding up showing elegant thighs encased in sheer tights. 'Any other questions, Frank? Is it all right to call you Frank? Do call me Carol.'

His throat was tightening again. He decided to ignore the last question and ploughed on. 'One piece of information which would be useful. Could you give me the names and addresses of David's last two tutors? We may need to interview them.'

Her eyes widened and her right hand moved to her throat. 'Why? Why do you want to know that? What could they possibly tell you about David's disappearance?'

His heart constricted, disappointment and jealousy welled up, blocking his throat. Ann Fenner had told the truth. Carol was frightened at the thought of the tutors revealing ... he coughed, trying to regain speech. 'It's possible if David was fond of one of his tutors he might have got in touch with him; they might have some snippets of information that might give us a clue to where he is, or what happened to him. Believe me it's surprising how sometimes the smallest fact can lead to other more important clues being revealed.'

Carol looked at him, her eyes shimmering, as though she was about to cry; she looked young and vulnerable.

'Are you all right?' He got up and sat next to her on the settee.

'I'm sorry,' she whispered, taking his hand. 'I find it all too much, sometimes. Where is my boy?' she sobbed, and rested her head on his shoulder.

Her hand was small, fluttering like a trapped bird in his hand, and the heady perfume was overpowering. He wanted to hold her tight, tell her he'd find David. She looked up at him, her mouth close to his, lips slightly parted, her pupils dark pools in her blue eyes. He bent his head and gently kissed her. Her mouth opened and her tongue, flickering like a lizard's, tried to enter his mouth. Frank drew back. 'I'm sorry. I shouldn't have taken advantage of you. Please forgive me,' he said.

She smiled up at him. 'We'll pretend it didn't happen, shall we? I'm afraid I do get upset sometimes. All these questions bring back the pain and worry. You've been so kind.' She moved away and put a hand to her forehead. 'I'm sorry, I don't feel well, a horrid headache. I need to lie down.'

Frank didn't know what to do or say. He wasn't in full control of himself. First she'd seemed frightened, then vulnerable; when he'd kissed her, her reaction had shocked and thrilled him. Why he'd reacted as he did he couldn't understand.

'I haven't answered your question about the tutors, have I?'

'No, you haven't.'

She leant towards him again, smiling, in spite of her headache. 'I'll look up the addresses. Perhaps we could meet tomorrow? Not here. Where do you live? I have the car.'

No. This was not wise. 'Near Dunwich.'

'Tomorrow afternoon?'

His chest tightened. He hesitated. 'Do you know the National Trust car park above Minsmere beach?'

She nodded, her eyes sparkling.

'Park there at two. I'll find you.'

'Do you live near there or at Dunwich?'

'Dunwich,' he lied. 'Our agency is based there, as you know.'

There was a knock on the door. After a delay of several seconds Ann Fenner came in. 'Sorry to bother you, madam. I'm going out, now. I won't be back until late. Is that all right?'

Carol got up, pulling her dress down. 'I told you to take the rest of the day off, Ann. Please don't bother me again.'

Ann Fenner looked at Frank anxiously. Was she afraid he was about to join the tutors and maybe other men, who had fallen for Carol? She could be right. He also got up, put his notebook and biro into the briefcase and walked towards the door.

'Goodbye, Mrs Pemberton. If you'd look up the addresses, I'd be grateful.'

Ann Fenner went into the hall.

'Tomorrow?' Carol whispered.

'Tomorrow,' he said.

Chapter 16

Laurel stopped on her way to her car and looked at the front garden. Everything at Greyfriars was spring-like: the sunny day had opened the crocus flowers, bees were diving in for nectar and pollen, and a soft sea breeze moved the daffodils in the grass. All this should have lifted her spirits. It didn't. She tried to analyse her feelings. She didn't have to look far: Frank. Something was wrong. It was after he'd been to the Pembertons on Monday. Something happened there. What? On Wednesday evening when Stuart told them about Ann Fenner's discovery of Carol Pemberton having sex with one of David's tutors, she'd seen different emotions flicker over his face: he looked hurt and … angry? … jealous? She wasn't sure. David's drawing of Carol showed she was beautiful. She'd thought Frank was too professional to become involved with a client, but how much did she know about him as a man? She knew him as a policeman, a private detective and a friend and colleague. She'd first met him as the detective sergeant investigating the murder of her younger sister, Angela; then as a detective inspector on the Nicholson case, now they were partners. But as a man? He was attractive; not only his good looks and green eyes, but his sense of humour, his intelligence and the ability to make leaps of imagination, tying one fact with another.

There'd been times when his magnetism made her wish their relationship would take a different direction, usually when she'd been in danger, or more prosaically after a few whiskies. She didn't want to go down that road, she preferred his friendship and their relationship as working colleagues. She'd learnt how shallow a bond built on sexual attraction could be: deeply consuming and important for a time, but then bitter disappointment when you realise the man you desired and gave yourself to, was not the man you thought he was, and deep chasms of shame and anger opened up. She cherished all her relationships with the team, but especially those with Frank and Dorothy. These last few days she hadn't felt their normal easy camaraderie, he didn't hold her gaze like he used to, didn't explain his thoughts.

He was going to the Pembertons today. She shook her head. Was she becoming paranoid? Was she letting her imagination run away with her? Was she jealous? Ugh! Nothing worse than jealousy. She opened the car door.

'Laurel!' Stuart Elderkin puffed towards her. 'You look nice.'

To try and cheer herself up she'd put on her favourite suede jacket, a green polo-necked sweater and new trousers. 'Stuart, thank you. I'm going into Aldeburgh to see Nancy. Want a lift?' She looked at her watch. 'It'll be getting on for lunch time when I get there, we could have a bite at the Cross Keys.' Perhaps she could talk to Stuart about Frank, he was such a comfortable man.

'Thanks, Laurel, but Mabel's just said she'll rustle up some lunch. Don't think I better turn the offer down.'

'No, that wouldn't be politic! So how can I help? Something you want me to buy for you in Aldeburgh?'

Stuart leant towards her, grasping her arm. 'Can I come with you for a hundred yards? I need to ask you a favour and I don't want Mabel to see me speaking to you.'

Laurel's shoulders slumped. She wasn't sure if she wanted to be involved with another set of relationship problems. Not at this moment. Stuart's pleading expression changed her mind. She wanted him and Mabel to be happy, she loved both of them and their engagement after Mabel nearly died, was a highlight at the time, and an expression of life after the deaths of last September. 'Hop in. I'll help if I can.'

She drove to Dunwich's car park at the sea's edge. There were a few cars there and two couples were walking towards the beach café, no doubt ready for large helpings of the famous fish and chips.

She turned to him. 'What do you want me to do, Stuart?'

He was biting his lip. 'Mind if I light up?'

He needed the support of his pipe. This was not going to be a simple request. 'No, but I'll open my window.'

It took several minutes of preparation and fiddling before he was puffing away. He hall-turned so he was facing her. 'This is difficult for me to ask, Laurel. To tell you the truth I'm embarrassed.'

'Will I be embarrassed too?'

'Possibly.'

'Is it something to do with Mabel? She's worried as well.'

'Is she? Worrying how to get out of our engagement?' he said, his voice harsh and bitter.

'No, Stuart. She thinks you're fed up with her.'

He grimaced. 'She's right there. Everything I do is wrong. One minute she's as nice as pie and the next she's like a cat who's had its tail pulled. Laurel, do you know why she's like this?'

There was pain in his voice and on his face. 'No, Stuart I don't, neither does Dorothy. We're all puzzled by her change towards you, but I'm convinced by what she said the other night she still cares about you and doesn't want to lose you.'

Stuart unclenched his teeth from the stem of his pipe. Hope lit his eyes. 'You do? What did she say?'

Laurel told him.

'You think she really thought I'd leave her for Ann Fenner?'

'She was upset to hear not only were you having a meal with her, but you looked as though you were enjoying yourself.'

Stuart leant back and thoughtfully took a few more puffs. 'If she feels jealous then she must still fancy me, even if she doesn't love me.'

She patted his free hand. 'I think she loves you.'

'Laurel, will you try and find out what's wrong? Why she avoids being alone with me? Why she suddenly says nasty things? If there's something I can do, something I can change to make it all right, I'll do it.' He glared at his pipe. 'I'll even give up this, if that's the problem. Will you do that for me?'

She didn't think it would be as easy as that. 'Yes, I will, Stuart. Shall I let Mabel know I'm speaking for you?'

He shook his head, like an old grizzly woken from its

winter slumber. 'No, not at first, only if you have to. I'll leave it to your judgement.'

'Supposing I make it worse? That could happen, Stuart.'

He pushed out his lower lip and let out a stream of smoke. 'I won't blame you. We can't go on like this. Something's got to happen, one way or another. I can't stand it and I don't think it's doing our detective agency any good either.'

Laurel silently agreed.

'I'd better get back. Could you drop me off before we get to the house?'

She smiled at him. She wasn't looking forward to talking to Mabel.

Laurel found a parking spot in Aldeburgh High Street, nearly opposite Nancy's cottage. It was twelve-thirty and the town was busy with Saturday shoppers and people out for lunch, either queuing for fish and chips or entering the several cafés and restaurants. She crossed the wide street and knocked on Nancy's door. No reply. She waited a few minutes and knocked again.

An elderly woman pushing a shopping trolley stopped beside her. 'Mrs Wintle isn't in.'

'I'll knock again, just to make sure, 'Laurel replied.

'I said she isn't in.' The woman's cultivated voice implied Laurel was an idiot. 'Her son's taken her out for luncheon. I doubt she'll be able to eat anything after what happened to her brother.' She took a key from her pocket and opened the door of the house next to Nancy's. 'It's no good you standing there. Have you a card?'

'A card?'

'A calling card!'

Blimey, an Aldeburgh resident of the first water. This was 1971 not 1871. 'No.'

'Shall I inform Mrs Wintle you called?'

Laurel admitted defeat. 'No, thank you. I'll call on her later.'

The woman gave a nod of her head worthy of the old Queen Mary, and entered her cottage pulling her shopping trolley behind her.

Laurel walked away, irritated and feeling at a loose end. What should she do now? It was time to eat and she did feel hungry; the seductive smells from Smith's Bakery of fresh bread, fruited scones and savoury Cornish pasties made her stomach clench, not to mention the smells from the open bags of fish and chips as people walked past. She could go back to Greyfriars. She hated feeling like this: indecisive and in need of some company; she liked to be independent and in charge of her life. She decided to go back to Greyfriars.

As she was about to cross the road to her car she heard her name called.

'Laurel, Miss Bowman.'

It was Mr Tucker, the gallery owner. He was outside his shop, waving a newspaper at her. She walked towards him. 'Hello, Mr Tucker, we meet again.'

'Good to see you. Are you looking for Nancy? She's out with her son.'

Laurel smiled. 'Yes, I know. Everyone seems to be keeping an eye on her. The woman who lives next door to her told me.'

Tucker giggled. 'Miss Evans, or as she is known, The Lady Evans. I expect she gave you short shrift?'

'I was berated for not having a calling card.'

'Why don't you come in?' He pointed to the gallery. 'I just nipped out for a paper.' He paused. 'Or have you plans for lunch?'

'No, I was wondering what to do, I think I'll go back to Greyfriars.'

'Ah, your base. May I offer you lunch? I need to let Kelvin know I'll be out for an hour, then we can go and enjoy ourselves. What do you say?'

Such a round, jolly man, smiling at her, obviously pleased to see her again. 'That's a lovely idea, Mr Tucker. I accept.'

'Ben, please. Let's go in and I'll introduce you to my assistant, Kelvin. He's a friend as well as an employee, been with me for ages. I've a gallery in London, and we box and cox the two places between us.' He opened the glass-panelled door and ushered her in. A bell tinkled and a tall man came out of the back showroom. He was younger than Ben, in his late forties, Laurel guessed, well built, with broad shoulders. He held himself well, and moved gracefully. They were a contrast: roly-poly Ben and tall, muscular Kelvin.

'Laurel, this is Kelvin Hagar, my right-hand man. Kelvin, Miss Laurel Bowman; I told you how quickly she acted when there was an emergency at the meeting last night.'

Kelvin shook her hand. His grip was firm, brief, and strong. He was a couple of inches taller than her, so about six one or two, with a long, narrow face, dark eyes and well-defined eyebrows.

'Very pleased to meet you, Miss Bowman.' His speech was clipped, his accent neutral.

'Laurel, I need to have a few words with Kelvin in the office. Won't be long.'

They went into the back showroom and a door opened and closed. She looked round. The front showroom was filled with light from the wide windows on both sides of the door, the shelves held displays of paintings and sculpture and the walls of the room were hung with larger pictures. By a pale wood desk a gilt easel displayed a beautiful painting of a Venetian scene. Each picture and sculpture had a tastefully written card giving the artist's name, the date it was done, the medium used, and the price. Some of the works were priced at several thousand pounds. She didn't know any of the artists, and the dates were all after 1930. Benjamin Tucker must be a rich man to be able to buy so many paintings and to also have a gallery in London. She must find out where it was.

Tucker came into the room.

'There are some lovely paintings, Ben. I see most of them are modern; I'm afraid I don't know any of the artists.'

He beamed at her. 'I'm glad you like them. I enjoy discovering new artists and setting them on their journey. It's much more exciting than selling the work of dead men. And much more profitable when one of your artists takes off.'

'You said you have a gallery in London. Where is it?'

'Old Bond Street.'

'Gosh, that's a posh address. Why do you need a gallery here? I'd have thought you're much more likely to make sales in London than Aldeburgh.'

Ben tapped his nose. 'There are a lot of rich people in this neck of the woods, and many of them love art and music. It's surprising the number of holidaymakers who buy art as a memento of their time in Aldeburgh, especially those who come for the music festivals.'

She was changing her opinion of Ben Tucker; he wasn't the kindly, slightly bumbling owner of a small art gallery, he was a rich art dealer with many connections in the art world and moneyed, and probably influential, customers. She wondered what he would make of David's work. Pity she couldn't show him the drawings, but as they weren't supposed to have them that wasn't possible. Or was it? Would there be any point in getting his opinion? She'd ask Frank.

'Interrogation over, Laurel?' Ben chuckled.

Laurel put a hand to her face. 'Sorry, I didn't mean to … I was interested. I've never met an art dealer before.'

Hagar came into the room.

'We're off to have lunch, Kelvin,' Ben said. 'I'll be back in about an hour.' He looked at Laurel. 'Possibly two.'

'Very well, Mr Tucker. Then perhaps we can discuss the best way of dealing with our little problem. I have a few ideas.'

Ben smiled. 'Kelvin always solves my problems. Such a good organiser. It's your army training, Kelvin, isn't it?'

Laurel looked from one to the other. It was as though the conversation had a secret code, as though they were talking in some sort of shorthand. 'Were you in the army long, Mr Hagar?' she asked.

'The army was my home. Then Mr Tucker employed me. Now my first loyalty is to Mr Tucker.'

What a strange answer. A bit of a fanatic. His face hadn't changed during his answer, there was no smile lighting up his narrow face with its long, bony nose and pointed chin. He hadn't answered the question.

'Which regiment were you in? Let me guess ... Special Forces? A commando?' Why had she said that? It was something about the way he moved, his height and strength.

Hagar's face darkened. He didn't reply but shot a look at Ben.

'You'll have to remember Miss Bowman is a detective, Kelvin. It's in her nature to ask questions.'

'I'm sorry, Mr Hagar, I didn't mean to embarrass you. Please forgive me.'

He shot her a baleful look. 'I'm afraid I'm not very good at small talk, Miss Bowman.'

The answer was innocuous but she sensed his dislike of her.

Ben took her arm. 'Lunch calls. Goodbye, Kelvin.'

'Goodbye, Mr Tucker, Miss Bowman,' Hagar said as he opened the door of the gallery.

It was a relief to step into the busy High Street; she'd taken a dislike to Mr Hagar and she was sure the feeling was mutual.

Laurel had an excellent lunch with Ben at a fish restaurant, where she'd had to refuse more than one glass of Muscadet. After lunch she'd walked to Thorpeness and stood by the Mere watching couples and families row over the shallow waters. Now she was able to think of Angela without guilt or anger.

She watched the boats skim over the water, the swans and ducks gathering at the edge of the mere in search of food. She smiled as she thought of her and Angela as children, holidaying with Mum and Dad in a rented house at Thorpeness. How happy they'd been, how innocent.

When she arrived back at Greyfriars the day was nearly over, the sun was low in the sky, painting the clouds with mackerel colours. There were no other cars in the drive. She was glad, as she didn't want to talk to anyone at the moment; she wanted to preserve her inner peace. She decided she'd have a cup of tea and then read in her bedroom.

There was a light in the kitchen. Mabel must be by herself. She remembered her promise to Stuart. She wasn't in the mood for a heart to heart but she might not get an opportunity like this for some time. Better get on with it before someone came back.

She pushed open the kitchen door. Mabel was sitting at the table nursing a mug of tea; there was a row of scones cooling on a wire rack. She looked up.

'Thought I heard a car. Did you see Nancy?'

Laurel sat down, poured herself a cup and told Mabel what had happened in Aldeburgh.

'I know that Miss Evans. She doesn't half give herself airs, I don't know why, 'cause she comes from a working-class family from Leiston. She got a scholarship to that private school near Southwold, went to Oxford or somewhere, and taught at a posh school. I can remember when her family hadn't two halfpennies to rub together, and her dad was out of work. Doesn't do to forget your roots, does it?'

'No, it doesn't.' Laurel smiled and touched one of the scones. 'Still too warm to eat, pity. Although I had a good lunch.' She told Mabel about Ben Tucker and meeting Kelvin Hager.

'He's been with Mr Tucker ever since he started the gallery. Keeps himself to himself. Doesn't mix like Ben Tucker does.'

'He said he was in the army. Do you any more about him, Mabel?'

She frowned. 'Why the interest? Or is it your natural nosiness?'

''Fraid so. He's such a contrast to Ben, I can't imagine them working together. Does Ben always stop at a hotel when he's in Aldeburgh? It must get expensive.'

Mabel got up and opened a cupboard door and took out a cake tin. 'No, he's got a house somewhere not too far away, not sure where. Sometimes he has house parties at the weekend or during the Festival. He brings people down from London, so I'm told. Likes a bit of life, does Ben Tucker.' She felt the scones. 'You're right, not quite cool enough to store.' She looked at Laurel. 'Do you ever wish you weren't so tall? I know I've difficulty in getting clothes and shoes to fit, and you're a good few inches taller.'

'What's brought this on, Mabel? Are you thinking about a new wardrobe?'

Mabel plucked at the sleeve of her green jumper. 'Perhaps I should smarten up a bit. That Ann Fenner always looks well dressed and groomed.'

'I bet she's not such a good cook.'

Mabel frowned. 'I think she could hold her own.'

Laurel decided to try and cheer her up. 'Talking about my height, did I ever tell you about the time my mum took me to the doctors when I was a child because she was worried how tall I'd grown; I was seven?'

Mabel sat up. 'No.'

'Yes. I couldn't understand why she was taking me, "I'm not ill," I said. "I beat all the girls at skipping at playtime."

'My mum said to the doctor, "Look at her, Doctor, there must be something wrong."

'The doctor looked at me. "How old is she? Twelve?"

'"There!" said Mum, "She's seven!"

'The doctor measured my height, then went to his desk and did some calculations. I thought if I was twelve I could stay up and watch *Match of the Day*.'

Mabel roared.

'The doctor said, "If she keeps growing at this rate she'll be six feet, give or take an inch by the time she's sixteen, unless puberty comes early."

'"Who's puberty?" I asked.

The doctor laughed and my Mum nearly fainted.'

Mabel was laughing so much she was holding her sides. 'He wasn't far off, was he?'

'Very accurate. I've never minded being taller than average. If any boy made rude remarks I just gave him a quick punch or a kick. Later I realised not many men would fall for a six-footer; actually, I'm only five feet eleven. Yes, there are disadvantages, and it can be difficult to find clothes and shoes that fit me.'

'Have you told Frank that story?' Mabel was wiping her eyes with a tea towel.

Laurel shook her head. 'Perhaps I will, one day.' She wasn't sure how to start asking about what was wrong between her and Stuart, but if she left it any longer someone was bound to come back in the middle of their conversation – if they got that far. Mabel looked relaxed; she decided to risk it and hoped Mabel wouldn't take

174

offence. She'd tell the truth and not go round in circles.

'Mabel, can I talk to you about Stuart? If you don't want to, I'll understand, but he asked me to help him this morning.' There, she'd said it.

Mabel's face flushed. 'What do you mean, asked you to help him?'

She swallowed and rubbed her hand nervously under her nose. 'He's really worried you want to finish with him, to call off the engagement. He doesn't know what he's done to upset you and he's afraid if he brings it up you'll just take off that engagement ring and throw it in the sea. He asked me to act as a go-between. He says he'll do anything to keep you – even give up his pipe.'

Mabel rested a hand on her heaving bosom. 'He said that? He still loves me even though I've been so awful to him?' Her eyes were full of tears, but she looked happier than Laurel had seen her in a long time. 'It's nothing Stuart's done. It's me, it's my fault.'

Laurel took her free hand. 'Can you tell me, Mabel? I'll help if I can.'

Mabel quivered. 'I can't find the words. I'm so much older than you. I've been married, I've had children and you …'

Laurel thought she knew where this was going. 'Mabel, I'm not a virgin and I studied human anatomy at college. Is this something to do with sex?'

Mabel clasped her hand to her mouth, tipped her head back and looked at the ceiling. 'Laurel Bowman, it's a good job your mother can't hear you!'

Laurel laughed. 'My mother's no fool. She knows what goes on between young people – and older people. Come on, Mabel, grit your teeth and tell me what the problem is.' Mabel must have passed through the menopause by now, or was she still menopausal? Was it something to do with that?

Mabel took a deep breath, sat up straight and placed her hands on the table, palms down. 'Promise you won't say anything to anyone else?'

'Stuart may have to know if he's going to understand what's wrong. If you do marry him, I presume you'll both want to have a physical relationship?'

Mabel shuddered. 'That's the problem, I'm not sure if I can do it. When we've been alone ... and, well, you know, I was afraid, and I put him off.'

'Why are you afraid, Mabel? Didn't you like making love with your husband?'

Mabel's face turned puce. 'Laurel Bowman, you don't care what you say, do you?'

Laurel laughed. 'All I can say is lucky you, I wish I had a man in my life. Come on, we've got this far, tell me what's frightening you.'

'It's ... I went through the change a few years ago, it wasn't too bad, but it's left me a bit ...' Her face was gradually getting redder.

'Dry?' Laurel guessed.

Mabel hung her head and nodded.

'Is that it? Do you want Stuart to make love to you?'

Mabel kept her head down and nodded again. 'I do love him.'

'I think we can sort this out without too many problems, Mabel.'

She raised her head. 'Really?'

'All you need is a lubricant. You could use baby oil, but there are better things you can get at a chemist. Would you like me to buy some for you?'

'Would you do that for me? But what will the chemist think? They'll think you're having sex with someone. They might think it's Frank!'

Chance would be a fine thing, she thought. 'Chemists are discreet and it's none of their business what I want a lubricant for, I might need it for mending a puncture.'

Mabel laughed. 'Oh, Laurel, I feel so much better. Thank you.'

'Shall I tell Stuart?'

Mabel cringed. 'Does he have to know?'

'Yes, I think so. I'll try and put it delicately, unless you want to tell him?'

Mabel's eyes widened in horror. 'I couldn't, I'd be too embarrassed. It'll be bad enough when he knows. Perhaps he'll want to call it all off, think I'm over the hill, needing help with ... you know what.'

'He's been married, his wife might have had the same problems; it's very common, Mabel. You just need a bit of help, that's all.'

'You won't tell him while I'm around, will you?'

'No, but I think the sooner the better. Is he coming here tomorrow?'

'No, and there's another thing, I don't want us to start our married life here at Greyfriars, I think we need a bit of privacy. Can you tell him that? I know we said we'd let out his bungalow to make a bit more money, but I don't think I could brace myself if I knew someone was in the next bedroom.'

Laurel spluttered. 'There's only Dorothy and me, we won't have glasses against the bedroom walls, Mabel; but I can see your point of view. I think I'd feel the same.'

'Frank had the right idea, keeping his cottage. He can get up to what he likes and we won't be any the wiser.'

Laurel's good mood started to disappear. 'That's true. I'll drive over to Leiston tomorrow and see if I can talk to Stuart. Believe me he'll be over the moon.'

Mabel simpered. 'I feel a bit that way myself.'

Chapter 17

Sunday, March 14th, 1971

Frank closed the door of his cottage, squinting as the cold, horizontal rain, straight off the North Sea, slashed into his face. Perhaps the weather would put her off. The thought was a relief, balanced by a sense of loss. What was he doing meeting Carol like this? The pretence she was bringing him the names and addresses of the last two of David's tutors was laughable. What was driving him to act in such a stupid way? Lust? He didn't want to admit he couldn't control his desires; he'd always been able to in the past. Perhaps he was getting what he deserved. There'd been several women he'd had affairs with; some had ended amicably, but with at least two, as soon as the woman became serious, even when he'd still liked and wanted her, he'd ended the affair. Was he frightened of being …? What was he frightened of? Responsibility? The thought of children? His brain was a mess. He didn't like it. What would happen if she was there, in her car? Was he reading her wrong? Perhaps all this was quite innocent. Perhaps she was lonely, glad to escape from the house with its memories of her missing son. Perhaps he was imagining she was attracted to him.

He pulled the hood of his waterproof over his head

and, with the wind on his back, walked to the car park. He knew she drove a black Rover. There were only two parked cars. One was hers. He went to the passenger door and opened it.

'Frank! I was afraid you wouldn't come.'

She was pale, her hair loose, its blackness making her white skin gleam like alabaster, the red lipstick on her full mouth a sharp contrast. Her blue mohair coat was open, showing a short skirt, bare legs and feet clad in ballet pumps.

Frank pulled his door shut. She was close, beautiful and vulnerable.

'Where's your car?' she said.

'I parked off the road, just before the cottages.'

'Shall we stay here and talk, or do you want to drive somewhere else? Perhaps we could go to your house.'

'I told you, I live on the agency premises, other people live there as well.'

'You mean your partners?'

'Yes.'

'I think it would be better if we went somewhere less public.'

'I don't think many people are taking walks today, Carol, but if you want to move …'

'I do. It's lovely to hear you call me Carol. I'll drive towards Westleton, there are some pull-ins on the right leading onto the heath.'

How does she know that?

She turned on the ignition, put the car into first gear and drove smoothly over the rutted surface of the car park and turned right, on the road to Dunwich.

As they passed the deserted site of Blackfriars School,

she nodded her head towards it. 'You solved that case, didn't you? When you were in the police.'

'Yes. Six months ago, but it seems like another life.'

'Why did you leave the police?'

He shrugged. That was something he didn't want to share with her. Something he couldn't share with anyone except Laurel. He would probably have left the force in the near future, but Laurel's predicament catalysed him into action. It was Laurel's and his secret. He'd never betray her.

After turning left onto the Westleton road and driving for a few minutes, Carol turned right into a rough area of gravel behind gorse hedges. It was a spot popular with people bringing their dogs for a run over Westleton Heath. There were no other cars today.

She turned towards him, pushing the edges of her coat wider, her skirt riding up. Her legs were smooth, as pale as her face, long and slender; the same subtle perfume she'd worn yesterday rose from her hair and body.

'Did you bring the names and addresses of the tutors?' he asked, retreating slightly.

She laughed and reached out a hand, touching his face, caressing him from his temple, down his cheek, and circling his lips. Her deft fingers and the look of mischief in her eyes deepened his breathing and aroused him.

'I didn't even bother to look for them. I think we both know why we've met today.' The tone of her voice told all.

Words seemed to stick on his lips. His body wanted to do one thing, his brain another. Everything important to him seemed to be disappearing and the world only existed here, in this car, with her. He didn't know what was going to happen, he couldn't be sure what he would do. Her beauty, her sexuality, overwhelmed him. His mind was losing the battle. His urge to kiss her, not only her lips, but everywhere, her neck, the blue hollows near her clavicle, the desire to see her naked, to sculpt her body with his hands, to possess her, was too much. He was lost.

Her eyes widened, her pupils enlarging, probably mirroring his own. They moved towards each other and she pulled his head down to hers, her mouth opening greedily, her tongue darting. He held her tight, kissing her back.

She unlocked her arms from round his neck. 'Let's go in the back. There's more room there.'

She wants to do it now. Christ, Frank thought, I'm thirty-two, I haven't had sex in the back of a car for a decade. As she moved to open her door her skirt rode up and there was a brief glimpse of black hair. It was as if a fist had punched him in the gut. No tights and no knickers. Like a tart preparing for a night's work she'd come ready for easy access. This was no romance, no sudden passion. He was wanted for one thing only: to satisfy her sexual needs. He was virile and available. A wave of shame and revulsion washed over him. They say no fool like an old fool, but he was a young fool with no control over his body and mind.

She climbed into the back and took off her coat. 'Hurry up, Frank.' Her eyes were glittering, the urgency in her voice spoke of a desperate need. Shame and revulsion were replaced by pity, and the worry of how he was going to get out of this situation. He was an idiot. What would be the effect of this debacle on the case? He'd forgotten his responsibilities: to the missing boy,

David Pemberton, and to his team.

He leant over the front seat towards her. 'Carol, I'm sorry, but I can't do this. It's wrong. You're very beautiful, very desirable, I wanted to make love to you, but I can't.' He was expecting and he deserved a scene. He'd gone down the same path as her. She thought he was more than willing, and he had been.

She looked bewildered, obviously unable to believe what she was hearing; her mouth quivered and her face puckered with hurt and frustration. She pulled her coat back on, as though suddenly cold.

'Why? Why does it always happen? Why won't people love me?' Tears slowly trickled down her marble cheeks.

Frank breathed out. She looked like a child whose favourite doll had been taken away. He wanted to take her in his arms and comfort her. He didn't.

'Carol, you know this isn't right, for several reasons. You're married, if your husband found out he'd be terribly hurt. I'm sure he loves you.'

She sniffed and wiped away the tears with the back of her hand. Frank passed her a handkerchief. 'He doesn't care. He knows I need someone to love me.'

Her husband knows of her affairs? He condones them? Frank didn't believe Adam Pemberton would turn a blind eye to her infidelity.

'You mean you've been unfaithful to him before?'

She pouted. 'Not very often.'

He didn't think he'd better mention the tutors.

'Why haven't you left him?'

Her eyes widened. 'I love him, he's David's father. I don't want to leave him.'

'You say he knows about …? How can he go on as

183

normal if he can't trust you?'

She shook her head in irritation. 'You don't understand. I *think* he knows, but he won't ask me because he's afraid of the truth. He loves me. If he had proof he'd have to do something about it.'

This was beyond Frank's understanding, and all he wanted to do was to finish this scene and get back to normality. He was out of his depth. 'I think we ought to move out of here. Could you drop me off at the car park?'

She flushed, her eyes narrowing. 'What are you going to do about David? I expect you'll want to stop investigating the case.'

'No, on the contrary, Carol. I want to find David, for you, for your husband and for David himself. I'd understand if you didn't want to see me again and if you asked your husband to drop the case, but I hope you won't do that. All this is my fault. I haven't been professional.' How would he explain to Laurel and the others if the case was closed?

She leant back, her face expressionless, all tears gone. 'No, I want you to go on with it, but I don't want to see you again, send one of the other detectives if you want to ask any more questions.'

'How will you explain that to your husband?'

'I won't. If he wants to see you, then I suppose you'll have to come to the house, but I won't see you again.' She got out of the back seat and moved behind the driving wheel. 'If you think I'm driving you back to Minsmere beach, you can think again. The rain's eased. You can walk.'

That put him in his place. He opened the car door, climbed out, then turned. 'Are you OK to drive back to

Aldeburgh? I could drive you.'

'I don't want to be with you anymore. Goodbye.'

Frank zipped up his waterproof and walked away from the car, turning left onto the road leading to Dunwich. He'd walked a few yards when he heard the noise of Carol's car engine and the sound of wheels on gravel. He looked back; the Rover was speeding off. The wind increased and the rain started again, as cold and horizontal as before. He deserved it. He took his punishment with the same humility as the Abbey monks centuries ago took punishments for their transgressions.

Chapter 18

Laurel and Stuart sat opposite each other on comfy armchairs in the lounge of his bungalow in Leiston. She'd told him what Mabel's problem was.

'We can take it slowly. I'm a bit rusty myself,' he said, grinning like a naughty schoolboy. 'Will you have a word with her when you get back? Tell her I'll be over tonight and I'll take her out for a meal, if she'd like that. Mind you, not sure what's open on a Sunday evening in March.'

'Of course, I will, Stuart. But we'd arranged to have a brief meeting tonight before going to the school tomorrow.'

Stuart grimaced. 'Damn, forgot all about that. You going straight back?'

Laurel was unsure; she didn't want to go back to Greyfriars. 'No. I thought I'd have a drive. I need to do some thinking.'

Stuart looked at her quizzically. 'Worried about something? Wouldn't be Frank, would it?'

Laurel avoided his gaze. 'No. I just need a bit of space, that's all. I'm still upset about Nancy's brother; I wish I'd followed my instincts and broken into the house and rescued him. It's shaken my confidence and I feel I've let Nancy down.' She hadn't opened up to any of the others, even Frank, about how she felt, but Stuart was such a comforting person; you could trust him to give a balanced and truthful answer. Perhaps not the one that would give you a false sense of relief, that it wasn't your fault and you couldn't have done anything else, but he'd tell you truthfully what he felt.

'You made an assumption it was Nancy coming back with Clara. I think if I'd been in your shoes I'd have done the same. It was just fate Nancy wasn't at home and couldn't contact you. You'll have to accept what happened. You can't play it over again. I wouldn't say forget it, Laurel, I'd say learn from it. It's a bad experience, but in this line of work, we're going to have those. You're a strong-minded woman. Use that gift and get over it. Get over it, but don't forget it.'

She leant towards him. 'You're a wise man, Stuart. Thank you.' She kissed his cheek.

Stuart coloured. 'I'll have to confess to Mabel I've been getting intimate with a ravishing blonde.'

She laughed. 'This ravishing blonde could do with being ravished.' She laughed again at the expression on his face. 'That was not an invitation, Mr Elderkin; you need to save your sexual energies for Mabel. Time I went!'

He got up and helped her into her waterproof. 'I think it is. You'd better go for a long walk and cool down. What with Mrs Pemberton and her liking for young tutors, and now you fancying a fat ex-cop, my faith in womanhood's taken a beating.'

She gave him a playful punch on the shoulder. 'See you later.'

Laurel waved to Stuart who was standing at the gate of his bungalow despite the rain driving in from the east.

He waved back, a broad smile on his face. She turned on the ignition. Stuart gave a last salute and turned back to his open front door. Their conversation hadn't been as embarrassing as she'd feared; he'd quickly latched on to Mabel's fears and difficulties.

Her car faced towards Aldeburgh and she decided to drive that way rather than turn it round and go back to Dunwich. As she approached the left turning to Thorpeness, just as she'd done in September, last year, when she was meeting Frank to persuade him not to tell the school her sister had been murdered, she hesitated, then signalled left, and steered the car towards the sea and Thorpeness.

When she'd moved to the area last September, she'd avoided the place, after finding it brought back too many memories of Angela, but now she'd started to find visits to the village, and especially taking a boat out onto the mere, were soothing, and the memories pleasant. No chance of boating today. The place was deserted and even the swans and ducks had disappeared, taking shelter in the undergrowth of the islands dotted about the lake.

She parked in the public car park on the sea side of the road going to Aldeburgh. It was empty. She tied the hood of her waterproof under her chin and pulled on gloves. As she opened the door a gust of wind almost pulled it from her hand. The rain was lashing horizontally, cold and stinging. She made her way to the mere; the surface of the normally peaceful water was disturbed, waves rippling away from the grassy shore, willow trees and alder bushes pushed down to meet the water. She turned, facing the rain and wind, and struggled to the beach, making slow progress.

It was deserted, the sea pounding the shingle; she put a hand over her mouth as the gusts were taking her breath away. Steel grey waves rushed in, piling on top of each other in their anxiety to reach land. A few gulls were riding the wind, banking and turning, like planes in a dog fight. Bubbles of exhilaration coursed through her blood; worries about Frank and Nancy were forgotten in her joy of the elements.

She remembered a similar day with Angela: they'd loved the storms, racing each other over the beach, skipping on the edge of surging waves, chased by Dad shouting at them to stop and get back to their cottage. Mum's horror at the state they were in, but not even a dressing down could stop their crazy laughter, whipped up by the rain and wind. Smiling she turned and half-ran to the car park, the wind helping her.

Another car, a Land Rover, pulled in, sending up spray from puddles. A tall man got out, followed by a black Labrador. It rushed up to her, wagging its tail and bouncing with pleasure. Perfect weather for Labradors.

She laughed and patted its head. 'Good boy.'

'Miss Bowman,' the man said, 'what are you doing out in this weather? Although you look as if you're enjoying it as much as Billy.'

Laurel squinted at him; he was dressed in oilskins and walking boots. 'Dr Neave?'

'The same.' He grasped her gloved hand in his.

'It's a long way from Aldeburgh to give your dog a walk.'

He nodded. 'Come into my car for a minute and I'll explain. Perhaps you may have seen him. Have you been in Thorpeness long?'

Laurel frowned. 'I'm not sure, about half-an-hour, maybe more.' What was he going on about?

He opened the passenger door and she got in. Billy whined as he was made to jump back in the car. Dr Neave faced her, his face serious. 'Have you seen Dr Luxton at all?'

'In Thorpeness?'

'Yes. He lives here.'

'No, I haven't seen him since Friday night. What's the matter? Is he all right?'

Dr Neave pulled off his hood, his thick, dark hair was messed up and Laurel had an urge to run her fingers through it and get him into shape.

'I got a phone call this morning from his deputy. You remember Dr Luxton went home with him on Friday night. I examined Luxton yesterday and he seemed much better. His deputy phoned me about an hour ago. It seems Dr Luxton returned home on Saturday night. He insisted he'd recovered. The deputy was relieved as he'd promised to take his family to relatives for Sunday lunch in Bury St Edmunds. He phoned Luxton several times this morning from there, but no one picked up the phone. So he contacted me.'

She saw Neave was worried; she could understand why. 'Where does he live?'

Neave pointed in the direction of Aldeburgh. 'He's got one of the houses that face the beach; that's why I parked here. Billy needed a run, so I thought I'd walk to his house.'

She'd lusted after one of those beach houses. There was a long line of them strung out from the village, perched above the beach and sea, each with a large plot of land. Laurel imagined living with the North Sea and its birds as neighbours, isolated but near enough to a shop and a pub if you needed a loaf of bread or a pint of beer. Lucky Dr Luxton. Or not so lucky, Dr Luxton?

'Would you like me to go with you?'

He smiled at her. 'Would you? You seemed to have a good influence on him on Friday night. I'd appreciate your company.' He smiled. 'So would Billy.' The dog's front paws were on the back of Laurel's seat and he was trying to lick her to death.

She ruffled his ears. 'Nice to have one fan.'

'Make that two,' Neave said, looking her straight in the eyes.

Laurel knew she was a mess, a very wet mess. Perhaps he was keen on mermaids. If he liked her in this state, how would he behave when she was scrubbed up and in her best blue suit? She needed a bit of flattery. Every woman does.

'Shall we go? Are you taking Billy?' She hoped so, he seemed a lot of fun.

'If I don't he'll rip up the seats in frustration.'

They slowly battled their way from the car park, along the main road to Aldeburgh; soon the line of houses came into view.

'Which one is his?' Laurel shouted, the wind gobbling up her words.

Neave moved closer, nearly tripping as Billy pranced round his legs. He was on a lead and obviously wanted to be set free. 'Get down, you stupid mutt. Sorry, not you, Laurel. Is it all right if I call you Laurel? My name's Oliver.'

She smiled and nodded. Oliver, not her favourite

name, but he was attractive: taller than her, which always helped, with dark, rugged good looks. She'd seen first-hand his skill as a doctor. He seemed a sensible and capable man, and he'd come out of his way to check on Dr Luxton, showing a caring and compassionate nature.

'It's next to the last house. I don't think many are occupied at this time of the year. We'll keep to the road, shall we?'

'Billy doesn't think that's a good idea.'

'He'll get a proper walk once we've checked on Luxton.'

They struggled on, strong gusts of wind pushing them sideways.

'Straight from the Urals,' he muttered. 'Glad it's not January, we'd be in a snow blizzard.'

They came to the house and turned their faces to the wind. It was an effort to move forwards.

'There could be flooding at high tide if this wind doesn't drop,' Laurel said.

'Sorry, what did you say?' Oliver shouted.

She shook her head. Billy crouched down and relieved himself, his ears blown horizontal, Snoopy-like; then he bounced up and gave a tuft of marram grass a good going over. She wondered if Dorothy would let her have a dog at Greyfriars.

The single-storey house was well built with wooden steps leading to a veranda which seemed to circle the house. There was a central glass door, with a porcelain door bell set in the right-hand brick wall. Laurel sighed with relief as the house sheltered them from the howling wind. She pushed back her hood and shook her head, Oliver did the same and Billy gave the wooden floor of the veranda a thorough sniffing.

Oliver pushed the door bell and the faint sound of its chimes could be heard from inside. There was no movement. He pressed the bell again, keeping his finger on the button.

'That should get him up, if he's having a nap,' he said.

Laurel went to the window to the right of the door. The curtains were drawn back; there was a dark leather three-piece suite, a coffee table, shelves full of books and at the far end, under a full-length window, a table and six chairs. Beyond the sea was boiling, the sky full of dark rain clouds. Oliver was still pressing the bell. She moved to the window to the left of the door, the curtains were closed. She banged on the glass. Perhaps it was his bedroom and he was in a deep sleep. Possibly induced by drugs.

'Let's brave the wind and go round to the beach side,' Oliver said. He looked increasingly worried.

The boarding continued round the sides of the house and there was another door on the sea side, a flight of steps leading down to the beach. The door was locked.

'Was the other door locked?' Laurel asked.

'Yes, I tried it,' he shouted, the wind once more kidnapping his words.

The room to the right of the door was the kitchen. No sign of anyone, but everything neat and tidy.

Oliver took her arm. 'Let's go round the back again. We'll be able to talk.' Billy seemed to have given up on a proper walk: his tail was down.

'His deputy said he phoned him last night, about nine-thirty. He said he seemed fine. He didn't phone again until after eleven this morning, when they got to Bury St

Edmunds. He'd told Luxton he was going to phone, and Luxton said he didn't mind him making sure he was OK, in fact he thanked the chap for his concern. Luxton said he would stay at home resting. They knew the weather was going to be atrocious. I'm worried.'

Laurel nodded. 'I think we should either contact the police and ambulance services or break in and call them if we need to.'

'And your choice would be?'

'Break in now. If we wait it might be too late.' This time she was going to trust her instinct. If she, or hopefully they, had to pay for the repairs to a door or window, so be it. Oliver could give first aid while she phoned for an ambulance. There was a phone in Luxton's house, the deputy talked to him last night.

'Agreed. Door or window?'

Laurel looked through the keyhole. 'I can't see a key in the lock. The glass looks thicker than the windows. Window has it.'

'Hold Billy, I'll find a stone from the beach. I've a few tools in my car if that doesn't work.'

He loped off, and Billy pulled at the lead in an attempt to follow. She crouched down and hugged him, burying her face in his fur. Eau de wet dog. It should be bottled.

Neave returned clutching a large stone in his gloved hand; he wrapped his scarf round his wrist.

'Stand well back, Laurel, and hold Billy tight. He might get agitated by the noise.'

She didn't think Billy would get agitated by anything, unless it was food. You couldn't have hoped for a steadier companion.

Neave half-turned his head and grimacing, smashed

the stone into the window near the handle. The glass cracked. He raised the stone again and hit with greater force. The window exploded, slivers of glass shooting to the ground, but mostly erupting into the room.

'That should wake him up,' Neave said.

Billy gave her a slobbery lick on the face, as if saying, 'There it's all over.' If only it was. The memory of going into Sam Harrop's house and finding those dead bodies was still crystal clear.

Neave knocked out the remaining glass from the frame of the window and opened it. 'I'll climb in; you stay with Billy.'

No. She didn't want him to be alone with whatever was in the house. She needed to see herself. 'No. I think we should go in together. You tie up Billy.' She pointed to one of the wooden rails.

He looked at her, puzzled and unsure. 'Most women would be glad to be left outside.'

'I'm not most women.'

'So I'm beginning to see.'

He sounded cross. Another knight looking for a fair maiden? Another admirer biting the dust? She'd worry about that later.

'Perhaps you'd like to go in first?'

Definitely a touch of sarcasm. 'Thank you.' She took the scarf from him for extra protection from any glass remaining in the frames and, placing her gloved hands on the bottom of the window, she pulled herself up and executed a neat entrance to the room. She turned round and passed the scarf back to him.

His mouth was open. 'God, you're fit.'

'I'll help you shall I?'

They struggled as she pulled on his shoulders as he squeezed through the window. He brushed himself down.

'We could get arrested for breaking and entering.'

'I'll claim you did it. I think they might believe me, after all *most* women wouldn't do this kind of thing, would they?'

He shook his head, smiling ruefully. 'Touché. That'll teach me.'

'I hope so.'

'Ready to explore?'

She nodded.

They moved from the lounge to a wide, green-carpeted passageway, running from the front to back doors. There were four interior doors. One to the room they'd left, and three on the opposite wall. One into the kitchen, the next a bathroom; the open door showed a white bath and lavatory, and the last door was to the room with the closed curtains.

Neave checked the bathroom. 'He's not in there.'

As she started to move towards the bedroom he held up a hand. 'I'll check the electricity's on.' He pushed down a switch. Bulbs in a three-light wooden fixture lit up the cream walls and a phone on a small table. He pointed. 'Good.'

They looked at each other and nodded. He opened the door of the bedroom.

She flinched and put a hand over her nose and mouth. The metallic stench of blood filled her nostrils, catching at her throat, making her stomach contract.

'Damn,' Neave hissed. He felt for the bedroom light switch.

Lying on the floor in front of a double bed, wearing

striped pyjamas, was Luxton. His throat was a gaping wound, the skin of his neck furled back showing red muscles and the severed edges of his wind pipe, protruding like the obscene tube of a vacuum cleaner. There was a great pool of congealed blood round his head and upper body, dark as the deepest ruby. His face was drained of all colour, all life; his wide-open eyes stared at nothing. His arms were spread out, as though in supplication. On the palm of his right hand was a cut-throat razor, its blade and handle thick with partly dried blood.

Neave pushed Laurel back. He moved to Luxton and crouched down, avoiding the pool of blood. 'Nothing we can do for him now,' he said, his voice low and bitter. He straightened up and turned back to Laurel. 'I'll phone the police.'

Sounds of him picking up the phone in the hall, then mutterings.

'It's not working. I'll stay here with him. Can you find a phone? Get the police and the ambulance service. Take Billy with you.'

His words penetrated her brain. If you wanted to take your life, why choose this violent and awful end? What courage was needed to make such a devastating cut? She edged nearer the body. She couldn't be sure, there was so much blood, but it looked as though there was one deep cut. Why not choose an easier death? Why not a mixture of alcohol and sleeping tablets? Dr Luxton seemed a nervous man. A scared man. A man who was more scared when he'd seen the headmaster of Chillingworth School, Mr Baron, at the back of the hall.

'Laurel, did you hear me? Are you OK? Do you feel

197

faint?'

Yes. That would be a good excuse. What did she know about Neave? Nothing. Did she want to leave him with the corpse of Luxton? Did she trust him not to alter something? If there was a connection between Luxton and Baron, could there be another connection between Neave and Luxton, or between Neave and Baron? Frank had told them of his suspicions that the Harrops had been murdered.

She pretended to wobble and Neave took hold of her arm.

'I think I'd better sit down.'

He helped her to the kitchen and she leant on him as he seated her on a chair. When he tried to push her head between her knees she resisted.

'A glass of water would help.'

He found a glass in a cupboard and filled it from the kitchen tap.

'Thank you.' She sipped. 'I'll stay here. You find a phone. The shop or pub would be the best bets. Ask for Inspector Revie and tell him to contact Dr Ansell.'

'Dr Ansell?'

'He's a pathologist, he's excellent.' It was Frank's word, excellent. She needed Frank here. He'd know what to look for, just as he'd known when they found the Harrops. She'd have to do the best she could once Neave was out of the way.

He frowned. 'You may be faint but your brain's still working.'

Oh, dear. She gave a pathetic smile. 'I'm trying to help.'

He sighed. 'Right. Don't move from here. I'll see if I

can find a key, save the police breaking one of the doors down. They won't want to climb in a window.'

And you don't want to climb out of one, she thought. She hoped her suspicions about him were unfounded. He was attractive, but so had Nicholson, the headmaster of Blackfriars School been; he'd impressed her when they first met. It was a lesson she wasn't going to forget in a hurry. Don't let your hormones affect your judgement.

She took another sip of water. Wonder if there's any alcohol in a cupboard? she thought. She could do with a slug of something stronger than this.

'Will you be all right, Laurel? You could come with me. We can't do anything for poor Luxton now.'

She shook her head. 'I feel shattered. I'm not sure I'd make it to the village. I'd slow you down.'

'Right. I'll look for a key.' There were the sounds of drawers opening and closing. He came back into the kitchen. 'No good, I'll have to climb through the window.'

'Sorry I can't help you this time.'

Neave took hold of a kitchen chair. 'This should help me get out. I'll get back as soon as I can. I'll take Billy with me. As soon as I've phoned I'll put him in the Land Rover and drive back to you as quickly as possible.'

Poor Billy, no walk for him today.

'Thank you, Oliver.'

Sounds of Neave's exit were accompanied by muttered swear words. She waited a few minutes and got up. What should she be looking for? First, she'd have to look at Luxton's body again. She needed to fix in her memory all the details. Think what Frank would say to her. 'I want to know everything you could see. Do you think this death

199

looks suspicious? From your knowledge of Luxton do you think this is the death he'd have chosen?' She could answer that one already. No. 'Look for evidence of suicide or murder, but if possible don't touch anything. Examine the other rooms and go through any papers. Look in cupboards, waste bins and bathroom cabinets.' That's enough, Frank, she thought. Before she knew it Neave would be back. At least the noise he'd make climbing in would give her warning. She'd be able to make it back to the kitchen and her glass of water.

She braced herself and took a handkerchief from her waterproof pocket to hold over her nose; her gloves would protect any evidence, such as fingerprints, and as she couldn't think of anything else to put off the moment, she went into the bedroom. It was hard to believe this lifeless shell had been a living man. He seemed like a dummy prepared for a horror film or a frightening sight as a ghost train trundled through dark tunnels on its rackety tracks. Poor man. How he would hate his body being examined and dissected, his life looked at in minute detail, his secrets exposed; that's if he had secrets. But everyone has secrets.

She avoided the pool of blood which was coagulating to a jelly. She searched the chest of drawers and the wardrobes. There was nothing but clothes and a few mothballs. She was relieved to move to the main room. She switched on the light and decided to draw the curtains. She'd explain to the police she'd been frightened of someone seeing her. She looked in a desk. Its drawers were empty except for some pencils, a rubber and a few mathematical instruments. There were no papers. She frowned. She remembered Frank hypothesising the amount of ash in the Harrop's fireplace didn't match up with the amount of paper that may have been in the filing cabinet in Sam's study. She'd have expected Luxton to have papers, possibly relating to his work, here. There were many books in a bookcase, the majority scientific, but also some classical novels and poetry books. There was something about the arrangement of the books: they were uneven, as though they'd been put back in a hurry. It didn't match the obsessive neatness of the kitchen. She took out several books and shook them. Nothing fluttered to the floor. She was wasting her time. Someone had done the same actions recently. Luxton? She didn't think so.

She moved to the bathroom. There was nothing in the medicine chest of interest: the usual cold remedies, a tube of ointment for treating haemorrhoids, plasters, and an eyebath. All in neat order. She moved swiftly to the kitchen. She couldn't imagine she'd find anything here. She flung open cupboard doors and quickly moved tins, packets of biscuits and tea, but nothing was hidden. The cupboard under the sink held a bucket, several cloths and bottles of bleach, washing-up liquid and Dettol. She pulled out the cutlery drawer. The knives, forks and spoons were neatly grouped in their respective places. Each piece of cutlery nestling against its neighbour. Nothing had been touched here. She lifted out the wooden box, its divisions lined with green felt. It was heavy and she gripped it tightly to stop it tipping and scattering the contents on the floor. She placed it on the kitchen table, next to her glass of water.

Lying on the waxed paper lining the drawer was something wrapped in transparent plastic. She carefully removed the plastic. It was a black-and-white photograph,

201

about four by three inches. A young boy smiled at her. An attractive boy. She'd seen his face before. Then he'd not been smiling. He'd looked terrified. She was sure it was the same boy David had drawn. The boy who looked as though something terrible was going to happen to him.

Chapter 19

It was after seven before Laurel drove away from the Thorpeness car park. She and Neave had been questioned by Detective Inspector Revie and they'd been ordered to attend Leiston police station the following day to give detailed statements. She was bone-tired and wanted a shower to wash away the particles of death sticking to her skin. She couldn't go back to Greyfriars yet, she had to see Frank and tell him about the photograph. She decided she'd call at his cottage and hope he hadn't left for the meeting.

From Westleton she took the road to Minsmere beach, were Frank lived in the end cottage of a row of former coastguard houses, his being the one nearest the sea, looking over sandy cliffs to the North Sea. The lambent moon was a smudge of light behind clouds; the car's headlights revealed trees guarding the deserted site of Blackfriars School. She shuddered. The line of trees ended and was replaced by the heath with its stunted oaks and black mounds of gorse. She heaved a sigh of relief: there was a light on in Frank's cottage.

The night was calmer than the day, it was dry and the easterly wind had died. Sounds of rock music, loud enough to penetrate the solid door, meant Frank was either in a good mood or he was getting in one. The

Faces? She raised the anchor-shaped knocker and gave several raps. The music stopped.

'Laurel! God, you look awful. Come in. Where've you been? Dorothy phoned to ask if I'd seen you. The meeting's been cancelled. We'll have a brief session before we go to the school tomorrow morning.'

She didn't reply. He wouldn't look so good if he'd spent an afternoon with a corpse with its throat cut. She followed him down a narrow corridor into the kitchen.

'I was just about to cook my supper, but that'll wait. Sit down, you look shattered.'

That was better than awful. 'I need to talk to you, Frank. Dr Luxton's dead.' She sat down on a chair next to a pine table.

Frank's face stiffened. 'Accident?'

'No. Could be suicide. His throat was cut.'

Frank took a bottle of white wine from the fridge and two glasses from a cupboard. He poured a good measure into each. 'Tell me about it, Laurel.'

'I need to wash my hands, and have you some bread? I need something to eat, or I'll be drunk before you know it.'

He pointed to the sink and cut her a thick slice from a loaf, spreading it thickly with butter. 'Eat this. I'll cook for both of us when you've told me what happened.'

At last she was going to get dinner à deux. What a way to get him to cook for her!

The bread was sourdough and the butter cold and soothing. She was ravenous. Stuart Elderkin said murder always made him hungry, although she hadn't seen any difference between his normal hunger and that brought on by violence. She swallowed the bread and took a mouthful of wine.

'Ready?' Frank asked.

'I'd better phone Dorothy first and tell her what's happened.'

'Phone's in the front room.'

She came back, picked up her glass and sat down. She told him everything, from meeting Dr Neave in the car park to the discovery of the photograph of the terrified boy.

'The same boy? You're sure?'

'Yes. He was smiling, but it wasn't a casual snap. I'm sure it was posed. You know the look: the cheeks are tight, the smile forced. The other interesting thing was the background. It was an interior shot; behind him was a tapestry, the kind you find in old houses. There was a border of acorns surrounding a hunting scene, with a stag and dogs. I couldn't see all of it because of the boy's body.'

Frank placed his empty glass on the draining board. 'Was it a full-length photo?'

'No, head and upper body. He was naked, Frank. He looked young and vulnerable, his bones sticking out – an immature boy. What was his photo doing in Luxton's house? Why was it hidden?'

'You put it back?'

'Yes. I was still looking at it when I heard Neave climbing in through the window. I put it back where I found it, under the cutlery box. When he came into the kitchen he found me as he'd left me: sitting in a chair looking faint.'

'Did you do drama at school?'

'No, but I was in a few school plays; my big role was

205

in *Major Barbara*; they thought they needed someone tall for the main female character.'

Frank pulled a face. 'Can't stand Shaw.'

'Frank, what are we going to do? You know what this means?'

He pulled another face. 'I need to tell Revie about David's drawings of people, or put them back and somehow tip him off where they are. That *would* be difficult.'

She wondered why? Had something happened she didn't know about? 'There must be a connection between the school and Luxton. He looked scared when he saw Baron at the back of the hall on Friday night. Also, we'll have to tell Revie about the boy's photograph if the police don't find it.'

He sighed. 'I'd thought I'd built up a reasonable relationship with Revie, but this could put the kibosh on it. How was he with you this afternoon?'

Laurel drained the last of the wine. She felt better with something in her stomach. 'He remarked on my being involved in the discovery of three bodies in five days and hoped I wouldn't make a habit of it. He also thought my choice of companion was improving.' She watched his face closely.

He raised his eyebrows. 'Is that your opinion as well?'

She pursed her lips. 'I haven't decided. I'll wait until after dinner before I give you my answer.'

Frank got up. 'In that case I'd better get on with it.' He busied himself getting food out of the fridge and a cast-iron frying pan from its hook on the white-washed wall. 'Laurel, I've got something to tell you. In fact, two things. I'm not proud of either. I need to confess. I'm going to cook dinner while I tell you. That way I don't have to look at your face. Is fillet steak OK? There's plenty for two.'

He showed her a large steak on a white plate. It was bloody. Recent memories flooded back. She gulped.

'Sorry. Was there lots of blood?'

She nodded. 'As long as it's not rare, I can manage. Another glass of wine wouldn't harm. What's bothering you, Frank? Whatever it is, I'll try and help.'

'You've got a strong stomach.' He refilled her glass. 'I'll start with my first mistake.' As he washed lettuce leaves, chopped up celery and radishes he told her about keeping back the drawing of the woman having sex with a man.

'Could you see it was Mrs Pemberton?'

'No, but I thought it might be.'

'She's really got to you, hasn't she?' That pain under her ribs was back.

'Make that *had* got to me.'

She didn't answer and took a sip of wine.

'I'll have to tell the others, won't I?' He put the salad into a glass bowl, added a dressing and tossed it using salad servers.

'Yes. But they'll understand.'

'Do *you* understand, Laurel?'

'I think so. She's a very beautiful woman, or so her drawing showed. Everyone has one moment of madness, at least one, when all you can think about is the person you've fallen in love with. Do you love her, Frank? After knowing her such a short time? Is that possible? Or is it just lust? Or a mixture of both?'

He didn't answer.

207

'I'm trying to understand. Although we haven't known each other for that long, this isn't like you. You're normally in control, and I've got the impression you'd hate to hand control to another person.' Had she said too much? She couldn't see his face as he was cutting chunks of bread and putting it on a plate.

He lit the gas under the frying pan. 'Would you lay the table? Cutlery in the table drawer.'

She got up and followed his instructions.

He held his hand over the pan, flinched at the heat, then put the steak into it. It sizzled, giving out an appetizing smell. He was right, she had a strong stomach, saliva was already collecting in her mouth. 'Shouldn't you have some fat or oil in the pan?'

'That comes later. Five minutes and it'll be done. Just time for my second confession. I don't want to share this with the rest of the team, perhaps Stuart, but not Dorothy or Mabel, unless everything goes bottom-up and I'm thrown off the case.'

What had he done?

He told her about Carol Pemberton, their meeting and the result. 'Don't say anything yet. I'll finish cooking, we'll eat and then you can tell me what you think I should do.' He put a good lump of butter in the pan; it frothed up, the sizzling and the mouth-watering smell increased. He turned the steak over, revealing a charred underside. A few minutes later he put the steak on a board, cut it in two, and placed the pieces onto warm plates. He poured something from a bottle into the pan, it hissed as it hit the hot pan and fizzed as he stirred it into the blackened butter.

'What's that?'

'Madeira.' He poured the sauce over the steaks. 'Tuck in. I hope this won't be our last supper.' He looked at her and raised a quizzical eyebrow.

Laurel placed the paper napkin he handed her over her lap. 'Not if they're going to be as delicious as this.' She raised her glass which he'd filled with red wine. 'Cheers!'

The green of his eyes seemed to darken. 'Chin-chin. Thank you, Laurel. I'm glad you came round.'

After they'd eaten they moved to the small front room. Frank removed a fireguard and poked the smouldering log into life. She sank into an old but comfortable armchair; the meal, wine and the return of their former relationship made her aware how much she valued Frank's friendship. His confession of his desire for Carol, although it produced those under-the-ribs pains, made her see him in a different light. He wasn't perfect, he could lose control, he was as vulnerable as anyone else to human frailty. At times she'd wanted to have a different, physically closer relationship with him, but now she wondered whether it would be worth risking losing his friendship. Friendships sometimes lasted longer than love.

'Well, Laurel. I've told you, I'll tell Stuart, and I'll tell Dorothy and Mabel about keeping back the drawing. Do you think I should do anything else?'

She shook her head. 'No. We'll have to hope Carol Pemberton doesn't decide to call us off the case. Frank, what I did to try and uncover my sister's murderer was far worse than your indiscretion. I'll never be able to repay you for your support. You risked a great deal for me.' When she told him how she'd made the killer of her sister, Angela, confess to her murder, and how he'd died, she'd expected Frank to arrest her; she thought he couldn't do anything else: he was a policeman. When he told her he was resigning from the force and she must never tell anyone else about what she'd done, her relief was unforgettable. He'd taken a great burden from her. No, she could never repay him.

'I think we ought to forget that, Laurel. Thanks for being so understanding. Shall I make you a coffee? I'd offer you a whisky, but I think you've had a bit too much to drink; you've got to drive home.'

Laurel looked at her watch. 'Crimes! It's nearly eleven.' She stood up, swaying as she moved towards the door. 'I don't usually feel so squiffy after a few glasses of wine. I'd better get on my way.'

Frank got up and took hold of her arm. 'Sit down. I don't think you can drive. It's not far but the roads are narrow and there are no lights. I don't want to find you in a hedge as I drive to work tomorrow morning.'

She flopped back into the armchair. 'Well, I can't stay here.'

'Why not? I've a spare room and a pair of my pyjamas might be big enough for you.'

Gosh, dinner à deux, and now an invitation to stay the night. She giggled.

'You're definitely the worse for wear. I'll ring Dorothy and tell her you're staying with me.'

She giggled again. 'She'll make you marry me!' The giggles turned into guffaws.

Frank shook his head and went out of the room. He returned with a bottle and two glasses. 'All sorted. Dorothy trusts me not to ravish *you*, but she was worried about *me*. I said I'd lock my bedroom door.'

She tried to throw a cushion at him, but failed

miserably. 'Is that Jameson's?'

'It is. You're allowed a small one, then I'll tuck you up in bed.'

Laurel smiled. 'Will you read me a bedtime story?'

Frank shook his head and poured whiskey into the glasses.

'Frank, could I have a bath? I feel … contaminated. I wouldn't want to get into a clean bed without washing today away.'

He passed her the glass. 'Of course, or a shower, I had one fitted.'

A hot cleansing shower – bliss. 'Thanks.'

Later, when she was in bed, clean, in a pair of blue cotton pyjamas, there was a knock on the door.

Frank came in. 'Everything OK? Bed long enough?'

She felt vulnerable lying beneath the sheet and blankets. 'Thanks, Frank. The bed's very comfortable.'

He came over to her and ruffled her damp hair. 'Thanks for being so understanding, Laurel. Sometimes I forget you're a woman, you're such good company and so non-judgemental.' He bent down and kissed her cheek. 'Sleep well.'

So he forgets I'm a woman. Perhaps she'd better remind him. She turned off the bedside lamp. What would she have done if the goodnight kiss had been the first of many?

Chapter 20

Monday, 15th March, 1971

On Monday morning, after a short meeting at Greyfriars, Frank and Stuart arrived at Chillingworth School at eleven. They'd agreed their questioning would concentrate on getting as much information as they could on David and his friend, Peter. Laurel wasn't with them; she was at Leiston police station making a statement about finding Luxton's body. Frank asked her, if possible, to talk to Inspector Revie and tell him he needed to speak to him urgently.

Frank had asked for two rooms and he was given a small room off the Headmaster's office on the ground floor, not a place he would have chosen, as Baron might be able to listen in. The room was sparsely furnished with two wooden chairs and a battered desk. He'd asked to see Gary Salmon, the PE master first, and as he arranged the chairs on each side of the desk, he heard Baron say, 'Go through, Salmon, he's waiting for you.'

The man was tall, about six feet, with dark hair and eyes, heavy eyebrows and regular features. He was dressed in tracksuit bottoms and a yellow athletic vest, showing off his broad shoulders and lean torso.

Frank held out his hand. 'Please sit down, Mr Salmon.

I'm Frank Diamond. As you know I'm investigating the disappearance of David Pemberton.'

Salmon gripped his hand and squeezed.

Frank squeezed back. 'That's quite a grip, Mr Salmon. I hope you're gentler with the pupils.'

Salmon frowned, his eyebrows meeting in the middle of his forehead. He sat down, back straight, legs wide apart.

I should have grinned and borne it, Frank thought. Not a good beginning. Try again.

'I saw you with the pupils on the playing fields when I first visited the school. You looked as though you had them well under control. It must be difficult achieving high athletic standards with pupils of varied disabilities.'

Salmon seemed to be having trouble following his line of thought. 'What do you mean?'

Frank searched for different words. 'Do you have any problems teaching the boys games?'

'No.'

'None at all? Do some of them have coordination problems? Can't catch balls, things like that?'

'Yes.'

This was impossible. He decided to cut to the chase. 'Did you teach David Pemberton?'

'Yes.'

'What was he like? Did he enjoy games?'

Salmon widened the space between his legs and leant forward. 'He didn't do much PE, he did extra art. He joined in when we went for cross-country runs. He seemed to like that, he was a good runner, could keep going when the other boys slowed down.'

'What did you make of him?'

'Make of him?'

'Yes. Was he a pleasant boy? Or was he troublesome?' It was like getting blood out of a stone. Or a lump of concrete.

'He was all right, didn't say much.'

'He was friendly with Peter, wasn't he?'

The eyebrows came together again. 'Who told you that?'

He tried to look puzzled. 'Mr Baron? The school matron? I can't remember.'

'Oh.' The caterpillars above his eyes crawled apart. 'I suppose they told you he died?'

Frank tried not to show his surprise and consternation. Peter dead? 'Yes. I can't remember what they said he died of. Was it a heart problem?'

Salmon laughed. 'Yes, it stopped. They usually do when you die.' He continued laughing.

Frank took a chance. 'When was that? The end of April, 1969, wasn't it?' That was near the date David ran away.

'Something like that. Epileptic fit, died in his sleep. He had diabetes as well. Always trying to get out of games, saying he didn't feel well.'

'What was his surname, I've forgotten.'

'Mobbs ... you seem to have a bad memory, Mr Diamond. Anything else you've forgotten?'

Frank decided to change tack. He waved his notebook and biro. 'That's why I write a lot of notes, Mr Salmon. Do you teach any other subjects?'

'Geography.'

'Have you always been a teacher? You look like a military man, to me.'

Salmon flushed and pushed his shoulders back. 'Army. Best years of my life.'

'Why didn't you stay? Why go into education/'

'That's none of your business. They treat you great at first, but if your face doesn't fit … they treat you like shit.'

'Are there any other military men on the staff?'

'No, but …'

Frank looked at him questioningly. 'Yes?'

Salmon moved uncomfortably on his seat. 'No. No one else.'

'What was Peter like?'

'I thought you were here to ask about David Pemberton?'

'That's true, but I believe David was close to Peter. I wonder if David heard about his death and was so upset he ran away.'

Salmon pulled at his lower lip and nodded. 'Could be; makes sense.'

'What was Peter like?' Frank persisted.

'Daft as a brush, like all those slitty-eyed kids. We've got several, you know. Most come from the orphanage.'

Frank resisted saying something. 'The orphanage?'

'Don't you know? Thought you were supposed to be a detective?'

'That's what I'm trying to do – detect. Tell me about the orphanage.'

'Not sure which one it is, but the governors always accept two or three boys each year, all fees paid. Sometimes it works out but sometimes they get sent back—'

Baron poked his head round the door. 'Sorry to

interrupt, but you're late for your lesson, Mr Salmon. Had you forgotten?'

Salmon flushed and got up.

'Sorry, Mr Diamond. I'm afraid Mr Salmon must leave now. I'll send in the next person.'

'Thank you, Mr Salmon, you've been most helpful.'

'Goodbye.' He stalked off, shoulders back. All he needed was a peaked cap and a swagger stick.

Stuart Elderkin pulled out a chair and smiled at the matron, who didn't respond in a like manner. He hoped this interview would be more productive than the last three.

'Very kind of you to give me your time, Miss Gammell.'

'Nurse Gammell.'

He smiled and nodded. 'Of course.'

'So how are the boys at the moment?' Perhaps some small talk might oil the wheels.

'What do you mean? How are the boys?' Her sharp voice and pinched nostrils suggested she wasn't impressed. The clipped speech and slight accent reminded him of a film he'd seen where a female Nazi concentration guard was being beastly to the women prisoners. It would be good casting.

'Are they all well? No outbreaks of boils, or ingrown toe-nails?' He laughed, hoping to lighten the mood.

She glared at him. 'We do not allow boils; all the boys are inspected every week for any skin problems, insect infestations and finger and toe nails are regularly cut. Without fail.'

One step below torture and nails being pulled out. He

gave up any idea of establishing a rapport.

'Can you tell me about David Pemberton? What was he like? Who were his friends? Did he have any illnesses?' He leant back in his chair, trying to look relaxed, but probably failing. God, Mabel was like an angel, even in her worse moods, compared to this she-devil.

'David Pemberton? Why do you want to know about him?'

'Didn't the headmaster explain? We're trying to find out what happened to him.'

She sniffed. 'I can tell you nothing.'

'You must have had some dealings with him; you must have seen him around the school.' His blood pressure was rising.

She pursed her lips and looked upwards as though racking her brains. 'No. He was not ill while he was here. I did not know him.'

'You said a minute ago all the boys were inspected regularly. You must have come across him then. There aren't that many boys at the school.'

Red patches formed above her cheek bones. 'You are trying to confuse me.'

'Why don't you want to talk about David? Have you been told not to?' See how she handles that.

She half-rose from the chair. 'You are a rude man. No one tells me anything. Certainly *not*, Mr Baron.' There was a contemptuous tone when she mentioned the headmaster. Interesting. He decided this conversation was not a waste of time.

'Nurse Gammell, I do apologise if I've upset you. No offence intended,' he grovelled. It seemed to have the right effect as she gave a swift nod of her head and settled back in her seat.

'Did David ever speak to you? Did he ever ask your advice? I imagine many of the boys might seek your help.'

This remark seemed to puzzle her. He could understand why. He'd rather consult a witch doctor than ask Nurse Gammell for help.

She shook her head. 'No. He did not.'

'That's a very attractive accent you've got.' She frowned. He decided to modify that remark. 'Just a trace, now and then. Your English is impeccable. Are you German?'

Her bosom heaved. 'German! I hate the Germans! Murderers and rapists! I am Russian.' She seemed to grow about two inches as she declaimed her nationality. Stuart decided not to follow that up … just yet.

He smiled at her. 'Wonderful. Our staunchest allies. Great fighters – the Russians.'

Her bottom lip curled. 'We won the war, without us you would be under the jackboot.'

'I'm sorry you can't tell me about David. What about Peter, David's friend? What can you tell me about him?'

The nationalism in her eyes faded. 'Who is this Peter? We do not have a Peter.'

'Really? I'm sure Mr Báron mentioned him.'

'What does *he* know?'

'He *is* the headmaster, surely he knows all the pupils.'

She shrugged. 'There was a Peter, Peter Mobbs but he is no longer with us.'

'He left?'

'Yes. He died. Nearly two years ago. He had many

problems, he was a Down's syndrome boy, also a diabetic and he had epilepsy.' Her cold tone didn't suggest any sympathy for Peter.

Nearly two years. About the time David ran away. 'The parents must have been grateful there was someone at the school who could give him proper care. I expect you had a lot to do with him?'

She shrugged. 'I monitored his insulin injections, tested his urine for glucose levels, made sure he ate the right foods.'

'Did he die at home?'

'No. Here. He had no parents. He was from the orphanage.'

After trying, and failing, to get information about that institution Stuart Elderkin decided to finish the interview. He needed to see Frank. There were two matters to follow up. The orphanage and the death of Peter Mobbs.

Frank waited for Stuart at the front of the school. He walked round the mini-bus, which was a new, powerful machine, with blackened windows and no school logo on its sides. He'd asked Baron about that and he'd said it was easier for the pupils if they weren't stared at when they were taken out on visits, which was also the reason for the lack of a school logo. Baron finished by saying they couldn't spare any more time for further interviews and after consulting parents, no children would be seen. There was nothing Frank could do about that; he had no clout. He was no longer a detective inspector. But Revie was. Could he get him onside? He'd show him the drawings, tell him about Luxton's possible connection with the school, and suggest a visit to Chillingworth by the police.

He had to try. If Laurel was right, and Luxton was connected to the school by the photograph of the boy, plus his reaction on seeing Baron, then even if David 's disappearance wasn't tied to the school, something nasty was probably going on there, and needed to be stopped. Pronto.

Stuart walked towards him and they both got into the car.

'Sorry to keep you, Frank. Well that's a rum do. I don't like the smell of this.'

'Shall we stop for a pint and a sandwich? Then we can swap details.'

Stuart tapped the dashboard with his small hands. 'Best news I've had today. That was completely unsatisfactory. No, I lie. Despite the lack of cooperation a few things did emerge.'

Frank started the car. 'Save it until we've eaten. I'm starving. Where shall we lunch?'

Stuart pursed his lips. 'Might as well go back to Aldeburgh and the Cross Keys, we'll be halfway home then.'

They chose a table near the window looking out to Crabbe Street. After polishing off several crab sandwiches and a few pints of Adnams, Frank decided it was the right time to confess to Stuart. It would make it easier to tell Dorothy and Mabel if Stuart knew his transgressions first. He told him not only about the drawing he'd kept back, but also his meeting with Carol, and Laurel knew everything.

'I'd rather not tell Dorothy and Mabel about meeting Carol.'

Stuart's face was grave. 'So how do you feel about her now?'

Frank bit his lip. 'I couldn't say this to Laurel, but when I saw how Carol was dressed, well, undressed, my desire deflated like a burst balloon.'

Stuart sniggered. 'Sorry.'

'I suppose I'm a romantic at heart, I don't like women leaping on me. It makes you realise how women must feel like when no sooner are they alone with a man than he forgets foreplay and heads directly for the vital parts. I thought perhaps I was falling in love, but I'm afraid it was lust.'

'But not very strong lust, or you'd have, er … carried on, wouldn't you?'

'Perhaps my male hormones aren't up to scratch.'

Stuart slowly sipped the last of his pint. 'Join the party! I'm not sure I'm up to it. Been a bit since I made the four-legged beast.'

Frank turned to him. 'Don't think of it like that, Stuart. You love Mabel, she's a lovely woman, and she seemed to be thawing the other night.'

'I hope you're right.' He picked at a bit of crab meat he'd missed.

Frank decided he couldn't take any more personal relationships issues. 'I'll get some drinks in.' He came back with two half-pints. 'We need to do some thinking.'

Stuart pulled a face. 'Half-pints do nothing for my brain.'

'Let's get back to the case. What did you find out?'

They exchanged information.

'We've got to get Revie onside, make him see the connections between the school and Luxton,' Frank said.

'Could be difficult. Wonder if he found the photograph Laurel told us about. He'll go hairless if his team missed that one. We don't want to get his dander up.'

'What do you think about the Harrops' deaths? Can *they* be connected to Luxton's?'

Stuart slowly shook his head. 'Can't see it, but if they were murdered and if Luxton was murdered, I can't believe we've got two different killers in the area who are expert at making a murder look like suicide.'

'It almost looks like someone is tidying up. Removing people who might be a danger to them. But I don't get the connection with the Harrops. If Luxton was a paedophile, and the school was involved, then he won't be the only one, will he?'

'No. We know Sam Harrop was a homosexual. Do you think he was also interested in young boys?' Stuart asked.

Frank looked down into his glass as though the bitter would reveal the answer. 'Remember, when we first took on the case, you told us about another boy who died at the school?

'Yes.'

'You said there was a post-mortem. Can you remember the names of the doctors who signed the death certificate?'

Stuart's eyes widened. 'You don't think it could have been …?'

'It's a thought.'

'We need to examine the two death certificates: Peter's and the other boy, I think his name was Roy Franks.'

'We've got to see Revie. Let's hope I can eat enough humble pie to satisfy him.'

'Offer him humble pie and a side order of fame and

promotion if he cracks this case,' Stuart said.

'But where does David fit into all this? Now we can understand why he didn't want to go back to school. But what happened to him, and where is he?'

David, Age 13 years

I have a friend. The first friend I've ever had. His name is Peter. He has Down's syndrome. I like him so much. He is the same age as me. He's at Chillingworth School. I was frightened when I went there. Peter hasn't got a daddy or a mummy. He's an orphan. He lives in a place called an orphanage with other orphan boys. He doesn't like it. We came to the school together. He was scared, too.

He likes to watch me draw and paint. He tries to do the same but he makes a mess. We laugh together at his drawings. I like it when he laughs. He throws back his head and all his body shakes. When he does that he makes me laugh and I can't stop. It makes me happy. I like feeling happy. It's good.

When I went home for half-term I told Mummy and Daddy about Peter. I asked if he could come to stay for Christmas. Daddy looked pleased. Mummy said she would see. Before I went back to school she said no. I think she rang the school. I drew Peter and put him with the secret drawings.

I wish I hadn't told Peter I'd ask if he could come home with me for Christmas. I said we could sleep together in my room. I told him about Miss Fenner and her puddings. We talked about what we would like for Christmas dinner.

Peter wanted lots of roast potatoes and I wanted a pudding with flames. I have to tell him he can't come. He is upset. I am upset. Why didn't she let him come? She fusses round me. She comes in my room when I'm drawing. She's always looking in my desk and tidying up. What would she say if she saw my secret drawings? The one of her with the tutor? Or the one of her I see in my head? When I go to school I miss Daddy and Miss Fenner, but I don't miss Mummy. When I'm at home I miss Peter.

I like the art teacher. I don't like the PE teacher. He's a bully. Peter doesn't like him. The headmaster, Mr Baron, comes and looks at my drawings and paintings. He says nice things. He lets me miss PE and do art instead. I like him, but he won't let Peter miss PE. I go to Mr Baron's room with the art teacher. We have tea and cakes. They aren't as nice as Miss Fenner's. Mr Baron has lots of paintings on the walls. He takes me round them and he talks and talks. My art teacher says I am a lucky boy.

When I go home for Christmas I draw Mr Baron. I also draw the nurse. I don't like her. Peter is afraid of her. When he feels ill he won't tell in case they send him to her. He says she made him take of all of his clothes. She examined him all over and looked at his willy and made him bend over and prodded him. He cried when he told me. Why did she do that? I'm not going to let her do that to me. Peter is sad he has to stay at school for Christmas. I'm going to talk to Daddy and see if Peter can come home with me at half-term.

I want to show him my secret drawings. I don't think I can show him the one with my mummy and the tutor. I feel my face go red as I think of doing that. It's a bad secret. I wish it wasn't true.

225

Chapter 21

Laurel looked round the dining table at Greyfriars. Supper was over and Frank was helping Mabel and Dorothy clear up. Stuart filled his pipe, looking happy and relaxed. Laurel was nervous because Frank was going to tell Dorothy and Mabel about keeping back the drawing of Carol and the tutor; because of that she couldn't do justice to cold beef, sauté potatoes and salad. Frank hadn't eaten much either. How would they react? What would happen if one or both of them were so upset they wanted to end their association with him? If Mabel was disgusted, would she take Stuart with her? It was wonderful to see Stuart and Mabel happy together again. Why did you do that, Frank? Why jeopardise the partnership? She'd said she understood, and she did. She couldn't criticise him; he'd taken a great risk when he didn't inform anyone of her part in the death of her sister's murderer. The other three didn't know what a debt she owed him. One she could never repay. What she'd done was on a different level to his indiscretions. But she couldn't tell them. She couldn't tell anyone. It was her and Frank's secret.

Mabel and Dorothy came back into the room with the coffee tray.

'That apple pie was the best I've ever tasted,' Stuart said, taking Mabel's hand as she passed him. 'And as for that custard!'

Mabel laughed. 'I broke the housekeeping budget buying apples at this time of the year, and real cream went into the custard.'

'So, it's bread-and-pull-it for the rest of the week, is it, Mabel?' Frank asked as he came in and went to his seat.

'I think I can do better than that.'

Coffee was poured and Stuart puffed away contentedly.

Frank looked at Laurel, then Stuart. They both nodded. Frank looked pale.

'Dorothy, Mabel. There's something I have to tell you,' he said.

At the serious tone of his voice their faces tensed.

'Not bad news, I hope, Frank?' Dorothy said.

'Not in the sense you mean, but yes, it is serious. I'm afraid I've let you all down. I've told Laurel and Stuart, and now I must tell you.' He went to his desk and came back with the drawing of Carol and the tutor. He laid it on the table in front of Dorothy.

'This is just as Ann Fenner described,' she said, passing it to Mabel. 'You can see it's drawn by David. The boy must have seen them making love, if that's what you can call it. Where did you get it, Frank?'

He told them.

'Why didn't you show it to us with the others?' Mabel asked, looking puzzled.

'You didn't want it to be her, did you, Frank?' Dorothy asked, sighing and shaking her head. 'I must say I am surprised. I had you down as a hard-to-seduce kind of chap.'

Stuart snorted. Frank looked shocked. Mabel looked

227

confused.

'I can only apologise. It was extremely foolish of me,' Frank said.

'I don't understand. Why did you do it, Frank?' Mabel asked.

Frank's face reddened and he couldn't seem to find the words.

Laurel decided to step in. 'Frank was attracted to Mrs Pemberton; she's a very beautiful woman. We all do crazy things at times. Don't we, Mabel?'

Mabel shot a glance at Stuart, who gave her a broad grin. 'I suppose we do. Right, anyone want some more coffee?' she said. Stuart passed his cup.

Frank looked from Mabel to Dorothy. 'You'll forgive me?'

'Silly boy, let that be a lesson to you. I hope you haven't got tangled up with her. I didn't say before but she's got a bit of a reputation in Aldeburgh. Been seen with men who weren't her husband. I should have mentioned it before, but it's only gossip. If I'd known you were feeling frisky I'd have warned you off,' Dorothy said, lowering her spectacles and giving Frank an old-fashioned look.

It was the first time Laurel had seen Frank blush.

Dorothy shook her head. 'Tsch, tsch tsch.'

'That's enough, Dorothy. From what I hear, your time in the WAAF wasn't all it should have been,' Laurel said.

Dorothy lit a cigarette, blew a stream of smoke at Laurel and smirked. 'I can't remember. That's the blessing of getting older.'

Stuart rapped on the table with a coffee spoon. 'Any more confessions? No? Then I'd like to say on behalf of myself and Mabel that we're both grateful the way you've put up with our problems. They're over now. We're both happy again, aren't we, love?'

Mabel smiled. 'Yes, thank you. Frank, don't worry about the drawing; you've shown it to us now. Boys will be boys.'

Laurel was sure Frank wouldn't like being equated with men who behaved like randy goats.

'Thank you,' Frank said, 'you've all been very understanding. Shall we begin the meeting? Laurel would you start?'

She told them about finding Luxton's body and the photograph of the frightened boy in the cutlery drawer. The mood darkened as the implications of a possible connection between Luxton and the school became clear.

Mabel took a deep breath. 'I hope what you're implying, Laurel, isn't true. There's nothing I hate more than children being messed with. If I'd ever caught a man touching my son, well, I'd probably still be in gaol.'

'We have no proof of this, but we must inform the police of our suspicions. Laurel managed to get a word with Inspector Revie this morning,' Frank said. He turned to her.

'I didn't say why you wanted to see him, but I told him it was urgent. He was involved with the post-mortem on Luxton at Ipswich this afternoon. I gave him our phone number and he said he'd contact Frank as soon as possible.'

'Sam Harrop was a homosexual. Do you think he was a paedophile, Frank?' Dorothy asked. 'Could his death have something to do with the school and Luxton? I never heard he was like that. If it's true and he was, then Nancy didn't know about it. At least I don't think so. I'm finding all this very confusing.'

Mabel thumped the table. 'We've got to do something. Those kiddies at the school could be in danger, if they aren't all ready. What are you going to do?' She glared at Frank and Stuart.

Stuart reached out and took her hand. 'Calm down, Mabel. No good going off half-cocked.'

Laurel bit her lip. She looked at Frank who had his hand over his mouth. She knew it was no laughing matter, but she was grateful for some light relief after the past few days.

Mabel gripped Stuart's hand. 'Sorry. It's got me in a tizzy. I'll shut up.'

'Stuart, would you tell them what we found out at the school this morning,' Frank said.

Stuart laid down his now dead pipe. 'Mabel, you won't like this either. Brace yourself.'

He told them about Peter's death, the time it happened and how he and Frank felt it was important to see not only Peter's death certificate, but also the boy's who'd died at the school a few years ago.

Laurel looked at Frank. 'You think it could have been– –'

Her words were interrupted by the shrill ring of a phone.

Frank picked it up.

'Yes. Thank you for ringing me … Yes, I do need to see you urgently … tonight? … Yes … Hold on.' He turned to the others. 'Revie is willing to drive here now from Ipswich. Is that OK with everyone?' He spoke into the phone. 'Thank you. We'll expect you in …? I'm grateful, Inspector Revie.' He gave instructions on how to get to Greyfriars. He put the phone down.

'I think something must have happened at the post-mortem. He's on his way.'

Frank stared intently at the rest of the team seated round the dining table. They'd gone over the facts they'd present to Revie in minute detail. 'Excellent. I think we've made a tight case to give to him. We know what we want him to do, but if he can reach those conclusions by himself, so much the better.'

'He's had a long day,' Stuart said, 'he'll be tired, so he might be on a short fuse.'

Dorothy bristled. 'We haven't been shirking, you know. I'll soon sort him out if he gets ratty with any of you.'

Laurel sighed. 'No, Dorothy, this is the time for diplomacy and a bit of buttering up.'

'Perhaps I'd be better off to bed,' Dorothy said, looking hurt.

Frank turned to her. 'No, we need you here. You're an important member of the team. It's vital Revie sees we're a well-organised, efficient and professional unit. Which we are. You'll have to be gracious, offer to take notes, which he'll refuse if he has any sense, and look every inch the organiser you are.'

Dorothy smiled at him. 'If you put it like that.'

'You could try a bit of lipstick, I hear he's not married,' Stuart said.

'Stuart Elderkin, mind your manners. Dorothy's not like that,' Mabel said. 'I expect he'll be hungry. I'll see what I can rustle up for him. That should help to calm him

231

down.'

'Are we all getting supper?' Stuart asked.

Mabel shook her head and went to the kitchen.

They waited in the sitting room. Frank lit a fire, and Laurel had glasses and bottles of whisky and beer ready. The scene was set for the seduction of Inspector Revie. Frank was worried: if Revie didn't play ball their hope of finding out what happened to David Pemberton would be so much more difficult. There were possible threads linking the deaths of the Harrops and Luxton to the school; they were poking out of the substrata, waving their cut-ends, like earthworms emerging from their burrows, looking for a partner to connect with. There weren't any hard clues, just suspicious deaths and gut feelings. He didn't know enough about Revie, how he worked, his ambitions, his integrity or his lack of it. From his meetings with him over the Harrops' deaths, he thought he had a sharp mind, quick to catch on to the possibilities of possible murder of not only Sam, but Clara as well. Was he a risk taker, or would he play it by the book? When he saw him with Ansell he'd been willing to share the details of the Harrops' post-mortems.

The ringing of the front door bell ended his reverie. Dorothy, complete with freshly combed hair, a clean white blouse and bright red lipstick went to the door.

'Inspector Revie. How good of you to come so late at night. I'm Dorothy Piff, the administrator of Anglian Detective Agency. Do come and meet the rest of the team. We're in the sitting room. Can I take you coat and hat? Oh, a Gannex, such a reliable coat. Ready for all weathers, as I'm sure you are.' There were mutterings from Revie.

'Tart,' Laurel said, smiling at the others.

Frank and Stuart rose as Revie barrelled into the room. Nicholas Revie looked tired, the skin of his face was grey, but the bright blue eyes flashed as he looked at them in turn. He nodded to Laurel and Elderkin and was introduced to Mabel.

'Inspector Revie, would you like a bite to eat? I know an important policeman like you won't get much chance to have proper meals. I cater for all our team so they can spend their time working. How about a bacon sandwich? I've got some lovely smoked back and fresh bread.'

Had she overdone it?

Revie pursed his lips. 'You've certainly got a treasure here,' he said to Frank. 'Thank you, I'd love a bacon sarnie. Got any HP sauce?'

Mabel nodded, looking satisfied with her effort to help the meeting go smoothly. She glided off to the kitchen.

'We were going to have a drink, Inspector. Would you like a whisky? Or is there anything else you'd fancy? Tea? Coffee?' Dorothy asked.

'I could murder a beer.'

'Bottle of Adnams?' Frank offered.

'I think you're all trying to worm yourselves into my good books,' Revie said, parking his solid girth into an armchair.

'I hope we're succeeding,' Frank said, passing him a full glass.

The smell of crispy bacon and the tang of the brown sauce Revie had liberally spread on his sandwiches lingered in the room. Frank could see Stuart was suffering. Revie sat

233

at the head of the dining-room table.

'You've got a good set up here. I'm impressed. I think I might kidnap you,' he eyed Mabel, 'and take you back to headquarters. That was the best bacon sandwich ever.'

Mabel simpered and Stuart glowered at him.

'Right, let's hear it. What have you got to tell me that's so important?'

Frank began by going over the David Pemberton case, including the finding of the drawings in David's bedroom. Revie spent time staring at each one, he frowned when he looked at the drawing of the frightened boy, and gave extra time to the woman having sex with a man. Stuart told him about Ann Fenner and her revelations.

'Interesting, but not relevant to the cases I'm dealing with,' he said.

Laurel explained her involvement with the Harrops, leading up to finding the bodies. 'Samuel Pemberton was a homosexual, which Nancy Wintle will confirm,' she said.

Revie narrowed his eyes. 'Did he like little boys?'

'We don't know, but it's a possibility.'

Stuart took up the story and told him about their findings at Chillingworth School.

Revie frowned, his features gathering towards the centre of his face. 'Two boys dead. We need to see the death certificates, don't we?'

Frank sighed with relief. 'Yes, and you can get your hands on them more quickly than we can.'

'And what if the name we think might be on those certificates, isn't there?'

'Then all we have are suspicions, and dead people who may or may not have been murdered. Can you tell us anything about Luxton's death? We'd be grateful if you could tell us what the post-mortem revealed,' Frank said.

Revie leant back, thrusting out his belly. 'If I had another of those bacon sarnies, my memory might get into gear.' He smiled lasciviously at Mabel.

She shook her head. 'First time I've heard of HP sauce being good for the grey cells.' She looked at Stuart. 'Bacon sandwiches all round? And lots of coffee as well.'

There were positive replies and Stuart's mouth turned up at the corners.

'Miss Mabel, you're a treasure,' Revie said. 'Would you mind if I told them about the post-mortem while you're busy in the kitchen?'

'I think that's a good idea. I don't want to hear details as I'm eating bacon.'

Somehow bacon sandwiches lost their allure.

'Ansell performed the PM,' Revie said. 'He's a thorough worker and I trust his findings.'

'Excellent,' Frank said.

'As you know, Luxton's throat was cut. I wanted to know whether he'd done it himself or someone else had killed him. Unfortunately, Ansell can't be sure, but he's favouring murder.'

Laurel gasped. 'Poor man. He must have been terrified. He didn't seem in control of himself on the Friday night. If only he'd stayed with his deputy, he might still be alive.'

Frank leant towards Revie. 'What made Ansell suspicious?'

Revie frowned. 'Not sure if I can remember all the details or the correct jargon, but the main suspicious factor was the cut in the throat. Ansell thought there was bruising in the region of the cut, but the tissue was so damaged he couldn't be sure. Also in most suicides the cut is upwards, left to right, for a right hander and right to left for a left hander. This cut was straight across and really deep.' He took a long drink of beer.

'The windpipe ... what do you call it?' he continued.

'Trachea,' Laurel replied.

'That's it. Cut right through. Happens sometimes, so not suspicious. Ansell said in suicides you don't usually get the deeper structures like the food pipe ... what do you call it?' He looked at Laurel

'Oesophagus,' Laurel replied.

'That's it, you don't get that or the vertebrae damaged. Luxton's oeso ... food pipe, was cut through and his neck bones were nicked.'

'All that blood was from the veins *and* arteries?' Laurel asked.

'That's right, arteries are deeper than veins. Those are the reasons Ansell thinks Luxton was murdered.'

'Inspector Revie, I've got a confession to make,' Laurel said.

'Call me Nick. You must come in handy, Laurel, knowing all the parts of the body. Perhaps I'll kidnap you as well as Mabel. Ever thought of joining the police?'

Laurel shook her head. 'When I tell you what I did while Dr Neave was phoning the police you may think differently. I found a photograph of a young boy under the cutlery drawer in the kitchen.'

'Had a snoop, did you?' Revie laughed. 'We did find it. Anything else you found?'

'No, but I thought some papers might have been removed.'

'I think you ought to join the force. You're wasted here with this lot.'

'Sorry, you can't have her, she's ours,' Frank said.

Laurel picked up the drawing of the frightened boy and placed it before Revie. He looked up at her, his eyes narrowing. 'Yes, I saw the likeness to the photograph. It could be him and this could be the connection. I think I'm going to have to see the chief constable. This could be tricky. First I need to get the death certificates of the two boys.'

Mabel came in with a tray of coffee and a plate of bacon sandwiches. Revie grabbed one and started devouring, Stuart joined in, Laurel shook her head and Frank said he'd prefer another whisky.

Revie gulped down the sandwich. 'I can't tell the chief about the involvement of you lot.' He wiped grease from his chin with a paper napkin. 'You keep quiet about what you've found and I'll help if I can, with information about this David Pemberton. Although I can't see the connection. He ran away from home, didn't he? Unless he went back to the school. But why would he do that?'

Chapter 22

Laurel parked her Cortina on the Pembertons' drive. She glanced at her wristwatch. Exactly ten. Adam Pemberton hadn't yet been interviewed and Frank had asked her if she'd do it. She hoped she wouldn't see Carol Pemberton, although part of her was curious to see her in the flesh. She hoped if she did she'd be able to hide her feelings about the woman; she shouldn't be biased, but she was on Frank's side.

It was only as she got out of the car she felt the biting north-easterly wind. It was a cold but bright late winter day; as she'd driven into Aldeburgh on the Thorpeness road the sea had glittered below an almost cloudless sky.

The door was opened by Ann Fenner, who Laurel recognised from David's drawing and Stuart's description.

'Miss Bowman? Mr Pemberton is waiting for you in the library. Would you like some coffee?' Her smile was warm and welcoming. Stuart had made a good impression.

'Yes, thank you.'

Ann Fenner opened a door. 'Mr Pemberton, Miss Bowman is here. Shall I bring in coffee for two?'

'Please, Ann,' a tall, serious-faced man said, getting up from a leather armchair, and putting a newspaper down on an occasional table. 'Miss Bowman. Please take a seat.' He shook hands then waved to an armchair.

He looked tired and strained. She wondered if he knew about his wife's unfaithfulness. It was hard to imagine he wouldn't have any suspicions, although often the husband or wife was the last to know what their other half had been up to.

'I understand you want to ask me some questions? Where is Mr Diamond today?'

'He had another line of enquiry to follow up. I'm sorry he couldn't be here. I'm afraid you'll have to make do with me.' She gave him her best smile, implying that it wasn't such a bad bargain.

'My dear Miss Bowman, I assure you, you are a more than adequate substitute.' His face creased in a warm smile, lighting up his brown eyes.

He wasn't as bad as Frank had described him, but then Frank was biased.

'Before you begin I must ask you if there's been any progress? I know it's only just over a week since Mr Diamond came to see us, but …'

Laurel hesitated, unsure how much she should reveal. 'I can't go into details, Mr Pemberton, but although we aren't any closer to finding out what happened to David, our investigations are taking us into new territory and we hope what we find out will throw light onto David's disappearance.' What a lot of words for so few, if any, facts.

Pemberton shook his head and smiled. 'Very diplomatic, you'd have made an excellent lawyer.'

Laurel smiled. 'Someone said yesterday I should join the police force, and today it's a career in the law! What will tomorrow bring?'

Pemberton raised is eyebrows. 'Perhaps modelling? You have the height and if I may say, the face and figure.'

Not such a grumpy old solicitor after all. 'Thank you, but I think I'd get bored prancing up and down a catwalk. Is Mrs Pemberton available if I need to speak to her?'

The frown reappeared. 'I'm afraid she'd feeling under the weather, a nasty headache; she's lying down and doesn't want to be disturbed.'

'I'm sorry.'

The door opened and a delicious smell of fresh coffee preceded Ann Fenner, who was carrying a loaded try.

'Thank you, Ann.'

Laurel noticed the smiles exchanged between them, and Ann Fenner blushed as Adam Pemberton praised some fairy cakes she'd brought in. She poured out the coffee and Pemberton watched her as she left the room.

'I don't know what we'd do without her. She's so calm and efficient.'

Unlike your wife? 'Mr Pemberton, I know Mr Diamond talked to you briefly, but I do need to ask you a few questions. I have read your statements to the police and the other detective agency, but they don't tell me about your feelings, your, if you'll pardon the phrase, gut response at the time David ran away.' She took a sip of coffee; as good as it smelt.

Adam Pemberton looked alarmed. 'Gut response? I'm not sure we should place much weight on such things, Miss Bowman. I prefer to work from hard facts when I'm dealing with a client. I don't think a gut response would warrant a reasonable fee.' He smiled at her. 'I presume you aren't talking about indigestion?' He gave a tight laugh at his own witticism.

She laughed politely. 'Mr Pemberton, bear with me. Haven't you sometimes made decisions based on how you felt about someone, rather than on references, or someone else's opinion? For example, when you appointed Miss Fenner. How did you feel when you interviewed her?'

Pemberton rubbed his cheek. 'Yes, I see what you mean. Miss Fenner made a good impression on me and I was sure she'd be an asset. That was before I read her testimonials and references. Now Carol wasn't too keen on her, but when she read her references she agreed to take her on. She's been excellent.'

She wondered why Carol Pemberton didn't like Ann Fenner. 'This proves you're a good judge of character, Mr Pemberton. I know this may be painful, but I'd be interested to know your feelings about your son, and also how you felt when he ran away from home. Are you willing to tell me?'

'Do you think it will help?' He moved uneasily in his seat. 'I'm not very good at this sort of thing. Carol says I hold all my feelings bottled up inside me. I'm afraid that's the way I was brought up, and I'm not sure I hold with all this flower power, and love everybody philosophy which is so popular nowadays. It seems very false to me.' His brown eyes were unhappy, his shoulders drooping.

Laurel wished she didn't have to press him, but it was needed. They had to find out if David had run away. So far there was no evidence of his survival, and they had to keep in mind, terrible as it would seem, that David could have been murdered by one or both of his parents. Going on her own gut responses she couldn't see this unhappy, hide-bound man being a murderer, but you could never be sure how anyone would react in unusual or dangerous circumstances. Look what she'd done when her sister was murdered – she'd lost all sense of judgement, and if it hadn't been for Frank, where would she be now?

'But are you willing? I do think it's worth it, otherwise I wouldn't put you through such questioning.'

He smiled at her, a sad, rather sweet smile. 'You're a very sincere woman, Miss Bowman. Ask away.'

Laurel took her notebook and biro from her briefcase. 'Do you love your son, Mr Pemberton?' She kept eye contact and spoke softly and kindly.

He gulped and looked at the floor. He slowly raised his head looking into her eyes. 'Yes, I love him.'

'How did you feel when you realised he had a disability? Did you love lessen?'

He shook his head. 'You can't turn love on and off, Miss Bowman. You haven't yet had children, if you had you'd realise love for a child is a different, stronger love than you have for, say, your parents, your brothers and sisters. Although that love, whatever they do, also cannot be set aside. The love you have for your own child is …' He hesitated as though trying to find the right words. 'A primal love, the love any mammal has for its young: a need to nurture, protect, to see them grow to maturity and to see them replace you one day as they form their own families. They are your future. I was upset when we discovered David's problems with reading, writing and normal relationships. He is my only child. I am fifty-two, Miss Bowman. Carol can't have any more children. I was devastated. Especially for him. I worried what would

242

happen to him when I was gone. Who would look after him? How was he going to cope in this difficult world? I think I probably showed my anxiety and grief too openly to him, and this meant we weren't close. I've thought of little else since he left.'

'Do you think he's dead?'

He closed his eyes and the lines either side of his mouth deepened. 'It's nearly two years. If he's alive, where could he be? Every Sunday in church I pray to God and to Jesus to look after him if he is alive. I pray he will come home, however many years pass, and I pray for God's strength to help me be a better father to him than I have been, if he returns.' He lowered his head, exhausted, as though these confessions had squeezed every drop of energy from his body and mind.

She wanted to stop, to give him some comfort, but she pressed on. 'What was your reaction to his artistic abilities? Were you proud of him?'

He sat in silence, then took a deep breath and looked up. 'I couldn't understand how he did it. At first, to me, it was another manifestation of his lack of normality. I wished that instead of that gift, he'd been a normal child. I didn't wish he was a bright child, one who would go to university, I'd have been happy if he'd been a normal little chap, not a brain box, just a naughty boy who got up to the usual childhood tricks with his rascally friends. I was slow to appreciate how talented he was. What an unusual gift he had. Now I can see how I could have helped him more than I did, to nurture this gift, and hopefully base a successful life on who he is, not who I wanted him to be. I've thought about it a lot since …'

Laurel was upset by his confessions; she knew how

much it had cost him to talk in such a way about his feelings, but there was one last question.

'Mr Pemberton, do you think your son loves you?'

He recoiled from her. 'That is a terrible thing to ask. It is a question I have asked myself, time after time. If he'd loved me, surely he'd have confided in me? Told me his troubles. That is what a parent is for, isn't it? To help their children in times of difficulty. There was one thing that made me hope.' He leant forward, his eyes desperate. 'I've never told anyone before, not even Carol. It was a small thing but it gave me hope. I didn't want to tell her because she'd have derided me and taken away my one comfort.'

Laurel was near to tears herself, the story was heart-rending. 'What was it, Mr Pemberton?'

He rose from his chair and went to the desk. He took a key ring from his pocket and unlocked the middle drawer on the right of the knee-hole desk. He brought a brown envelope to her and opened it. Without comment he passed the contents to her.

It was a pencil drawing of himself. Drawn by David. The man in the drawing was smiling, his eyes kind, his lips parted as though about to say something. Underneath, in the same childish hand that had written Peter on his friend's drawing, were the words: To Daddy from David.

'Where did you find this?'

'It was in that drawer.' He pointed to the desk. 'It was not there the day before he left.' He shook his head, his eyes watery. He took out a handkerchief and blew his nose. 'It's silly, I know, but I look at it every day. I wonder what was in his mind when he drew me, and why did he leave it for me? I want to believe it's because he cared for me, and knew I'd be hurt by what he was going to do.'

She wanted to tell him about Peter's drawing and how it was the only one with a name and Peter meant so much to David. But, how could she? 'I think it must have been his way of showing you it wasn't *you* that made him run away. It shows he cared how you would feel.' She didn't know if she should have said that, it wasn't professional, but the poor man was bereft. And *sh*e was responsible for this outpouring of grief.

There was hope in his eyes. 'Do you think so?'

'I do.'

'Thank you, Miss Bowman. I don't know if what I've told you will help in your search, but I must admit I feel better for talking about him. You have given me renewed hope.'

'We'll do everything we can to find him.'

He took the drawing and placed it back in the envelope and put it back in the desk, carefully locking the drawer.

Why hadn't he showed it to his wife? What did he say – deriding him? Her opinion of Carol Pemberton decreased even further.

'One last thing, Mr Pemberton.'

He looked pleadingly at her.

She smiled. 'No more awful questions. Would it be possible for me to take one or two examples of David's work with me? We'd return them as soon as possible.'

His face relaxed. 'Yes, of course. What do you want them for?'

'It's a recent thought: I'd like to show them to Mr Tucker, the art gallery owner. It occurred to me if David is … he won't stop drawing. It's a compulsion, isn't it?

Mr Tucker has many contacts; he's got a gallery in London. It's just a small chance, but he might hear something about a young gifted artist. I think it's worth a try.'

'Yes, he's got a lot of contacts. I've heard he invites potential buyers down for weekends, that kind of thing. Of course, he knows about David. He asked a few years ago, if he could have a show for David. Just a small affair, he felt his drawings would sell, especially as he was so young.'

'And did he have a show?'

Pemberton shook his head. 'No, I wasn't happy about it, although Carol was keen. I felt he was too young and people would be buying his work for the wrong reason.'

'What did David think about it?'

He grimaced. 'I'm afraid I didn't discuss it with him. Perhaps I should have.'

'Did Mr Tucker say anything after David disappeared?'

'Yes. He called about a week later. He seemed very upset. Said what a talent David was. He was keen to buy some of his drawings. I refused. They're all I have left of him. Would you like to come up to his bedroom, that's where his drawings are kept? You can choose whatever you want to show to Mr Tucker, but I would like them back. I think I'll have more of them framed and put round the house. I didn't want to do that before, but after our talk I think I will, then if he ever comes home, he'll see them.'

Laurel drove away from the Pemberton's house and parked her car in the High Street. She wished Smith's

Bakery would stop sending out tempting smells every time she came to Nancy's; she longed to sink her teeth into a Cornish pasty or a meat and potato pie. She decided she needed to up the number of runs she did every week, also she wanted to join an athletic club and get back to throwing the javelin.

She knocked on Nancy's door. She wasn't sure what kind of reception she'd get after Nancy's reaction to her bossy behaviour on the night they found the Harrops' bodies. She'd seen her a couple of times after that, but she'd been with Frank, and Nancy's son was with her. He'd gone back to Carlisle, to return for the funerals when Sam's and Clara's bodies were released.

'Hello, Nancy can I come in?'

She was looking better than the last time she'd seen her: her hair was bright pink, and she was wearing her tartan trews and a white polo neck.

'Yes, come in, Laurel.'

Nancy pointed to a chair near the electric fire. 'Would you like a drink?'

'No thanks, Nancy. I came to see how you are and to apologise if I upset you the night ...' It seemed cruel to bring up Sam's death again.

Nancy came to her side and patted her hand. 'I'm the one who should apologise. I realise you were trying to get me away from what must have been an awful scene.' She put her hand to her mouth and closed her eyes. 'I should have acted sooner, been stronger, not let Clara frighten me. I hadn't realised how ill Sam was, he deteriorated so quickly.'

Laurel took hold of her hand. 'If there's anything I can do, Nancy, let me know.'

'I can't believe Clara would do that to Sam. Why didn't she give him an overdose of morphine? I know it's against the law, but no one would have blamed her. What do you think happened, Laurel?'

She didn't want to upset Nancy again, but there were questions she wanted to ask. 'I think we're beginning to have some theories, Nancy. I need to ask you more questions about Sam. You may find them distressing, but if we don't explore his life, we may never get to the truth. Are you prepared to answer them?' It was going to be another painful interview.

Nancy's eyes looked haunted. There was a long silence. 'Yes, I'll try and answer your questions.'

'Do you think Clara could have killed Sam to stop him telling people he was homosexual?'

'Why would he want to do that? Now? It's no longer illegal, you can't be arrested for loving someone of the same sex. Sam hid his homosexuality; Clara knew what he was when she married him. No, I can't see her doing that.' She paused. 'I'm going to have a whisky; do you want one?'

Laurel was pleased their former relationship was restored. 'Yes please, a small one with same amount of water.' Dare she take the questioning further? She had to.

Nancy busied herself at the sideboard and in the kitchen, returning with two glasses on a tray. 'Here you are, Laurel. Cheers!'

She raised her glass and took a sip. 'Nancy, can you think of anything Sam might have done that made him feel he must make amends for before he died? Did he ever confess anything to you that would have horrified Clara? Horrified her so much she murdered him to keep him quiet?'

Nancy looked shocked, and took a swig of whisky. 'Do you think that's what happened?'

'I don't know, Nancy. I'm trying to think of the reasons Clara might have killed Sam. That is if she did kill him.'

Nancy took another deep drink. 'If she didn't, who did? Did she hire someone to do it? Like you see in American films? But if she did that, why didn't she go out and get, what do they call it …?'

'An alibi?' Laurel offered.

'Yes, that's it. Oh, this is ridiculous, we don't have hit men in Suffolk, let alone Aldeburgh.'

Laurel took a deep breath. 'Nancy, I'm going to ask you something that might upset you. I wouldn't ask, but there is a possibility there might be a connection between Sam and young boys. Do you think he was attracted to young men or boys?'

She was prepared for Nancy to lose her temper, and ask her to leave, or burst into tears. Neither of these happened. Nancy frowned, her eyes moving from side to side, as though she was searching her memory. 'Why do you want to know that? Do you mean did he ever have sex with a boy?'

Laurel was shocked by Nancy's reaction. It wasn't what she'd expected; people were endlessly surprising and fascinating. 'Did you suspect he might be attracted to boys? Do you know if he'd had relationships with a boy?'

Nancy flushed. 'Goodness, no. I don't know what I'd have done if I'd found that out!' She shook her head, looking distressed. 'It would have been a terrible choice to make. Betray my brother or let a child be sodomised. See

249

my brother go to prison, or let a child be molested, and his young life be ruined.' She put her hand over her mouth. 'I would have had to save the child. Oh, I'm glad I never had to make such a decision.'

Laurel wanted to end her anguish, but she might never have such an opportunity again. Next time Nancy might not be so forthcoming. 'Did you ever think he might be attracted to children?'

Nancy drained her glass, then went to the sideboard and poured in a good finger of whisky. She waved the bottle at Laurel. She shook her head. Nancy came back to the fireplace and sat down.

'Why are you asking these questions, Laurel? I think I've a right to know.'

Laurel sighed. It was a risk and Frank might not be happy if she revealed too much. It was important not one iota about the cases got out. 'Nancy, I can't tell you everything, and I'd ask you not to repeat any of this conversation with anyone else, even your son. As you know we're also working on the disappearance of David Pemberton. There may be connections between his running away, Chillingworth School, Dr Luxton's death and the deaths of Sam and Clara. We don't know how all these tie together, but it may have something to do with the children at the school. Frank thinks Sam and Clara were both murdered. Anything you can tell me might help us, and the police, to uncover the truth behind all these happenings.'

Nancy's glass stopped halfway to her mouth, her eyes as round as pennies. 'I can't believe it! Who would do such dreadful things?'

'That's what we're trying to discover. Can you help

us?'

Nancy put down her glass on a side table and rubbed the bridge of her nose. She nodded. 'Yes. Sam had come back from London to Aldeburgh for a short holiday, it was before he married Clara; I suppose he was about thirty-four. I was on the beach with Sam; James was holding a surgery. It was August, the beach was crowded with families. It was a lovely hot, still day, the sea calm and for once as blue as a forget-me-not, not its usual muddy brown. We'd been swimming, the tide was on the turn. The beach dips steeply so you were soon in deep water. I was towelling down when there was a cry. A woman saw her child was in difficulties. Sam ran over the pebbles, dived in, swam to the boy, turned him onto his back and brought him back to the beach.

'Sam put his arms round the boy's chest and squeezed; water gushed form his mouth. Then the boy collapsed. Sam bent over him. "He's stopped breathing, get an ambulance," he shouted and someone rushed off. I comforted the mother and told her Sam was a doctor. I tried to move her and the other people who'd crowded round away, so Sam had room to work.

'Sam put the boy on his back and gave him the kiss of life. The boy was about eleven, slim with blond hair and a face, as far as I could see, like an angel. After a few minutes he began to breathe by himself, and the crowd cheered as Sam supported him. I saw the look on Sam's face, I was sure he wanted to go on kissing those soft lips, holding the slender body close to his. Sam was wearing tight swimming trunks and I could see he'd an erection. I glanced round, afraid someone would cry out in disgust, but all I could see on the faces of the mother and the

251

onlookers was relief and admiration. Sam saw my face and flushed. He knew I'd seen his desire.

'Afterwards I wondered what would have happened if the rescue had taken place on a deserted beach. Would Sam have been able to resist the temptation of the beautiful young boy? One of my mother's sayings was: no one knows what they'll do until the right temptation comes along. She used to say it when a trusted bank manager ran off with the contents of the bank, or a beloved vicar left his wife of thirty years to live with a trapeze artist. She was an avid reader of *The News of the World*.'

'Did you ever tell anyone about it?'

'No, never, not even James.'

'I presume you didn't talk to Sam about it?'

'No. I couldn't. The thought Sam might desire children chilled my body to its core. He hadn't deliberately sought out the boy, he'd saved his life. I decided Sam's body had reacted on being close to the boy and kissing him. His mind and morals would have stopped him from taking such a dreadful path.'

Laurel wasn't so sure. 'Sam did take risks, didn't he, before the laws on homosexuality were changed?'

Nancy nodded. 'But being homosexual doesn't mean you're a paedophile, does it? You told me about your friends who are homosexual, they're not paedophiles are they?

'No, Nancy, you're right. Paedophiles can be heterosexual, homosexual, male or female.'

Nancy shuddered. 'I find it hard to understand people like that. How can they place their desires above the innocence of children? I despise them. I can't believe Sam

252

would be like that. Can you?'

Laurel didn't know what to say. Nancy had lost her brother; he'd died a terrible death, now she was faced with possibly learning that Sam had abused children. 'I think your mother's saying, about the right temptation, is true of all of us. Hopefully we never meet it. But perhaps Sam did.' But she had met it; it was what she'd done when she tried to make Angela's killer confess to her murder. She'd given in to the temptation of believing she could bring him to justice.

'He did that day on the beach. It was the right temptation, but luckily the wrong place.' Nancy rose from her chair and looked at the clock on the sideboard. 'I'm supposed to be meeting a friend for lunch, I'm not sure if I'll be able to eat anything. Would you like to join us?'

'That's kind of you, Nancy, but there's another person I need to see.'

'I do hope you and that nice Mr Diamond can sort all this out soon.' She hesitated. 'If Sam had done something wrong, would it have to come out?'

'I don't know, it would depend on the police and the people who were prosecuted. That's all a long way off, Nancy, we may never know what really happened to Sam and Clara.'

Nancy collected the glasses and took them into the kitchen.

She got up and waited for her to come back. 'I have one last favour to ask. Could I borrow a key to Sam's house? Frank, Mr Diamond, wants to have another look round. Have the police finished there?'

Nancy put on a blue wool short coat and wound a cerise scarf round her neck. 'Yes, they've given me the keys so I can sort out Sam and Clara's things. The solicitor says I'll be a very rich woman when all this is over. Sam left everything to me. He'd made an allowance to Clara and the right to live in the house until she died, but then the house would have come to me, or my son if I died. I'm surprised the police didn't have me down as the chief suspect.'

She smiled; Frank told her what Revie had said about Nancy not being able to peg out clothes, let alone string someone up.

Nancy went to the sideboard and passed a set of keys to Laurel. 'There you are, my dear. Perhaps Mr Diamond will find something that will solve the mystery.'

She took them and put them in her handbag. 'I doubt it, Inspector Revie seems a thorough person, but Frank likes to mooch about a crime scene, he says it gets his mind working. I'll get them back to you as quickly as possible.'

'No rush, I don't feel up to clearing out clothes just yet.' She smiled up at Laurel. 'Frank ... he seems a good man, er, are you and he ...?'

Laurel laughed. 'We're good friends and partners. You can squash any rumours you hear.'

'What a pity, you look good together.'

But not good enough, Laurel thought.

Laurel decided she needed something to eat before she saw Nicholas Tucker, so she bought some fish and chips and found a sheltered spot near the lifeboat station to eat them. She frowned, her fingers were greasy and she was concerned she'd soil David's drawings when she showed them to Tucker. She walked quickly to the public toilets

254

near the Moot House, and made the best of a bad job with cold water, no soap and her handkerchief.

She walked back to Tucker's gallery. Damn! It was closed. A sign hanging in the front door said it would open when the new summer collection was ready. No date was given. How could she contact him? Was he staying at the hotel? She would walk there and see. She peered in at the window: there were packing cases, some closed and ready for moving, and others empty. Brown paper and boxes were heaped in one corner. She thought she saw movement in the far room, so she knocked on the door. Several times.

Nicholas Tucker appeared; he was frowning, as though concentrating on solving a problem. The frown disappeared when he saw her, replaced by a smile. He opened the door.

'Laurel, what a lovely surprise. Do come in. We're in a mess I'm afraid. I heard about Dr Luxton. That was dreadful, and so awful for you, finding three dead people in a few days. Let's go into my office, shall we? If the denizens of Aldeburgh see the door open they'll be in like a shot wanting to know when we'll be opening again.'

He led her through the second gallery and upstairs to the floor above. This was also in a state of flux: more packing cases, and strong smells of glue and turpentine. He opened a door to a spacious office and drew out a chair in front of a modern desk.

'Sit down, can I offer you a drink?'

Laurel refused. 'I'm sorry to bother you when you're so busy, but I wanted to show you some drawings.'

He cocked his head. 'Yours?'

She laughed. 'No. I wish they were.'

She took out three drawings she'd selected from the Manilla envelope Adam Pemberton had put them in. 'These are by David Pemberton.' They were drawings he'd done in the year before he ran away. One was of the Moot Hall, another a fisherman's hut and the third was of Aldeburgh High Street.

Tucker laid them on the desk and looked at them intently. 'Did Mr Pemberton tell you I wanted to show some of his work in the gallery?'

'Yes, he did.'

'Mrs Pemberton came to see me with some of his drawings when he was, oh, about eleven, I think. He's a remarkable talent.'

'You don't think he's dead, then?'

He gazed up at her. 'I hope not. It would be a great crime if such a talent, possibly genius, were to die so young.'

'It's a great loss if any child dies, whether they're a genius or not, whether they're clever or with a disability, such as Down's syndrome.' What made her say that?

He nodded his head. 'True, true. All loss of life is sad.'

'I wanted to ask you if you would ask some of your art colleagues and see if any of them had come across a young boy with a talent like David's, or if they'd heard about such a person. If he's alive, he won't be able to stop drawing. At least that's what I believe. What do you think?'

'I'll certainly do that. A good idea, Laurel.'

She got up. 'Thanks for seeing me. You seem to have a lot of work to do. Do you usually change your paintings at this time of the year?'

He followed her out of the office. 'We need to get

ready for the summer visitors. The displays must appeal to their tastes, which are often different to the locals. The locals tend to buy in the winter.'

'Why? Do you put your prices up for the summer?'

He tapped his nose. 'You're a shrewd lady.' He paused, as though a thought had struck him. 'Are you doing anything tomorrow?'

She hesitated. The Harrops' house would be searched tomorrow. 'There's always more work.'

'More sleuthing?'

She shrugged her shoulders.

'I've a few friends staying with me at the moment. They might be able to help. And they have more contacts than I do. It would spread the word about David. I'm sure if they met you, and saw the drawings, they'd be only too pleased to help. Come for lunch.'

Why not? She didn't have anything planned for tomorrow, and it would get her out of going back to the Harrops' house with Frank and Stuart. It was a long shot, but she couldn't afford to turn the offer down. Perhaps when Tucker's friends saw the drawings, it might spark off something. 'Thank you, that's very kind.'

'Splendid. Twelve thirty for one?' He sketched a map to help her find his house and wrote down the address and phone number. 'In case you can't make it for any reason. I hope you can, my friends are leaving the day after. It'd be a pity to miss them.'

He escorted her to the door of the gallery. 'Until tomorrow. I hope the weather is as good as today. I'll be able to show you my garden. I'm so fond of it.' He sounded wistful.

'I'm not much of a gardener I'm afraid. It's Mr

Diamond, my partner, who'd appreciate your plants. He's got a degree in botany, would you believe. Always pointing out different wild flowers to me.'

Tucker looked bemused. 'Goodness. Wasn't he a policeman?'

'Yes. The best one I've met.'

'So what's he making of all the dead bodies? Does he think everything is above board and tickety-boo?'

'I'm afraid he has a suspicious mind.'

'And you, my dear?'

'I always think the best of everyone.'

He shook his head and laughed, his jowls shaking. 'That's no good for a detective. You'd better find another career.' Still laughing he waved goodbye and closed the door of the gallery.

Chapter 23

Stuart Elderkin stood outside the kitchen door in Greyfriars House. There were sounds of Mabel moving round, and the muted clash of baking tins, and a sweet, nutty smell crept under the door. It made his mouth water and his stomach felt hollow. Everyone else was out, this was his opportunity to get Mabel to finally commit herself. Their relationship had improved after Laurel talked with Mabel, and then relayed her findings back to him, but he and Mabel hadn't yet talked about her fears, and Stuart was careful not to press her, either for a discussion about getting married, or to be too intimate. He thought he'd waited long enough and now he wanted to be sure they had a future together.

He opened the door. 'Hello, love. That smells good.'

She turned. 'Hello, Stuart. Hold on while I test the cake.' She pulled a large cake out of the oven and placed it on an iron trivet. She pierced it in the centre with a knitting needle, pulled it out and examined it closely. 'Needs another five minutes.' She replaced the tin in the oven. 'Not sleuthing?'

He sat down on a chair at the table. 'No. Thought I'd come and see my best girl.'

Mabel took off her apron and ran a hand through her hair. 'Who's your second-best girl? Hope her name isn't

Ann Fenner.'

He shook his head. 'You're not going to let me live that one down, are you?'

'I should think not. Want a cup of tea? I'm afraid the walnut cake won't be ready for a bit, but I've got some scones left. I thought I'd make a cake as we're only having sandwiches tonight.'

'Perhaps a bit later. I think we need to have a talk, Mabel. A talk about our future. Everyone's out, even Dorothy; she's gone to see a friend. This is a good time. What do you say?'

Mabel stared at him. 'All right. Let me finish off this cake, then we'll talk.'

He watched her as she busied herself at the sink, checked the clock on the wall, took out the cake and tested it again. 'That's fine. I'll let it sit in the tin for twenty minutes before I turn it out. Thought I'd put cream-frost on the top and some extra walnuts. What do you think?'

He got up and inspected the cake. 'Looks perfect to me without all the other stuff. Almost as perfect as you.' He put an arm round Mabel's waist and gently pulled her to him.

'Stuart Elderkin, flattery will get you anywhere.'

'I hope so.' He kissed her and she put her arms round his neck and kissed him back. 'That was better than any cake.'

Mabel chuckled. 'Knowing you, you want to have your cake and eat it!'

'You know sweet things are my downfall, and you taste sweet today.'

Mabel pushed him away gently. 'We were going to

260

talk, remember?'

He took hold of her hand. 'We did, but I think I prefer action myself.'

Mabel sat down and pointed to a chair on the opposite side of the table. 'You go first. You start off.'

Stuart breathed deeply, remembered the warmth of Mabel's kiss and took courage. 'I love you, Mabel Grill. I've told you that before, and I want to marry you. You've driven me potty this last month or so, but now Laurel's explained what's the matter I understand. How do *you* feel? Do you love me and do you want to get married? If you don't want to … be intimate, I have to tell you I'm willing to give married life a go even if we can't …I'd rather be with you, even if we couldn't … you know, than be without you. I'm no Casanova, and I'd try and control myself, but you might have to smack me down now and then, 'cos you're a lovely looking woman, Mabel and I am only human, after all.' He slumped back in his chair exhausted by the effort.

Mabel put a hand to her mouth.

He couldn't be sure if the sound she was making was a sob or a laugh. 'What do you say, Mabel?'

She reached across the table for his hand. 'Stuart Elderkin, that was the loveliest speech I've ever heard. I do love you and I will marry you. As for the other thing … Laurel's got me something to help … you know.' She hung her head, 'I think it'll be all right. We may have to take it slowly.'

He squeezed her hand. 'That's all right, love, I was always a slow burner.'

'I think we'd be better starting off in your bungalow. It's not too far from here. I'd be nervous making love with all the others round us, well Laurel and Dorothy. I know they'd be discreet, but that's what I'd prefer.'

He gave her hand another squeeze. 'Then that's what we'll do. I'll get someone in to do some decorating; it needs a few coats of paint. Would you like a new kitchen?'

Her eyes sparkled. 'I certainly would! Can I choose it?'

He smiled broadly. 'Of course, I'll get you the best kitchen I can.'

'Thank you, Stuart.'

'So, can we set a date for the wedding?'

'I don't see why not. Spring's a lovely time to get married.' She jumped up. 'All this talk of love and marriage has made me forget my cake. I don't want it sticking to the tin.'

The sandwich supper was over and they'd moved to the sitting room. It was a chilly evening and Frank put another log on the fire. It was seven, the end of the day, and a clear sky was full of stars. Dorothy pulled the curtains together.

'Nancy had no objections to lending you the key to the Harrops' house?' Frank asked Laurel.

'No. We had a long talk. I asked her if she knew if Sam was attracted to children.' She told them of their conversation.

Dorothy blew her nose. 'That must have been hard for her, to think Sam was a pervert, I can't believe it myself, but I suppose after finding out the headmaster I worked closely with for years was a mass murderer, I should know better.'

'One thing Nancy said has stuck in my mind; one of her mother's sayings was: no one knows what they'll do until the right temptation comes along. We might think we'd never do something dreadful, until something unexpected happens and then it's too late. I find that frightening.'

Was that aimed at him? Frank thought. But she was right. It had been the right temptation, and he'd nearly given in to it. If Carol had been subtle, less pushy, he could easily have taken the next step. His throat tightened as he imagined making love to her, and immediately he was thankful he hadn't gone that far. His balls said yes, his heart and mind said no. 'Revie's said he'd phone me with details of the death certificates this evening.'

'He's being very cooperative. It must have been all the bacon sandwiches I gave him,' Mabel said.

Stuart puffed on his pipe. 'Frank told him we were going to have another look at the Harrops' house. He didn't object but asked to be informed if we found anything of interest. Said he couldn't see it as they'd been through it with a fine toothcomb. He's certainly playing along, which I didn't think would happen.'

'Revie doesn't mind using us if it helps him climb the greasy pole. As long as we don't let on to the top brass that we're working together, he'll be cooperative.' Frank turned to Mabel. 'I'm sure the bacon butties were the winning factor.'

'Flatterer,' Mabel said.

Laurel told them about Tucker and his invitation to lunch the next day.

'It could be useful, Laurel,' Dorothy said. 'We haven't any idea what happened to David. If something awful is happening at the school, that's a reason for David not wanting to go back there, but it doesn't help us find him.'

'I feel sorry for his parents; it must be awful not knowing what happened to him. Even finding his body, although that would be the end of hope, would be better than nothing,' Mabel said.

'Where does Tucker live?' Frank asked.

Laurel passed him the sketch map and instructions Tucker had given to her.

'It's out of the way,' Frank commented. 'Anyone been there?'

The rest shook their heads.

'Can I see?' Dorothy asked. Frank passed the piece of paper to her, and Mabel, who was sitting on the sofa next to her, looked at it as well. 'It's quite close to the Maltings.' Dorothy got up and left the room and came back with an Ordnance Survey map of the area. 'Look, Laurel, if you take the B1069 to Snape, keep going past the Maltings, then soon after, take the right fork down a narrow road to Blaxhall, and then another right to his house. If you get to Tunstall you've missed it.'

'Thanks. Can I borrow the map?' Laurel asked.

Frank put out a hand. 'Can I see?' He studied it for a few minutes, tapped on part of it and passed it to Stuart.

Stuart pursed his lips. 'Laurel, his house isn't far from Chillingworth School. Three, or four miles at the most along narrow roads.' He frowned. 'Any possible connection?'

Laurel slowly shook her head. 'None whatever. Except for the art connection with David. He was open about inviting me, and if I can interest these arty friends it may be of some help. I know it's a tentative hope, but as we haven't got any other way of finding David at the moment, a long shot is better than nothing. What do you think, Frank?'

Frank rubbed his chin; it'd been smooth after his morning shave but now the bristles irritated him. Would he ever discover a decent razor? 'It just seems a bit of a coincidence his house being so close to the school, but, as you say, there's nothing else to connect him with the case. We know where you'll be. What time will you be back?'

'I'm not sure.' She pulled a face, presumably adding up the time. 'Say by four at the latest. Will you still be at the Harrops'?'

Frank looked at Stuart. 'Who knows? You could call in on your way back; go to Aldeburgh instead of heading for Dunwich.'

Laurel nodded. 'OK, I'll do that.'

The phone in the hall rang. Frank jumped up.

'Frank Diamond speaking.'

Revie's Birmingham accent twanged in his ear. 'It's Revie here. I've got some interesting news for you.'

'Yes?' Come on man, spit it out.

'We've got copies of the two death certificates.'

'Yes?' God, Revie was enjoying this.

'Peter Mobbs and the other boy, Roy Franks.'

'Yes? Come on, Revie, stop farting around.'

There was a wheezy chuckle on the other end of the line. 'My mother said I enjoyed power.'

'If you don't cough up soon, I'm going to crawl down this phone line, get hold of your tonsils and turn you inside out!'

More wheezy laughter. Then silence. 'I shouldn't be laughing. The man was a disgrace to his profession.'

265

'Who was?' He knew, but he needed to have it confirmed.

'Dr Samuel Harrop. His name is on both death certificates.'

When Frank told them they sat in shocked silence. Both Laurel and Stuart had half-expected the news, but Dorothy and Mabel were stunned.

'Who can you trust if you can't trust doctors?' Mabel asked. 'Does that mean those boys were murdered?'

'Possibly,' Frank said, 'but it will be difficult to prove. They were both orphanage boys and both bodies, Revie tells me, were cremated.'

'So now we have the connection between Harrop and the school, plus the connection between Luxton and the school. Harrop knew he was dying and possibly wanted to confess, Luxton was almost having a nervous breakdown, he nearly told Laurel why he was scared; he'd have been a danger to someone,' Frank said.

'Who do you think that someone is?' Laurel asked the others.

'Someone at the school?' Dorothy queried.

'Baron, the headmaster, was at the back of the hall when Luxton collapsed. He'd have seen how frail and nervous he was,' Stuart said.

'Baron's lifestyle: his collection of art work, his clothes and watch, suggest someone with an income far above that of a headteacher of a small school. Did you find out any more about his background, Stuart?'

'I put out a few feelers; asked round some of my ex-colleagues. Haven't heard anything back yet.'

Frank stood up. 'I'm off for an early night. Want a lift,

Stuart?'

'No, I've got my car here, thanks. But before you go, Frank, Mabel and me, we've got some news for all of you.'

Frank stopped at the door and smiled at him. 'Good news, I hope?'

Stuart went to Mabel and took her hand and she stood up beside him. He nudged her.

'Stuart and me, we've set a date. We're getting married on Saturday, 29th May, and you're all invited, so I don't want any more murders or suicides round that date. It's not quite definite as we don't know if the church will be free. We'd like to get married here, at Dunwich.'

'Don't worry,' Dorothy said, 'I'll talk to the vicar, it'll be free!'

Laurel laughed. 'Dorothy Piff, you're a bully.'

Frank walked back into the centre of the room. 'I think I'll forget the early night, this calls for a celebration. Got anything interesting, Dorothy?'

Dorothy squared her shoulders. 'I always keep a bottle of bubbly on ice, just in case something special comes along.'

'And if it doesn't?' Laurel asked.

'Then I've been known to invent a happening. Sometimes it's good to celebrate the first snowdrop, a returning swallow, or the first log fire of the winter.' She marched to the kitchen.

'Frank,' Stuart asked, 'would you do me the honour of being my best man?'

Frank bit his lip, then rubbed his finger over it. 'Stuart, I'd be honoured. Thank you.'

'You'll have to wear a suit,' Laurel said and Mabel

laughed.

'I'll wear tails, if it'll make you both happy.'

Dorothy returned with a bottle and five champagne glasses. Frank pushed up the cork and toasted Mabel and Stuart. Champagne wasn't his favourite drink, but the liquid bubbles scoured his tongue and helped to partly erase the foul taste of young lives wasted.

Chapter 24

Wednesday, 17th March, 1971

Frank unlocked the front door of the Harrops' house; he should think of it as Nancy's house now. He was sure she'd never want to live in it, and because of its recent history he couldn't imagine anyone else would. He pushed open the heavy door, half-expecting to see the hanging body of Clara Harrop in front of him. He turned and held the door open for Stuart, who was carrying a shopping bag.

'Mabel packed us some sandwiches and a thermos of coffee,' he said.

'All's well that ends well?'

Stuart smirked. 'I feel a new man. I can tell you she put me through the wringer, but I think we'll be all right now.'

'Women, eh?' Frank said, pulling a face.

Stuart stared at him. 'What about, you know … Mrs Pemberton? Is that all finished?'

Frank closed the door behind them. 'Yes. As far as I'm concerned, but who knows what might happen if she chooses to be vindictive? I was a fool, or to more precise, I let lust win over common sense.'

'You're only human, and she is a cracker.'

'I let my infatuation with her cloud my judgement. I took an instant dislike to her husband for no good reason, and because of that I may have missed some vital clues. We're no nearer to finding David, or what happened to him, than at the beginning of the investigation.'

They went to the kitchen and Stuart placed the shopping bag on the table. 'I don't know, we've got a connection between the school, Harrop and Luxton, and we think we know why David didn't want to go back there. Hopefully Revie will be able to search the school. Who knows what he may find?'

'Let's hope it's not dead bodies. At least some of the children may be saved from molestation, or even death. I wish we'd known when we went there.'

Stuart grimaced and struck his right fist into his left palm. 'Too right. From what you told me, that Gary Salmon is a nutcase.' He peeped into the shopping bag. 'Not sure if I feel like having a picnic in this house.'

Frank nodded in agreement. 'I'm with you there. We'll search the house from the proverbial top to bottom, and break for lunch at the Cross Keys when we've finished upstairs. Or we can picnic on the beach?'

Stuart shuddered. 'Too cold. We can eat the sandwiches in the car on the way home. I daren't take them back. Got to keep in her good books.'

Frank looked at his watch. 'Right, it's ten o'clock. Let's make a start.' He passed a pair of cotton gloves to Stuart. 'I promised Revie we'd wear these. He was pretty scathing, said if we found anything of value he'd buy the five of us a slap-up lunch at The Wentworth.'

'That's made my eyesight sharper. By the way, what are we looking for?'

Frank blew out his lips. 'God knows, I certainly don't.'

Laurel drove past The Maltings at Snape; it was a wonderful setting for the concert hall: close to the river Alde and surrounded by marshes. She must book and go to one of the concerts at the Music Festival in June. She took a right-hand fork into a narrow lane, wide enough for one vehicle. The dense, overhanging hedgerows were bare, except for stretches of blackthorn blossom. She slowed down and turned right between two brick pillars into a short, tarmacked drive with mown grass on each side. At the end was a Georgian house; its regimented architecture didn't appeal to her, but it had its admirers, and Tucker must be one of them. A Land Rover and a Mercedes sat on a parking space in front of the house, which she had to admit was handsomely proportioned. There was an imposing central door, with two long windows on each side. The house was topped off with a gently sloping tiled roof with chimneys at each end. The art business must be good.

As she walked to the door it was opened by Hager, Tucker's assistant. He bowed slightly. She felt like the visiting lady from the next-door manor.

She held out her hand. 'Hello, Mr Hager.'

He gave her a brief and painful handshake. She felt the bones crunch.

'You don't know your own strength, Mr Hager.'

'I'm sorry, Miss Bowman. Did I hurt you?'

He didn't sound sorry. 'Hardly at all. Where is Mr Tucker?'

'This way, please.'

He led her into a marble-floored hall, sparsely furnished with three hall chairs and a two-tiered hat and coat stand. A wide central staircase led to the first floor. He opened a door on the right.

'This is the parlour. Please take a seat, Mr Tucker will be with you in a few minutes.'

The ceiling was high, and the two sash windows made the room light and airy. The mahogany furniture matched the period of the house: a tall bookcase, three settees and a couple of armchairs on either side of a marble fireplace. Over this was an oil painting; it showed a young boy playing a musical instrument – a lute? He was dark-haired with peachy skin, his ruby-red lips half-open. The light from an oil lamp lit his face and created shadows. A man, half-hidden, watched him. It was beautifully and skilfully painted, but disturbing.

'Miss Bowman, Laurel, I see you're admiring my Caravaggio.'

She hadn't heard him come into the room. 'Mr Tucker, Ben. Is it really a Caravaggio?'

He laughed. 'I wish it was; it's a good copy, not modern. Perhaps by one of his followers.'

It was the only painting in the room, but there were light patches on the walls where other paintings had hung. 'Are you changing your collection here as well as Aldeburgh?'

'Ever the detective, eh? Yes, I've moved some to my gallery in London. My collection is an ever-changing scene. I might keep a painting for a few months, a few years, then if the price is right I sell it.'

She wondered where the other guests were. There was no sign of any one else. 'Are your guests in the garden?'

'I have to apologise, Miss Bowman, my friends had to leave this morning. Such a pity. I tried to phone you but couldn't get through. However, I have briefed them about David and his particular style. They've promised to let me know immediately if they come across any of his work. If they do, I'll get in touch with you or Mr Diamond.'

Prickles of suspicion raced down her backbone. Why hadn't he been able to phone her? The telephones were working at Greyfriars.

'That's a pity. Perhaps, if you don't mind, I'll not stay for lunch. I need to meet Mr Diamond and Mr Elderkin in Aldeburgh.'

He pulled a distressed face. 'Oh, but you *must* stay, poor Hager has spent all morning preparing the food. He'll be dreadfully hurt if you go, and I won't be able to eat everything. Please stay.'

'I didn't realise Hager was also your cook as well as your assistant in the gallery.'

'He's a wonder, can turn his hand to anything.'

Including trying to break *my* hand, she thought.

'You will stay, won't you? Oysters from Orford for the first course,' he said, looking like a schoolboy who wanted his favourite catapult returned.

She laughed. 'Thank you, I will.' What harm was there in a few hours eating delicious food? Frank would be jealous when she recited the menu.

'Thank you. Let's go to the eating room, to give it it's Georgian title.' He led her to the room opposite the parlour. It was a similar size and again filled with mahogany furniture: an elegant table and six dining chairs, a sideboard displaying silver dishes and a wine cooler holding two bottles of wine. The table was set with silver cutlery and sparkling glasses.

Dining at Greyfriars was always civilised, but this was over the top for a casual lunch. She was pleased she was wearing her best blue suit and high heels.

'Goodness, Mr Tucker, this is very impressive. The table looks beautiful.'

'Thank you. I do like having guests, especially one whose beauty matches the surroundings. It's my weakness – beauty.'

Laurel smiled at him, not sure what to say. Was that

his right temptation? Beautiful objects? Somehow, although he'd paid her a compliment, she didn't get the feeling women would interest him. Would men? What was his relationship with Hager? She couldn't see it herself – Hager wasn't ugly, but she didn't find him attractive.

He pulled out one of the chairs for her, and Hager appeared carrying two oyster dishes. Frank would be mad.

He placed one of the dishes in front of her. His animosity seemed to seep across the air between them. He was not happy playing at waiter.

'Thank you, Mr Hager. They look delicious. A real treat.'

He nodded curtly, served Tucker, and took one of the bottles from the wine cooler. The ice clinked against the lead liner. He poured some into her wine glass.

'Thank you, not too much, I've got to drive back to Aldeburgh.'

He didn't reply, poured wine into Tucker's glass and left the room.

She chewed on an oyster, savouring its unique flavour, then took a sip of wine. Goodness, that was good. She looked at Tucker who was tipping an oyster down his throat: a swallower, such a waste.

'I'm not sure of the wine; it isn't Muscadet, is it?'

Tucker wiped his chin with a napkin. 'Certainly not, Sancerre, a much better match.'

She looked forward to re-educating Frank. 'I thought Mr Hager would be eating with us.'

Tucker, an oyster on its way to his mouth, paused. 'He's been too busy in the kitchen. My cook is on holiday, Hager's cooking is a temporary measure, but he has enough basic culinary training to fill in for a time.'

This was why the house seemed empty, Tucker and Hager the only occupants. A house this size would need a housekeeper, a cook, and certainly a gardener. It looked well-maintained so the lack of staff must be recent. It was unsettling, no one else in the house but herself, Tucker and Hager, the missing pictures, the copy of the Caravaggio with the boy looking at you with knowing eyes. But the oysters were delicious.

Tucker chatted away as Hager came back to clear the plates and then brought each of them a grilled Dover sole, sauté potatoes and some spinach. The flesh slid away from the bones and was perfectly cooked. Ten out of ten to Hager.

'I'm afraid Hager's culinary skills don't rise to puddings, so the last course is cheese,' Tucker said, as Hager, face like a frozen cod, placed a wooden board with several cheeses on it, in front of her. She cut two pieces, Camembert and a blue cheese. Hager was getting on her nerves and she noticed Tucker giving him an old-fashioned look and a slight shake of the head. What had she done to annoy him so much?

Laurel folded her napkin and placed it on the side plate. The meal was over as far as she was concerned; she needed to get back to Aldeburgh and see if Frank and Stuart had discovered anything. 'That was a delicious lunch, Ben. Mr Diamond will be upset when I tell him about the magnificence off the oysters and Dover sole.'

Tucker nibbled at a piece of Stilton. 'He's a bon viveur, is he, your Mr Diamond?'

Laurel smiled. 'He's a good cook.' She waited until Ben put down his knife. 'I must be off, but thank you once again.'

Tucker got up. 'A quick cup of coffee before you depart? Hager's already made it. We'll go back to the parlour, shall we?'

She would have liked to have given it a miss, but it would seem rude to refuse; and she'd drunk two glasses of wine, so perhaps it would be a good idea to have a coffee.

'Thank you.' The hours spent here had been a waste as

far as helping to find David. If she could have met Tucker's friends perhaps something might have come of it.

Kelvin Hager spooned freshly ground coffee into the cafetiere and filled it to the maximum mark with water which was just off the boil; he stirred it and placed the lid on, waited a few minutes and then pushed down the handle. He placed two cups and saucers on a tray with hot milk in a silver jug, and a bowl containing lumps of brown sugar.

He took two bottles from a cupboard. Which one should he use? Rohypnol or GHB? He'd have preferred to use the side of this hand and have done with it. Why had Tucker invited her here? He'd said it was a back-up, a bargaining tool, in case things went arse over tit. He didn't believe him. He felt like giving them both a dose and then finishing them off, but if Tucker died he'd be left as high and dry as a jellyfish on a beach.

He decided to use Rohypnol as GHB didn't mix well with alcohol, and the bitch had drunk two glasses of wine. She was a smug bastard, thought she was as good as a man. Because she'd bettered the headmaster everyone treated her like a hero. Pity the headmaster hadn't added her to his list of victims. But never mind, *he'd* add her to his list, which was much longer than the headmaster's. Nicholson was an amateur; *he* was a professional, a trained killer. How many had he seen off? He wasn't sure, he didn't keep a score, didn't put notches on his bedpost, or stick gold stars in a diary. He'd been cashiered from the army for violence – what did they expect? He'd met Tucker, or to put it another way, Tucker had engineered the meeting. He'd served him faithfully for fifteen years, with the promise when the time came for them to leave the country, he'd be well looked after. He'd have a high-level job in the government, one which suited his skills, plus a luxurious apartment and the finest whores Moscow could provide. He'd even learnt bloody Russian. Now he was suspicious. Tucker's attitude to him had recently changed. Did he intend to travel solo and leave him holding the can?

He wasn't sure. But if he found Tucker was double crossing him …Why make things more difficult by involving this bitch? What was Tucker up to making him cook lunch for her? Treating him like a servant? At the beginning, he'd enjoyed fooling the suckers who came to the house, because he knew what they were in for. How he'd scared them to death when they realised the shit they'd were in. The bluster soon stopped when they saw the evidence and he mentioned the names and addresses of their wives, children or lovers. A few cracks of his knuckles and a squeeze round their throats were enough to make them shit their trousers. Yes, he'd enjoyed that. Then Tucker made him nursemaid to that squit upstairs and now he was adding Miss Bloody Bowman to the menagerie.

He carefully measured some liquid from one of the bottles and poured it into a coffee cup. He poured out the coffee and picked up the tray. He entered the parlour and placed it on a low table; he handed one cup to the bitch.

'Cream? Sugar?'

'Cream, please, no sugar. Thank you for the lunch, Mr Hager.'

He smiled at her. She frowned.

277

'My pleasure, Miss Bowman.'

He half-bowed and silently left the room. He washed up while he waited. Waiting. Waiting. Fifteen years waiting. He was sick of mixing with old queens, buttering them up, listening to them braying away to Tucker, seeing their faces when after aphrodisiacs in their drinks, they'd been offered what they most desired. He was sick of filming them buggering children, although some of the old ones could only manage kissing and fondling. But it was enough. He was ready for a proper job. Searching out dissidents and making them squeal out their secrets. That was a proper work.

Tucker came into the kitchen. 'She's unconscious. What did you use? Rohypnol?'

Hager nodded.

'Minimal dose?'

'As you said.'

'Good. Take her upstairs, put her with him. Make sure you place her on her side.'

They went to the parlour. The bitch was lying on the settee, her head on a cushion, her mouth open, breathing heavily. She wasn't bad looking, good figure. He hadn't had a woman for a few weeks. The whores of Ipswich avoided him, didn't like his idea of playful sex. Tucker was looking at him. He picked her up, she was warm against him, her head lolling against his shoulder.

'You're not to touch her, that's an order,' Tucker barked. 'You'll have plenty of women soon enough.'

'Yes, sir.'

'I'll come up with you. I'll unlock the door.'

He doesn't trust me. And I don't trust him.

David, Age 13 Years and Seven Months

I don't want to go back. I won't go back. Daddy says I must. He asks me why I don't want to. I can't tell him. I promised Peter. He said if I tell, they will kill him. They will do terrible things to him. There's another boy. His name is John. Sometimes he sits with us. I don't like him as much as Peter. He is not happy. He never laughs. Even though Peter is scared he still makes me happy. I don't know what to do. If I tell they will kill Peter. If I don't tell they will keep on doing bad things to him. I know I should go back to school for Peter. He will be alone except for John. They've done things to him, too. Peter told me. John won't say. Peter tells me they go in the minibus to a big house. They're made to have drinks. It makes them all funny. There is a tall man and a short man, they are always there. The tall man gives them the drinks. Peter is more frightened of him than the short man. Then they go in a room and there are other men. Sometimes the same man, sometimes new men. The tall man and the short man go out of the room and the men do things to them, or they have to do things to the men. Sometimes the men kiss them and tell them they love them. Sometimes the men hurt them. If they tell anyone they will die.

Next week I have to go back to school. I draw John

and put him with my secrets. He is frightened. Why do these men do this? Why doesn't Mr Baron stop it? Does he know? Mr Salmon drives the mini-bus. He must know it's wrong. The men do it to them because they are orphans. John is an orphan. They have no mummies or daddies to tell. I'm afraid but I am angry. I hate all the teachers and the nurse. I'm not going back. I am going to run away, then I will go to the school at night and I will rescue Peter. If John wants to come with us he can. We'll run away together. We'll be happy. I can do drawings and sell them. We will live in a hut in the woods. We can catch rabbits and eat them.

I will find my way to the school. I can run and walk. I'll take a knife and if they try to stop me I'll stick it in them. They are bad so I think it's all right to do that. I'll plan what to take and when to go.

Daddy will be upset. I don't want him to worry. I'll do a drawing for him and send him a postcard and say I'm all right. I will write a sentence to Miss Fenner. I will not write to Mummy. Perhaps after a bit we can come home, I will tell Daddy what happened and the bad men will go to prison. Peter will live with us. Miss Fenner will make a special cake. We'll all be happy.

Chapter 25

Tucker followed Hager up the stairway to a first-floor room at the back of the house. Hager carried Laurel without any effort; Tucker would never cease to be amazed by his strength. He unlocked the door; beneath its veneer of mahogany was solid steel. Hager would never be able to break it down, and Tucker would have both the keys on him when he left.

Hager slid Laurel onto the single bed and put her in the recovery position. The room was empty; David must be in the bathroom. He often hid in there when he heard the door opening. No time to coax him out today.

'Good. Go downstairs, check the seals on the envelopes and put them in the hall. We don't want them splitting open in the post office. I'll lock the door. Have you everything ready for tonight?'

'Yes.'

'Please don't wear your protective vest.'

Hager glowered. 'Why not?'

'If we get stopped and searched at Customs it will raise questions.'

'OK.'

'You're quite sure this is what you want? There'll be no going back, Kelvin. Once the newspapers get the information all hell will be let loose.'

Hager stared at him, his face blank. 'We've talked about this many times. I want out. I want the job you promised me. Why would I change my mind now?'

It was a mistake to have brought it up. Trying to prevent Hager from killing them was taking his mind away from the main task. 'Just making sure. I don't want any last-minute regrets.'

'I don't do regrets.'

How true. 'Very well. Carry on.'

Hager took one last glance at Laurel Bowman, his gaze lingering over her long legs, which were exposed to the thighs as her skirt had ridden up. He turned abruptly and left the room. Tucker gently pulled down her skirt. It had been an impulse to involve her in his plans, but he knew when she didn't return to Greyfriars, or the meeting in Aldeburgh, someone from the agency would come here to find her. They knew where she was and when they found her, they would find David.

Hager had no regrets, but did he? Should he have settled for a life of mediocrity? One of many small cogs in London's art world? A safe life, but one where he'd have been consumed by perpetual jealousy as other people took the posts that should have been his. He'd been passed over so often; first the Tate, then the Royal Academy, the Victoria and Albert and even some provincial galleries. His face didn't fit. He wasn't friends with cabinet ministers who had the power to open doors. He wasn't part of the old boys' network. The bloody establishment. They were going to pay. He wished he could be here, in England, when the scandal broke.

Their approach had been subtle. Sympathising, flattering; saying he wasn't appreciated in his own country. He wasn't so naïve he didn't know what they were up to, but he wanted to see what they proposed, what was in it for him. The offer had to be worth taking such enormous risks for. When they explained their plan his mind was blown away. It was ingenious, breath-taking, and the power he's been denied by the establishment would be his. It was a long-term plan, nothing was rushed, and money was no object. He'd thought of nothing else once he accepted their offer. The meetings with agents and the attention to details was exciting, and after the success of the gallery in London, it's sister gallery in Aldeburgh and the setting up of the school, everything was in place.

Regrets? Yes, regrets it was finished. He'd been ordered to bring the project to a conclusion. The time was right. Great Britain was entering a period of strikes and unrest, fomented by left-wing activists. Some of the men he'd blackmailed, like Sam Harrop, were remorseful, or plain shit-scared, like Luxton. They had to be silenced. He couldn't afford premature discovery. By the time the police found out they'd been murdered he'd be away. He wasn't looking forward to a life in the Soviet Union, but they'd promised him control of one of the prestigious art museums.

Hager, what about him? He'd be glad to see the back of him. His usefulness was over. Russia had more than enough top-class killers to want another one. If and when he realised he'd been deserted and left to fend for himself, he'd look to destroy anything he could. He'd want to make it personal, kill someone he treasured, and because she was with David, Laurel Bowman would also die. He thought Hager would try to kill them, even before he

283

discovered he'd been double-crossed. But he had both keys to the steel door, and Laurel Bowman to protect David. Diamond, or another colleague, would come to find her. He would have saved one he held dear.

He looked at Laurel Bowman. He liked her: she was decent, intelligent, with a positive attitude to life. He hoped Hager didn't manage to get through the door. She'd shown great courage fighting Nicholson, but he was an amateur killer, driven by lust for young girls. Hager was a killing machine, with no sympathy for any man, woman or child. Tucker had seen what he was prepared to do. What's more Hager enjoyed his work.

Tucker took a parcel from inside his jacket and placed it beside Laurel. He put two fingers on her neck – her pulse was steady. She groaned. Was she coming to? Time to leave. Good luck, Laurel Bowman. He was hoping he wouldn't have to depend on her fighting spirit. If he did, she'd be fighting not only for her life, but for someone else's, too.

David, 15 years Old

The door thuds. I can't hear them talking. They've gone. Why did they come? Why both together? I'm glad Hager didn't come alone. He hates me. I hate him. I hate both of them, but him most of all. I open the bathroom door just a little. If he's there I'll shut the door and push it tight. There's no lock. When I do that he laughs and goes out, but sometimes he shouts and forces the door open. He doesn't hit me. He isn't allowed. He shouts horrible things. What he'll do to me one day. How he'll kill me. He tells me what he did to Peter, because it makes me cry. Peter is dead. I saw him when I went back to the school. He was on a bed in the sick room. All cold and white.

I look into the room. They've gone but there's someone on my bed. Is it a trap? Will this person spring up and kill me? It's a woman. She is the first new person I've seen for nearly two years. I go closer. She is asleep. She is tall with fair hair. Why is she here? Have they drugged her like they drugged me? I like her face. She reminds me of someone in a painting. It's in one of the books Tucker gave me. I have an easel, paper, paints, pencils, anything I want. I have newspapers, books, a record player and a tape cassette. I have a colour television. I have nice meals, and lots of tea and coffee, also lemonade, chocolates and sweets. He gives me everything except the one thing I long for. I cannot leave this room. I want to go home.

I ask Tucker why he doesn't let Hager kill me like Peter? He says I am a genius. It would be sacrilege to kill me. He promises one day I will be free again. When all he has to do is over. Hager says he will kill me. But first he will make me hurt. I have been here so long I don't care anymore. No, that's a lie. I'm scared of Hager and what he might do.

I go to the bathroom, wet a flannel and wipe her face. I would like to draw her. I will when there is time. If there ever is. Why have they brought her here? Did she come to rescue me? She moans. Her eyelids flutter open. She has blue eyes. She tries to focus on me. She looks shocked. Her mouth opens wide; her eyes stare at me.

'David?' she asks.

She knows who I am. 'Yes, I'm David.'

Chapter 26

Laurel felt something rough and wet moving over her face, like the tongue of a gentle dog. Was it Billy, Dr Neave's Labrador? Was he licking her back to life? She tried to move her head, it was full of lead shot, rattling round her brain, rolling from one side to the other, hurting, making her head heavy. Her tongue was stuck to the roof of her mouth, which was full of a horrible salty taste. Water. She needed water. She felt a movement as someone sat down beside her. She was on a bed. Who was next to her? Where was she? What had happened?

Having coffee. Drinking it. The chair under her starting to move. Her eyes unable to focus. The face of Ben Tucker, close to her, changing shape like a reflection in a fairground mirror. Staring. Then blackness. Drugged. She'd been drugged.

Who was he, the person beside her? Was she ill? Was she in hospital? The lunch. Hager waiting on them. Waves of dislike pouring from him. Was it Hager next to her? Panic surged from her guts to her throat. Must open her eyes. Her eyelids were sticky. She blinked several times as she tried to open them. The light hurt them. A face was looking at her. It wasn't Tucker. It wasn't Hager. It wasn't Frank.

The bright light made it difficult to see his face. She

blinked again. He was a boy, a teenager, with black hair down to the collar of his jumper. His eyes were dark blue, his face as pale as milk. Was he the Caravaggio boy, the one in the painting in Tucker's parlour? Had he come to life and stepped down from the picture? This boy was as beautiful. Her breath stopped. No. It couldn't be. But it was. It was him. She knew his face. He wasn't the boy in the painting. She'd seen him in a photograph in his file. Mounting excitement pushed away the pain in her head. Bubbles of joy exploded in her heart and brain. She couldn't believe who she was seeing. She thought he would be dead, lying in some cold grave. He was alive.

'David?'

'Yes, I'm David.'

'David Pemberton?'

'Yes. How do you know who I am?'

She tried to sit up. Her brain whirled round and she collapsed back.

He put a pillow behind her head.

'Thank you. Have you any water? My mouth tastes as though it's full of chicken shit.'

He laughed, went into another room and came back with a glass full of water. He held it as she drank. It tasted wonderful and washed away the stale salty taste.

'Thank you. My name is Laurel Bowman, I'm a private detective. We've been looking for you.'

He looked at her as though he couldn't believe her words. 'After all this time? I'd given up hope anyone would find me.'

'Your parents have never given up hope. The police searched for you, and we're the second firm of detectives your parents have hired.'

His eyes filled with tears. 'I should have told Daddy … If I'd told him this wouldn't have happened … Peter would be alive.'

'You know about Peter? How do you know?' God, she felt as weak as a young child. She took several deep breaths

He opened his mouth as if to say something, his lips trembling, opening and closing.

She remembered about his dislike of speaking; but he'd spoken fluently, with only small hesitancies between words.

'David, I know you don't like talking, but we're in a serious situation. I need you to tell me about how you came to be here, and as much as you can about Tucker and Hager.' A wave of panic passed through her. She wasn't either physically or mentally up to dealing with this. 'The good news is the other detectives know where I am. They'll come here when I don't go back.' She had a horrible thought. 'Are we in Tucker's house? Or have they moved me?'

He stared at her.

She tried to smile, willing him to speak.

He opened his mouth, his lips trembling. 'I don't know where we are … I've only been out of the house a few times. Tucker drove me in his car, but Hager was in the back with me all the time … They took me to places where I could see old buildings … I wasn't allowed out of the car. Tucker wanted me to draw what I saw, but I was frightened of Hager, and I didn't see why I should draw what Tucker wanted. I only draw what I want to draw.' His voice gained in strength as he spoke.

They hadn't broken his spirit, he still had that

determined look she'd seen in the photograph. She must try to seem confident for his sake. 'What did the house look like from the outside?'

He described the house she'd entered that day. 'Thank goodness. We're in the same place, that's something.'

'You mean we'll be rescued?'

'Yes, I'm sure we will.' She made her voice strong and definite. 'But, I need you to tell me why they brought you here and why they've kept you here all this time.'

'You mean why haven't they killed me? Hager wants to kill me, but Tucker doesn't and he's the boss … He says I'm a genius and he'll make sure when the project is over I'll be freed.'

'What's the project?'

'I don't know, but I think it's nearly complete. Tucker is getting edgy and Hager's angry and keeps telling me how he's going to kill me … He doesn't say that when Tucker's there.'

'David, we know you ran away from home, and you didn't want to go back to the school. Where did you go to?'

'I did go to the school. I was going to rescue Peter. Then we would run away together.'

Dear Lord, what a brave and foolish boy. 'What happened?'

David gulped. He shook his head.

'Please try, David. I need all the information you can give me, and I need it quickly.'

'Does it matter if your friends are coming?'

She decided to tell him her fears. 'We can't depend on Tucker leaving us alive. We need to make plans in case things go wrong. My friends will come, but perhaps not for several hours. We need to be prepared for anything. Does that make sense to you?'

The urgency of her voice seemed to have got through to him. 'Yes. If Hager has his way, he'll kill me.'

Me as well, she thought. 'I don't know why they've involved me. I think it must have been Tucker's idea. Hager can't stand the sight of me. Perhaps Tucker thinks my friends will come to find me, and if they find me, they'll find you.' She looked into his frightened eyes, willing him to put aside his phobias and fears. 'David, I need to know.'

He swallowed, his adolescent Adam's apple bobbing up and down. She wanted to hug him close and tell him everything would be all right, but there wasn't time and she'd remembered he didn't like being touched.

'I ran and walked to the school. I'd planned a way there using lanes and going across fields. It took me ages; I slept in a barn. It was the evening of the next day when I got there. I went in through a back door and I hid until it was night and everyone was in bed. I went up the stairs to the dormitory where Peter slept with the other boys from the orphanage. It was the holidays so there weren't many staff about. There was only John there, he said Peter was in the sick room, he wasn't well. I told John about my plan and asked him if he'd like to come with us. He told me to go away. He'd get into trouble. He pulled a sheet over his head.'

He was agitated, his eyes flickering with pain. 'I went to the sick room. There was a light on. I opened the door a little. On a bed was a body covered with a sheet. My heart was trying to escape from my chest. I couldn't breathe. Who was it? Was he dead? My legs wouldn't move. I was

291

stuck in the doorway. Then as I looked at the shape under the white sheet something happened to me. It was like a boiling in my guts, it bubbled and steamed up through my chest, up my throat to my head. I was hot with anger. I went to the bed and turned down the sheet. It was Peter. He was cold and when I put my hand on his face my skin seemed to sizzle. My best friend. My only friend. Dead. There was a great roaring sound. It was me. I howled.

'They came running in. The nurse and Mr Salmon. They grabbed me. He hit me and I went down. The nurse got a needle and stuck it in me. It went black. When I came round I was here in this room. With Tucker.'

Her skin turned into a sheet of ice. Such words from a child's lips. She'd loved working with children. Seeing their adult characters emerge from childish bodies. Rejoicing in them as they started out on their journeys through life. To hear this. She wouldn't let another life be wasted. She reached for the water and took another drink.

'Thank you for telling me, David.' She was beginning to feel more human; she risked putting her feet on the carpeted floor and, grasping the side of the bed, made a few tentative steps. 'Could I have some more water?' she asked, holding out the glass to him. She looked round the room. It was spacious, with a chest of drawers, a bookcase stuffed with books, a television, and a record player with piles of 45s and 78s beside it. This part of the room was carpeted, the rest was bare boards, with an easel, shelves for paper, paints, brushes, pencils, charcoal. Everything an artist would need. A large window let in light. She staggered over to it – no sign of the sun. A northerly aspect? Perfect for an artist. Except for the steel bars running vertically from top to bottom.

David came into the room carrying the glass of water. She drank half of it.

'Bathroom?' she asked.

'Yes. Do you want to use it?'

'Please.' Thank God for that. It was well equipped with a washbasin, shower and lavatory. She used the loo, then threw cold water over her face. She looked at her reflection in the mirror over the basin. What a fright! Her hair was wild, and the pupils of her eyes dilated. She tried to contain the anger surging through her body. The slimy bastards. Keeping David prisoner all this time. What had that done to him? How was he going to cope with life after what he knew had happened to Peter, after Hager's frightening taunts and the perpetual fear of his own death? How dare Tucker drug her and imprison her here in this room? She threw more cold water over her face and shook her body. No time for anger now. She must think what they would do, could do, if either of the bastards came to finish them off.

She went back to David and drank more water. She must try to get rid of the poisons in her body. Flush them down the loo.

David came towards her with a long slim parcel. 'Tucker left this. I think it's for you.'

Laurel took it and squeezed the packaging. Something long and hard. 'Is he fond of giving presents?'

David waved a hand at the TV, record player and radio. 'Anything I asked for he gave me, except the one thing I really wanted.'

She tore at the packaging.

'Sorry, I haven't got anything sharp. He wouldn't give me scissors.'

She looked up. 'In case ...?'

'Yes, in case I tried to kill myself.'

'Do you think you would have done?'

His face was grave. 'I might have. It was sucking me dry. I wasn't even doing much drawing. I drew a few things I saw on the television. I don't feel like that now. Now you've come'

'Good.' Laurel continued to rip at the paper. At last the Sellotape submitted. She unwrapped the brown paper. Inside was a long, slender knife. Its blade sharpened on both sides. A stiletto dagger. She showed it to David.

'It's a message, isn't it?'

'Yes, it means we may have to fight.'

Chapter 27

Frank and Stuart returned from the Cross Keys to continue their search of the house. They'd limited their alcoholic intake to half a pint each of Adnams' Best Bitter, but hadn't held back on the food. Cod and chips, twice, and a large piece of Black Forest gateaux for Stuart. They drank the coffee Mabel had made for them in the kitchen.

Frank wasn't sure if it was the amount of carbohydrates he'd eaten, or the fruitlessness of the morning search, but he felt low. Why were they doing this? The police had gone through it with a fine toothcomb. All they'd discovered in Clara's bedroom was a wardrobe full of expensive clothing, and a dressing table covered with perfumes, lotions and unguents by Nina Ricci, Dior and Worth. In contrast Sam's bedroom was as Spartan as a monk's cell. Frank wouldn't have been surprised to find a hair shirt.

'Which room shall we start in?' Stuart asked.

'I don't think we'll find anything in the kitchen and there isn't much left in Sam's study, so we may as well start with the sitting room.'

'Where he listened to music?'

'Yes. Gloves on.' He passed Stuart a pair. 'We'll do this room while we're reasonably fresh, but I must say I think we're wasting our time.'

'Come on, Frank. That's not like you. There must be some link between Sam and the school. His signing the death certificates of those two boys can't be a coincidence.'

Frank bit his lip. 'Sam Harrop was riddled with guilt; he wanted to see Nancy, perhaps to confess. He knew his time was nearly up. I was hoping he might have hidden a written confession, one that would nail the people at the school, especially Baron and Gary Salmon.'

'Not to mention that foul matron, I didn't like her at all.'

They went into the sitting room. Already it had an air of desertion, of lives over. There was the settee, the resting place of Sam Harrop's body. Bile rose in Frank's throat at the memory of his rictus grin and swollen belly. A famous surgeon, a respected member of his profession, a man to whom the residents of Aldeburgh looked up, a lover of opera and classical music. A paedophile?

He went over to the music centre. 'What did Laurel say about Sam when she first saw him through the French windows?'

Stuart frowned. 'She said she didn't see him at first as his dressing gown blended in with the wallpaper.'

'That's right. Where was he?'

Stuart shook his head. 'Why are you asking me? You know perfectly well what she said. Also, she wrote it in her report.'

He smiled at him. 'I know, Stuart, but I like you telling me.'

Stuart took out his pipe and tobacco pouch. 'In that case, I'm having a few puffs. Helps me to concentrate.'

He tamped down the shag tobacco and lit a match. He drew in air through the pipe until a satisfactory glow was produced. 'That's better.' He sat down in one of the armchairs. 'She said he was by the music centre with his hand over the cassettes.'

He looked at the record player, and cassette machine. Expensive equipment. The cassette machine had an external microphone; probably Sam used it to tape music recitals from Radio 3. 'The police looked inside all the LP covers, didn't they?'

Stuart nodded, sending plumes of smoke towards the ceiling. 'Worth going through them again?'

'No. But what about the cassettes?'

'They looked in all of those as well, didn't find anything, though you couldn't get much in them.'

Frank rubbed his chin. The bristles told him he needed another shave. He looked at his watch. Two o'clock. He'd shaved at seven that morning. He must have a high testosterone level, or more likely a rotten shaver. Perhaps he'd try a cut-throat razor. He shuddered. No, perhaps not. 'Stuart, there's equipment here for recording. This machine can record as well as play tape cassettes.'

'So?'

'Supposing Samuel Harrop recorded something onto a blank cassette?'

'You mean from an LP?'

'No, supposing he left a message. It's a possibility. He could hide it in one of the cassette covers.'

Stuart chewed on the end of his pipe. 'Possible. From the look of that equipment and all those LPs and tapes, he was keen on his music and well up with the technology. So how do we go about this?'

Frank raised his shoulders, then let them fall, emitting a long sigh. 'There's only one way. We have to methodically play every tape. It's a long shot. What do you think?'

Stuart got up, went to the fireplace, now empty of burnt papers, and banged out his pipe. 'Let's get on with it.'

Frank switched on the machine at the wall.

Stuart handed him the first tape. 'Mahler Symphony Number Four, the Royal Philharmonic Orchestra.'

He pressed the triangular start button and strains of a full orchestra filled the room. He pressed the square stop button. 'Next.'

'Puccini, *La Bohème*.'

A few seconds later. 'Next.'

'This could take some time,' Stuart said.

'Come on, next!'

'Keep your hair on. Here you are, Sir Adrian Boult conducts Vaughan Williams.'

Frank groaned.

An hour-and-a-half later they'd ploughed through half the cassettes.

'Handel arias by City of London Baroque Sinfonia,' Stuart said, wearily passing it to Frank. They listened. 'I always liked Handel, he was a good man. Did a lot of work with orphans in London.'

Frank didn't reply but took the cassette out of the machine and added it to the other rejects. Depression was setting in.

Stuart started on the next seam. 'Ah, English composers. Here you are, try this. Elgar, Symphony Number One.' They listened and it was ejected.

'OK, what about some Delius. Bit of a mixture this one.' The same result.

Stuart passed another cassette to Frank. 'Our local composer, Benjamin Britten. *Billy Budd*, London Symphony Orchestra.'

Frank held the cassette in his hand. *Billy Budd*, the opera. The fight between good and evil. In Laurel's report she'd noted Nancy had said he was Harrop's favourite composer. He looked at Stuart.

'Got a feeling about this one?'

'It's about an old sea captain recalling his part in the hanging of a young sailor, Billy Budd, and Claggart, the evil Master-at-Arms who wants Billy dead. We'll see.' The cover under the clear plastic showed the title, the names of the main singers and orchestra. He opened the plastic case. Inside was a cassette. It had no distinguishing labels to match the cover. Time seemed to stop as they looked at it. Frank almost didn't want to put it into the machine for fear of disappointment.

'For God's sake, put it in,' Stuart said. 'If it's blank, we'll just press on.'

Frank's fingers turned to putty, but he managed to click it in and to press the triangular play button.

Nothing, just the whirring of the tape. The day seemed to darken. Stuart groaned.

Then a voice. A reedy, hesitant, man's voice.

'My name is Samuel Harrop. I was born on the twenty-first of May, 1906, in Aldeburgh, Suffolk. This is my confession.'

Chapter 28

Laurel took hold of the stiletto by the ridged handle; it gave a good grip, and there was a short guard to protect the hand. She'd never used a knife as an offensive weapon; she wasn't sure she was up to sticking this one into either Tucker or Hager. If push came to shove – very appropriate – she'd have to.

David looked at her and then the dagger. 'Do you know how to use it?'

She tried to look confident. 'I haven't stabbed anyone lately, but I'm willing to do it if we need to defend ourselves.'

'I think you're supposed to stick it in and then move it round, so you damage the organs.'

Her back straightened. 'How do you know that?'

'Hager told me. He used to come to my room at night when Tucker was in bed. He liked to frighten me. He told me how he killed different people. That's how I know he'll kill me. He's told me too much.'

Bile rose in her throat. She grasped the handle tightly. A truly despicable man. 'Right. We need to make a plan so we can fight if one, or both of them, come for us. I hope we won't need to; Frank and Stuart should be here soon.' She glanced at her watch. Thank goodness they hadn't taken it. It was ten past four. She brought it to her

300

ear and heard its steady tick. They'd be expecting her soon. How long before they realised she should have returned? She tried not to let her worry show. It could be several hours before they became concerned. Why should they think anything was wrong? Tucker's invitation was open, and there was a good reason for going to his house.

'We've got a weapon. Hager won't be expecting that. I think we've got to presume Tucker is only interested in making sure you live, as he values your artistic skills. It will be Hager who comes to kill us. What else can we use as weapons? What can we throw at him?'

David seemed to come out of his reverie. 'I've got some heavy books.'

'Excellent!' Frank's word. Hurry up Frank.

'We could use LPs. I can take them out of their sleeves and we could slice them through the air.'

'Great. I'm rather handy with a discus so I can show you a few tricks. Have you got any chemicals? Things you use in your painting?'

David frowned. 'I've only got water colours. He wouldn't let me have oils, also I'm not keen on them.. We could mix some up with water. You mean to throw at him?'

She nodded. 'Into his eyes. Or we could dissolve some soap in water.' All this would be no use against a trained killer like Hager, but she had to try and raise David's morale. Make him think they had a chance.

'The basic plan is this. If you think of anything more, chip in. OK?'

David nodded.

She looked at the bed. There was a space underneath it. 'If we hear the door being unlocked this is what we must

301

do. You must go to the bathroom. Shut the door and keep him out for as long as you can. OK?'

David gulped.

'I'll get under the bed with the stiletto. We'll pull the covers down so I'm hidden. When he comes into the room it will look empty.' She hoped to God he would think so. 'He'll assume we're both in the bathroom and he'll try to get to us.'

David's face twisted with fear. 'Supposing he doesn't. He might look under the bed straight away.'

'That's a risk we'll have to take. Anyway, I'll have the dagger and I'm fit and strong.'

'You're not as strong as him. He likes to karate chop people. He told me. He said he killed a woman last week. He chopped her unconscious and hanged her from her own banisters.'

Clara Harrop. Her stomach tightened with fear. 'You mustn't believe everything he says. He's trying to frighten you. Come on, let me tell you the rest of the plan.'

'All right.' He didn't seem convinced. She desperately needed him to work with her. It was their only chance.

'You want to avenge Peter, don't you? He's worth fighting for. And all the other children.'

He sat with his head down. A tear wound its way from eye to mouth. He licked it. His head came up. 'Yes. They killed Peter. I hate them for that. I hate them for keeping me here. I hate Hager most of all. I wish he was dead. Then we'd be safe.'

'Good.' She risked reaching out her hand to him. She looked into his dark eyes. 'We'll fight him together.'

He took her hand and she pumped it up and down a few times. 'We're a team. David and Laurel. Fighters for

302

justice.'

'The two musketeers?'

'And soon there'll be four, when Frank and Stuart get here. Repeat the plan to me.'

David took a deep breath and pushed out his chest. 'You'll be under the bed and I'll be in the bathroom, I'll push on the door so he can't get in.'

'Excellent. We'll look and see if there's anything we can jam it with. He'll have his back to me as he tries to break into the bathroom. I'll creep out from the bed and stick the stiletto into him.'

David grimaced. 'Ugh! Where will you stick it?'

'I'll go for the heart. Left side.'

'Don't forget to waggle it round once it's in.'

She wanted to say ugh too, but she kept a stern face. 'I'll give it a good old waggle.'

David laughed.

Had she the bottle to do it? She wished she had her giant wooden spoon, the one she'd whacked Nicholson with when he'd attacked her in her cottage. Even then she should have given him another whack. Was she capable of deliberately killing Hager? She'd have to get her dander up. She'd need to be furious but icy calm. She wasn't sure if that combination was possible.

Chapter 29

Tucker closed his brief case. He was ready. Ready to leave this house, this country and to start his new life. Regrets? He wished he was like the chanteuse, Edith Piaf, and have no regrets, but that wasn't possible. He'd thought this day would never arrive, but he'd been instructed the operation must be wound up immediately. The time was right for the greatest scandal of all times to hit the headlines: Edward Heath's government was unpopular, unemployment had reached a million, the highest figure since the 1930s, the unofficial miners' strike had brought unrest, and political violence in Northern Ireland had shocked the nation. The time to bring this expensive and lengthy plot to fruition had arrived.

The government would fall. There would be a General Election. Communists within the Labour Party and the trade unions would foment unrest, mob rule would be encouraged. Who knew what might happen? These were not his problems. His work was nearly done.

Regrets? His art collection. He was already missing his beautiful pictures. He'd sold many of the best works. Was life in Moscow going to be to his taste? It would have to be. There would be a lot of rules and regulations; he would have to fit in, make sure he stayed on the right side of the rulers. Life was so much more relaxed here in comparison. If only he'd been recognised by the establishment and given a post he deserved, he'd never had given in to the temptation of revenge. He was apprehensive about the downfall of the government and following chaos. Not for the people, but what would happen to the great museums and art galleries? He hated the people running them, but he loved their contents. Would works of art be destroyed by the proletariat in revenge for dominance of the upper classes? At least he'd saved David. His Moscow bosses didn't know David was alive, the Russian staff at the school thought he'd been killed; he'd sworn Hager to silence. Those staff would be leaving the school tonight, making their way back to Russia by different routes. He smiled as he thought of the headmaster, Baron, and the stupid PE teacher, Salmon, waking up tomorrow to find they were left holding the baby. What a baby!

Tucker checked the contents of his briefcase: various passports, all but his UK passport hidden in a secret pocket; the ticket for the boat from Newcastle to Bergen. From Norway he'd make his way to Sweden, and from there he'd take a boat to the Russian port of St Petersburg. He patted his pocket. He'd both keys to David's room. Even if Hager became suspicious when he didn't return from Aldeburgh, he wouldn't be able to get into the room and harm David.

He smiled again. Involving Laurel was a master stroke. Her colleagues would be looking for her. That way he'd be sure David would be found. If Hager decided to make a run for it, the boy might die before anyone found him. It was also an insurance, in case Hager somehow managed to get in the room. She was a brave, strong woman. She'd proved her courage in tackling the insane headmaster, Philip Nicholson. She had a weapon. He sighed, wishing he could take one of David's pictures with him, but he mustn't arouse Hager's suspicions. He'd become increasingly unstable over the past few weeks. Killing the Harrops and then Luxton seemed to have emboldened him, and Tucker had felt his hold over Hager weakening.

He checked the briefcase again. The gun was there, safety catch on, on top of the other contents. He needed to have it handy in case Hager turned nasty. Once he was safely away from Hager he'd get rid of it.

He took a last look round his bedroom: the four-poster bed with its feather mattress and pillows, the luxurious piled carpet, the antique walnut furniture. He sighed. He did like the very best and he'd been able to afford just that.

He went down the stairs, his hand brushing the mahogany rail. In the hall were a pile of large envelopes. Each containing names of all the men who'd been invited at various times over the years to this house. Men of power and influence: judges, newspaper magnates, MPs, minor royalty, a few dukes and earls, a bishop or two, men of science and medicine, heads of charities, members of the armed forces, famous actors and television presenters, and of course the director of the local nuclear power station and Sam Harrop. It had taken years to build up this dossier. There were photographs of them, photographs that would send them to prison, but even worse, a catalogue of the secrets they had been blackmailed into revealing, and the illegal tasks they had carried out. The envelopes were addressed to the editors of the *Mirror, Express, Mail, Guardian, Observer, Telegraph, Times* and for good measure, the *Glasgow Herald,* and to the embassies of every country in Europe and also the USA.

In his bedroom, Hager was packing for the journey they would make that night. He placed the light-weight bullet-proof vest he'd had imported from the USA in the suitcase. Tucker had told him not to wear it. Why? Better on him than to be found by a Customs' search. He undressed and strapped it to his body under his shirt. That was better. He was a professional and liked to be fully prepared for any eventuality. It was all he need for his job: his steel-capped shoes, his vest and his hands. He didn't mind the occasional use of knives, razors and guns, but he took pride in his work and liked to improvise with whatever was at hand at the site. But the real pleasure, the intense pleasure, came with the perfect movement of his body, the swift blow and the satisfying contact between the edge of his hand and the neck of the victim. One stroke and they were dead. Sometimes he didn't want to give them a swift death. Sometimes it was personal. He wanted to see their faces as he tortured them, before finishing them off. For the Harrops it had been in and out as quickly as possible. The old guy put up more of a fight than he'd thought possible. Suffocation, No skill in that, only brute force. The woman had been more satisfying, some skill had been needed to make it look like suicide.

Tucker had told him they would drive to Dover, take the night car ferry to Calais and then drive northwards. They'd abandon the car at the German border and be taken on to Russia. He hadn't given him more details although he'd asked for them. It seemed vague. Tucker was usually meticulous in his preparation and plans. He supposed it had been taken out of Tucker's hands and he was following instructions.

The special reinforced and tightly sealed envelopes were ready. He'd enjoyed preparing them. Some of the photographs were sensational, so sensational the newspapers wouldn't dare print them. He'd bet money there'd be a rash of suicides in the next few days. That or the special forces might be kept busy arranging them.

He'd be glad to kick the dirt of this crap country from his feet. He wouldn't miss a thing. The nation had gone soft. The dock strike last year, making the government call a state of emergency. The country he was going to wouldn't put up with such behaviour. They'd shoot the bastards. One thing stuck in his craw. That little shite David Pemberton. And now the bitch Bowman. It didn't seem right leaving the house without wiping them out. But Tucker was determined David should live. If he hadn't involved Bowman, there was the hope David might die of starvation before they found him. He'd cut down on his food these past few weeks.

He might get the opportunity to get in the room before they left, perhaps just as they were about to go. He'd pretend he'd forgotten something vital, his passport. It wouldn't take long. He'd have to forgo playing round with the boy. One swift chop and he'd break his neck. Damn. The woman. He'd have two to deal with. Kill her first. She was the strongest. Then him. No time to play with her either. A pity. She'd be thankful for a swift death. He decided he'd get the spare key to David's room.

He listened at Tucker's bedroom door. He could hear

movement. He ran down the stairs. He looked at the hook on the kitchen wall were the spare key to the room was kept. It wasn't there.

Chapter 30

Frank looked at Stuart. 'Make notes of any important details, please.'

Stuart whipped out notebook and biro from his jacket and sat down on the armchair nearest to the music centre, his shoulders hunched. Frank took the other armchair, staring at the whirring machine as though it might explode. The reedy voice continued.

'The reason I'm talking into this machine is this is the only way I can hope to tell you, Nancy, what I've done. I wanted to tell you face to face. No, wanted isn't the right word. I needed to tell you. I've committed a crime, a terrible crime. If you find this tape when you are going through my effects, you must take it to the police. You must do this, Nancy. Never mind my good name, I shall be dead. I know it will hurt you to tell everyone what I've done, but if you don't more children will suffer and possibly be murdered. I am *not* exaggerating.'

Frank's breath stopped. Would they learn the full story?

'I haven't much time. Clara won't let me see you. I'm a prisoner in my own home. She won't let anyone into the house and she's hidden the telephones. I haven't many days to live. I wish I'd been able to speak to you, because after that I'd be able to take my own life and end the agony and degradation. Now I must try to live as long as possible until I am sure someone will stop them. I apologise if my words are jumbled or my thoughts unclear, it's a combination of pain and the morphine. I'm going to start from the beginning in case the tape is found by someone else. I'll try and tell my story in the right order.'

There was a pause and Frank could hear ragged breathing. 'He seems to be thinking clearly,' he said. Stuart nodded in agreement.

There was a dry cough and the voice continued. 'I am a homosexual. Nancy knows this, but she still loved me when she found out; I loved her more than ever for the generosity of her spirit. I married Clara as a cover; Clara and I got on well together and we both enjoyed the opera and classical music. She knew what she was getting into when she married me, and was prepared to exchange a physical relationship and true love for the kudos of my name, and the comfortable living I could give her. She's ignored my various affairs. I would have reciprocated, but she is uninterested in sex, and my presence by her side at functions and a generous allowance, is enough for her.

'When I became ill it didn't take me long to diagnose what was the matter. Cancer of the liver. One of my colleagues confirmed the diagnosis. I decided I wouldn't have any treatment, even palliative care. My life is over. As the disease progressed and my body became weaker, my conscience grew stronger, and I thought of the terrible things I'd done. I have no excuse. I know it's only because I'm close to death I want to confess. Would I be saying this if I still had my health? I doubt it.

'When we moved to Aldeburgh after my retirement as

a surgeon, I remained licensed as a doctor and helped out as a locum at some of the local practices. I enjoyed the occasional work. I often think of your husband, Nancy, dear James; he was the first man I fell in love with. What a generous soul. He discovered I was homosexual, but he didn't turn away from me in disgust. You both loved me, and it was James who inspired me to go into medicine.

'It was at a local surgery I first met Tucker ...'

Frank looked at Stuart, his heart seemed to stop. Laurel.

Stuart's biro froze above his notepad. 'Laurel!' he shouted, echoing Frank's thoughts. 'Switch it off!'

Frank shook his head. 'No. We need more information.'

'He seemed a charming man, erudite, amusing, and also a lover of opera and classical music. He invited Clara and me to dinner at his house near Snape. We had a lovely evening. There were four other people, two of them a local couple we knew and the other two were his assistant, Kelvin Hager, and a young man from London. He was ravishing, dark soulful eyes, skin the colour of caramel, and a slender adolescent body. He could have been the boy in the Caravaggio painting above Tucker's mantelpiece. He told me he was nineteen, and I must admit I lusted after him, even at my age.

'I haven't time to go into all the details, but Tucker acted as go-between and soon I was meeting the man at Tucker's house and we became lovers. I trusted Tucker: he was sympathetic, understanding, broadminded and with such a warm personality.

'Then one night I got a phone call from Tucker saying he needed my help. It was urgent, would I please come to

312

his house immediately. Of course, I went. I took my medical bag with me. I couldn't see what other kind of emergency it might be.

'When I got there Tucker was waiting in the parlour, as he liked to call the sitting room; Hager was with him. I could see no signs of an emergency. I hadn't paid much attention to Hager before, he didn't say much, and wasn't interested in music, indeed I never saw him show much interest in art, although he ran the gallery when Tucker was away. That night he was different: he sneered at me, with looks of satisfaction, dislike, and even contempt.

'Tucker showed me photographs. They were explicit. The man I thought was nineteen was only fifteen. A well-developed Italian, Tucker said.

'"How much do you want?" I asked, filled with disgust at myself and Tucker. All my working life I'd been careful to avoid scandal.

'"I'm afraid it isn't that simple," Tucker said. "We need your medical skills, not your money."

'I thought they must want me to carry out an abortion on some young girl one of them had got into trouble, although Tucker had never shown any interest in a sexual relationship, as far as I knew.

'"Unfortunately, a boy has died at a nearby school. We need your name on the death certificate, plus someone you know, a young doctor perhaps who will not question your medical opinion."

'The school was Chillingworth, a few miles from Tucker's house. I complied with their orders. This happened again, a few years later. A Down's syndrome boy ...'

Frank pressed the stop button. 'Laurel's gone to

313

Tucker's house for lunch.'

'I know,' Stuart said. 'What should we do?'

Frank's chest grew tighter with every second that passed and his guts twisted as he thought of the danger Laurel might be in. 'Why did he ask her to go to his house? What could he want from her? Surely he was inviting danger for no good reason.'

'The gallery. Laurel said it looked as though it was closing down. Tucker said it was a changeover of paintings,' Stuart said.

Frank looked at his watch. 'We'll listen to a bit more of the tape. See if it gives us any information about Tucker and Hager. They're into blackmail. They're using boys from the school. Who else are they blackmailing? Five minutes, then we'll act.'

'Shouldn't we go and get her now?' Stuart pleaded.

Frank held up his hand then he pressed the play button.

'I'm not sure how the first boy died, but he was bruised below the right ear. His anus and rectum were torn and he'd lost a lot of blood. I thought there would be internal injuries. I signed the death certificate and got a local doctor to sign without seeing the body. The boy had suffered. I felt as filthy as if I'd bathed in stinking excrement.

'Hager took me aside before I left the school. He pinned me against a wall and hissed in my ear, "If you utter one word about this to anyone I'll kill you. Not just you, but your wife as well, and for good measure your beloved sister, Nancy. Her death I'll make especially unpleasant. I'll strip her, tie her up and rape her with a handy kitchen implement. Don't fancy doing it myself, she's a bit too old and scrawny for me. Although you

314

never know, I sometimes get excited before I kill someone." I was physically sick.

'It was only a few months after I signed the death certificate of the Down's syndrome boy when I first noticed the signs of my own illness. Divine retribution? Many people would say so. I believed Hager. The man is a killer. Nancy, if it's you who finds the tape you must go straight to the police. You will need protection until Hager is caught.'

Frank switched off the tape and ejected it. He held it out to Stuart. 'You must contact Revie. Tell him the details and he must go, with as many men as possible, to Tucker's house. They'll need firearms. Keep the tape safe. I'll take my car and get to Laurel as soon as possible. You remember where the house is?'

'Yes. Laurel talked about it last night. Frank, I think I ought to go with you. There are two of them and Hager sounds like a professional killer.'

Frank shook his head. 'She might not be in danger. I can't understand why Tucker invited her. It isn't a secret where she is. I might be able to get her out without any trouble and Revie can make the arrests.'

'I don't like it.'

Frank grimaced. 'Not sure I do. Can you see anything I can use as a weapon?'

They scoured the room and went into the hall. There was a cast-iron umbrella stand, in it were two walking sticks and a cricket bat. Frank picked up the bat and gave a swing. He wished he had Laurels' monster spoon – that had given good service. 'This'll do.'

'Ever played cricket?'

'Mid-order bat at uni. My cover drive wasn't bad.'

'Let's hope you don't need to use it. I'll phone from a neighbour's, the phones in the house haven't been reinstalled. I'll get hold of a car if I have to steal one. I'll be with you as soon as I can. Good luck, Frank.' Stuart crushed him in a tight embrace.

Frank felt as if he were going to face a firing squad. He ran out of the house and towards his car.

Chapter 31

Laurel looked round the room. She couldn't think of any other ways of preparing for a visit by Hager. She and David had piled the heaviest books, along with some LPs, in a pile behind the bed where Hager couldn't see them if he came into the room. They'd collected containers, mugs, cups, glasses (some held brushes and pencils, which they discarded), and filled them with various concoctions: soap and water, pigments and water, and there were even a few full of urine. They'd giggled over that.

It was pathetic, but it had kept David busy, and she hoped given him confidence.

'David, what about sharpening the handles of some of your brushes? We could use the stiletto.'

He took a brush from a collection in a pot. 'You could try. Hey, here's another one for peeing in!' He dumped the remaining brushes onto the desk and held up the pot.

'How did we miss that? Do you think you can fill it?'

He shook his head. 'I don't think I'll ever pee again.'

She laughed. 'Me, too. Fill it with some pigment and water. Hager will look like a rainbow by the time we've finished with him.' She picked up the brush and tried to sharpen the wooden handle with the stiletto. After a few strokes she gave up. 'No good, I'm afraid, I might damage or blunt the dagger. That won't do, it's our main weapon.'

He came out of the bathroom, stirring the contents of the pot with a pencil. 'We could use pencils to stab him. Shall I sharpen some? I've got a pencil sharpener.'

'Good idea. I think we need to take up our positions soon.' She tugged at her skirt. It was restricting. 'David, I don't want you to be embarrassed, but I'm going to take off my skirt and tights. I can't move freely in them. OK?' Her high heels had disappeared.

David stopped stirring. 'That's a good idea. Would you like one of my tops? It would be better than that blouse. I've got some t-shirts.'

Her heart swelled with pride at his easy acceptance of her striptease and his thoughtfulness trying to find better clothes for the job she had to do. 'Thank you, David. The looser the better.' She took off her jacket, unzipped her skirt, rolled off her tights, hiding them under the bedclothes.

David pulled several tops from a drawer. She chose an oversized t-shirt with short sleeves. Luckily it covered her knickers.

'Right. I want you to go to the bathroom and wedge the door as tight as you can.'

David nodded, his face paling. 'I don't want to leave you.'

She wished she could pick him up, cast a spell, dissolve the bars at the window, and fly away with him to safety. 'I know. I don't want to leave you either. But we have to do this. As much as we'd rather be together, this is the only way we can escape.'

'I know, but I'm scared. Hager's a terrible person. I don't think he's ever liked anyone in the whole of his

318

life.'

'Then he's to be pitied. Remember Hager may never come into this room. My friends will arrive soon. We're taking precautions. Listen carefully, please. You must do as I say. If you hear shouting or noises like people fighting, you are not to come out of that bathroom. I forbid it.' She sounded as if she was giving the riot act to rebellious fourth formers. 'Understand?'

David took a deep breath. 'Yes, Laurel.'

It was the first time he's used her name. She wanted to hug him close and tell him it would be all right. 'Good. Hold the door tightly closed. Push hard if anyone tries to get in. Whatever you hear, even if it's me shouting for help, you are not to open the door. That's an order.'

He tossed his head and rolled his eyes. 'You've already said that.'

Teenage rebellion. 'Sorry to repeat myself but it's really important. Only open the door if it's me. If it's someone you don't know, ask them their names. If they say Diamond or Elderkin, they're my friends. Or it might be the police. You know Hager's and Tucker's voices. Use your common sense.'

'Diamond, Elderkin,' he muttered.

She went to the bathroom and opened the door. She looked in. There were a few books, LPs and filled cups in the bath and on the floor. God knows what use they'd be to him if Hager got to him, but they gave him some comfort. She'd spent a few minutes showing him how to throw LPs for maximum effect. A wave of panic swept over her; she knew the only chance they had if Hager came to kill them, was for her to attack him with the stiletto. All the other preparations they'd made would be as good as the straw house when the wolf came calling.

'Go into the bathroom and try the stool as a wedge. Is there anything else you want to take in with you? Got any sweets or chocolate?'

He went to a drawer and came back with a bar of Cadbury's Fruit and Nut chocolate and a bag of caramels. He broke the bar in two and gave her half, put some of the caramels in his pocket and gave her the rest. 'I'll take my sketch pad and some pencils. I'll try and draw while we wait.'

'Good. In you go. See you soon.' She gave him the bravest smile she could.

'Thank you for helping me, Laurel.'

They stood looking at each other. She pointed into the bathroom, not trusting herself to speak.

He turned and closed the door.

Sounds of wood against wood. He'd jammed the door.

'David? I'm going to test it. OK?'

'OK.'

She pushed against the door. It was holding. It would give her a few precious minutes, perhaps only seconds, to run across the room and stab Hager.

'You've done a good job. I'm getting under the bed. Good luck. Remember what I told you. Don't come out until you're sure it's safe.'

A groan from the other side of the door.

'Cheeky boy! It'll be detention for you tomorrow.'

A laugh. 'Thanks, Laurel.'

She wanted to stay by the door and keep talking. 'See you soon.' She walked away before he could reply. The bed was made of pine with a slatted bottom and a ten-inch gap between floor and the slats. She arranged the bedding to hide herself. She eased herself under the bed with her head at the bottom of the bed, her feet at its head. Through the draped bedclothes she had a good view of the room and the bathroom door. She practised getting in and out a few times. It wasn't easy, but she would be able to get out without Hager seeing her. She moved the pile of books farther away to give her more room to manoeuvre, and placed the stiletto under the bed. She prayed Frank and Stuart would come soon. But they would be unprepared for Hager. Hopefully Frank's antennae would be twitching. A terrible thought crashed through her mind. Hager might kill them before they realised she was a prisoner. God, what had she got them into this time?

Chapter 32

Hager stared at the empty hook on which the spare key to David's room normally hung. Why had Tucker removed it? He had the only other key. Footsteps on the stairs. Tucker was coming down. Hager moved into the hall.

'Ah, there you are, Hager. All the envelopes checked?'

'Yes, sir. When will we post them?'

Tucker was carrying two empty canvas bags as well as his briefcase. 'I've decided to take them into Aldeburgh now. I'll get to the post office with plenty of time to spare before they close. You can get on with the final clearing up. Are you packed ready to leave?'

'Yes, sir.'

'Good. As soon as I'm back we'll leave for Dover. No point in waiting for Laurel Bowman's friends to turn up.'

Tucker was blustering. 'Why don't we both leave now? Stop in Aldeburgh on our way to Dover. It would save you coming back.'

The skin under Tucker's left eye twitched. 'Yes, that would make sense, but this is how I've been ordered to carry out this part of the operation. I won't be long, although I do need to go into the gallery and collect a few things.'

'What about the woman and the boy? Shall I make sure they've got some food in case no one comes for a few days? You never know, her friends might not be worried when she doesn't turn up. Perhaps she sometimes goes off by herself.'

Tucker placed the canvas bags on the floor near the envelopes on the hall table. He rubbed his right index finger over his top lip. 'We can do that when I get back.' He turned and went into the parlour. 'I need to check I've got enough money for the postage.'

Hager followed him, tensing his muscles, flexing his shoulders, his right hand by his side, fingers in line. Tucker had his back to him, opening his briefcase.

'Where is the key to David's room?' Tucker's back stiffened. 'It isn't on the hook in the kitchen.' Hager edged towards Tucker, his hand moving from his side.

Tucker turned. In his right hand was a semi-automatic pistol. Before he could aim and fire, Hagar leapt towards him, right arm leading, and with great force hit him a downward blow with the edge of his hand below Tucker's ear.

There was a gasp of expelling air. Tucker's knees buckled and he slumped to the floor, the pistol falling from his hand. Hager kicked the gun away, then booted Tucker's body straight, cursing him as the steel caps of his shoe thudded into flesh and bone. Tucker's head lolled obscenely to one side. Hager stopped; breathing deeply he rubbed the edge of his hand. Tucker's lifeless eyes stared at him. As dead as a dodo, whatever one of those was. He picked up the pistol. A Makarov. Bloody useless gun. Heavy and clumsy. Cheap-skate Russians. Give him a Luger any day. Where was the skill and fun in shooting someone dead? He preferred to use his hands. To feel the flesh, the direct contact between him and his victims, and hear the crunch of bones breaking. That's what turned him on. Shooting someone? No fun at all. He threw the gun onto the floor beside Tucker.

He emptied Tucker's briefcase onto the sofa. Tickets for a boat from Newcastle to Bergen. His British passport. A wallet of money. He'd been right. Tucker was sodding off leaving him here with the bloody boy and woman. Thinking he wouldn't be able to get at them because he hadn't a key and he couldn't get through the steel door. His heart was beating faster than its normal fifty-five a minute and he felt blood suffusing his face. He looked down at the avuncular face of Nicholas Tucker, his boss for all these years, the man he'd looked up to, and respected. Who'd betrayed him. Lied to him. All the dirty work Hagar had done, all the perverts he's fed and watered, photographed and scared to death. Tucker had been going to leave him up to the neck in shit. He turned and kicked Tucker's head until it was a ball of pulp. He looked at his steel-capped boots and grimaced with disgust. Tucker had even made a mess of them.

He gave one last vicious kick into the body on the floor, and smiled as he heard ribs crack. Pity the shite wasn't alive. He looked again at the contents of the briefcase. Where were they? He bent down and rummaged through Tucker's jacket pockets. He touched the cold steel of the two keys and smiled in anticipation.

Now for those two bastards upstairs.

Chapter 33

Frank had never missed his Mustang as much as he did now. The Avenger was quick, but the Mustang had been quicker. He wished Stuart was with him. Last September they'd speeded in the Mustang to Dunwich to arrest Nicholson for the murder of several girls and women. Then he hadn't realised how close Laurel was to being murdered. Now she might be in greater danger. She was strong, but no match for a professional killer.

Coming out of Aldeburgh on the A1094 he floored the accelerator, pushing the speedo up to over eighty. He hoped he didn't meet a tractor. He braked as he came to the left turn for Snape. Christ, he'd have to slow down through the village, he didn't want to kill someone. His heart was pounding against his ribs, his mouth dry, tongue cleaving to his palate. He passed through the village and when he got to The Crown, on the outskirts, he speeded up until he was at Snape Maltings. As he passed The Plough and Sail on his left, he slowed down; he didn't want to miss the turning.

The road forked; to the left to Orford, to the right Tunstall. He took the right fork and then another right fork to Blaxhall. A short distance down this narrow road he should find Tucker's house. There it was. Should he drive up to it? He decided to leave his car in the lane. He grabbed the cricket bat from the passenger seat, and risking no one was looking out of the front windows, ran towards the house.

There were three cars in the drive. One was Laurel's. She was still here. She should have left by now. Where was she? The front door was closed. He pushed gently. Locked. He ducked down and edged to the left so he could look in the front windows. The room was empty. It was a dining room. If Laurel had come here for lunch this is where she'd have eaten. There was no sign of anyone and the table was bare, its dark mahogany surface glowing red in the sunlight.

He retraced his steps and moved to the window to the right of the front door. No one there either. Perhaps they'd gone for a walk. Perhaps Laurel was all right. As he straightened up he saw a leg sticking out from behind a sofa. He stopped breathing. It was a clothed man's leg with a brogue on the foot. He wanted to break the window with the bat and climb in. Instead he ran around the side of the house to the back. He prayed there would be another door and it would be open.

Who did the leg belong to? Tucker? Hager? He hoped it was Hager. He thought he could deal with Tucker, from Laurel's description of him. But Hager? Sam Harrop had described him as a killer. He, himself, was fit, and not above violence if it was needed, but he didn't fancy his chances against a trained assassin. He wished he had something more lethal than a cricket bat.

At the back of the house the windows were smaller and there was a central wooden door. He ducked below the windows and grasped the brass door knob. The door opened smoothly. He slid into a tiled passageway, leaving the door open – they might need a quick getaway. Holding the cricket bat with both hands, ready to hit out, he moved slowly up the passageway.

It bifurcated around what was probably a staircase. He took the left turn and came to the main entrance hall. The body of the man was in the left front room. He looked round, all senses on alert. There didn't seem to be anyone on the ground floor. On a hall table was a pile of large envelopes, nearby, on the floor, two canvas sacks. He glanced at the top envelope. The editor of the *Daily Telegraph*? What on earth was going on?

The door of the left front room was ajar. Using the bat, he pushed the door wide open and slowly moved into the room. He winced. The head of the body had been beaten or kicked to a pulp. From the body's size and girth, he thought it must be Tucker. Who'd killed him? Not Laurel. It must be Hager. Why would Hager kill his boss? Where was Laurel? Had she escaped? Was Hager chasing Laurel? He needed to search the rest of the house.

As he was turning to leave the room he saw a gun on the floor next to Tucker. He bent down and picked it up. Was it loaded? It was a make he didn't know. He'd trained as an authorised firearms officer and knew how to use it, but that was a few years ago. Think. Think. The gun would give him an edge if he met Hager, unless he was also armed. The gun was heavy, about a pound and a half, a semi-automatic pistol. It looked as if you had to pull the trigger hard to fire it. Yes, there was a magazine of bullets in it. He picked up the bat with his left hand and, holding the gun in front of him, moved into the hall and towards the stairs.

Chapter 34

Hager climbed the stairs, his mind red with rage. All his dreams of living like a lord in the Soviet Union were shattered. Shattered by that bastard Tucker. What should he do next? He'd have to get out of this country as fast as possible. Where could he go? The Ruskies would be after him when they found out their plan had failed and he'd killed Tucker. Could he fool them into thinking Tucker had played a double game? That he worked for MI5? Could he risk using the boat ticket to Bergen and then wait for them to contact him? If he did that he'd need to post the envelopes. If their plan worked would they care if Tucker was dead?

The other alternative was to set out on his own. Get to a corrupt state in Africa, and offer himself as a mercenary. There'd been good pickings in the Congo, Angola, Mozambique, and news was Libya was hotting up. If you enjoyed killing this was an ideal way to indulge yourself and not get sent to prison. But that was not what he'd been looking forward to. Tucker had assured him he'd have a job for life in the KGB, and his special skills would be appreciated. He'd fooled him, talking about the life style he'd have: the important post, the luxury apartment and the best whores in Moscow. The Russians mustn't have wanted him. Or had Tucker lied about him?

Not told them he was the man who did all the dangerous and difficult work?

The veins in his forehead throbbed as he realised what he'd lost. He stood before David Pemberton's door, the little shite – spoilt rotten by Tucker. He'd feel better when he'd killed them. Wash away the boiling fury with their blood. They'd be cowering in the bathroom. That's what he usually did. He could easily kick *that* door in. It was a confined space, but he could manage. He'd kill the woman first, she was tall and fit, but no match for him. No. He'd kill the boy, then he'd play with her. She was a fighter. She'd fought the mad headmaster. It would be a pleasure to take her. Then he'd strangle her – slowly. He took one of the keys he'd found in Tucker's jacket and pushed it into the lock.

Chapter 35

Laurel was cold and stiff. Not only from being confined under the bed, but stiff and cold with fear. She'd never felt so scared. She remembered being left with the unconscious Mabel on the beach, guarding her against the return of the person who'd tried to kill her while Frank went for help. She'd crouched beside her, talking, trying to help her survive, a stone in her hand, ready to lash out if the murderer came back. She'd been scared then. She'd been scared when Nicholson had attacked her. But this was different. She'd had too much time to think.

She tried to rub her arms and legs to keep the circulation going, but the space under the bed was constricting her movements. She wasn't just fighting for her life, she'd be fighting for David's, too. It was still difficult to take in what Tucker had done. He'd saved David's life by imprisoning him, but at what cost to the young boy? What damage had been done to his psyche? Locked in a room for nearly two years. Yet he seemed remarkably resilient. It was incredible how he'd coped with the isolation and perpetual fear.

She knew she'd only have one chance. If Hager came into the room and thought they were both in the bathroom, then she must act. Close her mind to what she had to do. No thinking – just do it. She must stab him with deadly intent. Thrust quickly and deeply. She decided to go underarm, like throwing a rounder's ball, thrusting upwards into his heart.

There was a metallic click. Her body went rigid. She peered between the draped bedclothes. The door slowly opened.

Hager used his right palm to push open the door. He made sure it went as far as it could go in case one of them was hiding behind it, waiting to jump him. His mouth twitched at the thought. Surely, they weren't idiots? He waited on the threshold for a few seconds, senses alert. The room was silent. He walked in. He was right. The room was empty. They were in the bathroom. He flexed his shoulders, then his right leg, loosening it ready to kick the door in. Perhaps he wouldn't have to do that, he might be able to trick them into coming out. He smiled. That would be nice.

He looked round. The bed was unmade, the bookshelves untidy. The room looked a shambles. He sniffed. Give a woman a couple of hours and she'd create chaos. He put his ear to the bathroom door and listened. No sound. He tapped on the wood.

'Miss Bowman, David, it's Mr Hager here. It'll be safe for you to come out in a few minutes. Mr Tucker has sent me to say we're leaving. Miss Bowman, there's been a phone call from your friend, Mr Diamond. Mr Tucker's told him to come and collect you. I'm leaving now. Goodbye, Miss Bowman and David. I'm sorry you've been kept here, but it was Mr Tucker's orders. Wait two minutes and then you can come out.' He walked to the bedroom door, closed it with a thud, then tiptoed back to the bathroom door.

Laurel tried to swallow her fear. Slowly and carefully she edged from under the bed. She lay on the carpet trying to flex her limbs, conscious of the silence and that the faintest sound would alert Hager. She got into a kneeling position and focused her mind on what she had to do. Don't think of him as human, imagine he's a dummy. You're a new recruit in the army and you've been given the command to stick the stiletto into the dummy, a dummy full of sawdust, not muscle, bone and blood. She raised her head. He was standing by the bathroom door. Talking to what he believed were the occupants. She prayed David wouldn't be taken in by his soft, reasonable words. She ducked down as Hager crossed to the bedroom door, slammed it, turned and tiptoed back to the bathroom, poised like a panther waiting for its prey to emerge.

He was looking at his watch, his back to her. His body tensed, he rolled his shoulders and flexed his legs. He was preparing for action. Time seemed endless. She couldn't breathe.

'Well, Miss Bowman and David. I'm growing impatient. I've given you five minutes. Come out in thirty seconds or I'll have to come in for you.' He started to count.

Now was the time. She steadied herself, resting her left hand on the bed, and grasping the stiletto with her right. She crouched, as though she was on the starting blocks for a race, then launched herself across the room, the stiletto held waist high and slightly behind her. She flung herself on him, put an arm round his neck and thrust the dagger into the left side of his back. His body arced. He screamed. There was resistance. The dagger wasn't going in.

Hager was preparing to take the door down when a body hurtled into him, throwing him against the door. An arm shot round his throat and something thudded into his back, partly penetrating the protective vest and sending a red-hot pain through his muscles.

He screamed with rage, caught hold of the arm and twisted it, forcing the attacker onto the floor. The woman. She was fighting and kicking. She slashed his face with the knife. In an instant he'd wrapped his legs round hers and put a lock on them and pinned her wrists to the floor. He squeezed the right wrist so hard she cried out and the knife dropped from her grasp. Her head was thrashing from side to side, her eyes full of hate.

She must have been under the bed. He winced at the pain from his back and face. She'd been aiming for his heart. If he hadn't worn the vest she'd have killed him. Tucker hadn't wanted him to wear the vest. He must have given her the knife. Betrayed again and again. Sod the lot of them. He felt hot blood running down his back and trickling down his face. The vest should have done better than this. His breathing slowed. He had her. Now he could take his time. And after, he'd deal with the little shite in the bathroom.

He looked down at her face. Her fury was fading. What was taking its place? Fear? He hoped so. If she wasn't frightened now, she soon would be. He looked down. Her legs were bare. No skirt.

'You've prepared yourself for me, have you, Miss

Bowman? So you mustn't blame me if I become a little excited. Shall we complete the striptease? See what the rest of you looks like?' He leant down, putting his full body weight onto her, and pulled her left arm across so he was holding both wrists in his left hand. She tried to fight back, he increased the pressure on her legs and wrists. She *was* a fighter. He'd never had a woman fight back like this. Some men. He could knock her unconscious, but he wanted to see her eyes as he took her. Should he rip her top off? He glanced down. The t-shirt, obviously one of David's, had ridden up, showing her flat stomach and flimsy knickers. His breathing increased and he smiled. He pressed his swollen cock against her belly and saw the terror in her eyes. He reached down and grabbed the edge of the blue knickers.

She bucked like a wild horse, jerking a knee into his balls. He lost his grip on her left wrist. She threw back her head and screamed blue murder.

Frank was on the fifth stair. There was a terrible scream.

'Get off me! Get off me! You filthy bastard.'

Laurel.

'You bitch!'

Hager?

A thud.

Then silence.

Frank ran up the stairs. One door was open. There were grunting sounds. He raised the revolver, and with the cricket bat in his left hand, silently entered the room.

Hager was on top of Laurel. She wasn't moving. He was astride her, looking down at his crotch, his hands in front of him.

334

Blood pulsed through Frank's forehead, his veins bulging with rage and hate. He wanted to pull the trigger and keep pulling it until Hagen was no more than a heap of dead flesh. The years of training and discipline took over. He needed to get him away from Laurel. He put the bat on the carpet and held the gun with both hands.

'Hager. Police. I have you covered and if you don't get up I'll shoot you. This is a warning. Now get up,' he shouted.

Hager's back went rigid. For a second Frank thought he'd turned to stone. Then with a roar he sprang up and faced Frank, flies open, eyes bulging. He leapt towards him, his right arm raised, hand horizontal.

Frank aimed for his chest and pulled the trigger. The sound of the gunshot in the restricted space was deafening. Hager staggered backwards, clutching his left breast, his knees buckling. Then he seemed to summon up strength and stumbled towards Frank.

Christ! He's not going down. He pulled the trigger again. The second shot was as loud as the first. Hager tottered back, almost falling over Laurel. Frank was desperate to get to her. Had he killed her? Hager was coming at him again. What was the man made of? Then it dawned. He was wearing body armour. He pulled the trigger for the third time. There was a click, but nothing happened. Jammed.

He dropped the gun, picked up the cricket bat and strode towards Hager, as though preparing for a full toss. He drew back the bat and hit him under the chin with the hardest drive he'd ever made. Willow connected with jaw bone. Hager's head seemed to lose contact with his neck. His body hit the floor and Frank knew he'd killed him.

Cricket bat in hand, he bent over Hager and checked for a pulse. He'd seen too many scary movies were the villain popped back into life when you thought they were dead. There was no pulse.

He threw down the bat and rushed to Laurel, pressing the tips of the two fingers against her neck. A steady beat. Blood was running down her face from her scalp. He placed his ear close to her mouth. She was breathing. Tears of relief welled from his eyes. He gently turned her into the recovery position, and pulled a blanket from the bed and wrapped it round her.

He held her gently. 'Laurel? Laurel? Can you hear me? It's Frank. You're safe. Hager's dead.' He stroked her hair into some semblance of order and kissed her cheek. He needed to get an ambulance. Hopefully Stuart and Revie would be arriving soon, but he daren't wait.

There was a banging on the bathroom door. He jumped up and grabbed the bat. Who was in there? It couldn't be Tucker, he was dead. Were there three of them? Had he got to kill someone else?

'Laurel! Laurel! Are you all right?' the voice cried. It was a young, male voice.

He went to the bathroom door and knocked. 'Come out. I won't hurt you.'

'Who are you?'

'Frank Diamond.'

'Laurel's friend?'

'Yes.'

'Where's Hager?'

'He's dead.'

'Really?' The voice sounded pleased.

'Yes, he's dead.'

'Where's Laurel?'

'She's here, but she's unconscious. Could you come out and look after her? I need to call an ambulance.'

There were sounds of something being moved, muttering and swearing. 'Damn, can't move it. Ah, yes!' A cry of triumph and the door swung inwards.

A tall, thin teenager came out. His long, black hair was dishevelled round his pale face. Deep blue eyes stared at Frank.

No, it couldn't be!

The boy looked at Laurel; he rushed to her, and knelt down.

'Laurel, Laurel,' he cried, echoing Frank's words. 'Please don't die. Not now. I wouldn't want to live if you died. It wouldn't be right.'

His words seemed to have more potency than his, for Laurel raised her head and groaned.

The boy grasped her hand; tears splashing onto her face.

'David. Brave man. We did it,' Laurel croaked, then her head fell back and her eyes closed.

David! He looked at the boy again. Those eyes. The same eyes as Carol's. It was David Pemberton. Frank couldn't take any more and he flopped onto the floor beside them.

'Are you David Pemberton?'

He was still holding Laurel's hand and her fingers had curled round his. 'Yes. Shall I get Laurel some water?'

'If you would, thank you.'

David got up. He pointed at Hager's body. 'Are you sure he's dead?'

'Yes. He's dead.' He couldn't believe he'd killed him.

337

He felt like joining Laurel and passing into oblivion. His stomach clenched. He'd killed someone. What would happen now? God, he hoped there wouldn't be a trial. When he'd decided to leave the police and become a private investigator he'd never imagined he'd encounter someone like Hager. A professional killer. He shivered. What might have happened to Laurel if they hadn't discovered the cassette, and heard the dead voice of Sam Harrop? What if he hadn't found the gun? The bullets hadn't killed Hager, but they'd slowed him down, allowing him to finish him off. Death by a cricket stroke. Would that be a first? Would he be in the *Guinness Book of Records*? The shivering increased. He shook his head. This was delayed shock. He heaved himself upright. He needed to get Laurel to a hospital.

David came back from the bathroom with a cup of water. 'Sorry it took so long, we'd filled all the mugs and glasses with water and paints to throw at Hager.'

What was the boy talking about?

David giggled. 'We filled some with pee. Pity I didn't get a chance to douse him in that.'

Frank was dying to ask him how he came to be here, but he thought it would be a long story. 'I'll find a phone and get—'

'I can hear sirens.'

It was true. There was the sound of the front door being broken down. Frank smiled. They could have gone round the back, but Revie would have enjoyed forcing his way in. Footsteps pounded up the stairs. Revie barrelled into the room. Stuart was behind him. He pushed Revie aside, his face grey with worry. He bear-hugged Frank. Then he looked at Laurel. Her eyes were open.

'Laurel.' He knelt beside her and gently took her hand.

She tried to smile. 'I'm all right, Stuart. Frank came in time. Saved me from a fate worse than death. So they say,' she whispered.

Stuart pointed to the body. 'Him?'

She nodded.

He turned to Frank. 'Did *you* kill him?'

He was conscious of Revie glowering behind Stuart. Could he claim someone else was responsible? 'Yes, I shot him twice and finished him off with the cricket bat when the gun jammed.' He looked at Revie. 'Going to arrest me?'

Revie smirked. 'No. I'll see you get a bloody medal. Who's this?' He pointed to David.

'Allow me to introduce you to David Pemberton, the missing boy.'

Revie's mouth opened and his chin dropped. 'Well, I'll go to our back door!'

The floor seemed to be undulating, the walls rippling. He sat on a chair. 'I think I'll join you,' he said.

Chapter 36

Stuart watched as an ambulance, with a police escort, took Frank, Laurel, and David to a hospital in Ipswich. Tucker's house was swarming with police.

Revie put down the phone in the hall. 'Ansell, the pathologist, is on his way.' He pointed to the pile of large envelopes on the hall table. 'What's all this about?

'I was wondering that, myself,' Stuart said. He rifled through the pile. 'Seems every major newspaper's been covered. Shall I open one?' He was dying to know what they contained.

Revie frowned. 'Best if I do it.' He opened an envelope addressed to the editor of the *Daily Telegraph*. He pulled out a sheaf of papers and photographs. He moved away from Stuart, shielding the contents. But his face showed disgust, astonishment and then concern.

'Can I have a look?' Stuart asked.

Revie shook his head. 'I'm sorry, Elderkin. This is really bad. I wish I hadn't opened it. Left it to my chief constable. This is going to cause a stink.'

He picked up the telephone. 'Sorry, I need to make this call in private.'

He'd never seen Revie so serious or so worried. What was in the envelopes? Blackmail details? Why send them to newspapers? He couldn't imagine what the contents were to cause Revie such consternation.

Stuart returned the car he'd borrowed from Mabel's son at the fish and chip shop in Aldeburgh, and got into the police car which had followed him from Tucker's house. They drove to the Pemberton's, and pulled up outside. Frank, with Revie's permission, had asked Stuart if he would go to the Pembertons to give them the good news David was alive and well.

Stuart opened the police car door. 'I think it's best if I go by myself. I don't think there's any need for you to come with me,' he said to the PC at the wheel. 'I'm presuming they'll want to go directly to the hospital to see David, so I shouldn't be long. OK?'

The PC looked disappointed. 'Pity. Makes a change to bring someone good news, I was looking forward to doing that.'

'Sorry, mate, but the sight of a uniform might give them the wrong impression, at least to begin with. You can have a chat with them on the way to the hospital. Remember this was our case, and we did find him.' Even if it was inadvertent, he thought.

He rang the bell. He was looking forward to seeing the Pembertons in the flesh, and especially Carol Pemberton. Was she as beautiful as her drawing? He didn't suppose she'd fancy him: too old and too fat for her tastes. He wondered if Mr Pemberton had any inkling of what she was up to.

The door opened.

'Mr Elderkin! Stuart! What a nice surprise.' Ann Fenner beamed at him.

'Can I see Mr and Mrs Pemberton, please? It's urgent,

Ann.'

Her smile disappeared and a hand covered her mouth. 'Is it David?' she whispered, moving back and letting him into the hall.

Stuart patted her hand. 'I need to tell his parents first.'

She tried to compose herself, but he could see she was near to tears. She must have a real soft spot for the lad.

'Mr Pemberton's in the library. Mrs Pemberton isn't in.'

Just my luck, he thought.

Ann led him to the library and opened the door. 'Mr Elderkin from the detective agency to see you, Mr Pemberton.'

Adam Pemberton was seated in an armchair before a lively fire, a newspaper in his hands. He shot up, his face paling, the paper trembling. 'David? Is it David? You've found him?'

He moved towards him, holding out his hand. 'I'm Stuart Elderkin, Mr Pemberton. Frank Diamond would have come to give you the news, but he—'

Adam Pemberton grasped his arm. 'My boy, where did you find him? Where was he buried? Was he murdered?' His body was shaking, his eyes filled with tears.

Stuart took hold of him and held him firmly by the shoulders. 'Hold on, sir. We have found David, and he's alive. He's been taken to the hospital in Ipswich. I'm here to take you to him.'

Adam Pemberton stared at him, his mouth open, he shook his head from side to side. 'No. It's not possible. Are you sure? Is it really David?' His chest was heaving and he staggered backwards, taking Stuart with him.

Stuart manoeuvred him back to his chair, looked

around, saw a whisky decanter on a sideboard and poured out a good measure into a glass. He gave it into the shaking hands of Mr Pemberton, hesitated, then poured one for himself. He wasn't driving.

The glass chattered against Mr Pemberton's teeth as he swallowed the whisky.

'I helped myself, hope you don't mind, but we've had a hell of a time today.'

Adam saluted him with his glass. 'If what you say is true you can have as much whisky as you like.'

He'd remember that.

'Why is he in hospital? Is he injured? Where did you find him? What has he been doing all this time? Why didn't he contact us? Does he want to come home? Dear God, how I've prayed for this day. A day I never thought would happen. I was sure if we ever found him, it would be his body.' He put down his glass and buried his face in his hands, great sobs shaking his body.

Stuart put an arm round his shoulders and blinked back a few tears himself. 'He's alive, and as far as I can see, he's in pretty good shape. He couldn't contact you. He's been imprisoned all the time he's been missing. He's looking forward so much to seeing you and his mother.'

Adam Pemberton looked up, tears still running down his face. 'Imprisoned? Who did that?'

Stuart stepped back. 'Why don't you get ready? There's a police car waiting to take us to the hospital. I'll tell you as much as I can on the journey there.'

Mr Pemberton found a handkerchief and wiped his face. 'Yes. Yes. Let's go at once.'

'What about Mrs Pemberton? Can you contact her?'

He shook his head. 'I don't know where she is.'

He decided not to pursue where, and who, Carol Pemberton was with. 'Would you mind if I told Anne Fenner about David? She's thinking the worse at the moment.'

Adam Pemberton's expression was changing as the news finally sank in. There was a smile on his lips and a laugh came bubbling up from his chest. 'No, ask her to come in. I want to tell her. I want to see the look on her face.' He was hysterical with happiness.

Stuart found her in the kitchen, sitting on a chair, her head in her hands. She'd been crying.

'Ann, Mr Pemberton wants to see you.' It seemed cruel not to tell her, but it was Adam Pemberton who wanted to make her happy.

She wiped her face, straightened her hair and silently followed him into the library. When she saw the look on Mr Pemberton's face, she turned to Stuart. 'What's happened?'

He shook his head.

Adam Pemberton came up and took her hands. 'Ann. They've found David and he's alive.'

She raised her head, a look of astonishment on her face, then she threw back her head and laughed and cried at the same time. 'Praise be to God. Where is he?' She turned to him. 'How can we thank you for finding him?' Then back to Mr Pemberton. 'Oh, sir. I'm so happy for you.'

Adam Pemberton regained his composure as Ann lost hers. 'There, there, Ann. I'll have him back as soon as possible, and you can make him one of the puddings he loves so much. I'm going with Mr Elderkin to the hospital in Ipswich. There, don't look worried. Mr Elderkin says

344

he's well. I'll tell you everything when I come back. If I decide to stay in Ipswich, I'll phone you.'

She withdrew her hands from his. 'Thank you, sir. Will you give him my love?'

Adam smiled. 'I certainly will. Right, Mr Elderkin, shall we go?'

There was no mention of Mrs Pemberton.

Chapter 37

Laurel was propped up in her hospital bed in a single room; David was next door and an armed policeman was positioned outside guarding both of them. She wasn't sure what the threat was as Hager and Tucker were dead, but she supposed the police knew what they were doing. She'd been x-rayed, and her various injuries treated; the main damage was to her throat, where Hager had hit her, but an unpleasant internal examination had shown there was no lasting damage, and the ice-cream she was eating not only tasted delicious, but was soothing as well.

A nurse smoothed her already smooth bedcover. 'Is there anything else I can get you?'

Laurel took the spoon out of her mouth. 'That was lovely,' she whispered. 'Any chance of a cup of tea? I'm really thirsty.'

'Certainly.' The nurse disappeared and returned a few minutes later with the tea. 'Are you up to seeing anyone? David Pemberton is back in his room, and Mr Diamond is with him. They asked if you were fit enough for them to pay a visit.'

'Do I look awful?' she croaked.

The nurse raised her eyebrows. 'Considering what you've been through you look amazing. Would you like me to comb your hair? I'll try and miss the stitches.'

'Please.'

The nurse fussed round her for a few minutes. 'There, it's the best I can do. I'm sure they'll understand if you're not your sparkling best. Shall I bring them in? I think just half an hour, then you must rest.'

Laurel smiled at her. Everyone had been so kind, praising her courage and resourcefulness. 'Thank you.'

'They'll be glad to see you. David's been really worried. We can't believe he's been found alive, it's as though he's back from the dead. I remember reading about his disappearance in the papers, and feeling so sorry for his parents. I know how I'd feel if any of my kids went missing.' She left the room.

Laurel knew she was still in shock. She hadn't fully come to terms with all that had happened, but the main feelings were relief and joy. Relief she and David were still alive and joy he'd be reunited with his parents. The way he's worked with her as they prepared for Hager, his courage, his boyish camaraderie; she would treasure those memories always. His fears for her and his relief when he realised she was alive were touching. She desperately hoped he'd be able to cope with the stress of the attack and long captivity, and he'd be able to have a happy life ahead of him.

The door opened and Frank and David, dressed in hospital pyjamas and dressing gown, came in. They stood on the threshold staring at her.

She beckoned them. 'It is me. I know I look awful, but I'm OK.'

Frank strode to her bedside. 'I'd give you a kiss, but I'm not sure which bit of you is injury-free.'

She pointed to her right cheek. 'Try that bit.'

Frank bent down and put his lips gently on the spot. He whispered, 'Laurel, you frightened me to death. Please don't accept any more lunch invitations from mass murderers.'

She laughed, then winced at the pain in her throat. 'It would have helped if you'd got to me a bit sooner. How did you know I was in danger?'

'It's a long and complicated story and there's a young man who wants to talk to you.'

Frank stepped back and ushered David towards the bed. He shuffled forwards, looking shy and hesitant.

She held out her hand. It was a calculated risk. She knew he didn't like being touched, but during the danger they'd shared, he'd shown he cared for her.

He reached out and grasped her hand briefly. 'Laurel. You look awful.'

Frank laughed. 'A ladies' man.'

She and David giggled, then she started coughing.

Frank held out a glass of water. 'Try this.'

David brought a piece of paper from behind his back. 'This is for you. I drew it in the bathroom when we were waiting for Hager to come.' He handed it to her.

The sketch showed her standing, legs astride, dressed in David's t-shirt, bare legs tensed for action, hair flowing out as though caught in a wind, a warrior look on her face and right arm raised, the stiletto clenched in her fist. Gosh, she did look fierce. Her chest swelled with pride. She felt much better already, and waved the paper at Frank.

'What do you think about that? David's a genius!' She turned to the boy. 'That's the best present you could have given me, David. I was feeling a bit wimpy, but you've made me feel one hundred per cent better.'

David flushed and grinned at her. 'You saved my life. If you hadn't come, I'm sure Hager would have killed me.'

Frank turned to him. 'I haven't got it clear yet. Why did Tucker keep you a prisoner? How did he get hold of you?' He pulled two chairs from near the wall and positioned them near her bed. He sat on one and waved to David to take the other.

David pulled the chair near to the bed and reached out for her hand. She smiled at him and took it. 'I went to the school after I ran away from home. I went there to rescue Peter. I knew they were doing horrible things to him. I went into the sick room and he was lying on a bed, his face covered. He was dead. I think I must have cried out. They came and she stuck a needle in me.'

'The matron?' Frank asked.

David nodded. 'And Salmon. When I woke up I was in the room at Tucker's house. Tucker was kind to me but he wouldn't let me go home. At first, when he gave me everything I needed to draw and paint, and I got anything I asked for, it wasn't too bad. I thought Tucker had saved me. Which he had. I didn't know he'd anything to do with Peter or John. But Hager started coming at night. He didn't touch me, but he'd stand close to the bed and tell me all the awful things he'd done and what the men had done to Peter and John. Then I knew Tucker must be bad as well. Worse, because he was Hager's boss.' He pursed his lips and blew out a long breath. 'That's the most I've spoken in two years.'

From everything she knew about David, his inability to talk at length, his dislike of being touched, it appeared that

349

somehow, during his captivity, he'd changed. Could she ask him about it? 'David, thank you for telling us that. It makes a lot of things clearer.' He smiled at her, still holding her hand. 'You can speak very clearly now. How have you managed to do that? It seems like a miracle to me.'

David blinked and gave a wry smile. 'When I was young, I could speak quite well, but I wouldn't do it. I don't know why.' A frown clouded his face. 'Are my parents coming?'

'Yes,' Frank said. 'Stuart Elderkin has gone in a police car to fetch them. They'll be overjoyed. They didn't give up on you, David. The police investigated your disappearance, then when they couldn't find you, your parents hired a detective agency. They weren't successful and so they came to us.'

David frowned. 'I don't want to see my mother.'

She shot a glance at Frank. She couldn't ask David why, but if she didn't, perhaps he'd guess they knew the reason. Frank made a slight inclination of his head.

'Why is that, David? She never gave up hope of finding you alive. She'll be overjoyed to have you back,' she said.

David stuck out his lower lip. 'I can't tell you. I haven't told anyone, not even Daddy.'

She didn't know what to say without giving away their knowledge of his mother's infidelities. She could see Frank was feeling indecisive, wanting to say something to help the boy, but unsure of his words.

'David, your mother has obviously done something which has upset you,' Frank said. 'I don't know if what she did was right or wrong, but she does love you. What you've been through for the past two years is unimaginable. Your parents have suffered, too. Perhaps you'll be able to forgive your mother, talk to her, now you are older and more mature. You'll be able to make a fresh start as a family.'

David glared at him. 'You don't know what she did.'

Frank didn't reply.

There were the sounds of voices approaching. She could hear Elderkin and another man. The man was laughing.

David stood up, his eyes widening. 'That's Daddy!'

The door opened and Adam Pemberton burst into the room, followed by Stuart Elderkin.

Adam, laughing with joy, opened his arms and David flew into them.

'My boy! My boy!' Adam buried his face in David's hair and David hugged his father as though he'd never let go of him. Adam's shoulders started to heave as laughter turned to jagged bursts of tears.

David raised his head. 'Don't cry, Daddy, I won't ever leave you. I promise I won't run away again.'

Adam smiled through his tears and kissed him on the forehead. He seemed too choked to say any more.

'Mr Pemberton, let me introduce Laurel Bowman,' Frank said.

Adam, an arm still round his son, moved to the bed and shook her hand. 'Mr Elderkin told me how you saved David. I can't really understand everything that's happened, but I thank you from the bottom of my heart.'

Tears ran down her cheeks. 'I'm so glad David is alive and with you. He deserves a lot of the credit. We worked well together, didn't we?'

David, leaning against his father, wiped tears from his cheeks and grinned. 'We were prepared to fight, Daddy. We were going to throw books and records at him, and pots of paint and water and, er ...pee.' He dissolved into a fit of giggles against his father's chest.

Adam was looking at him in astonishment. 'David, you're speaking so well.'

David pulled a face. 'Sorry, Daddy, I was a bit naughty, I could speak but I didn't. I've been practising for two years. The telly helped, I used to talk to the people on the screen. Tucker gave me a lot of books, and at first he used to help me. When I found out what he was really like, I wouldn't let him.'

Adam looked at him in amazement, shaking his head.

He's a one off, she thought. Such a strong will. That's how he managed to survive the isolation. She looked round. In the heat of their reunion she hadn't realised Mrs Pemberton was not here.

David seemed to have made the same connection. 'Where's Mummy?'

Adam's face changed. 'She wasn't at home when Mr Elderkin came. Ann will tell her when she gets in.'

'Is Ann still with us?'

'Yes, she's overjoyed. She sends her love and she'll be making your favourite pudding.'

David's face split into a wide smile. 'I'm glad she's at home. I like Ann.'

'Yes, she's a good woman.'

At these words David's face darkened. 'Daddy, I need to talk to you alone.'

She shivered. Surely the boy wasn't going to tell his father about his mother?

Adam looked puzzled.

'We can go to my room. It's next door,' David said.

'Please excuse us. Once more thank you, all of you, for what you've done. I can never tell you how much this means to me.' Adam put a hand on his son's shoulders. 'Show me the way, David.'

Chapter 38

Monday, 5th April, 1971

Frank held his breath and lowered his head below the soapy bath water. He blew out air, then sat up, water rolling down his shoulders. He'd escaped to his cottage, to try to make sense of everything that had happened. The last nine days had been the longest of his life.

He, Laurel, and also David Pemberton had been questioned non-stop. One statement being followed by others, culminating in interviews with people who were obviously either in MI5 or MI6, or both. The deaths of Tucker and Hager and the operation they had run, had sent shock waves right to the top of the establishment. Frank thought he knew what they'd been up to, and he'd told his questioners his suspicions. Blackmail. From what Sam Harrop had said on the cassette tape, he'd been blackmailed into certifying death certificates of murdered children. The technique used on him was probably used on other people. People like Dr Luxton. Had he been blackmailed for money? Or more likely for information. What secrets had he passed on to Tucker? It was the contents of the envelopes addressed to the editors of the main daily papers, and others, that was causing concern.

According to Stuart, Revie had opened one of the

envelopes and immediately phoned his superior. He'd secured all the envelopes and refused to discuss their contents with anyone. Frank was frustrated by the lack of information coming back to him, Laurel and all the team. He wanted to know what had happened at the school. Had Baron been arrested? Were all the children at the school safe? And David? What had he told his father? Adam Pemberton hadn't come back to Laurel's room after Frank and Stuart had left the hospital. When Frank came back the next morning David had gone home.

How was he coping? What effect would the last two years have on his future life? And Laurel? After a check-up and a night in hospital, she'd insisted on coming back to Greyfriars, but the repeated questioning about her time in Tucker's house hadn't given her a chance to come to terms with nearly being raped and murdered by Hager. In six months she'd been attacked by two killers. Could he expect her to be able, or want, to go on working at their agency? *He* was finding it difficult coming to terms with deliberately killing a human being. A terrible man. But he'd pulled the trigger and he'd dealt him a fatal blow – the post-mortem revealed he'd broken Hager's neck.

If Hager hadn't worn a bullet-proof vest would Laurel have killed him with the stiletto? If she'd killed him, he wouldn't have attacked and nearly raped her, but how would she have coped with taking someone's life? She already carried the guilt of her part in the death of her sister's murderer. Would she have been able to add to that burden and go on with her life?

The bath water was cooling, and a soapy scum clung to the edges of the bath. Time to move. He stood up and reached for the hand-held shower, flipped the controls and sprayed cold water over his head and body. Revie was coming to Greyfriars this evening.

Laurel helped Mabel and Dorothy clear the supper table, Frank was lighting the fire in the sitting room and Stuart was making coffee. Conversation over their meal had been desultory, everyone had seemed to be engrossed in their own thoughts. In the days since coming back from hospital, Laurel had tried to keep busy, so she couldn't think about Hager and what might have happened. She'd upped the mileage of her daily run, bought a set of weights in Ipswich, and added them to her keep-fit routine. She'd mowed the lawn within a millimetre of its life, until Dorothy protested, and got Mabel to teach her how to bake bread. She knew her manic behaviour was disturbing the others, but they hadn't said anything. They understood the reasons behind it.

She went into the sitting room; a log fire was burning brightly, the kindling crackling and throwing red sparks against the fire-bricks, the apple log on top catching fire and sending a sweet smell into the room. Frank was crouched in front of it, poker in hand, staring into the yellow flames.

'Good fire,' she said.

Frank straightened up. 'You can't beat a fire, there's something primal and atavistic about leaping flames. Central heating is civilized, but doesn't warm the soul.'

She joined him, stretching out her hands to the heat. 'I like the central heating in the morning. I'm not keen on getting up to icy windows and cold clothes.'

Frank put the poker back in the companion set. 'Thought you were a tough guy.'

'In case you haven't noticed I'm a gal not a guy, and I don't feel too tough at the moment.'

'Is that why you've taken to body building?'

She retreated to an armchair. 'I wasn't quite strong enough, was I?'

'Laurel, if he hadn't been wearing the body armour, you'd have nailed him. You're strong enough for me, if you get any stronger I'll get an inferiority complex.'

She glared at him. 'That I would like to see.'

Stuart came into the room carrying a tray with several glasses. 'Having another spat, are we?'

She gave him a glare as well. 'We can't all be lovebirds,' she snarled, then she saw his face. 'Sorry, Stuart. I'm afraid I'm a bit edgy.'

He put the tray on a sideboard. 'No need to apologise. You've every right to be upset. Like a whisky?'

'Yes, please. The usual: half and half.'

Stuart poured a measure into a glass and topped it up with water. 'Frank?'

'Same. Please.'

She relaxed as Dorothy and Mabel joined them and they settled before the fire, sipping their drinks, waiting for Revie to come.

'How much will he be able to tell us?' Dorothy asked.

Stuart shook his head. 'I don't know, perhaps very little. Something stinks. We've all been told not to discuss the case with anyone, or else!'

'I have heard one thing, it's all over Aldeburgh,' Mabel said.

Dorothy looked miffed. 'What? I've not heard anything.'

'My son rang me up today. Seems Mrs Pemberton's

left the town. The rumour is her husband has given her the heave-ho and he's filing for a divorce. What do you think about that?'

Laurel's heart plummeted. 'David must have told his father. How awful.' Carol would be free. She glanced at Frank. His eyebrows were raised.

'And Ann Fenner has moved out of the house and has taken a cottage near Nancy Wintle, paid for by Mr Pemberton. It seems he didn't think it was right for her to sleep in the house now his wife's gone.'

'Is she still the housekeeper?' Dorothy asked.

'Yes. Gets on like a house on fire with David,' Mabel replied.

'I thought they looked well together, her and Mr Pemberton, when I went to fetch him to the hospital,' Stuart ruminated, having lit up his pipe, sitting close to Mabel on the sofa.

'You're jumping the gun, Stuart Elderkin,' Mabel said, digging him in the ribs.

Stuart tapped his nose. 'I know a romance when I see one.'

Mabel threw back her head and hooted with laughter. 'Well, you could have fooled me.'

They were all laughing when the sound of the front door bell made them freeze.

Mabel showed in Revie.

For once he had a solemn face, with none of the old bluster and aggression. 'This is cosy.' He nodded as Frank waved a bottle at him. He sat down with a heavy sigh and lifted the glass to them. 'Here's to you all.' He drank the contents of the glass in one quick movement and held it out for a refill.

Frank gave him a good amount. 'Hope that will last longer than the first. I don't want to be up and down like a yo-yo.'

'Feeling chipper, are you?'

'Yes, shouldn't I be?'

'It depends.'

Frank looked at him quizzically.

'On what you'll all think, once I've told you everything I'm allowed to tell you.' He took a sip of whisky, 'Ready?'

They all nodded.

'It's big. So big I've had to sign the Official Secrets Act and I think you'll all have to, as well. What I'm going to say is confidential, if it gets back I've told you too much, they'll have my guts for garters. Have I got your words?'

They looked at each other. They all nodded.

'What about the children at the school? Are they safe? Are they being taken care of?' Frank asked.

'Yes, they're safe. The children from the orphanage have been taken to other homes. They'll be kept under surveillance and if possible they'll be found foster parents, and hopefully adopted. The rest of the pupils, who weren't in danger, as far as we can make out, have been returned to their parents and they'll be given help to find new schools.'

'What about John, the frightened boy? Is he safe?' she asked.

Revie slowly shook his head. 'No sign of him. We're searching the school and grounds. Doesn't look good.'

There was silence.

Her eyes filled with tears.

'What about Baron and the other staff who were involved?' Frank asked.

'Baron and Salmon, the PE teacher, have been arrested, but some of the other staff, the matron and the school cook, have disappeared. Out of the country and back to Mother Russia, I should think.'

'Mother Russia?' she said. 'I don't understand.'

Revie grimaced and pulled at his nose with thumb and forefinger. 'Right, what I'm telling you now, I'll deny I've said. Understood?'

They nodded.

'It was blackmail for secrets, and not money?' Frank said.

'I told them you'd probably worked it out. Yes. From the investigations over the past few days it seems Tucker, with his arty connections in London, and no doubt information from his controllers, invited influential men, with known vices, down to his house near Snape Maltings. Narcotics and aphrodisiacs were found in the house, and using these, and presenting the men with temptations they couldn't resist, they were photographed performing acts on young boys that would have landed them in gaol and obviously ruined their careers. An upstairs room was used; it has a two-way mirror, and also … a large tapestry.' He looked at Laurel.

She closed her eyes. John, the frightened boy, standing in front of a tapestry in the photograph in Luxton's house. Waves of sickness washed over her. She gripped her glass tightly.

'What was in the envelopes?' Frank asked.

Revie nodded. 'Ah, the envelopes.'

Waves of anger competed with nausea. Her breathing deepened. 'What will happen to these men? Whoever they are they should be brought to justice. I don't know what they did to those poor children, but we know one, Peter, was murdered. They can't be allowed to escape without being brought to book.'

Revie turned his gaze on her, his eyes like stones. 'I couldn't agree more. It seems there was more to it than blackmailing these men for secrets that might be useful to the USSR. The big idea, as far as we can tell, was to bring down the government. Things are dodgy as you know, and the men who'd be exposed are well-known men in all spheres of society, from cabinet ministers to men of the cloth.'

Her mouth felt full of ash.

Dorothy looked sick and Mabel's head was in her hands; Stuart stared at the fire.

'They can't let the government fall. It would be too dangerous,' Revie said.

'But what will happen to these men? They can't be allowed to get away with what they've done.' Her insides were burning.

'Look, I'm just the messenger. I agree with everything you're saying. I persuaded them to let me tell you something of what all this means. I thought if I could talk to you, I might persuade you not to go off at half-cock. If you try and do anything about this, if you try to get justice by the usual methods, you'll be stopped. I mean stopped. Permanently. There's nothing you can do. All I can say is that various men will be removed from their positions; I wouldn't be surprised if we don't hear of some suicides in the next few weeks.' His voice was anxious, his face worried.

Frank clenched his jaws. He looked furious.

'You're a good bunch. You saved David and you've saved some of the kids in the school. The two main culprits are dead. Baron and Salmon will never get to trial. What will happen to them? I don't know. I don't want to know. I think you're going to have to swallow this, as I've had to.'

'It's not right,' Mabel said.

'I know,' Revie said, 'but you need to go on working. Helping people.'

Stuart got up and tapped his pipe against the fireplace. 'You've put your head on the block for us, haven't you?'

Revie pulled a face. 'Perhaps. I'll tell you something, I'm making copious notes, with as much detail as I can remember. I saw some of the photos of the men involved. I'm going to make those notes and I'm going to put them in a safe place. The time will come when all this will come to light. Sometimes justice is slow, but it's my belief in the end it usually brings home the bacon.' He looked at Mabel. 'Speaking of bacon, Mabel, any chance of a few butties? All this trauma's given me an appetite.'

Laurel shook her head, she wished she could feel the same.

Chapter 39

Saturday, 29th May, 1971

Laurel and Dorothy entered the church together. They'd tossed a coin before they left Greyfriars to see which side of the church they'd each sit on: she sat in a pew to the left of the aisle, Dorothy to the right, in the pew directly behind Stuart, the groom, and his best man, Frank.

The church was crowded with guests and local people, keen to get a glimpse of not only the bride and groom, but the detectives who'd rescued David Pemberton and been involved in the deaths of five local people.

She looked at Stuart and Frank. Stuart looked nervous, continually turning round as though he expected Mabel to appear in a puff of smoke. He looked smart and substantial in a new dark suit, a red carnation in his buttonhole, matching his red tie. Frank looked handsome. She'd never seen him in a suit before. His hair looked as though it had been trimmed, but it still skimmed his collar. Stuart caught her eye and waved. He turned to Frank, and nudged him. Frank flashed her a bright smile and his lips formed a silent word. She thought it was 'Stunning!' She smiled back at him. She'd bought a new blue, wild silk dress; she'd never wear the blue suit again. It had only been creased from hiding it under the bedclothes, but it was associated with murder. She'd given it to Dorothy who said she couldn't throw it away; she'd find a good home for it. She hoped she wouldn't meet it again on some other woman.

Nancy Wintle was in the congregation with a friend. Laurel had visited her a few times and gradually Nancy was getting to grips with her brother's death, and all the terrible things she'd learnt about him. Nancy told her she was selling Sam's house, though she wasn't sure anyone would want to buy it. She assured her if the price was right, you could always find a buyer, and it was in a lovely part of the town. Nancy said she was going on a luxury cruise with a friend in September. It was something she'd always wanted to do, now she could afford it. She'd asked Dorothy if she'd like to go with her, but Dorothy had declined; she was too busy with the agency. Dorothy said she was fond of Nancy, but the thought of a cruise, trapped with possibly boring people at your table every night was her idea of hell.

Laurel's eyes widened. Oliver Neave was sitting at the back of the church on Stuart's side. She hadn't seen him for weeks, not since the death of Dr Luxton. He smiled at her, a warm admiring smile. The blue dress was paying for itself. Should she invite him back to the reception at Greyfriars? One more wouldn't matter and she knew Mabel and Stuart wouldn't mind. But would Frank? She hoped so.

Inspector Revie was also on Stuart's side of the church, looking smart but grumpy. Why had he come? Did he have a heart after all? He seemed to have gone up in Frank's and Stuart's estimation, but she wasn't completely won over. Her back stiffened. Adam and

364

David Pemberton came into the church, pausing as Adam talked to a steward. He led them to a pew on the groom's side. Adam was formally dressed as usual, but David looked different and grown up in a grey suit; a handsome, almost beautiful boy. Heads turned and people whispered as they sat down. It must be hard for them to cope with all the interest and gossip. She wondered where Carol was. She must be heartbroken: her lost son found, and then lost again to her as he refused to see her. Her marriage was over. Laurel hoped she wouldn't contact Frank. Carol must have realised how much he wanted her. Now she was free. How would he feel if he saw her again? Laurel's stomach clenched.

The organ music soared through the church. She turned. Mabel, in a lilac suit, high heels and a fetching hat, was led down the aisle by her son. She looked supremely happy, smiling and nodding to all her friends. Stuart had turned and his face was a picture of joy. Laurel bit her lip, trying to stem tears. She was so happy for them and there seemed to be a swelling of good will from all the people here. Would she ever marry? After the end of her engagement she'd decided she'd concentrate on a career, but when you saw two people so happy to be together, and willing to give themselves to each other, a longing to do the same surged through her. Would she ever find her soul mate? Could it be Oliver Neave? Or was her soul mate the unattainable Frank?

* * *

In a marquee on the lawn of Greyfriars house, Frank was seated at the top table, next to Stuart. The speeches were over, the meal eaten, some people were leaving, the rest chatting and sipping the dregs of wine or coffee. Laurel was on his other side. She looked beautiful in a shimmering blue dress, hatless, her hair swept up in a style he hadn't seen before. It was a happy day for Stuart and Mabel, and now the church service was over, they seemed relaxed, talking to each other and occasionally getting up and chatting to their guests.

He was able to see all the other people who were seated at the two long tables at right angles to the top table. Somehow Revie had managed to wangle his way in. He was chatting away to a woman wearing a basket of fruit on her head. Perhaps he was partial to a few cherries. Revie had told him, because of the help and cooperation the police had received from the Anglian Detective Agency, it had been decided a special relationship between the Suffolk constabulary and their firm, with Inspector Revie as the intermediary, would be established. This was to be an informal relationship; no official announcement would be made. He didn't have to look far to understand the secrecy. Too many questions would be asked. It was a sop to them for their cooperation. A cooperation they didn't have any choice in. He'd been disillusioned with various aspects of policing when he'd resigned and set up the detective agency, but that disillusionment had spread to politics and other areas of power. However, if they'd have police help and cooperation for future cases, that couldn't be bad and he didn't mind working with Revie. He thought, just thought, his heart might be in the right place.

Stuart was laughing at something Mabel said.

Frank turned towards them. 'Don't use up all the good times too soon, Stuart.'

'You're in a cynical mood today. Is that what

weddings do to you?' Stuart asked.

Frank raised an eyebrow. 'Everything's going smoothly. No one's had a row with their neighbour, or thrown trifle over the vicar. Bit boring, isn't it?'

Stuart shook his head. 'I'm quite happy with boring. We've had enough excitement lately.'

'Nonsense,' Frank said. 'It's nearly two months at least, since we've had a murder.'

Stuart leant across Frank. 'Laurel! Can you do something about this man; he's in a most peculiar mood. Talk some sense into him.'

Laurel was talking to Oliver Neave who was on her right, another unexpected guest, though how she'd sneaked him onto the top table he wasn't sure. Probably Dorothy's doing. Little Miss Fix-it.

Laurel said something to Neave and leant over Frank to talk to Stuart. The warmth of her body through the fine fabric and her light floral perfume made him flinch. He remembered how it had felt when Carol was close to him; her heady perfume seemed to replace Laurel's.

'I've given up on him, Stuart. He's been in this mood for weeks. The sooner we start another case the better.'

Frank didn't say anything.

'We did well financially out of the last one. Mr Pemberton was more than generous. We've had a few small cases over the past few weeks; kept everything ticking over nicely. Hope you'll be able to manage without me and Mabel for a week. Who's doing the cooking? You could make a few omelettes, Frank.'

He couldn't stand it anymore. He had to get into the fresh air. 'We'll manage, Stuart. I hope you and Mabel have a lovely honeymoon in London.'

'Thanks, Frank, and thank you for being my best man. Mabel's looking forward to seeing some shows and doing a bit of shopping. Not my favourite place, London, but she didn't fancy Blackpool.'

Frank stood up. 'I'm going to get a breath of fresh air. I'll see you before you go.'

Laurel placed a hand on his arm. 'Are you all right, Frank? Would you like some company?'

'No thanks, Laurel. See you later.'

He walked towards the beach. He wanted to get away from people and the way they looked at him. A man who had killed another man. He sensed people felt differently about him: wary, unsure – frightened? Although the verdicts on the three people murdered by Hager had been given as a mercy killing and two suicides, rumours were rife. The official line was David was kidnapped by Tucker and Hager, motives unknown, and Laurel had suffered the same fate. Hager had killed Tucker – that was true, and Frank had killed Hager in self-defence. This information didn't stop local and national speculation. David being returned safe to his parents after being missing for two years was also a big story. Both Adam and David refused to talk to the papers, having been bound to silence like the rest of them. The lies made Frank sick to his stomach, and the fact he couldn't do anything about it made it worse.

He turned into the road leading to the beach car park and the café. He walked over the pebbles, some as large as duck eggs, the soles of his new shoes slipping on the smooth surfaces. Ahead, and to his left, the marshes stretched out towards Southwold. The grey of the alders matched his mood.

How must Carol feel? All she knew was David was safe at home. Perhaps when he was older and realised everyone makes mistakes, he'd be more understanding, and a reconciliation might be possible. Would she go to court to seek justice for herself? Or had Adam made a bargain with her: a good settlement if she gave up all rights to see David? He could imagine Adam doing that; he would know how to manipulate the law.

What of David himself? Was he concerned about the men who'd ruined and caused the death of his friend, Peter? How could he understand why the men who'd used young boys for their pleasure, weren't brought to justice? What effect would that have on his character?

He walked towards the sea, flat waves hissing against the shore, picked up some flat pebbles and skimmed them over the waves. Time to go back and wave goodbye to Mabel and Stuart. Perhaps he'd persuade Laurel to go for a walk over the heath to the Eel's Foot at Eastbridge. He wanted to find the easy companionship they'd shared before this case started.

By the time he got back. Stuart was loading two cases into the back of his Humber Hawk.

'Thought we were going to miss saying goodbye to you.' Stuart grasped his hand. 'Look after yourself, Frank, while we're away.'

'I will. Where's Laurel?'

'Gone off with that nice Dr Neave, I shouldn't wonder,' Mabel said.

Stuart raised his eyebrows.

Dorothy rushed out of the house, waving a piece of paper.

'We'll have a brand-new case for you when you get

369

back,' she said triumphantly.

Frank cocked his head. 'What have you been up to?'

She waved the paper under their noses. 'It could be very profitable. A telephone call from a very important person. He needs our help and he doesn't care how much it costs him. He wants the best. He wants the Anglian Detective Agency.'

He smiled. 'The best, eh? That's what I like to hear.'

Laurel came out of the house. 'I can see Dorothy's told you. It'll be good to have something to get our teeth into.'

Stuart and Mabel were looking undecided, as though they weren't sure if they should take a honeymoon.

Frank opened the car door. 'Off you go. We'll get the details and talk it over when you get back. No decisions will be made without you.'

They got in quickly, as though he might change his mind. Stuart tooted his horn and they were off, everyone waving furiously.

'I'll supervise the cleaning up,' Dorothy said. 'What are you two going to do?'

'Would you like a walk, Frank?'

The burdens of frustration, guilt and sadness seemed to slip from his shoulders. 'Yes, I would. Over the heath and through the woods to the Eel's Foot?'

'Perfect. Give me two minutes to change. You're not going in that suit, are you?'

'We'll drive to my cottage, I can change there'

She hugged him. 'Just like old times.'

He laughed back. 'If you can call last September old times.'

'It seems an age ago.' She turned and ran into the house.

'She looks lovely today, doesn't she?' Dorothy said.

'Always looks lovely to me,' he replied.

Dorothy cocked her head, smirking.

'No, Dorothy. We're friends and partners. Nothing else.'

'She's been through a lot; it's hurt her, perhaps more than any of us.'

'I know.'

'I'm very fond of Laurel. She's a brave girl, but she feels for people.'

'That's why she's a good detective.'

Dorothy shook her head. 'I'm fond of you too, Frank Diamond.'

'Dorothy Piff, you've drunk too much champagne.'

She kissed him on the cheek. 'It's been a wonderful day. Cleansed my soul. Right, I'll get started.'

He waited by his car.

Laurel, in a track suit, her hair in a pony-tail, ran from the house. The evening light was behind her, she seemed to be on fire. How full of life she was.

'What a marvellous day, Frank. Think of Mabel and Stuart on their way to the flesh pots of London.'

'A walk to Eastbridge seems small beer,' he said.

'Suits me. But I'm looking forward to a pint of Adnams at the Eel's Foot.'

He opened the passenger door of his car. 'Hop in, the sooner I can get out of this suit the better. Tonight, the beer's on me.'

She looked at him and smiled. 'I think you're weakening, Frank.'

She could be right. He smiled back but didn't say anything.

371

David, Age 15 years

I didn't want to go to the wedding. I knew I'd hear the buzz, buzz, buzz of people talking about me behind their hands. They'd stare. 'They had him for two years. What did they do to him? Poor boy, he must be damaged.' They'd imagine in their secret minds what they did to me. I know what they'd be thinking.

Hager came at night when Tucker had gone to bed. He'd stand close to me. I pulled the blankets over my head, but he'd rip them off. He'd tell me over and over everything the men had done to Peter. How they adored his smooth skin, how Hager held him down, forced his legs apart, and the men would take turns to rape him. How Peter had suffered. Hager told me who the men were. He told me because I'd never be able to tell anyone. I would be as dead as Peter. Hager never missed any detail: the excruciating pain, the mutilation, the gut-wrenching fear.

It's locked in my brain forever. The only way I can get rid of it is to get rid of them. I'll have to wait. I mustn't tell anyone I know the names. It is my secret. I like secrets. The police and the men from the secret service, they told my father he must be silent. I must be silent. It's a case of national security. Tucker was working for the USSR. He was a spy, passing on information from the men he blackmailed. We boys don't matter. All the boys who were used for the sexual pleasure of the men whose names I know, don't matter. I don't matter. I was imprisoned for nearly two years, but that doesn't matter. What matters is the government and the country.

Why hasn't Laurel done something? Without her I would be dead. When I saw her lying on my bed, a beautiful woman, I thought they'd given her to me. Was she to be my toy? When she woke up she knew who I was and realised we might be murdered. She plotted and planned. She used everything we had to fight Hager. She was brave, she made me feel brave. She was like the goddess Diana, the huntress: brave, bold and intelligent. Now she is silent. Why?

My rage boils. The bubbles of hate expand, wanting to burst. One day, I don't know when, I'll let those bubbles pour over the rim and they will scald those men. The men whose names I know.

The End

Acknowledgements

My thanks to:

My cousin, Gladys, for her support and friendship.

Members of the South Chiltern Writing Circle, Reading Writers and The Dunford Novelists for their friendship, helpful criticism, and craic.

To my editor, Jay Dixon, for her continuing scrupulous work in smoothing the edges of this novel, also her support and dry humour. Still a pleasure to work with!

To Accent Press for publishing this novel and to all the staff for their encouragement and professional help, especially Hazel and Katrin.

To Michael O'Bryne, a retired chief constable, author of *The Crime Writers' Guide*, for his helpful advice, especially on fingerprinting in the 1970s.

To Mr Fryer, fisherman of Aldeburgh, for allowing me to use his name for a fictional fisherman in this novel. A name so appropriate for a man who catches and sells fish, I couldn't resist it!

To Mr T, who gave me space to think and write, and provided me with various tinctures, as needed. I miss him.

Author's Note

Henning Mankell wrote in the Afterword to *The Troubled Man*:

'In the world of fiction it is possible to take many liberties. For instance, it is not unusual for me to change a landscape slightly so that nobody can say: "It is exactly there! That's where the action took place!"'

I have also taken liberties in moving some of the houses and shops of Aldeburgh from their true settings and placing them where I wanted and needed them to be. After all, this is a work of fiction!

For more information about **Vera Morris**

and other **Accent Press** titles

please visit

www.accentpress.co.uk